Gaard's hand tou_____ that it was as if a warm, swe_____ _____ had caressed her. A warm tingling began in the place his hand lay and radiated out, down to her fingertips, up her arm to her shoulder and neck.

Slowly Dawnlyn turned to look into his eyes. They were a clear gray now, untouched by storm, and they held her mesmerized for an endless moment. Gaard's lips came down on hers, his large hands came up to cup her face, holding her as one would a delicate flower.

He kissed carefully along the slim column of her neck, then slowly eased her onto her back, his lips brushing her neck, her chin, her cheek. Her body arched inadvertently toward him but she was not aware of it. She knew only an all-consuming need.

"It is not so terrible, is it?" he whispered gently, moving his mouth across hers with infinite lightness.

"No," Dawnlyn breathed weakly.

Books by Lynn Erickson

High Country Pride

Published by TAPESTRY BOOKS

Dawnfire

Published by POCKET BOOKS

Dawnfire
Lynn Erickson

PUBLISHED BY POCKET BOOKS NEW YORK

An *Original* publication of POCKET BOOKS

POCKET BOOKS, a division of Simon & Schuster, Inc.
1230 Avenue of the Americas, New York, N.Y. 10020

Copyright © 1984 by Carla Peltonen and Molly Swanton

ISBN: 0-671-46969-X

First Pocket Books printing March, 1984

10 9 8 7 6 5 4 3 2 1

Printed in the U.S.A.

This book is dedicated to Kate Duffy who gave me the chance to write about a subject that everyone else rejected. My undying thanks, Kate.

What has become of the steed?
What has become of the warrior?
What has become of the seats of banquet?
Where are the joys of the hall?
O for the bright cup!
O for the mailclad warrior!
O for the glory of the prince!
How that time has passed away
And grown dark under the cover of night,
As if it had never been.

From "The Wanderer"
anonymous Anglo-Saxon poem

Chapter One

The Northumbrian Coast of Scotland, 1072 A.D.

THE SKY OVER THE NORTH SEA HAD BARELY BEGUN TO PALE. Heavy gun-metal gray seas rolled, lumbering, to the foot of the cliffs and broke there, dashing themselves endlessly against the staunch wall of St. Abb's Head, booming and hissing their displeasure as they had been doing, futilely, since the beginning of time.

Against the roiling, inky-purple night sky stood the ancient tower of St. Abb's, its tall, portentous silhouette commanding the headland. In the thick stone walls, the tiny windows were slits of darkness like the eyes of a sleeping beast, and puncturing the writhing clouds was the fantastically turreted and dormered profile, its stepped gables and massive parapets a clear warning to any would-be violator.

The Scots sentry, huddled out of the salty wind on a turret of the tower, stared out eastward over the water with little enthusiasm as he stifled a yawn. In his many years of service to the earl there had not been a seaward raid, and there was no reason to believe one would come this night. In truth, he thought pridefully, St. Abb's had never been taken by surprise, had never been overrun during the few Viking attacks of the past two centuries. There had always been a steadfast laird at St. Abb's, and Robert Renfrew, even

1

though he was growing old, was still a good man. His son, Ian, although hotheaded, would someday be a proper laird, too.

The sentry scratched at the chafed skin under his wool tunic, then abruptly tensed. Something did not quite fit the pattern of empty sky, empty seas, to which he had grown accustomed these many nights he'd stood watch. Fully alert now, he walked into the raw April wind to the edge of the turret and strained his eyes into the awakening sky, scanning the dark sea.

Yes! A black shadow fled before the wind, scudding noiselessly over the foam-tipped waves, like an ominous, dark bird of prey.

Another shadow followed, and another.

The sentry counted five before he sounded the frantic alarm to wake the sleeping Hall: "Vikings! The Northmen attack! To arms! Vikings!"

Dawnlyn Renfrew was awakened by her brother's rough hands. Instantly she sat up, holding the eiderdown modestly to her chin, her heart thudding with unaccustomed apprehension. "What is it, Ian?"

"Dawnlyn, for God's sake, rise! There are five Viking ships off the Head. Father and I must organize the men. Take care of the women and children, hurry!" Ian's normally jaunty tone was harsh with purpose; his blue eyes were shadowed, cold. But not afraid.

Dawnlyn took a deep breath. If Ian wasn't afraid, then *she* wouldn't be, either. She'd had to do this before, twice in her eighteen years, and each time the dreaded dragon ships had passed by harmlessly, never daring to scale the inhospitable heights of St. Abb's Head, or unable to breach the high walls that protected the leeward side of the tower.

"Hand me my robe, then," she said levelly, determined not to panic or cause any of the Hall's women to do so. "Go on back to Father. I'll see to the women and children." She pulled the rich, gold-velvet robe around her shoulders, freeing her single, long, copper-colored braid with a hand,

and slid gracefully out of the huge bed. "I should have stayed at Coldingham," she said, making a valiant attempt at humor. "At least, I'd have gotten a better night's sleep."

"Not likely," growled Ian. "Those accursed ships are headed for Coldingham landing, no doubt, and the nunnery there will be the first to catch their eye. Well, it might save us, if they stay there . . ."

"Ian!" Dawnlyn crossed herself with a slim white hand. "Pray to God nothing befalls them."

"Better them than us!" And he was off, striding out of her chamber door, his sword slapping against his thigh as he moved.

Quickly, Dawnlyn belted her fur-lined robe around her narrow waist with a gold chain. She'd dress later, when the danger was past. Then she turned to Meg, her maid, who was crouching on her pallet, her thin face terrified. "Meg, get up. We're all going to the chapel now and you needn't worry—those pagan Northmen won't get into the Hall. They never have before. Now go down to the kitchen and fetch the cook and her women." Dawnlyn thought for a moment —she mustn't forget anything. "Send the boys out to Ian. He may have need of them. And bring along some loaves of bread in case we have to stay there for a time." She gave the young girl a gentle push. "Hurry, Meg. And don't be afraid. Naught will happen to us."

When Meg was gone, Dawnlyn took another deep breath and glanced quickly around her with large, uptilted, tawny eyes. There was nothing of value in her room, really, except her rosary. All of her remaining belongings were a few miles away at Coldingham, at the nunnery there. This had been her last visit home before taking her final vows, and she would leave on the morrow to return there, never to enter the walls of St. Abb's Head again as Dawnlyn Renfrew. From now on, she'd be Sister Ebba, a wife of Christ, a woman holding an honored position in society. A woman of authority, education and perhaps, someday, power, like her Aunt Gabriella, the Mother Abbess.

Hastily, she snatched the rosary and her ring of keys and

strode purposefully out her door, going to one of the narrow windows that looked out over the courtyard. There was confusion below her in the yard: men milling and shouting, horses neighing, their iron hooves ringing on the cobblestones, the slap of sword against thigh, the ring of a metal blade tested by its owner.

The sight below brought a small stab of fear to her breast, but the battle preparations were not her affair. She shook off her trepidation quickly and bustled to the end of the corridor and down the curving stone steps to the lower reaches of the tower.

Meg had preceded her and the kitchen was deserted except for Gerta, the stout cook.

"Lord above, Lady Dawnlyn!" she said, panting. "Everyone just ran away when that little twit of yours came in here crying and bawling. You'd think she'd have better sense! Fighting men need food."

Gerta moved as fast as her bulk would allow. "Those men haven't even broken their fast." She piled wheels of cheese, loaves of bread, butter, cold chickens on a trestle table with the kegs of mead and cider. "Someone's got to take these things out to the courtyard, my lady." Gerta turned, surprisingly agile for all her weight. "Ah, there you are, you no-good child!" She grabbed a small boy's ear, wrenching it and dragging him over to face Dawnlyn. "Thought you'd get away, did you? And here's your mistress, boy. Aren't you ashamed? Now, get busy and take this food out to the men who are to defend you!"

"Go on, boy," coaxed Dawnlyn, far more kindly than the cook. "Quickly, now. And ask Ian for some men to help you." She turned to Gerta. "Come along, now, you've done your best, the rest is up to the men."

Gerta trundled along behind Dawnlyn, still mumbling that servants nowadays were cowardly, useless and uppity and never were where they were needed. Dawnlyn had heard it all before and smiled to herself at the cook's grumbling. The Hall could do with more servants like the staunch Gerta and

4

less like the timid, fearful Meg. And yet, she knew, the very word *Viking* was enough to terrify any woman in Scotland or, for that matter, in England or France or Ireland. The very word conjured up nightmarish images, hushed whispers, fearful tales of rape and dismemberment, of pagan cries and brutish, heathen warriors who were impervious to pain and wounds when they turned into berserkers in their wild battle frenzy. But to Dawnlyn, who knew little else save St. Abb's Hall and the peaceful Coldingham nunnery, these were but horror tales—the reality of such nightmares had not touched her serene world.

Shaking off her dark thoughts as they hurried along the damp, half-lit stone corridor, Dawnlyn ushered Gerta ahead of her into the chapel and closed the stout oaken door behind her.

The chapel was full. She glanced around at the familiar chamber—it was as old as Christianity itself in Northumbria with its huge, unmortared blocks of gray stone, its altar and basin for holy water carved from a single slab of living rock. She became aware of the sudden hush as she stood facing the crowd of women and children, the many pale ovals that lifted toward her, expectant, as if she were their savior, and then the wailing and keening began again, filling the small, thick-walled chapel with tangible fear. And she thought to herself then that it wasn't fair—she was not without fear herself and yet, as always, the people expected her to be the strong one, to be their anchor in the storm. They were ever placing burdens on her shoulders, ever looking to her as if she were already a mother abbess.

Shaking off her agitation, she walked toward the altar, squeezing a hand here, talking quietly to a sobbing woman, a wailing child there. When they finally grew less fearful, she forced a confident smile to her lips. "Aye, that's better," she said softly. "There is no reason to shed tears." She turned to Gerta; at least *she* was dependable. "Gerta, be so kind as to divide up the bread evenly, and the cider. We will all break our fast together and pray for safe deliverance from the

Vikings. There shall be no more crying in here. We are Scotswomen and must be brave. Remember that. No one has ever conquered St. Abb's Hall and no one shall."

And then the serious-minded young girl went dutifully among the women, calming them, quietly alleviating their fears, until the chapel was filled with the sound of women's chatter, even a child's giggle here and there.

The time passed slowly.

Very little could be heard through the thick stone walls, and Dawnlyn was perishing to unlatch the heavy plank door and see what was happening outside. Waiting, she decided, was the most difficult part. Suddenly she wished she were a man and could fight, do *something*. Waiting was so hard. And to put on a cheerful face in front of the other women, to smile and seem unconcerned when her heart leaped at every sound, when her ear was cocked toward the door, wondering, not knowing.

After an endless two hours, Dawnlyn began to doubt her own brave words. By now, surely, someone should have come to tell her that the danger was past. She dared not show her own fear, dared not voice her doubts. They all looked to her . . .

"Here, my lady," said Gerta softly, padding over to her mistress. "Eat something. You need your strength."

Dawnlyn met the stout woman's kind gaze and her heart gave a great thud. Gerta knew! Gerta had always known how great the burden was to the young girl. She closed her eyes for a second and prayed, then took the crust of bread from the woman's hand. "Thank you, Gerta," was all she could force past the lump in her throat.

Gathering her long, heavy robe around her, Dawnlyn sat on one of the wooden benches and tried to chew on the crust of bread. Her imagination began to best her iron control and she felt her hands begin to tremble slightly. With all her inner strength she fought the mounting fear; she tried to recall the last time there had been Vikings sighted off the Head—it had been when she was ten, and she had waited in the chapel with the women then, too. But that time it had

6

seemed something of an adventure to her, an exciting event to break the monotony of her seemingly endless studies. The other children had cried and clung to their mothers' skirts, but not Dawnlyn; firstly because she had no mother to comfort her but mostly because she had been raised from birth to be serene and deliberate, to be a woman of God who would one day join the church and therein be afforded much satisfaction.

As she waited while the minutes ticked by unendingly, she watched as two small children played in the chapel close to their mothers' sides. Where had her own childhood gone? In truth, had there ever been time for play or had she always been studying dutifully, seriously to become a nun? Dawnlyn Renfrew, the people had always whispered, so sober-minded, so mature, so proud. And yet now she felt as weak as a fledgling, and where a Viking raid had once seemed an adventure, now her hands shook and her heart pounded in dread. She told herself, over and over, that St. Abb's Hall could not be penetrated, never had been. They were safe—shortly she would sit in the great hall with her father and Ian laughing at the foolish Vikings. Still . . .

What if the unthinkable happened?

It couldn't, she told herself sternly.

But, what if . . . ? What if the Vikings were right now scaling the walls of St. Abb's, killing and burning in their berserker's frenzy? What if the men couldn't stop them?

No, never, it couldn't happen to her home, or to her, Robert Renfrew's educated, refined daughter who was to be a nun. It couldn't.

Like a candle flame in an evening breeze, she felt her courage vacillating and suddenly she longed to run to the door, throw it open, scream for help. But she couldn't. Her pride and training would not allow her to show such weakness. And they all depended on her so much.

And then she heard a noise through the door. Her tawny gaze whipped around, widened. There were muffled shouts, the clang of metal on metal, a sudden harsh cry, then a terrible pounding on the stout planks.

7

All the women drew in their breath in one prolonged gasp.

Mighty as Stonehenge's enduring rocks, blond and ruddy, Gaard Wolftooth stood, feet straddled, over the body of the last man he'd laid low with *Lightning Bolt*—his broadsword —and glanced around him. The battle for this godforsaken spit of land went well, even though the defenders fought bravely.

Bravely for Scots, that is. Of course, not one of them was a match for his Viking warriors. No one in the known world was a match for *them*.

The familiar noise of battle surrounded him, held him in its bloody grip: shrieks and grunts, the slap of leather, the ring of metal, the whistling of arrows that could penetrate a man's body, armor and all, and come out at his back, the chop of the hand axe as it split flesh and bone. This was his world, his life. Perhaps many Norsemen had given up these ways ages past for a quieter life, but farming or trading or wielding the smooth tongue of the politician was not for him.

With eyes as forbidding as a bleak winter sky, Gaard surveyed the courtyard and saw that the last few defenders were huddled together in front of the main door, nearly done for now excepting a slim young man, whose dark red hair showed beneath his helmet. The young one fought valiantly, ferociously, standing over a body that he defended with what was obviously his last strength.

It was almost over.

Gaard smiled to himself grimly; it made him appear even more grisly than did his blood-spattered clothes, frightful-looking helm with its cruel nosepiece and the string of sharp-tipped, white fangs that hung around his corded neck.

If it hadn't been for his daring idea of climbing the very cliffs beneath the tower, they might have wasted weeks sieging the well-protected keep. As it was, they'd surprised the enemy totally, taking the Hall easily, with only the loss of one man on the dangerous, slippery, black climb up the sheer cliff. And that man would go to Valhalla proudly, having died in battle.

Gaard eyed his lieutenant, Sweyn, who had just brought down the red-haired one with a glancing blow to his head that dented the helmet but probably not the young man's skull. Well executed. Another man to do Gaard's bidding as the new lord.

Finally the remaining defenders lowered their swords; it was obvious that they could not prevail. Gaard surmised by the way the defeated men kept glancing at the fallen red-haired boy and the older one he had tried so hard to defend that they were the men of authority—the earl and his kinsman, perhaps.

Sweyn was rolling over the earl's body, pulling off his helmet, uncovering his gray hair. Yes, the man lived, struggling to his hands and knees as Gaard strode toward him.

"Yield! Tell your men to throw down their weapons." Gaard's deep voice rang out clearly in the now silent courtyard. The language came back to him, but slowly and rusty on his tongue. It had been years since he had answered his mother or her priest in their own language.

The gray-haired man tried to stand, his movements groggy and flaccid. He looked around at the bloody carnage and the tall, ruddy Norsemen who surrounded him, grinning wolfishly at his defeat.

"Yield!" repeated Gaard.

"I have but little choice," said the man finally and then, for the first time, he saw the red-haired youth stretched out at his feet. "Ian." His voice was filled with pain; he knelt at the boy's side, but Gaard jerked him roughly to his feet again.

"The whelp's yours?"

The earl nodded sadly.

"He's just been knocked cold. He'll be up soon enough." Gaard kept his voice harsh, unrelenting, but silently he acknowledged the man's fear for his son. "What is your title?" he asked the earl.

9

The man straightened up, wincing. He faced Gaard bravely, without cowering or pleading for mercy. "I am Robert Renfrew, Earl of St. Abb's Hall. This is my son, Ian." His voice was strong and proud.

"You are no longer earl of these lands. I am now the Jarl of St. Abb's Hall. I, Gaard Wolftooth of Thorkellhall, claim this land as my own. I have won it in fair battle."

Robert's gaze fell away. "Aye, that you have, Gaard Wolftooth."

"Swear allegiance to me and you will be allowed to go free, about your own business. I mean no more harm to anyone. I wish to rule in peace here."

"My own business," ground out Robert bitterly. "I have no business. You've taken it from me."

"No doubt we can find a place for you here in my Hall." Gaard watched the man carefully, gauging his mettle.

"I thank you, kind sir," said Robert sarcastically. Then, "May I take my retainers and go elsewhere?"

"Nay, I need men to work here."

"Then I have no choice at all. I place myself in your hands. I ask for mercy for my son and—" he stopped suddenly.

"Have you womenfolk here?" asked Gaard, guessing at the man's unfinished sentence.

"Just the servants," said Robert cautiously, "and I ask for your mercy on their behalf also."

"You'll have mercy, old man," growled Gaard, "if you behave yourself and keep that young one in line."

"Father, don't believe him," came a weak voice from behind them. "You know what he is. A liar! A Viking's word's not good enough to spit on! He'll take what he wants and kill us all anyway," called Ian from where he lay on the ground. He tried to rise, but Sweyn put a leather-shod foot on his shoulder and knocked him backwards roughly.

"Ian!" cautioned Robert, the light in his eyes restored now that he knew his son would live.

"Yes, warn your whelp to mind his ways," said Gaard,

10

turning back to Robert. "He misjudges my intent and insults me greatly."

Ian, unnoticed, had gathered his strength and suddenly flung himself at Sweyn, snatching the man's belt-dagger. "Killers! Heathens!" he shouted as he stabbed wildly at the lieutenant.

Effortlessly, Gaard stepped across the intervening space and knocked Ian's hand aside, then twisted his arm behind his back until the youth was brought to his knees, gasping in pain and humiliation.

"Yield!" Gaard's thin lips turned down into a snarl.

"Never, heathen pig!" shouted Ian, even as he felt the joints of his arm creak and begin to separate under the strain. Then he gathered what little spittle remained in his mouth and spat at the Viking's shoe that lay just under his nose.

Gaard flung him aside as one would a pup. "I have offered a just peace and see what I get? Put these men in the dungeon to cool their heels. I'll have no insubordination in *my* Hall."

"But the wounded—" began Robert.

"Let them sit and wallow in their own pain. No doubt it will do them all good, especially your insolent pup."

He shouted orders to his men to take the Scots to the dungeon, to post a sentry and see that no one, *no one,* saw the prisoners until he gave word.

The young upstart, Ian, was dragged off, still cursing impotently while blood ran down one side of his face, striping him savagely with crimson. The other men went more quietly, dejected, ignoring the ribald Norse laughter and joking around them, even though they did understand a few words of the foreign language.

The former earl turned just as he was about to enter the tower. His face was lined with worry. "The women," he said, "you promised mercy . . ."

Gaard looked for a moment into the man's eyes. "So I did," he said slowly. "I am a man of my word. Your women will come to no harm."

"But . . ." Robert's gaze swept the scene of Viking warriors collecting behind Gaard. "But your men . . ."

"Are no different from any others," said Gaard roughly, growing agitated by the old man's unnecessary concern. "My men will have their sport, old one, but we are not slayers of women and children. Begone, I tire of your prattle."

When the Scots were ushered away, Gaard turned and gestured for Sweyn to follow him into the great hall.

"Where do you expect they'll be?" asked Sweyn.

"In the chapel, of course," answered Gaard, smiling implacably, "where all good Christian women should be." Then he turned to face the warriors who crowded in behind them. With the careless authority of one who is used to being obeyed, he raised a silencing hand. "Take what you will within these walls," he said, "but there will be no more blood spilled this day, as we have need of the womenfolk to do our bidding. Now go," he gestured toward the corridor, "and heed my words well . . . no more bloodshed!"

"I hope they save a young one for me," mused Sweyn with a savage grin as he stood next to his leader.

"Don't fret, Sweyn, you'll receive your share of shrinking women-flesh."

"You'll join us this time?" asked Sweyn, looking wistfully toward the dark corridor.

"Perhaps." Gaard's thin lips curled into a frown. "As I plan to remain here, I may as well seek warmth for my bed."

Sweyn strode away, calling over his shoulder, "Perhaps the old earl has a daughter . . ."

"No doubt," Gaard muttered, looking pensively around his new holdings. "And no doubt she's married, toothless and ugly as a toad."

Chapter Two

WHEN THE FIRST RAMPANT VIKING BURST THROUGH THE chapel door, emitting a thunderous roar of victory, a great hush fell over the women; it was as if a glacial chill suddenly swept the air, freezing them in their stances.

Dawnlyn's eyes fixed in terror on the monstrous Viking who stood on the threshold, tall and menacing like all his breed, his lips split into a wide, lascivious grin in his thick blond beard. His shirt of chain mail was grimy, half-dried blood spotted his helmet, his face, his leather battle harness. The long, grooved broadsword sheathed in his belt still dripped with the blood of Scotsmen, and Dawnlyn's stomach lurched sickeningly at the sight. Then one of the women cowering in the corner let out a thin, eerie wail, breaking the heavy silence as if she had some private, awful knowledge of which no one else was as yet aware.

Then more of the Norsemen stood behind their fellow, some with swords and war axes in hand, others simply staring, their wild blue eyes wide with blood frenzy and anticipation.

They poured through the door until it seemed like dozens were pawing at the women, slinging them over their broad shoulders, heedless of the terrified shrieks and bawling children.

13

Dawnlyn remained frozen in mute dread, clutching the loose folds of her velvet robe around her small body, her heart pounding furiously with horror at the scene of brutality.

It was as if a terrible nightmare were unfolding before her eyes. She'd never seen men behave this way, never even realized they could be so bestial.

With a quavering breath she closed her eyes to the sight, telling herself that this was not really happening, that when she opened them again it would be her father and Ian who stood in the chapel.

Sounds of coarse laughter reached her ears and she blotted them out, striving desperately for some kind of control in the face of this horror.

And yet her mind rebelled against the icy control— scream, she told herself, fight against these brutes, show your terror to the world; it would hurt far less to respond than it would to hold in the fear and sickness.

, She opened her eyes and the terrible scene flooded her vision. Mindlessly, she shrank back against a damp stone wall, but the scream would not come, locking itself in her breast.

Her helplessness strangled her. Always, there had been something she could do to help her people in the face of their fear, but this time there was nothing in her thoughts but total futility. There was *nothing* she could do!

Then hot, blood-stained hands were on her, too, dragging her frigid body into a wall-like chest of chain mail, half crushing the breath from her lungs.

Though sickened by the blood-smeared clothes, the fierce pale eyes assaulting her while a gnarled hand pulled hard at her coppery braid, Dawnlyn still could not cry out in terror. She was a Renfrew. And if she were the only Renfrew left breathing, she would not give these vicious heathens her fear to mock.

Moist lips sought her neck while the huge Viking forced her head back, tearing at her hair. She felt a nightmare of dizziness sweep her and a moan stuck in her throat. The cries of the other women receded, blotted out by her own agony of fear as the Norseman pressed himself against her mercilessly. And all the while she couldn't quite fit her mind around the reality of what he planned to do with her.

Then suddenly she felt his hold slacken; she gasped for air while white dots swam momentarily before her eyes. His hands finally left the soft swell of her bosom; the paralyzing panic began to ebb. Then Dawnlyn slowly became aware of a change in the atmosphere—it was quiet now save for an occasional wail from one of the women. These terrible men had, for some as yet unknown reason, ceased their attack; their attention, to a man, was riveted on the threshold of the chapel.

Pushing against her captor's chest with small white hands, Dawnlyn saw over his shoulder a huge man in the portal, so tall and broad-shouldered that his figure seemed to fill the entrance way.

He was their leader—even though she knew nothing of men such as this, of that fact she had no doubt, as his deep, roaring voice sounded and stilled the room into a respectful hush. Dawnlyn had never seen a man so fearful looking. He fit every preconception she'd ever had about Vikings: tall, fair, savage, powerful. An alien being, covered with blood and sweat and battle soil. One big, war-scarred hand grasped his enormous broadsword—a sword that most men would need both hands to hold—and his eyes were dark pools of menace in the shadows of the chapel. His mouth was wide, the lips thin, finely chiseled, but they were drawn down grimly at the corners. Everything about the man shouted authority, strength, command and, to Dawnlyn, terror.

The awesome Viking took a step into the chapel; his keen gaze swept the room. And then he spoke again, only this time, much to her amazement, the tone of his voice was less threatening and his words were in her own tongue.

"Is there a Renfrew amongst you?" he demanded, his presence filling the small chapel with a terrible dominion.

Dawnlyn tried to collect her thoughts and swallowed with

difficulty. What could this Viking leader possibly want with her? She posed him no threat. Did he wish to rid himself of *all* the Renfrews?

Again his iron-gray eyes traveled slowly about the chapel; there were several warriors already climbing atop weeping women who lay helplessly sprawled on the cold stone floor; Meg was sobbing convulsively, pressed against a bench, her barely developed bosom showing beneath her torn linen shift. Everywhere there was agony. The room shimmered with the smell of sweat and blood and fear.

"Answer me!" came the thunder of his deep voice again. "If there be a Renfrew woman among you, I demand you make yourself known, or by Odin's breath I'll see this Hall torn down stone by stone!"

Her heart squeezed in dread. She had to answer him— dear God! She couldn't weaken now!

From her place behind the Viking, still pressed against the wall, Dawnlyn tried her voice. "I am daughter of Robert . . ." she choked, praying that God would grant her the courage to face this Norseman.

His steely gaze moved relentlessly to the shadowed wall. "Show yourself, woman!"

Her Viking captor stepped aside with a small grumble heard only by Dawnlyn. And then she was free, facing the leader, her knees threatening to buckle at any moment while her mind screamed questions at her: why did these men want to harm her women? And what did this tall man want with her?

"I am Gaard Wolftooth, the new Jarl of St. Abb's," he growled. "I claim the woman of this Hall. Come here to me, woman." He stood motionless, his legs apart, his arms folded across his chest, exuding the air of command.

Suddenly a rumble rose from his men as their eyes traveled from the feared leader to the small copper-haired woman. And all the while Dawnlyn cringed inwardly at his statement, "I claim the woman of this Hall."

"Come to me," he commanded again, his tone husky and forbidding.

Fear coiled in her stomach like a writhing serpent as a terrible truth came to her. The Viking wanted her . . . wanted to do that unspeakable *thing* to her. The enormity of her situation struck her with numbing force. But Dawnlyn couldn't go to him—not willingly. She shook her head slowly, barely moving her slim neck. Her tawny eyes held his unflinchingly.

"You cannot escape your fate," he taunted angrily. "Now come to me. I will have the daughter of Robert Renfrew."

Again, her heart pounding wildly, Dawnlyn shook her head. "Not in the house of my God," she whispered through trembling lips. It was as though this thought gave her courage an anchor, something to hold onto in this storm of madness.

For a brief moment his eyes turned dark, then abruptly Gaard Wolftooth tossed back his head and laughed. "Your God!" he roared. "Look about you, daughter of Robert! Whose god rules here?"

"Mine," she replied softly, feeling control embrace her. "My God is still here. He is *everywhere.*"

They stood many yards apart, separated by musky air, by words, by a chasm that could not be bridged. The rumble of talk had ebbed. The men awaited their leader's next move with greedy impatience—how could this tiny woman dare to defy the mighty Wolftooth? The air in the room quivered in anticipation like something alive while silence enshrouded the man and the woman.

For a moment they stood facing one another across an inviolable line she had created, and Dawnlyn thought he would kill her on the spot, so rabid was the look in those steel-gray eyes. But he made no move in her direction.

Finally he spoke in his native tongue—evidently making sport of her. The tension eased and husky laughter arose from his men. Their eyes fell to Dawnlyn's face, lingered, then lowered to her frame lasciviously.

Dawnlyn cringed. She knew nothing of men's lust, did not even really understand why they were glaring at her body, but still she felt somehow shamed beneath their lewd regard. She lowered her eyes. She would never give in to weeping and pleading—such a response was too deeply repressed in her. She sensed he wanted to abuse her—to violate her—but she could neither beg nor submit.

Drawing his helmet from his head and tossing it to the stones with a heavy clang, Gaard smiled wickedly. He began to stride toward her; his men moved from his path. With each step, Dawnlyn thought with horror, he grew a foot in height.

Then he stood over her, a giant blur of stained chain mail, a face made harsh with dirt, eyes the legendary color of stormy seas, unrelenting.

"Nay," she whispered, "I'd sooner kill myself . . . I'd rather join my father and brother before I let you—"

"Your father, your brother?" growled Gaard. "You think them dead?"

"They live?" came her soft voice, filled suddenly with hope.

"Yes. Now yield, woman. I do not wish to cause you harm. My gut is full of battling for one day."

So great was Dawnlyn's relief over her family that tears finally slid down her pale cheeks. The Viking leader mistook them for a woman's plea for mercy, and anger flared within him. He was offering this wench a reasonable solution, a secure position—she should come to him gladly. He meant her no harm.

Reaching out, he took hold of the gold velvet robe and pulled it down off her shoulder.

Dawnlyn's eyes flashed at him in terror; she put her hands up to cover herself in the thin linen shift. "No!" she cried. "Not in the chapel . . . please . . ."

Christians! he thought in anger. She was another like his mother, herself a captured woman, a Christian. He had no time for this—his men, too, were looking on with amusement playing on their scarred faces. Damn this wench! Why wouldn't she yield?

Clenching his teeth, Gaard took hold of the girl's arm and

gave her a sharp but calculated jerk bringing her up short against his rock-hard body.

Dawnlyn gasped in shock. "No!" she breathed. "Please!"

Cheers rose from the men who glared longingly at her proud carriage, her high, firm breasts molded revealingly against the linen. And then slowly they turned from the sight, their eyes feasting again on their own captive women. The noise of mingled cries and grunts once again filled the chapel as their attention was diverted from their chief and his innocent, tawny-eyed captive.

Gaard's gaze lingered on the upturned face of the girl, the wide hazel eyes, the springing red hair and trembling mouth. He sensed the depth of her courage and it struck a chord of respect within him.

In a last attempt to save herself, she forced her eyes to meet his. "I cannot yield. Not here. I would rather you killed me."

"Then you will yield outside this door?" he asked in a musing tone, still marveling at her determination in the face of his strength.

Dawnlyn stood back from him, pressing herself to the wall, covering her young breasts from his eyes. She could not answer him; there *was* no answer to his question. She compressed her lips and stood silently.

Gaard placed his hands on his hips and swept her with an insolent gaze, grumbling in his own tongue as if frustrated. She caught the word *Odin*.

The moment stretched out unendingly while he merely seemed to study her, making a fateful decision.

And then suddenly he moved and she gasped, feeling herself lifted high into the air and slung roughly over his shoulder as if she weighed no more than a fawn. When she finally caught her breath, he was carrying her aloft in the hall, up curving tower steps.

Her mind spun frantically. This pagan, this Viking warrior whose fierce looks struck terror into her very soul, had for some unknown reason given in to her plea. But why? Did it mean he understood her plight and was going to spare her?

Then they were inside the largest bed chamber and she was being lifted down from his shoulder, seemingly with more care than she had been hoisted up to the tall perch.

"Robert Renfrew's chamber?" he asked abruptly, viewing the room with curiosity.

"Yes," she murmured, fumbling with the folds of her gold robe. Perhaps, she thought quickly, all Viking men were not like those below. Perhaps this one did not seek to do that unholy *thing* to her. She held the robe's neck firmly closed.

"Do not bother yourself, little one," he observed, returning his gaze to her slender frame. He nodded ominously toward the bed, then began undoing his leather belt in which was sheathed his bloody sword.

Dawnlyn felt terror suck at her innards. The tremulous hope she had held only seconds before was dashed. If only she could convince him somehow, explain to him! "I cannot do that, that . . . lie with you," she stammered quickly. "I am not like the other women. I am a novice in my church. I am to wed Christ . . ."

"What have gods to do with this? Now disrobe." And he peeled off his chain mail shirt, dropping it in an irrevocable heap at his feet. Next came his woolen tunic, exposing the breadth of his chest with its triangle of blond hair and the strange necklace. He then undid the cross garters and slid off his leather shoes while his steely eyes never left her face. With each departing article of clothing, Dawnlyn's heart gave a sickening lurch of horror. She had never seen a man this way. When he began to slide down his pants, she whirled away from him, crying, "No! You can't!"

His voice reached her across the room to where she had fled. "I offer you a secure position here . . . I shall protect you as no other can, woman. Are you daft?"

Dear God, she thought in horror, he thinks me some common maid! He doesn't understand that for me to yield to such disgrace is not possible!

"Please," she begged, hands covering her face, "I am to become a nun! If you know my language, then you know of my faith! Don't shame me!"

She felt his large hands on her shoulders, deceptively gentle, and gasped. "Take off the shift and come to bed. I will have my way with you and do not intend to discuss it. Rape is not to my liking, but if I must . . ."

Rape! The word he had spoken so quietly stuck in her brain, brought hideous images to mind. "I won't!" cried Dawnlyn, knowing escape was impossible but knowing, too, that she couldn't let this happen.

When his voice came again, from behind her, it was lower, gentler in tone. "Be you a virgin?"

"I am to become a nun. I know nothing of men." Involuntary tears glistened in her eyes. Of course she was a virgin—didn't he understand anything she had told him?

"Then I will take you with care."

Take her! Ruin her! Dawnlyn's back stiffened. "How kind of you, my lord," she cried in sudden defiance. "I would rather throw myself from this tower window than have you touch me, you ungodly heathen!" She heard him growl, and his hands moved from her shoulders to the back of her filmy shift.

"Do you not fear me? Do you not know that to invite the wrath of Gaard Wolftooth is to invite doom?"

"Of course I fear you," she said bravely. "But God has given me strength to face whatever befalls me. I cannot willingly yield—"

Suddenly she felt the linen shift being torn from her back, and she shrank fearfully from him.

At the sight of her small back and tiny waist, the round, firm hips and slender legs, Gaard drew in a breath. "Lie beneath me willingly and I'll not mar this beauty."

Both frightened and shamed, her skin burning beneath his bold gaze, Dawnlyn quickly broke away and ran toward the bed, where she snatched up a quilt to cover her nakedness. She had never been so mortified!

Gaard viewed her form for a moment, then quietly walked toward the bed. She was a beauty, her teeth bared in desperation, her coppery hair loosened from the braid, springing down to her waist in wild disarray. What little he had seen of her naked flesh was enough to rob him of his senses. Yet the desire was tempered by acknowledgment of her innocence. He was no brute; it was not his way to defile innocent women. And, too, there was a purpose to this deed: it would serve him well to make the woman of the Hall his, and there was her sweet beauty . . .

Dawnlyn faced him—a David to his Goliath—fear and loathing spilling from her marigold eyes. She knew he would have to battle her every inch of the way and then, if he did rape her, she knew also that she would not cry out or beg for mercy.

Still, she could not quell the fear in her heart when her eyes saw his masculinity. She'd seen men partially naked before—a bare chest, muscled arms or legs—but this man, this Viking warrior, was seemingly not like any other. He was tall and tanned, and as muscled as a bull. Light hair sprang from his chest, his forearms, his long hair was matted with dried battle-sweat to his neck, making it hard to tell its true shade or texture. His features were bold and generous: a wide, grim mouth, a nose that reminded her of a hawk, yet not so stern as his flinty eyes, which struck a chord of fear in her.

But in spite of the awesome spectacle he presented, it was the sight of his tumescent manhood that caused her to dart for the door. She'd never dreamed a man would look this way. Her hand was reaching desperately for the latch when she felt herself being swept up into those corded arms, held against the surprisingly soft, warm skin, carried to the bed and dumped unceremoniously onto the eiderdown. Her own covering lay back at the door, unattainable.

For what seemed an eternity, she struggled uselessly against his overpowering strength while he evidently never tired of the sport. It was humiliating as she fought and scratched only to have his hand possess a breast and then squeeze a thigh. He touched her in intimate places with large, calloused hands; his eyes burned a leisurely path over her naked body. And all the while, she couldn't fathom why one human being would want to do this to another. What would he gain from hurting her, from seeing her reduced to abject degradation?

Dawnlyn shrieked and kicked, fighting him, but to no avail. Slowly, as her physical strength began to wane, she sensed that he was playing with her, waiting for her to tire and relent.

But that she would never do!

It came to her, when her strength was nearly exhausted, that somehow this kicking and scratching was exactly what he would expect her to do. Then, when she was so weak she could no longer fight him, he must think she would yield like a shrinking rabbit.

Suddenly she ceased the struggle. Her hair was pinned under her arms, which he held over her head, her eyes flashed boldly like golden spikes, her flesh was covered in a glistening sheen of perspiration. With her heart thudding wildly, her chest heaving with effort, she hissed, "Go ahead, you pagan, I'll not play your game. And when you're done," she rasped breathlessly, "you'll not have even touched me. My God will protect me and it will be like this never happened."

"Damn you," he muttered abruptly, his hand twisted in her hair, pulling her head back until their eyes met. While his legs still pinned hers to the quilt, he realized where he had heard those words before. "My God will protect me . . ."—they were his own mother's words!

Oddly angered by his thoughts, his mouth descended onto hers cruelly, but there was no pleasure in it now. What was there about these ardent Christian women that forged their morals with chains of iron? Why? How would it hurt this copper-haired woman to accept him?

He brought his head up sharply, his face lingering over hers. "Damn it!" he growled, "show me something! How can you just lie here like *this* and feel nothing?"

"Use my flesh as you will," she breathed, "but you'll get nothing from me. In my soul I can never yield."

Gaard's body stiffened above her while his hand twisted again in her hair. "I have fought hard this day

. . . journeyed across a sea! I am weary and angry and ache for relief . . ."

"Relief for you!" she bit out. "For me it is assault! Why do you want to harm me?"

"To pleasure myself!" he roared. "By thunder, woman, I am only human!"

"And I am a person, too!" she cried. "There can be no pleasure in this for you! Simply because you are stronger than me . . ." Her molten-copper eyes flashed up into his then, and Gaard was suddenly swept by the truth of this young girl's words. She had a storehouse of courage that strangely overwhelmed him. Of course he could force her . . . And yet, the quality of her courage was beyond his experience. Other women wailed, then yielded, but this one was as steadfast as stone.

And Gaard knew, then, that her defiance and strength were undermining his resolve. He wanted her, wanted to reap a response from those tender lips, but what pleasure was there in overwhelming this small woman with mere physical strength? What did *that* prove?

Angry, frustrated, he sat up abruptly, running an agitated hand through his rumpled hair. With grim lines grooved deeply in his cheeks, he pushed himself from the bed and strode to where her shift lay.

Throwing it to her with exaggerated insouciance, he said, "Here, cover yourself so that your charms have no effect on my brutish urges." His words were bitter and sarcastic. He pulled on his trousers and turned to face the girl as she struggled into her torn shift with great haste. "I suppose you consider yourself saved from a fate worse than death, don't you, girl?" Then, as her uncertain silence hung between them, "Well? Answer me! You were as full of words as a lawspeaker not so long ago!"

"Yes . . . no . . . I don't know how to answer you. I am afraid you will be angry no matter what I say." Her voice was soft and shaking, and he had to strain to hear her.

"The truth, little one! With me the truth will serve you best."

"Then I will tell you. I do feel fortunate. Thank you for sparing me." Her eyes met his, begged for understanding with an eloquence that squeezed his heart.

"Ah! You cold Scots have ice water in your veins. I would have had little pleasure from your skinny bones in any case." He saw her body stiffen with unbidden shock and felt a spurt of childish satisfaction. Then it struck him. "By Odin! I do not even know your name."

Her eyes narrowed. "My name is Lady Dawnlyn Renfrew and that you cannot take from me so easily."

Gaard tossed back his head suddenly and laughed. "A wondrous creature you are! In my land you would be cast into a peat bog for witchcraft, for I believe you have put a spell on me!" While he merely gazed at her, his anger apparently abated, Dawnlyn suddenly realized that she had no idea whatsoever why he had spared her. Still, she was immensely grateful and she thanked God for hearing her prayers.

"You look well pleased with yourself," he said, and she thought: there is no pleasure in what I feel, quite the contrary. He had stripped her of her clothes, touched her intimately in places no man had ever even seen, much less fondled! Nay, it was far from pleasure she was feeling. Degraded, soiled, confused—those were the things that weighed on her mind now.

He walked slowly toward the bed, still eyeing her in a bemused way. "This victory of the flesh I cede to you, Lady Dawnlyn," he said pensively. "But this is only the first battle between us, I think. There will be more . . ."

"I do not seek to battle with you, Gaard Wolftooth," she threw back at him, her chin held high. "I am to become a nun, and I ask of you to respect my position. You cannot have my flesh or my soul, for I am given to another . . ."

"Your God," he stated flatly; then his mouth turned down at the corners in a dark frown. "I should throw you to my wolves below, Dawnlyn Renfrew . . . let them take their sport with you. Yes," he taunted, "perhaps I shall. It would temper your steel."

Was he serious? Did all men wish to do this thing so much? she wondered dismally, fear creeping into her heart once more.

Seeing how her eyes had grown wide again, Gaard laughed knowledgeably. "Now go fetch me water for a bath and stir the flames in the hearth, for I want to soothe my sore muscles." It was an abrupt dismissal, as if he'd had enough of women and their follies. She realized that he had purposely tried to frighten her once more. "And fetch me mead and food while I rest," Gaard said, insultingly, stretching himself out on the bed with lithe, catlike arrogance.

Was he mad? What game was this he played? Didn't he know she would escape him now?

Realizing that she truly was free to leave the chamber, willing herself to think no more for the moment about what might still be done to her, she donned her robe and left the room quickly, glad to be gone from his sight.

She crept down the long, curving steps and through the great hall where the Viking men slept or drank her family's ale. Several of the women were still being pawed, others sat hunched in the far corners, weeping hysterically. To Dawnlyn's eyes the scene was a mad charade. She searched the hall for Meg, then spotted her in a corner, curled up into a fetal ball. She strode purposefully toward her.

Dawnlyn shook the girl's arm. "Are you all right?"

"I think so," came the girl's trembling reply. "The brute has done with me and sought another."

"Then try not to weep . . . the worst is over. Now come, we must make haste." Dawnlyn helped the girl to her feet. "We are all captives together, Meg. We must be strong and accept this fate as best we can." Dawnlyn led the girl down a corridor and stood at the narrow steps of the dungeon.

"Nay!" Meg wailed. "I cannot go down there!"

Dawnlyn shook her head in exasperation. "Then I shall." But she was stopped at the bottom of the cold stone steps by a fierce Viking guard. She tried to make him understand that her father was down there, that she had to see him, but the man stood in her path like an impregnable wall and refused to understand her.

Finally, at her wit's end, she called through the dimness, "Father! Are you there?" Moaning reached her ears from below; she steeled herself. "Father! It is Dawnlyn."

"Dawnlyn!" Robert's voice finally echoed up through the murk to reach her.

"Are you all right, Father?" Her heart throbbed hopefully.

"Aye, aye. But Ian's hurt and we need bandages, water. Can you help us, lass?"

And then she knew with utter clarity that she couldn't escape immediately to Coldingham, to the nunnery. She had to help the wounded, see to Ian and her father first. Later, later she would escape . . . "I'll return," she called, then retraced her path back up the dark stairwell. But, she realized suddenly, to help them meant to go back to that frightening Gaard, the leader. Would he allow her to aid them? Most likely he wouldn't care if her father and brother rotted in the dungeon. Yet duty beckoned, refusing to release her.

Dawnlyn instructed Meg to fetch Gaard his water and heat it on the hearth. She went for the mead and a roasted chicken—a serving wench now, herself. But, she told herself sternly, she would have to do his bidding with a minimum of rebellion if she wanted to help her kinsmen.

Before returning to her father's quarters, she stopped at her own chamber to change into a soft green velvet gown, which was roped loosely at the waist with a silken cord. Somehow the clean gown next to her skin felt safe and secure; she put from her mind again the fact of her position here. Soon she would flee to Coldingham—flee and forget in the embrace of her God. But first, she had her duty . . .

Meg, although trembling from head to toe, was already pouring warm water into the wooden tub when Dawnlyn arrived. Gaard was sitting naked on the side of the bed, a quilt barely covering his manhood, his long, muscular legs, covered with curling blond hairs, stretched comfortably out

27

in front of him. His back was to Dawnlyn and she saw a narrow white scar running from the thick muscle of his shoulder blade down in an arc, ending near his tapered waist. Inadvertently, she wished the stroke of the blade had finished him off, then just as quickly put the ungodly thought from her mind.

"Ah," he said lazily, "there you are. I was near ready to send someone to fetch you back."

Dawnlyn ignored him, placing the flagon and chicken on a rough-hewn wooden table next to the bed. When she came near him, he gave her soft rump a healthy slap and quickly she turned, glaring into his amused, heavy-lidded eyes.

Chuckling, Gaard rose, dropping the quilt, and spun Dawnlyn into his arms, nearly knocking her breath out when her breasts slammed against the obdurate wall of his chest. His lips descended onto hers in a demanding, searing kiss, and she steeled herself for the inevitable pain; but somehow his lips did not hurt her. Instead, they pressed hers with a kind of tender possessiveness that sent a strange thrill of faintness through her. She fought the feeling. Then just as swiftly he released her, causing her to stumble back against the bed.

She drew the full sleeve of her velvet gown across her mouth. "You pagan!" she hissed, wondering how she would ever keep up a civil front. The man seemed to goad her deliberately.

Ignoring her now, Gaard went naked, unashamedly, to the half-full tub and lowered himself into its warmth. "Bring me my food," he commanded.

Anger spurted dangerously within her and she hesitated.

"Have it as you will, Dawnlyn," he said, his eyes narrowed. "But if I have to rise from this comfort, then I shall take my wrath out on your flesh. Do you want a beating?"

Grasping at control, humiliated beyond bearing that Meg had heard his rude words, Dawnlyn carried his food and mead over to the tub while Meg, terrified, dragged the table over, too.

"Begone!" he commanded of Meg. "Your fair lady is quite capable of seeing to my needs."

And Dawnlyn did, furious at his taunts, unable to keep herself from giving some of her own back when he forced her to scrub his neck and hair. Yet as her hands worked lather unwillingly over his flesh she could not help but be amazed at his powerful build, and thoughts kept crowding her mind of that same body, only a short while ago, lying on top of her, pinning her to the quilts, those large, calloused hands touching her so intimately. Yet, strangely, he had not marked her flesh nor truly harmed her in any way . . .

A hot flush stained her cheeks a fiery crimson.

"What causes your sudden color?" observed Gaard, smirking.

Dawnlyn narrowed tilted eyes, scrubbing at his back, letting her nails, as if by accident, leave long red marks on the tanned skin. "Thoughts of your proximity, *great* Viking. Thoughts of how close I came to losing my virtue."

"Your ignorance is laughable. I would have done you a favor, if you'd the sense to see it," he said matter-of-factly.

She ignored his words, afraid to arouse his temper. She sought for a new topic, to turn his mind from her remarks. Her fingers caught in the strange necklace of white, glistening objects that lay on his smooth, muscled chest. "Your teeth?" she gibed, but knew they weren't, as his were white and healthy and quite obviously still in his mouth.

Gaard chuckled deeply, relieving her anxiety, then bade her bring him a sharp shaving blade so that he might scrape his whiskers. He was the only clean-shaven Viking she had seen, and she guessed it must set him apart from his warriors. She even offered to shave him herself.

"Nay!" he laughed easily. "Do you think me stupid?"

As he scraped away the light-colored whiskers, Dawnlyn saw another scar marring his chin. It appeared that a sword must have glanced off the jawbone in some long ago battle. His body, she saw, was a map of campaigns, and she wondered suddenly about his past life.

"Have you reached forty years?" she asked unthinkingly, studying the deep crinkle lines around his dark silver eyes. And abruptly she realized that she had just spoken to him civilly as if he were an honored guest in the Hall!

"No. My years are thirty-four. And you, Dawnlyn?"

"I am eighteen summers," she replied, still amazed at the turn of their conversation. Why, they could have been two ordinary people exchanging civilities.

"You should already be wed. Perhaps it is your rash tongue that keeps you single." But the tone of his voice was light, almost playful.

"I am to be wed to my church."

"I know of your ways. They are foolish. A woman belongs with a man, bearing his children." He tossed aside the blade, drank thirstily from the flagon, then rubbed soap over his face and asked for rinsing water.

It was a good thing he could not see her face just then, Dawnlyn thought, because surely her drawn brows and tight lips would have given away her anger at his thoughtless words. She reached deep within and struggled for control. She knew instinctively that to best this man who had total power over her, she could not give way to the anger she felt.

Dawnlyn took a deep breath as she fetched the water and began pouring it over his hair, his strong neck and powerful shoulders. She would try once again to reach this barbarian, to make him understand her plight. He did not seem unintelligent. Maybe she could convince him to let her go to Coldingham freely. "A nun is afforded much freedom and power . . . power that a woman married with babes suckling each year is denied."

"And you desire power, little one?"

"My due measure. All my life I have been raised and tutored toward one goal. I am not a meek lamb."

"You need not tell me," he mused.

Curiosity besting her now, Dawnlyn touched the necklace. "Why do you wear this . . . this thing?"

"This *thing* is a necklace of the teeth of Fenris, the Giant

30

Wolf. It is my talisman and my luck." He touched it with his long fingers, a lazy, slanted smile carved on his wide mouth.

"Fenris? A giant wolf? Surely you jest."

He turned on her his quicksilver glance full of roguish laughter and mock anger. "No one has dared to question my tale before," he said, an edge of humor barely concealed in his voice.

"What tale? Faith, you Vikings have strange customs."

"Shall I tell you the story? It is very impressive and full of Norse magic. It has been told and retold for nearly three decades now." His eyes glinted a kind of challenge at her.

"Yes, tell me. Then I will know better what kind of man has conquered my home."

Gaard settled back in the tub, his humor fading now, a faraway look in his eyes. "It happened when I was but a lad of seven. I wandered away into the dark forest, playing with my wooden sword. I played at being a fierce warrior, slashing a twig here, a flower there. Suddenly the wood was silent and there I was—alone—surrounded by a pack of fierce, blood-hungry wolves and Fenris, the Giant Wolf, Bone Gnasher, was their leader." He paused then, eyeing Dawnlyn carefully for a moment. Then he said of Fenris, "His tongue lolled out, dripping, and his red eyes met mine. He was taller than I and very, very hungry. He growled, deep in his shaggy throat."

"What happened?" burst from her lips. Her tawny eyes were wide with expectation.

A smile so slight that it went unnoticed touched Gaard's lips; he went on. "I was terrified. You can imagine. But the sons of the mighty Thorkell Gray Hair were taught courage with the first sip of their mother's milk, and so I stood staunchly, raised my little wooden sword . . ." Here he paused, the consummate storyteller.

"Yes?"

"And the glistening white fangs of Fenris fell at my feet like harmless pebbles, and he slunk away into the tall spruce with his deadly pack. I was left with these." Again, his fingers caressed the necklace.

31

Dawnlyn's eyes followed his fingers as if mesmerized, studied the white things that hung around his neck. They *did* look like teeth . . .

Then reality struck her and she glanced up abruptly to meet Gaard's droll gaze. "You mock me," she said stiffly, embarrassed to have been so gullible.

With that, he laughed heartily. "And your stories? This man, Moses, who parted the Red Sea waters. Am I to believe such a farfetched tale? I've been to the Red Sea and it appeared quite intact to me." His tone was light, bantering.

Dawnlyn was struck mute. How did this pagan know of her faith? And what did he mean, he had been to the Red Sea? And how could he *joke* about the story of Moses?

Tight-lipped, she walked toward the small window overlooking the headland far below. Gaard dressed in a clean, brown, wool tunic, forgoing the shirt of chain mail. When she finally turned around to face him, she was taken aback by his change of appearance.

Now that he was washed and his hair no longer matted from the helmet, she saw him quite differently. The strong, hard features were the same: lean carved chin, thin lips, generous nose and stormy eyes. But the cleansing had lent him a more civilized look and his hair was now the color of light honey, thick and unruly, hanging in waves below his ears, quite different from the Scots, who kept theirs cropped close to the head.

"What are you glaring at, woman?" he asked, sheathing his heavy sword in the leather belt.

"Your hair. Why do you not trim it?"

Gaard laughed proudly. "We Norsemen have golden hair and are pleased to show the world," he bragged. "Have you not noticed our fair color and great height?"

"Yes," she mused aloud, "there are none quite like you."

Gaard strode toward her, picked up a cascading lock of her copper hair. "Although not at all fair," he observed, "your hair is the color of maple leaves in autumn. It is quite rare. And your eyes"—he tipped her head to view them

32

better—"your eyes are nearly the same hue. 'Tis amazing, the effect . . ."

Unbidden, Dawnlyn's breath stopped in her throat. Swept by uncertainty, she spun away. "I must gather linen and water and see to our wounded." She spoke hastily, moving toward the door. "Will you tell the sentry to let me pass?"

"What?" he exploded.

"My brother is wounded and so are many others . . ."

"How can you know that?" He thrust his arms across his wide chest, waiting impatiently.

"I . . . I was there to see them."

"By Odin!" he roared. "Do you not realize the danger you placed yourself in? I'll have the guard's head for this!"

"If you wish," she said mildly. "But he did not let me see them. He only let me call out for a moment."

Gaard's eyes were a deep gray now, storming with fury.

Quickly Dawnlyn undid the latch. "I will go to my family. I will!"

"You won't. You cannot possibly think I'll relent on this, too . . ." But his words were lost in the empty room as Dawnlyn quietly slipped down the dark corridor.

Gaard stood alone, thunderstruck, his grim mouth hanging open in mute disbelief.

Chapter Three

DAWNLYN WAS SURE HIS HEAVY HAND WOULD COME DOWN upon her shoulder at any moment. It was utterly unnerving to keep walking, head held high, away from the room. But she did it, even though thrills of fear ran up her spine; and his hand never stopped her nor did he call on his men to restrain her.

Slowly, the tension ebbed from her body as she made her way back down the damp-walled steps towards the barred door of the dungeon. But even before she reached it, she knew the sentry was still there, as an oil lamp cast weird, flickering shadows around the final curve of the stairs.

She made up her mind, took a deep breath and descended the last few steps, rounded the corner.

"I must see the wounded men," she said, hoping he could understand her, hoping her voice sounded sufficiently authoritative.

The sentinel had been well supplied with food and drink for his lonely vigil. He wiped the froth of ale from his beard and stared at her. She could see he was half drunk. She'd have to be careful.

He shook his heavy head.

"I am the lady of this Hall. I have the authority." She made her voice sound forceful, took a step forward, but the guard narrowed his eyes and moved in front of her, resting his hand on the hilt of his sword threateningly. She tried to speak to him in the few words of Norse she knew, but none of the words fit together properly. "Let me pass," she finally managed in his tongue.

"Nay." His voice was rough.

"I *will* see them!" she cried, frustrated beyond measure. She stamped her foot in anger. "They're hurt. I must help them. You big, bloody fool! Cruel, heathen barbarian!" Her temper rose, shattering whatever calm she had managed to retain up to now. She could hear moans of pain beyond the barred door. Panic rose in her breast; she fought it down, but it threatened to choke her. She *had* to get to her father, to Ian, to all of them!

The sentry eyed her coldly, shook his head again. All the pent-up pain and fury of the day burst in her veins. Somewhere, deep in her consciousness, she was aware that the man was merely following orders, that she was no longer mistress in this Hall, that she was conquered, her family ruined, that Gaard was behind their ruination and *he* should pay. But the heavy-shouldered man before her bore the brunt of her present rage.

Seeing only Gaard's visage, she launched herself at the guard, beating with small fists against the rock wall of his chest, crying, shouting unintelligibly.

Pain and terror and hysteria drove her on, heedless of her danger. But it was all over in a moment; the huge man laughed harshly and grabbed her arms, pinning her wrists together with one hamlike hand, then threw her aside effortlessly.

Dawnlyn lay in a heap on the damp stone floor, her chest heaving with effort. Sudden cold logic flooded her as she lay there: force was useless. She had to be more clever than these brutes to get her way.

Silently she rose and ascended the stairs to the great hall where dozens of the Vikings ate St. Abb's food, drank the ale, fondled the women, all the while roaring with coarse laughter. Never had Dawnlyn heard such a racket within these walls; the dour Scots never deigned to laugh so freely or so loudly.

She looked around cautiously, not even certain of what she was searching for—someone to help her.

But in this foreign, boisterous army, there was not one she knew, or could trust, or could even talk to.

"My lady, you look lost. Do you search for Gaard?" An unknown voice, accented but intelligible, sounded in her ear. She whirled, startled.

A tall young Viking faced her, fair as the others, but clean shaven except for a blond, drooping mustache. He looked quite civilized, having obviously cleaned himself and donned clothes not stained by the battle. He eyed her, half-amused, half-appreciative. "Do you search for Gaard?" he repeated.

So they all must assume that *thing* had occurred between her and Gaard. Hot shame burned her face. "No!" she said, too loudly. "I'm trying to get to the wounded men in the dungeon. Surely your esteemed leader wishes them to live so they can swell the ranks of his subjects." Her voice rang with scorn. "And that *beast* on watch will not let me by!"

Laughter flickered in the young man's deep-set blue eyes for a speck of time. Dawnlyn fought down her anger once more. "He has orders, my lady," he said softly.

"Orders!"

"Yes, Gaard's orders. He'd be executed if he allowed you past. However, we shall see if something cannot be done. Allow me to introduce myself. I am Sweyn Ivarson, Gaard's lieutenant." Then Sweyn eyed her more soberly. "I can hardly believe Gaard would allow you to roam about so freely. The battle mood is still within the men."

Dawnlyn met his words with silence.

"Does Gaard know where you are? Does he know you wish to go to the dungeon?"

"He knows," she said finally, "I told him."

"I see," replied Sweyn pensively, studying her. He sensed the defiant streak in this softly beautiful girl and thought that it was no wonder at all Gaard let her have her way—what man could resist the combination of calm fortitude and such innocent, golden beauty?

Dawnlyn felt suddenly unnerved by this man's close scrutiny. "My men need help," she explained desperately. "I see you don't neglect your own!" She gestured at the wounded Vikings, lying on pallets in front of the hearth, bandaged, propped up on cushions, most joking and laughing and drinking as heartily as their uninjured companions.

"Patience," said Sweyn. "I will send a message to Gaard and we'll see what develops. Pray be seated while we wait, my lady, and share a cup of cider with me."

He called for quill and parchment and wrote, then sent a young serving wench aloft with it.

Dawnlyn seated herself stiffly on a wooden bench to wait. Sweyn sat casually next to her, poured cider into a cup for her, took up his own flagon of ale.

"You know how to write," Dawnlyn remarked haughtily.

"Yes, and cipher, too. I was raised with Gaard, and his mother's priest taught us as boys." His glance was tinged with humor.

"A priest! But I thought . . ."

"Norway is a Christian land now and has been for nearly a hundred years. At least *some* of Norway is. There are those who prefer the old ways, and some who combine the two and seem quite content."

"And you speak our language?"

"Again, the priest . . ."

"Unfortunately, your chief, Gaard, did not learn so much." Her voice was tight and hard, filled with smugness.

"There you are wrong, my lady. He learned more than I and was a far better pupil."

She turned to him in amazement. That barbarian upstairs! And then the girl returned, handed the rolled parchment to Sweyn, backed away warily.

"Ah," said Sweyn, "he allows you to treat your men. I rather thought he might. Gather what you will need and I will see you safely below to the dungeon."

Quickly, before Sweyn could change his mind, Dawnlyn gathered a great bundle of food and a keg of water, then ordered one of the hall women to bring clean linen and the chest of herbs left by her mother.

When all was ready, Sweyn carried a torch and led the way down the dungeon steps, where he spoke to the sentry and showed him Gaard's mark on the parchment.

Regally, Dawnlyn swept by the huge Viking, disdaining to meet his eyes as he opened the barred door. The girl, Mary, who carried the basket of cloths, was terrified, whimpering with fear in the cold, dank chamber that wept with the moisture of the ground that surrounded it. The low moans of the imprisoned men made Mary's eyes grow wilder with fear.

"Mary, you may return to the hall. I'll see to them myself. Go on, now," said Dawnlyn wearily. The girl would probably be of no help anyway.

"I shall leave you the light, my lady," said Sweyn. "The sentry has his orders. He will unlock the door when you ask. Will you be long?" he asked, impervious to the scene of misery around them.

"Probably, yes," answered Dawnlyn distractedly. She was trying to see into the gloom of the dungeon. Terrible odors and sounds assailed her senses. The heavy door clanged shut behind her, making her nerves jump with fright.

"Father?" she called tentatively.

"Dawnlyn! You've come." Robert's voice was weak. It came from across the echoing room, muffled by cold and damp and endlessly thick, dripping walls.

Raising the torch, Dawnlyn searched the dim room. There he was, trying to stand up against the far wall, blinking at the light of the torch.

Dawnlyn stuck the torch in a leather wall sconce, crossed to her father, embraced him, felt herself enfolded by his arms as she had been so many times as a child. His hand stroked her hair. She swallowed a lump in her throat, desperately blinked back hot tears. Her father was worse off

38

than she; he needed none of her problems to add to his own.

"I promised I'd come back," she whispered. "I brought food and water and bandages. How fares Ian?"

"Half out of his mind with rage. You know your brother. He has a nasty gash on his head that keeps bleeding. He's a bit dizzy, but he'll survive, lass. How'd you manage to get in here? I heard you earlier . . ."

"I managed," she said tightly.

"Are you . . . all right, Dawnlyn?" Her father's tone left no doubt as to what he meant.

"I'm fine," she said hastily, unable to meet his searching gaze. "I am unhurt."

Robert was silent, knowing his daughter well enough, recognizing all the small signs of her ordeal. He sighed. At least she showed no signs of a beating. He was powerless to help her now; she'd have to be strong enough to face it on her own.

Dawnlyn busied herself with the men, treating the most seriously wounded first, holding her stomach from emptying on the dank floor by pure fortitude. There were, fortunately, only a few serious wounds, the rest mainly cuts that needed cleaning and stitching, broken bones that had to be set, bruises, cracked heads, broken noses and teeth. Her main problem was not treating the men but the difficulty of seeing their wounds clearly in the murky light. One man had a stomach wound that she knew would be fatal; she made him as comfortable as she could. There was nothing to be done.

All the time she worked, the men spoke softly, thanking her, asking after her and speculating on what the Vikings meant to do with them. She could not answer them, except to say, "This Gaard Wolftooth means to be the new laird. He would have us believe that he wishes peace. But whether or not he can be trusted, I have no idea."

Finally, Ian let her treat his wound, having made her tend to all the others first.

"It's nothing," he insisted.

But Dawnlyn, straining to see, cleaned the cut, snipping

39

away the blood-clotted hair from its edges with her sharpest scissors, and put in several neat stitches while Ian cursed loudly at the needle pricks.

The men were eating ravenously and drinking the water. It had been a long, painful twelve hours or more since they'd fought. They'd lost their keep, their places in society, some even their women, all on this day. They were reduced to no more than the rats with whom they shared their rotting quarters. But still, rats must survive . . .

"Will he kill us?" Ian's voice reached through the darkness, disembodied.

"No, I don't think so," she answered. "He'd have done it by now, I should imagine. He no doubt wants men to follow him."

A collective sigh of relief rose from the shadowed figures around her. What if she were wrong? Did she have the right to give them hope if it was to be dashed?

Robert gestured Dawnlyn to a corner of the chamber; a black shadow darted across the ground as they made their way there. Dawnlyn shuddered, wondering for how long she could keep up this calm facade.

"Lass, tell me the truth. What's he done to you?"

Her glance fell away. "Nothing I can't bear. Don't worry about me. I think he means to keep me here, but I'll find a way to escape. I'll go to Coldingham and be finished with him."

Dawnlyn's voice was changed somehow; her father recognized a new tone, a new hardness beyond her normal maturity. And yet, this was no defeated woman. No matter what the heathen had done to his daughter, she still had her pride and her courage and even her wits about her.

"My poor lass, I've failed you, all of you. Never in two hundred and fifty years have the Vikings been able to take St. Abb's. It's a terrible thing to be defeated, maybe even worse for you . . ." Robert's voice was filled with unquenchable sorrow.

"No, Father. It wasn't your fault. I've never seen anything like them. They're like animals . . ."

"But in battle they're the cleverest, they pride themselves on it, outwitting their foes time and time again. Oh, well, it doesn't matter anymore. We must accept this burden God's laid on us."

"Not God! The Vikings laid the burden on us." Her words slashed the damp air like a flame. "Don't blame this on our Lord!"

"Dawnlyn, hear me. If this man, this Gaard, wants you"—he ignored the way she averted her face from his then—"you'll have to stay with him . . ."

"No!" she interrupted. "I'll see that you're all well and then I'll return to Coldingham. I'll hide there!"

"My child, you must try to understand—it's too late for that. You must stay here with him. I know it's hard to accept, but think: you're the only Renfrew left to see to the Hall, to take care of the people. They'll all look to you now. I can't help from this accursed hole in the earth. Don't you see? It's your responsibility as a Renfrew. And you can't leave it. These men would have died tonight but for you. You have always been so strong and done your duty." His words were low and Dawnlyn had to strain to hear, but they fell on her ears with the ring of terrible but unalterable truth.

There was no escape for her—nowhere to run. All those long years spent in preparation and now there would be no gentle life as a nun. Tears welled in her hazel eyes. She brushed them away relentlessly.

"I fear there is still more, lass. You're a beautiful woman. Any man would want you. Aye, I know it's a terrible thing for you. But for your protection, and for ours, think of my words: you must get this Viking to marry you, if you can." He went on, overriding her gasp of shock. "He'll have you anyway," his voice grew hard, "if he hasn't already. Face the truth. If you're his wedded wife, you'll have his protection and be able to help us all that much more. And if there are children from this man"—this time he had to stop for a while, give his poor, innocent child a chance to assimilate this burdensome revelation—"they will at least be legitimate heirs to St. Abb's. They will be Renfrews."

41

Dawnlyn was still; only her eyes revealed the tumult that threatened to engulf her. Children! She hadn't thought of that, hadn't had time to even consider that awful possibility. No, she had been born to be a nun, it couldn't happen to her . . .

Robert's hand reached out to rest on her shoulder. "I know, it's hard to accept. But, lass, there's no escape. So you must live the best way you can under their power. Unfortunately for you, that's as a married woman. Think on it, Dawnlyn . . . you've always been a sober-minded, dutiful girl . . ."

She'd had the rest of the endless night to think on it. Not wanting to upset her father any more, she hadn't argued with him, nor had she allowed him to see how shocked she'd been by his cold assessment of her situation. Surely he didn't *really* mean for her to enter into holy wedlock with this crude Viking, this heathen stranger. But when she thought back on his hard words, she was afraid that his solution was best for everyone. But, to *marry* that crude Viking? My dear Lord, she prayed, could she bear it? Was there no escape? How could a person's whole life be turned upside down so quickly, so savagely?

A terrible, bleak loneliness swept over her—she didn't *want* to marry. She wanted to be a nun, and she'd never even imagined another existence. She'd never be able to cope! Still, the decisions had to be made *now*, instantly; there was no time for prolonged thought, or prayer, no time, even, for a decent interval of mourning. The shock hadn't even worn off.

She wandered the cold dark corridors of the tower, seeing and hearing things that had never existed in the Hall before. It was as if she were a wraith, doomed forever to wander with no place to rest, no sanctuary. Desolation ate at her like a sharp-beaked vulture.

Eventually, she tried to find a chamber in which to sleep, but they were all taken by Vikings who snored or mounted women uncaringly as she pushed the doors open.

Gaard was nowhere to be seen, neither in the great hall with the ribald Vikings nor in the dark passages. She could only assume he'd retired already and prayed that he had no more interest in her . . . tonight. At first it had amazed her that she was able to wander about freely in the corridors, but then she had noticed the armed sentries at every door, the many fierce eyes that followed her every movement. And she knew then that they followed Gaard's orders to the letter: she was to be allowed the freedom of the tower and Gaard's so-called protection, but there would be no escape.

In her mind's eye an image formed, a terrible, frightening image that chilled her to the bone: the lengendary Viking leader as a deadly spider squatting placidly at the center of his web, waiting, ever conscious of all movement in his realm, aware even of the slightest stirring of the farthest one of his intricately woven silk strands. Dawnlyn felt the prickly web surround her—she was trapped, hopelessly entangled in Gaard's net.

Exhausted after the hours spent under unbearable tension, the fear, she now sought only a place to rest, to lay her head. Her muscles seemed to tremble uncontrollably from tiredness; tears were agonizingly close to the surface as she wandered the Hall of which she'd once been the proud and honored daughter.

Then she realized dismally that there was no place for her but one—the master chamber where she had last seen Gaard. Even though she couldn't bear the thought of willingly going near him again, plain exhaustion overruled her qualms. Perhaps he wasn't there at all . . .

Quiet as a mouse, she pushed open the door and peeked in. Gaard was indeed there and lay sprawled on the big bed, his long, naked limbs entangled in the eiderdown. She held her breath, praying he would not awaken, but he slept heavily, an empty flagon of ale on its side next to the bed.

His clothes were flung helter-skelter on the floor, and, as her eyes grew accustomed to the darkness, she saw his heavy sword lying by his side on the coverlet.

Such overwhelming arrogance these Vikings had! To

sleep, unguarded, while occupying an enemy keep. She slipped up to the bed, reached a hand out to touch the steel of the sword. Its cold whisper thrilled her. Suddenly she imagined herself lifting it, burying it deep in this man, the stranger who had taken from her so much she held dear. A sheen of moisture covered her brow; her fingers caressed the sword lovingly, sensually. She pictured him lying in his own blood, his flinty eyes meeting hers for a split second before the life left them, knowing she'd won.

Her eyes shifted to his body, so long, endlessly long, lying there on her father's bed. And so relaxed. The broad shoulders that rippled with muscle, the long, graceful arms, corded with iron strength, the fair, curling hairs on the chest that rose and fell gently. Then his face, closed and different in sleep, deceptively innocent, a slight frown clouding the high brow.

He was a handsome man, she hated to admit, but handsome only in repose. In action, he was cruel as Lucifer, a heathen who would undoubtedly take her as if she were no more than a brood mare.

She could kill him now.

But the heat of her intent ebbed. The sword was too heavy to lift, and even if she could lift it, he'd wake and wrest it from her. And, too, there was her gentle Christ, who taught "thou shalt not kill." It was not feasible.

Leaving him to his ill-earned sleep, Dawnlyn found a woolen cloak, wrapped it around her and curled up in her father's big chair.

Sometime, alone, so very alone in the fragile hours of the dawning, she slept.

Dawnlyn awakened the next morning sensing that something had happened within her during the course of the night. She opened her eyes finally, her head filled with the knowledge of what she had to do, recognizing the ultimate wisdom of her father's advice. She could not be selfish or undisciplined. She still longed to be a nun, but first she was a Renfrew. She had been educated and filled with pride in herself and her family. It would not do for her to run, hiding from her duty, from *him*. She had been taught to face life, to accept and deal with problems, not to hide under the covers like a child and cry. She wondered, for a moment, from whence had come this inner strength; was it truly because of her upbringing within the church, her lack of youthful folly, or had she been born with the strength to face reality squarely?

She felt cold and cramped from sleeping in the hard chair. Glancing over to the bed, she saw Gaard stretch, then sit up and shake his head as if to clear it. A cold clutch of fear grabbed her heart. Then desolation washed over her—the man was an utter stranger, a barbarian. And she was to be his woman . . . his wife? *Belong* to him? Let him use her body in that awful way? How could this be happening to her? How could her gentle Lord *let* this happen to her?

Then, as if reading her thoughts, Gaard looked over at her, his eyes bleary and red and dimmed by overindulgence.

"You wasted half of a comfortable bed," he growled. He ran a hand through his tousled, dark blond hair and winced.

"You were as drunk as a pig, my lord," Dawnlyn said sarcastically, "and I had no wish to be near you."

"Then why didn't you simply continue to wander about aimlessly or sleep in that dark hole with your menfolk?" he taunted. "Or did the rats put you off?"

"Better the rats, my lord," she bit out, "than you." But as soon as she saw the murderous scowl come to his face, she wished she hadn't spoken so hastily. She curled up into the chair as if for protection.

Gaard studied her for a moment; slowly the scowl softened. "Women have no sense," he remarked offhandedly, dismissing her with a glance.

"No sense?" she repeated, suddenly angry, but then remembered that she mustn't goad him into a rage—too many lives dear to her were held in his hands. "I do not wish to quarrel," she said, holding in her irritation.

"Nor do I. There is much to be done here this day, and

my life would be far easier if you would be biddable, Dawnlyn."

"I shall do my best," she replied sincerely now. "But before you see to your work, there is something I wish to ask of you, my lord." She uncurled her slender frame from the chair and sat straight-backed, her gaze holding his with a pride that cost her much.

"Ask, Dawnlyn, but come to the point quickly, woman, for I do not cherish female word games."

"Yes, my lord, I'll be brief and to the point. I wish for you to . . . to marry me." Her eyes fell away at the sight of his raised brow. She swallowed hard. "As the lady . . . former lady . . . of this Hall, I ask to be treated fairly. I believe a marriage between us would serve both Scots and Vikings alike."

Gaard's expression remained closed for an endless moment. Finally he spoke. "Well said, Lady Dawnlyn. And there is some wisdom to your words." And then he smiled. "But I have long since considered such an arrangement and concluded that, at this present time, I am far too involved to think on a marriage." He swung his long legs over the side of the bed, stood and stretched as if to dismiss her.

Heat rose to her cheeks and Dawnlyn quickly averted her gaze from his nakedness; her heart pounded slow drumbeats in her breast as he went to the washstand and she could hear water splashing.

She took a deep breath. "Because you have chosen to remain unwed up until now does not mean that you cannot change your mind. There must be a betrothal between us," she finished far more confidently than she felt.

Gaard's head was raised over the basin, water dripping from his hair, splashing back into the pewter vessel in tiny rivulets. He straightened slowly. His face wore an almost comical expression. "What?" he laughed, amazed.

"Now that you would have everyone believe you bedded me, I repeat, you owe me marriage." Her voice was exceptionally calm, even cool, belying her inner turmoil.

"I owe you?" He threw back his leonine head and

laughed, shaking the drops of water from his hair like so many careless diamonds in the morning sun. "You, a skinny little slip of a girl, *you* say I must marry you?"

"Yes, you must," she repeated, trying desperately to ignore his amusement. "If you wish to rule here without constant rebellion, you'd do well to honor me. The people of St. Abb's respect me and my family. They could make your life a merry hell."

"With you in the lead, no doubt," he grinned. "Well, by Odin's one eye, you do not lack for courage, Dawnlyn Renfrew."

"No, I do not," she conceded, eyeing him carefully. "Norsemen are known far and wide for their cleverness," she went on slowly while he dressed, "and if you are a wise leader, I think you'll see the advantage of an immediate betrothal to me."

"Not much advantage as yet when I shall be absent from the Hall a good deal of the time. I am a warrior, Dawnlyn, not a landlord who tends sheep and settles the squabbles of my subjects." He buckled his belt, sheathed his sword in its place as if to punctuate his words.

She thought furiously—there must be a way to convince this brute! "If you plan to be gone from the tower often, then would it not be wise to have a wife at home, one who knows much about the inner workings of your keep and can run things smoothly?"

"And who could lead these Scotsmen into rebellion while I'm away?" he threw in coolly.

"No!" she said, "not as your wife . . . I am a woman of God, I would never do such a treacherous thing. But as a woman dishonored . . . one who has been made to seem a whore . . ."

"A whore?" He looked at her with bewilderment. "But I have not touched your precious virginity! You are no whore!"

"In the eyes of my people, I am. By bringing me to this chamber you sealed my fate. I speak truthfully."

Gaard grumbled under his breath, then finished dressing.

Finally he turned his full attention back to Dawnlyn. "You say that as wife to me I could place trust in you?"

"Aye." She felt hope build within her and yet, at the same moment, she wished he would say 'no' and release her from this dreadful duty.

"And as my wife you would honor my position of jarl while I am gone and would seek to have your subjects do the same?"

"Aye," she whispered again. "I swear I would."

"I will think on it," he said finally, and Dawnlyn let out a deep, ragged breath. "Now I have much to tend to here in this new land and cannot dally here longer with you while the sun shines in the morning sky." He strode to the door and she again felt oddly dashed by his curt dismissal. And yet what he said was true: he was not a civilized landlord, nor was he used to mincing words with women—he was a warrior and he dealt with her as directly as he would with a man.

She fully expected him to leave then, but Gaard seemed to hesitate at the door. Finally he turned on his heel and strode back to where she sat, bewildered.

"Stand up, Dawnlyn," he stated, towering over her. "I have treated your proposal in too great a haste. We met only yesterday and I hardly know you. You are a stranger to me, woman. But let me look at you for a moment before I must go."

Dawnlyn blushed furiously; he treated her as if she were a mare on the auction block, as if he were deciding on just how much to spend.

"Come, Dawnlyn," he drew her up with a steady hand, "I think you misunderstand. In my life I have had little time for women and their ways. A female is to be protected and, except to share my bed, I have never looked upon one for more. I very much wish to know this woman who asks me to wed her."

So cool, so businesslike! And the way he spoke of women sharing his bed—how crude!

She shivered as his hand pulled away her cloak, then

48

cupped her face beneath her chin. Her blush warmed as he studied her from head to toe. From her long copper tresses down the graceful curve of her neck his eyes traveled leisurely, stopping now and again on the swell of a breast, a soft hip, the mold of a thigh beneath the gown.

His eyes returned to meet hers. "You are a beautiful creature," he stated levelly. "A man could do far worse."

"Thank you," she whispered uncertainly, wishing suddenly that she looked like an old crone. Why must *she* be the one to sacrifice her whole life? What if he did accept her offer and she was thrown into an unwanted marriage—how would she ever *be that person?*

Gaard's hand fell away from her chin. "I have discomfitted you," he said. "I did not mean to." He turned, retracing his steps to the door. Over his shoulder he called, "Well? Are you not coming below to break the fast? Should I decide in your favor, I do not wish to share my bed with a bag of bones, Dawnlyn." And he strode out abruptly, leaving her standing in the middle of the chamber, her face as pallid as a daytime moon, the phantom impression of his fingers on her still.

Chapter Four

AT FIRST DAWNLYN HAD THOUGHT TO DRESS FOR THE EVENING
meal like an old hag, for in truth her mood that day was
hardly one of gaiety. She had tried to put her feelings into
perspective, to give a name to her present predicament.
Whereas she did feel like a sacrificial lamb, it was more,
much more than that which distressed her. She felt rather
that a life-giving umbilical cord had been severed and she
was floundering, grasping for some kind of reality in this
suddenly turned-around world. Great waves of loneliness
and insecurity swept her. It simply wasn't fair.

But, perversely, she made up her mind that afternoon to
be as willing and attractive a consort as possible. She
decided that to cower away from her responsibilities would
be equally as horrible a mistake as a possibly disastrous
marriage—she had more sense of duty than that!

And strangely, too, she wanted Gaard to realize just
whom he was turning down, or at least whom he was
treating in an infuriatingly offhand manner. So she took
great care with her hair and her dressing after having Meg
drag innumerable buckets of water up to her chamber for a
long, leisurely bath.

She may have been raised to be a nun, and perhaps she
knew nothing of her own attractiveness, but instinct told her
to wear her most elegant and dignified gown, one that she
never would have worn again had she gone to Coldingham
—there it would have been cut up to use as a rich altar cloth.

It was a fine, soft wool gown of the deepest, richest royal purple. Banding the sleeves above the elbow and around the square-cut neck was a wide swathe of intricate gold embroidery. The gown fell in tight-fitting gussets over her hips to swirl beguilingly around her trim ankles. She let her hair flow loose in rich, rippling copper waves and put a thin gold circlet on her head to hold it in place.

She studied herself in the shining metal mirror and decided she'd do quite well. Purple was a daring hue to combine with her coloring, but somehow she carried it off with a flair.

She hadn't seen Gaard since breakfast, when he'd left her with the casual remark, "I've things to do. See to the dinner tonight. I wish to feast well with my men in the great hall. You will be there." And he hadn't even seen her eyes narrow, catlike, nor her hands clench whitely in her lap. He'd walked straight out with Sweyn, their heads together on warriors' matters, their easy male laughter wafting back to her across the room.

It must have been then that she'd decided to show him, to prove her worth in the face of his neglect. She might be all alone now, her very existence threatened, but she would hold her chin high. She knew she was indulging in the sin of pride, for it had been pointed out to her repeatedly by her Aunt Gabriella, the Mother Abbess, but this unholy mess she was in negated all normal rules of behavior, or so she reasoned.

She descended regally that evening to the great hall and proceeded to seat herself in the chair next to her father's, or rather Gaard's, carved wooden seat. He came in shortly, accompanied by Sweyn—were the two *never* apart?—and he had a ruddy, healthy glow on his lean cheeks. His fine gray eyes were bright and a smile curved his wide, mobile lips as he bantered with his lieutenant. Then he turned his head to say something to Sweyn and Dawnlyn saw, with a slight sense of shock, that he had a long red gash on his cheek that was clotted with dried blood. Had he been in a fight? Then why did he laugh? These Vikings—they were a mystery to her, laughing over wounds as if they were a mere tickle, then turning unimaginably savage over nothing at all.

Gaard seated himself in the carved chair with a lithe, pantherlike movement, then called loudly for ale. He neither greeted Dawnlyn nor acknowledged her in any way until he'd taken a great long draught of the stuff, then wiped the foam from his lips with the back of a tanned, supple-fingered hand. He leaned back in the seat, resting the flagon of ale on his flat stomach.

"And so, my lady," he finally turned to her, "were you kept busy today?"

"Aye, my lord," she replied with mock demureness, her eyes downcast so that they hid the sparks that played there. Then she turned toward him in her chair, tossing her hair back over her shoulder so that he would be sure to notice it and wondering from whence came such female coquetry. "I see that you have been hurt. Do you wish me to take care of it?"

"Of what?" he asked, then a wide smile split his lips and he gestured at the gash on his cheek. "Oh, that! Nay, don't touch it. It'll give me a nice scar, to match my others!" And then he turned to where Sweyn sat on his left and they both gave great guffaws of laughter that broke on her ears so harshly that she wanted to cover them with her hands. But she sat there rigidly, pretending not to notice his rudeness. Only the rose blush on her cheekbones gave away her anger.

The first course was brought and the men sliced off pieces of mutton with their long, wicked knives, tearing hunks of bread to act as trenchers for the meat. They talked loudly in Norse and laughed often, putting away enormous amounts of food and drink while Dawnlyn tried to eat her portion with exaggerated care.

It was just as they were starting on the honey cake that a commotion drew everyone's attention to the heavy front doors. The bagpipes that had been entertaining the men at their feast stopped, their haunted wailing fading away too slowly.

"What is this?" shouted Gaard across the great hall. "Who disturbs my dinner?"

Then, to Dawnlyn's growing horror, two Vikings in full battle gear burst into the hall, and sagging between them they carried a bloodied, unrecognizable thing that Dawnlyn supposed to be a man.

"We caught him firing the ships, my lord. He and another one who got away. I've sent the others after him, but this one I thought you'd like to see," said one of the men. "They barely had time to begin their sabotage before they were caught. They killed the sentry . . ."

Gaard rose from his seat, the easy laughter and camaraderie gone from his face, replaced by a merciless scowl that sent icy shivers of fear down Dawnlyn's spine. He seemed to unfold, taller and taller, until he towered, hovering over the two men and the poor wretch between them. Dawnlyn could almost see sparks of power crackling around his body, a power that was so intense she could not help but think of his story about the giant wolf. She could almost believe the tale now . . .

"What possessed you to harm my ships?" he asked in a quiet voice, but the menace in his flat, steely tone was that of a well-honed blade, wicked and lethal.

The man tried to stand between his two captors; Dawnlyn could see his struggle to straighten, to face Gaard. Finally his battered head raised and he looked Gaard in the eye, a cold snarl on his lips.

"I only regret we did not finish you and your ships off," he spat, but his voice was weaker than his will. "My luck has run out," he said more strongly. "I do not ask for mercy. I am Gull Larson, an honorable man and a Viking. Kill me quickly."

"Who put you up to this, Gull Larson?" asked Gaard, his voice velvet-soft, yet edged in steel.

"No one."

"We shall see. Cut him, Sweyn." The tone was as cold as the North Sea, as irrevocable as death.

Sweyn drew his sword, a glinting smile on his lips.

He is enjoying it! registered Dawnlyn in abhorrence. She wanted to get up, to run away, to scream, but deadly, implacable horror kept her rooted to the spot. She went cold all over and her stomach began to flutter with sickness.

Then the sword flashed and a fine white line was drawn across Larson's face. It only began to ooze red after the man started to scream.

"Whose lead do you follow?" asked Gaard again.

Still the man resisted. He fell staunchly silent again, but his breast rose and heaved in shuddering gasps. Then, as Dawnlyn looked on, Gaard called on another of his men to make their mark on Gull Larson and then another . . . and another. Soon the man was screaming without pause, a tatter of red stripes sliced him everywhere on his body. Then he sagged, unconscious, between his two captors.

"Throw a bucket of water on him. He's got a long way to go yet," grated out Gaard.

While someone went to fetch the required bucket, Dawnlyn seized the moment and rose from her chair.

Gaard whirled on her, as quick as a snake. "Where do you go, my lady?" he slashed.

"I wish to retire, please," she whispered, an involuntary tremor traveling down her limbs.

"No! You will stay and see this to the end, my gentle lady. It will be most educational to see what befalls Gaard Wolftooth's enemies!" His eyes were nearly black and he ground the words out as if she, too, had tried to burn his ships.

His rage shook Dawnlyn to the core. She knew a sudden, terrible fear of this man who had become another being, a totally alien being. She had an inkling of the Vikings' power to conquer everything in their path. And, too, she was hideously reminded of the deep chasm between their worlds. How would she survive marriage to this cruel man. She could not fit her mind around such a reality. She sank back into her seat, mute and shaken.

Gull Larson regained his senses with the splash of cold water. When he saw that he was not yet dead, he seemed to collapse in upon himself; his will leaked out of him as did his life's blood, slowly, inexorably.

"I will tell you," he breathed. "No more cuts. I wish to go to Valhalla with all my flesh about me."

His voice went on, weaker and weaker, naming his accomplice; then, bringing a rumble of fury from the gathered men, the name, Karl, came to Dawnlyn's ears.

"Your brother, Karl," Gull Larson was saying, "sent us with you, Gaard, in your banishment. He wished us to weaken you, destroy your ships, sabotage your forces in any way we could. We were well paid. He fears your power, Gaard Wolftooth, and well he may." The man's voice was a mere breath now. "I am done." His head fell forward, his breath panted in his chest. "Let me rest."

"You are a brave but misguided man, Gull Larson," said Gaard in a clear voice. "Stand before me so that I may judge you."

Someone held a cup of ale to Larson's lips, several hands helped him to his feet. He stood, weaving, welling blood from myriad slashes, a figure of horror and pity and fierce glory. He faced Gaard, raised his head, met the implacable iron-hued eyes.

"You are a traitor," said Gaard, drawing his sword, "and should not be accorded mercy, but I find nonetheless that I respect your courage."

He let the words rest on the air, imparting the faintest glimmer of hope to the prisoner. Dawnlyn could actually see the man take a freer breath, one swelled with hope. Would Gaard let him go? What kind of insane charade had they played with their prisoner?

The two men stood facing each other, one a bloody pillar of suffering, the other a powerful leader, an arbiter of life and death. Silence hung over them, breathless.

And then Gaard turned away from Gull Larson, his shoulders slumped infinitesimally. What? thought Dawnlyn, then the man is to live . . .

And in that precise moment, as her thought was still completing itself, Gaard spun around, swinging his sword in the same eye-blink of time, and Gull Larson's head was rolling and bumping across the rush-covered floor, its expression of near hope still on its lips.

A great roar of mirth rose from Gaard's men, deafening and unutterably savage. Sweyn clapped a congratulatory hand on Gaard's shoulder, grinning like a child at a mummer's act. "By Odin's beard, you outdid yourself that time, Gaard," he chuckled. "Never have I seen such a look on a man's face . . ."

Gaard glared down at the fallen body, gave it a nudge with his toe. "He didn't deserve to enter Valhalla in such a hopeful state. He deserved no such favor from me."

He turned his silver gaze onto Dawnlyn, triumphant and cold as a river in winter. "What say you now, my lady, of Viking justice?"

Dawnlyn straightened in her chair, as pallid and chilled as ice. "I can only wish I had not been forced to view it, my lord, and I am glad it is over. My God teaches a gentler way," she ventured carefully.

His stormy gaze caught and held hers. "Gentler, perhaps, but not nearly as successful." His voice was low and intimate.

She bowed her head in mute acquiescence, not catching the intent way his eyes rested on her clinging purple gown, her dainty, leather-shod foot, the pale circlet around her burnished copper hair, her breasts and hips and slim white hand as it lay half open in her lap like an averted glance.

Later, much later, when her nerves ceased their jumping, Gaard turned once more to her. His mere attention, however, caused her heart to begin a slow, apprehensive pound in her breast and she was unable to meet his eyes.

"Come, now," he said, placing a hand on her sleeve, "where is that courage I have seen in you?"

She stirred uneasily in her chair. "My courage is intact, my lord, it is merely that my stomach turns."

"Would you have thought better of me if I had spared the traitor's life?"

"Yes . . . no," she whispered. "I truly cannot say . . ."

"Then I shall answer for you." He took a long drink of ale. "What bothered you was actually *seeing* his fate. You knew he deserved death, however, didn't you?"

"Aye." Finally her glance met his. "It was just the way . . . the *way* he died."

"It is our way, Dawnlyn. As leader, it is something I must do, although I do not necessarily enjoy it. It is simply expected of me."

"Expected?" she breathed. "Then you say that the bloodlust I just saw in your eyes was an act?"

Gaard's lips curved into a frown. "You see much for one so naive . . ."

"I may be naive, my lord, but I have always been said to possess a good mind and a great maturity." She paused, then said, "Tell me you gleaned no pleasure from the act."

"I cannot." He met her gaze pensively. "There are certain times when a man loses himself to the lust of violence. No doubt this sounds alien to you, Dawnlyn, but it is true nonetheless. I have just cause for my anger. My brother had me banished. You have been overly sheltered in your life and there is much you will learn as the years pass. Do not deign to judge me."

While she tried to sleep in the chair in their chamber that night, his words came back to haunt her. She was highly educated, but was she sheltered from knowledge of the real world? Had her very strict upbringing robbed her of a true understanding of reality? Perhaps, she mused, trying to find a comfortable sleeping position, perhaps there were some things in life of which she knew nothing.

And then she wondered, as she listened for his footfalls in the corridor, if she knew the first thing about men. Why had Gaard spared her, then? Isn't that what cruel Vikings did to a woman—weren't they all the same?

And what of this night? Would he allow her to sleep in this chair or would he carry her to the bed? Just how much respect did he have for her and how long could it last? And then, without knowledge of where it came from, another thought seized her: if he *did* carry her to the bed, what would his lips feel like on her? Would his hard body be as strangely soft and warm as she recalled?

At daybreak, as she opened her eyes, she saw instantly that he was in the large bed and she wondered at what ungodly hour he had returned to the chamber. His back was to her and she could see the writhing scar on its breadth gently rising and falling in his slumber.

It did not seem possible that this sleeping man was the same as the fearsome warlord he'd been last night. She couldn't reconcile the two in her mind.

She dressed quickly and quietly, catching her hair back with ivory combs, and softly closed the door behind her as she left him sleeping as peacefully as a babe. She drew her first breath, it seemed, when the heavy door separated them.

Dawnlyn went directly to the great hall, where she took a loaf of bread, some cider and some salted fish and descended to the dungeon to see to her father and his men. Quickly, she told them of the grisly event of the previous evening and the men fell silent, their faces pale with foreboding in the dim light.

Ian cursed and stalked the confines of the room, restless and bored. "If he'd only let me free!" was his constant refrain.

"Then you're better off here," said Robert drily. "Hasn't your sister's tale put any sense in your head?"

"If only he'd let me *out!*" said Ian again, his blue eyes wild with frustration. Dawnlyn left them, heavy with fear for her father and brother and the other men. Gaard was capable of any brutality—now she knew that. What would he do to the men of St. Abb's?

When she reached the great hall, Gaard was there, dressed in a fine gray tunic, tall riding boots and his ubiquitous sword. He looked fresh and energetic standing by the hearth, one foot resting on a bench, a casual elbow on his knee as he listened to one of his men. Then both of them threw their heads back and laughed as if at some jest, and Dawnlyn saw the graceful way his neck arched and the cords of muscle that ran along it to his lean jaw.

Then he turned and noticed Dawnlyn standing uncertainly by the trestle table. She felt like shrinking away from him but forced her back straight and her chin high. Instinctively she knew that to let him cow her would make her life hell on earth.

"My lady Dawnlyn," he called across the intervening space, "good morn to you."

He could have been an old acquaintance, perhaps a friend of her family or a distant relation. How could he be so casual about everything?

She nodded coolly to him, then crossed the hall to break off a piece of Gerta's fresh baked bread. She was ravenously hungry this morning. With all the turmoil she couldn't remember when she'd last eaten—it certainly hadn't been the previous night!

But she was not to break her fast in peace. As soon as she sat down Gaard appeared next to her and slid lithely down into the seat beside hers.

"You will come riding with me this fine morning. I need you to show me the layout of these lands."

She could feel his quicksilver gaze on her as she stared straight ahead, chewing the fragrant bread. "Why me? Surely there are others . . ."

"*Others* will not do," said Gaard tranquilly. "I will have *you* to guide me, Dawnlyn." His manner left no room for argument. It was polite but unquestionably firm. "Come, finish your meal. I wish to leave shortly."

"I cannot just leave. There are things I must do. The servants—"

"The servants be damned!" he said laughing. "There is a time for leaving it. You must learn to relax and enjoy life, Dawnlyn."

"*Enjoy* life! I have been taught that life is a vale of tears, and that we all must fight the sin we were born with."

"Well, then, Dawnlyn Renfrew." He leaned close to her, tilting up her chin with one finger. "It's about time you learned differently. How fortunate you are that I am here to teach you!" He smiled into her eyes and she wondered whether he meant to frighten or console her with his arrogant words.

They set out after breakfast, having delayed only long enough to order a lunch made up and packed away in the saddle bags. Dawnlyn was very surprised that no one accompanied them. Even Robert Renfrew had always ridden out with at least a man-at-arms at hand. The arrogance of this man continually amazed her. But then, she had to admit, perhaps it was not arrogance but plain self-confidence that guided his actions. In truth, he had not made an ill-advised move yet.

"We're going to Coldingham first, as I wish to see how much damage was done to my ships," he said, his tone mild and conversational. "You must tell me the best way to go and indicate every point of interest along the way." His eyes, light in the spring sun, met hers squarely. "You must know everything about St. Abb's, Dawnlyn, for, if we are to wed, it will be your responsibility. I shall be gone much of the time."

"*If* we wed, my lord?" she asked insinuatingly.

"I have not yet decided."

"Is today some sort of test for me, then?"

"If you wish to view it so . . ."

They followed a narrow path away from the rocky coastline toward the valley of the River Tweed. Green hills, misted in the haze of the spring morning, rose about them. The earth smelled damp and fecund, ready to sprout with summer's plenty. Farmers were out working their fields, a young child chased a herd of fat-bellied cows from their path, fluffy white sheep grazed on the thick grass. It could have been before the Viking attack; nothing was changed and yet, Dawnlyn reflected, everything was changed . . . for her.

Chapter Five

THE TINY VILLAGE OF COLDINGHAM, ON THE BANKS OF THE
Tweed, came into view. And there, at its northern edge,
stood the cloister, with its ancient moss-covered stone walls,
its square, unadorned Romanesque church tower, its massive gates, closed now to Dawnlyn.

She stopped her mare at the edge of the village, suddenly
unable to ride on; she felt a sad ache fill her, her memories
as poignant as pressed flowers. She could not face seeing
those dear walls, knowing the life that was now forever
barred to her was continuing, secure and dignified within
them.

"Come," she heard Gaard say impatiently. Then, "The
nunnery is still there, Dawnlyn. But it will have to exist
without you. Your talents lie elsewhere. And be comforted
by this thought: you're well out of that sterile life."

He reached out and did a strange thing—he patted her
arm reassuringly, as if he knew exactly how she was feeling.
He led the way past the cloister, past the tiny clutter of
cottages and down to the shallow bay where his five dragon
ships lay at anchor.

A sentry called out to them, seemingly not a bit surprised
that the renowned Viking leader should arrive with no
fanfare, no men-at-arms, only a strange Scotswoman for

company. The Northmen's ways were peculiar—so casual, yet admittedly effective.

Swinging down effortlessly from the big gray destrier, he helped Dawnlyn dismount, then strode down the pebbled beach toward the ships, talking all the while with the sentry, asking questions, obviously about the attempt at sabotage the night before. He stood at the edge of the water, his hands on his hips, staring across the few yards to where one of the ships lay beached, one side blackened by fire.

"Have you ever seen a Viking ship before, Dawnlyn?" he asked, glancing around at her.

"No, my lord."

"Beautiful, aren't they? That one," he gestured to the largest ship that stood out a few hundred yards from shore, "is mine. She's called *Wind Eater*. You should see her with her canvas spread, flying across the waves. Someday, perhaps, you'll take a journey on her."

The ships did indeed look like dragons, Dawnlyn thought. Long, black, curved hulls, dangerous looking, tall bare masts, empty oar holes along the sides like dozens of dark, fathomless eyes. Dawnlyn gave an inadvertent shudder. Beautiful? No, she would not call them *that*. Deadly, yes, with a certain menacing grace. But never *beautiful*.

"Soon I shall sail back to Norway with these ships and battle my brother Karl. You see how he tries to destroy me even across the sea." His cool gray eyes met hers levelly. "The other spy, by the way, was caught last night. You were spared *his* end. It was not nearly so interesting as the first."

Then he spoke with some men who had just rowed to shore from one of the undamaged ships, giving them directions as to the repair of the burned vessel. They spoke for some time, the men seeming to feel equal to their chief, but yet standing back from him with intense respect. They listened to him, nodded, listened again, made suggestions, but always there was the distance of their respect between them and Gaard.

Dawnlyn tucked away this knowledge, adding it to the other small bits of information she had gleaned from watching this Viking warrior. Perhaps someday the pieces would fit together into a comprehensible pattern.

On the ride back to St. Abb's, Gaard was relaxed and talkative. It seemed that just as she was beginning to think she understood him, he changed, like quicksilver, into another being.

"I have spread the word that Mass will be held as usual on Sunday," he said after a while.

"Thank you, my lord," said Dawnlyn.

"It is not my wish to change your people's ways, you must understand."

"How kind of you, my lord," she retorted sarcastically, and then she could have bitten her tongue. She could not afford to antagonize the man.

But Gaard only shot her a quick, sidelong glance and went on to say, "I have called for a meeting of all the people after Mass on Sunday. I shall have some words for them so that they can know their new jarl. I have ordered a feast as well."

What exactly did he have to say to the Scots? she wondered. Was he merely consolidating his position here? She rode silently ahead of him, feeling his gaze rest lightly on her back.

They stopped for a picnic lunch by the banks of a stream that ran, gurgling, to empty into the River Tweed several miles below. Gaard seemed very comfortable and relaxed. The sun shone in a blue sky as if everything conspired to make this a pleasant day. And in spite of the constant threat his very existence presented, Dawnlyn could not resist the lure of contentment.

She was sitting under a tall oak tree, sipping her cup of ice-cold brook water. She'd thrown off her cloak, as the afternoon was warm, and her cheeks were pink from riding into the wind. A faint smile curved her mobile lips as she watched a baby lamb kick up its heels in the meadow.

How long had it been since she'd had the leisure to just sit and look at a pretty scene like this? When was it that she'd last watched a baby lamb or noticed how the edges of the clouds feathered iridescently against the blue sky or felt the sun's warmth without being preoccupied? Just when had her life turned into a chore, delineated utterly by obligations, responsibilities, by the whole gamut of duties? She couldn't remember the last time she'd had an entire morning of idleness. She felt curiously unfettered, as if the Vikings' conquest of St. Abb's had paradoxically set her free.

"Is it so bad to be conquered?" Gaard's voice broke Dawnlyn's reverie with the odd query.

She could only murmur, "What?" Her mind was unable, at first, to clothe the words with any meaning.

"You looked so content. I merely asked if it is so bad to be conquered." His tone was matter-of-fact.

"Aye, of course it is!" she answered, vaguely irritated. "You cannot possibly know how it feels to be at peace with the world, with yourself one moment," she mused aloud, "and then have your whole existence thrown into turmoil."

"Oh," he countered, "but I have known turmoil. You think it was easy to be unjustly banished from my home-land?"

"Nay," she replied honestly, "but it's not the same. My life is . . . *was* at the nunnery. I was so happy . . . I knew what it was that I wanted."

"And now?"

"How can I know? The future is a huge, black empty thing. I do not know where I fit into it. I cannot see myself nor my future anymore. I am possibly to marry a stranger and not even a Christian stranger. It is most . . . unsettling," she said quietly.

"But I do not take your God from you. You are welcome to him. I am not jealous, nor are my gods. There is room for all in this world."

"Yes, but still . . ." she murmured.

Gaard studied her for a moment, then turned away thoughtfully, looking about them at the serene setting. "Would you be happier than this," he gestured to the green meadow, the stream, the remains of their meal, "at Cold-ingham? Is that what you truly believe?"

"Aye, of course," she said, but her words were automatic

as the warm breeze touched her softly. "I had always planned to be a nun. It is my calling. I could have been the Abbess one day, as my aunt is, and I could have controlled my own destiny and that of the women under me. And I could have done much good as a nun." Even to herself, her tone sounded smug, even vaguely petulant.

Gaard lay stretched out on the green grass next to her, resting on his elbow, idly chewing on a blade of grass. He eyed her carefully; the sun reached under the branches and turned his eyes almost silver. She could not meet them; she gazed off across the meadow.

"Sometimes one must change the direction of one's life," he said quietly. "Sometimes there is sufficient reason to change what has been planned since childhood. Sometimes, there is even good to be derived from change. A man cannot afford to be set in his ways. If you don't bend with the wind, if you are brittle, you break."

"And did you also study philosophy?" asked Dawnlyn lightly, her mood relaxed for the first time in days.

"Yes, but that is not the issue here. I wish to point out a fact of life, that is all."

"And whence comes your vast experience on this subject? Why should I heed your words?"

"Dawnlyn, have you ever once thought why I came here, to this inhospitable coast, to this foreign land, to make a new home? It was not by choice, believe me. I had a fine home, a good father, a loving mother, a hall full of willing servant girls. Why should I leave there?"

"Why, indeed, if it was as you say?" asked Dawnlyn coolly.

"Because my father died of a festering wound last year and my older brother, Karl, who carries a deep jealousy and hate for me, trumped up a false charge against me and had me banished from my home. And so I speak from experience."

Dawnlyn could say nothing. She knew his words were sincere; the pain in his voice told her that. Somehow, the idea of Gaard being bested by another did not gladden her heart. Reluctantly, she began to see it from his point of view. "You can never go back?" she asked hesitantly.

"Not unless Karl is proven wrong, which, so far, I am unable to do."

She stole a look from under her lashes at Gaard. He stared, unseeing, out over the lea, and his brows were drawn together in a frown. His profile was noble, strong, his lips and chin and nose drawn by a bold but skillful hand. So, a Viking can feel pain and hurt, she thought. The knowledge did not console her as much as she would have surmised.

Suddenly he turned toward her and she quickly looked away in confusion. "So you see, I merely wish to show you that a person can be equally successful at more than one of life's tasks, if they are, indeed, a useful and intelligent person."

"And I suppose you mean that I am neither," asked Dawnlyn tartly.

"No, I mean just the opposite. That you would make an excellent wife and mother, just as, I'm sure, you would make an excellent nun."

"But there you are wrong," she replied softly. "I know not the first thing about marriage or motherhood. I was raised, since birth, to be a nun."

"I think, Dawnlyn," he said mildly, "that the idea of a marriage frightens you."

"That's not so," she said quickly, but knew it was a lie—the very notion of marriage to him was threatening beyond description. "It's simply that there are far better things for a woman to do in this life. Marriage, motherhood —any ignorant peasant woman can do *that.*"

"Nay, my sweet Dawnlyn. There you are as wrong as anyone's ever been. If not for good mothers, there would be no good children. The world would be a wild and unhappy place."

She had no clever rejoinder for his statement and had to content herself with pursing her lips and disagreeing silently.

"You are prettier when you smile." His tone was playful.

"Sometimes there is nothing to smile about," she said, knowing as the words emerged that they sounded as if she pouted like a child.

"Come now, Dawnlyn, I'm trying with all my might to be pleasant today. Can you not return my efforts in kind?"

She was silent, not wanting to anger him yet not wanting to appear to give in to him, either. Then she felt his sword-calloused hand on her arm. She could only stare stupidly at the spot, feeling her heart leap under her ribs.

His hand, hard as it was, touched her so lightly that it was as if a warm, sweet breeze had stopped and caressed her. The tender pressure, so gently insistent, made her flesh seem to melt, made her bones turn to water in her flesh, paralyzing even her will. A warm tingling began in the place his hand lay and radiated out, down to her fingertips, up her arm to her shoulder, then even up her neck until it began to bend like the stalk of a flower toward the source of its life, the sun.

Slowly she turned to look into his eyes. They were a clear gray now, untouched by storm, and they held her mesmerized for an endless moment. It seemed to Dawnlyn that some very great truth lay just behind the silver orbs of his eyes, but she could not say what it was.

"Come, Dawnlyn," he half-whispered, his hand not moving, yet seeming to lure her toward him compellingly.

A warm, strange pulsing filled her. A bee droned somewhere; then there was utter silence. Even the blood in her veins and the breath in her lungs seemed to stop for a moment. All the air seemed to have gone out of the world.

She closed her eyes to better feel the alien sensations that flooded her. Then, inevitably, Gaard's lips came down on hers. They were firm and soft at the same time, burning and cool, filling her with an exquisite pleasure that was utterly strange to her, yet utterly familiar, too, as if something she'd dreamed once long ago had taken shape in reality. His lips moved on hers, his large hands came up to cup her face, holding her as one would a delicate flower, a bloom of exotic beauty.

Tenderness rose from the core of her, a tide so over-whelming that she was swept away. It continued to well through her, a powerful, surging river.

He pulled back from her and she opened her eyes, oddly bereft, to meet his clear gaze. She tried, desperately, to read the message in his eyes, the message she knew must be there, but she could not decipher it.

Still, her body was weak with sensation and, amazingly, she only wanted to feel his lips on hers again. There was room for no other thought in her mind. It was as if something beyond her control were pushing her, propelling her toward an unknown destiny.

His lips touched hers again, seeking, finding, then all thought fled. She opened to his touch like a bud, feeling his tongue enter her, tease, withdraw, fill her again. Her body arched inadvertently toward him, but she was not aware of it. She knew only a need, an all-consuming need, for the security of the moment.

"Ah, Dawnlyn," he said finally, breaking into her daze, "you'd be a terrible waste as a nun."

Then he kissed her carefully along the slim column of her neck and her stomach fluttered delicately. Slowly, slowly he eased her onto her back, his lips brushing her neck, her chin, her cheek.

"It is not so terrible, is it?" he whispered gently, moving his mouth across hers with infinite lightness.

"No," she breathed weakly, wanting him to continue kissing her this way and yet sensing that if she did not stop him something beyond her control would have her in its grip. Then she felt his warm hand on her gown, touching the side of her breast through the material.

Suddenly she grew tense, afraid of Gaard.

"Oh, little Dawnlyn," he said, stroking the swell gently, "don't you truly wish to know what it is like? There is pleasure beyond words in the act of joining. Let yourself go . . . seek out the adventure . . ." And his mouth pressed to hers and slowly he parted her lips until she could feel his tongue enter the warmth of her mouth.

The mere sensation of tongue meeting tongue was enough to send a quiver of delight coursing down her limbs until she was faint with reaction. How was it possible for this stranger, this Norseman with such fierce eyes and cruel lips, to have cast this spell over her?

He moved his mouth away for a moment. "Put your arms around my neck, Dawnlyn. It's all right . . . Go on . . ."

Timidly, she obeyed. Her eyes closed and her lips fell apart expectantly. Then his mouth was over hers again, only his kiss was not gentle, but demanding and exciting this time. Wave after wave of strange delight washed over her and she opened her lips fully to him, receiving him, twisting her mouth against his. Even when his hand cupped a breast again, she did not stiffen as before but allowed her mind, instead, to explore the wondrous sensations.

Her thoughts spun without direction, each vying for ascendancy but none achieving it. One moment she told herself guiltily that she must stop him at once, stop herself— the next, she longed for something as yet unknown, some fulfillment that held itself before her like a haunting dream. Was it the adventure of which he had spoken that beckoned her? She did not know. All she knew was loss of control— her armor was falling away, her shield lowered. She had never, *never* let herself feel this way . . .

She sensed Gaard's hands at the silver fastenings of her gown, one by one undoing them, and with each small opening, she gasped in shock. Why didn't she fight him, stop him? What insanity had come over her?

"That's it," he coaxed, barely whispering. "Let yourself find pleasure in it. I'll try not to hurt you, Dawnlyn. I would never want to hurt you . . ." He began then to slip her gown away, bunching it beneath her against the prickly grass. It felt so wonderful to let someone else take control—always, before, it had been she who had to think of everything, see to all the little details of her existence.

Dawnlyn's eyes were still closed, her brain still whirling with indecision. Then she felt the warmth of the sun on her legs and was aware of her undershift being lifted away as

69

Gaard's words flowed over her and his hand stroked her with endless, tender care. It all felt so wonderful . . .

Then the sun, dappled through the trees, touched her intimately and her complete nakedness struck her. Her eyes flew open. If she didn't stop this madness now . . .

"Don't be afraid," he whispered, lying beside her, his head propped on a hand. "I haven't hurt you, have I?" Slowly his iron-hued eyes traveled the length of her, drank in her exquisite beauty as if she were water to a thirsty man.

"I . . . I don't know what has come over me," she said quietly, her flesh ablaze beneath his scrutiny.

"You are becoming a woman. It is long overdue and nothing to be afraid of."

"But . . ."

With a finger over her lips he silenced her then; his mouth was covering hers again and his hand found the soft young swell of her bosom. Sensation swept Dawnlyn; feelings deep within her were both terrifying and glorious at the same moment. Then his lips were on a breast and she drew in a surprised gasp. Gaard seemed to delight in kissing her there and she failed to understand why—all she knew was a great, consuming pleasure as his mouth kissed a breast, a pale shoulder, lowered to her abdomen.

Awareness of her naked state, of the sun pouring down on her flesh, slowly died away as he continued to fondle and caress every inch of her and she began to sense that there was more, much more he would do to her, but she had no idea how she should respond.

He sat up beside her slowly, a smile touching his sculpted lips, his gray eyes nearly blue, reflecting the pellucid sky. He pulled away his clothes, placing them beneath her, his gaze lingering on her leisurely as if he had no more desire in the world but to view a breast, the soft, white womanly curve of a hip, a firm, rounded thigh.

"Look at me," he said carefully, placing a gentle hand on her chin and bringing her head around toward his long, sun-darkened torso. And she did view him and her cheeks flamed at the sight of his powerful chest and the crisp, blond hair curling there. Then, in curiosity, her gaze lowered and her breath was snatched away.

"Don't fear," he chuckled lightly. "I am no different than any other."

But the sight of his manhood, swollen and awesome in the light of day, struck fear into her in spite of his words. She knew, from observing animals and their ways, what he planned to do, and surely it would harm her! Her strange desire to experience this adventure was quickly gone; she hadn't been thinking properly, so weakened was she by his gentle kisses, but now she was truly afraid and wondered how she could have let a single kiss, a warm, sun-blessed afternoon, rob her of her moral sense.

But Gaard was drawing her back into his embrace again, and as his lips covered hers in a thorough kiss, she lost the will to protest. He held her now so closely that her thigh was pressed against his manhood and a tremor passed through her at the contact.

She wanted to protest, and yet she could stay in these arms forever. It was all so confusing, so unsettling . . .

Slowly Gaard stroked the curve of her hip; then his hand moved and touched the white flesh on her inner thigh, carefully easing her onto her back, easing her legs apart so slowly that she barely realized the vulnerable position in which he had placed her.

Still his mouth covered hers, and any words she might have said were locked in her throat as she parted her mouth to his insistent kiss. Then she felt his hand, which still stroked her thigh, move upward and she started at the contact when a finger sought her intimately, deeply.

The pleasure she was experiencing became a kind of insistent ache, and her legs fell apart weakly while a soft moan escaped her lips. He moved his mouth onto the firm swell of her bosom and teased at a nipple that stood pert and waiting for his kiss. She could feel his hand move in rhythmic strokes against her inner flesh, and he sought more of her. Involuntarily, Dawnlyn began to move against his hand and felt hot waves of pleasure begin to build within her womb.

71

Suddenly his hand moved away and she was aware of him easing his large frame between her legs and she was aware, too, that his shaft stood at her opening, but no longer did she wish to stop him or even protest.

She wanted this union now. She sensed there would be great pleasure in it, and the years of strict upbringing, of staunchly taught morals, fell away like so many forgotten leaves in an autumn storm.

"Are you sure?" Gaard whispered, his clear eyes searching her face.

"Aye," she replied faintly, then squeezed her eyes shut, waiting, ready to receive him. "Aye . . ."

She felt his hands on her thighs again opening them fully, and then his fingers parted her and his shaft sought the entrance and he pressed against her until he gained a small entry.

Dawnlyn tensed, unable to stifle the reaction.

"No," he said in a husky, strange voice. "Relax, little one . . ." Then, "That's better . . ." And he pressed himself in farther, felt the warm wall of her virginity while he watched her face and saw her bite her lower lip, waiting, uncertain.

"I do not want to hurt you," he said, "but you must not tense, Dawnlyn." Still, he realized his words were impossible for her to comprehend. He would take her quickly, then. Gaard drove his member deep into her flesh, feeling the wetness of her torn virginity surround him.

A cry was wrenched from her lips and she tried to free herself. "You hurt me!" she gasped, and Gaard felt strangely ashamed of himself.

"I did not mean to," he breathed. "If only you were not so tense." Then with great, painful restraint, he stilled his movements within her, letting her discomfort subside slowly. When she was finally quiet beneath him, Gaard began to move against her again and kissed her eyes, her nose, her mouth until she was subdued.

All the while Dawnlyn lay there, feeling no more pain but too uncertain to fully enjoy his caresses now. She felt oddly lulled by his slow thrusting and it was, she admitted, not unpleasant.

Gaard continued to move within her, holding himself in check but sensing that this beautiful girl's first time would not be totally fulfilling to her—she was still too taut, still waiting for him to hurt her again. If only, he thought, he could convince her to thaw a little.

"Oh, Dawnlyn," he whispered in her ear, "if only you knew. Someday, someday I'll show you . . ." and his pace quickened. He lost himself to all rational thought in the sweet innocence of her exquisite body. Suddenly he met his moment of utmost pleasure and shuddered above her, crushing her to him as if he could not get enough of her young body.

Afterward, when he lay beside her, holding her against him, he said quietly, "You are so young, so innocent. Did I hurt you terribly?"

As he waited for her answer, he scrutinized her profile, trying to discover what there was about this too-serious young girl that stirred him so. He'd had many women in his thirty-four years, but never had he been troubled by a virgin's pain before. He could hardly believe he'd asked, or that he waited in suspense for her answer. Her face was half averted from him, and he saw the youthful curve of her cheek, the sweep of her dark lashes, the unblemished skin and the incredibly fine, sun-touched down that gilded it. She was lovely, but he'd seen and bedded more spectacular beauties. And yet not one had touched him as poignantly as this one.

At his soft words, Dawnlyn was abruptly aware of a bee buzzing nearby, an insect click in the tall grass—reality flooded back and sun was pounding down on her once more and Gaard's tousled hair was touching her shoulder, his hand warm on her damp belly.

Somewhere deep within her was a dull ache. "I am not hurt," she whispered. Finally a burst of realization flooded her senses. "Oh, dear Lord," her voice was abruptly stricken, "what have I done?"

Gaard was silent for a moment, then coiled a tendril of her hair around his finger. "Nothing any other girl wouldn't have done. Don't worry, Dawnlyn, it didn't touch your *soul.*"

Did she imagine it in her confusion or was there a tinge of humor in his voice? She was afraid that he was dreadfully wrong, that it had indeed touched her soul and that she'd never be quite the same again.

When they rode into the tower's courtyard that afternoon, Dawnlyn was still numb with bewilderment. She left her horse in the stableboy's hands and, without a word, went down the stairs to the dungeon.

She spoke to her father and Ian, saw to it that they had food and more oil for their lamp, but she barely heard what they said or what she answered. She didn't remember climbing the cold stone steps, passing through the great hall or entering her own chamber.

It wasn't until she sat down and leaned her arm on the table, nearly cutting herself on Gaard's war axe lying there, that she realized where she was. She drew in her breath sharply and snatched her arm away from the glinting edge, looked around wildly for a second; then comprehension returned. And with it came shattering recollection.

Chapter Six

DAWNLYN DRESSED FOR SUNDAY MASS SOMBERLY IN DOVE gray and pulled a gauze veil over her copper-bright hair. Taking up her rosary, she descended the stairs, holding herself composed and calm.

Yet, inwardly, grave doubts gnawed at her and had been eating away at her since she had been made truly a woman by Gaard. The blaze that had ignited within her body so suddenly brought to light a new side of her, one she never would have dreamed existed. On the one hand her stomach fluttered delicately remembering his quiet, careful caresses; yet, on the other hand, the loss of control that had consumed her was utterly devastating. How could she have given herself so shamelessly to a man—a virtual stranger—who would not even promise her marriage?

She entered the chapel silently, vowing to herself that she would put aside such earthly notions while in prayer.

But she could not control her thoughts; it was maddeningly painful to her that Gaard had not spent a single night in the Hall since that idyllic afternoon some days ago. She had even lowered herself to ask Sweyn his whereabouts and received only the offhand reply that Gaard was occupied with the repair to his ship at Coldingham. It galled her doubly: first because he ignored her, second because she couldn't control her own feelings of rejection.

Where was he at this moment? When would he appear, tall and virile, his storm-gray eyes searching for her across the great hall? How had he so quickly become the focus of her life?

Perhaps Gaard had found another who had caught his eye; perhaps at this very moment he was with another, looking at *her* with those cool, granite-hued eyes, cupping *her* face so tenderly in his hard hands, moving his lips over *hers* so expertly.

Biting her full lower lip, Dawnlyn bowed her head and began to pray fervently that she could quell such worldly notions. Certainly she had never been raised to think about such things; as a novice in her church, she had had no reason.

Prayer was difficult this Sunday morning—the words that she repeated automatically were, for once, meaningless, and her heart clutched each time her mind's eye insisted on envisioning Gaard: first as the fierce leader who had so easily slain that man, and then as the gentle lover, the sun glinting off his golden hair, his muscles gliding effortlessly beneath his tanned skin.

Eventually the soothing tradition of Mass, the flow of familiar Latin words, surrounded her and the inner turmoil lessened. The women of the keep were there and also a few Scotsmen who were not locked in the dungeon, who had not fought either due to age or infirmity. And there were several Vikings at prayer also. Dawnlyn surmised that they were Christians, for as Sweyn had told her, Norway was now a Christian land. It seemed impossible, yet here they were. Idly, she wondered if they prayed for absolution, having killed in battle so recently. She guessed that they would.

Gerta rose and left the chapel early ; no doubt she had many preparations for the feast that would follow Gaard's speech to the people.

Mass ended and Dawnlyn avoided the St. Abb's priest,

whose eyes sought hers. To face him now would be too humiliating; everyone in St. Abb's surely knew who had taken her from this very chapel that fateful day. No, she could not greet him.

She supposed she'd have to appear in the courtyard where Gaard was to speak. It was expected of her. Suddenly she shrank from facing him again, and a small pulse of anxiety began in the pit of her stomach as she walked out through the double doors of the tower.

After the calm of the chapel, the courtyard was a seething mass of noise and excitement. The mournful lamentation of a bagpipe echoed off the walls of the tower in counterpoint to the suspense of the day's events. Every man, woman and child had come from miles around to share in the new lord's bounty. Some were merely curious to see him, some wished to ingratiate themselves with him, some had a complaint or a problem they hoped to lay before him; but most considered the legendary Gaard Wolftooth with fascinated fear.

Dawnlyn spoke to many of the people, men and women she'd known since birth, and assured them all that Robert and Ian were well. To their questions regarding her father and brother's fate, she had no answer. No one asked what *her* fate was to be. They all seemed to treat her as the lady of the Hall; they all assumed that she was under Gaard's protection—his chattel now. It galled her to be viewed so casually.

And then a sudden hush fell over the crowd; every face turned towards the steps that led down from the great, thick front doors of the tower. Gaard appeared from within, flanked by Sweyn and another great, tall Viking with a full, reddish beard. Sweyn and the other man were dressed elegantly, in brightly colored garments, embroidered with gold and silver. Their hair shone, newly washed, in the morning sun, and their strong hands rested negligently on the hilts of their long, inlaid broadswords.

But Gaard drew every eye. He stood, tall and lithe and powerful, his feet slightly apart, his long, muscled legs in tight-fitting hose. He was dressed in stark, unadorned black, except for the string of gleaming white wolf's teeth around his neck.

Dawnlyn gasped silently at the sight of him. Never had he seemed so awesome to her. He had an alien strength about him, an aura of something more than the normal man. And everyone around her felt the same; every breath was snatched away in thrilled respect. Dawnlyn was grateful for the security of so many bodies surrounding her, pressed close in forced proximity—she was only another face in the throng.

He spoke to the people in a strong, ringing voice, telling them that there would be peace and prosperity in St. Abb's now, that they no longer had to fear him or his men.

"For I want to rule in peace here and I am petitioning King Malcolm in Edinburgh to bestow these lands on me legitimately. Every man that works fairly will be treated fairly. There shall be a court of twelve men convened in the case of wrongdoing. Each man will receive his due. I am prepared to compensate every family that lost a man to a Viking sword either in gold or in sheep or in cattle. My man Knute"—he indicated the hulking Viking behind him—"will take the names of all those families and will honor their claims."

A relieved murmur rose from the crowd. Dawnlyn had bitter thoughts about people's fickle natures, for they had cheered Robert Renfrew not so long ago.

When the courtyard grew quiet once more, Gaard swept the crowd with a cool gaze. "I tell you that all will be treated fairly and be protected against raiding Normans or other Vikings, true enough, and yet know this, my subjects"—he paused for effect—"if any one of you is caught in rebellion against my rule, or caught stealing on my land, I will show no mercy to that man or woman. Be assured that my power is above all others and I will not tolerate an enemy amongst my own people." Again he paused, then gazed over his shoulder to the turrets above.

Every eye turned in the direction of his stare, and there Dawnlyn discerned a heinous scene: perched on two poles were the heads of the Viking spies who had betrayed Gaard and set fire to his ship.

She gasped at the sight of the still drooping mouth of one and the other—the man Gaard had personally slain—whose mouth still held the quirk of near-hope.

"My temper, when aroused, knows no bounds!" Gaard's voice boomed in the courtyard, and the closely packed bodies trembled in fear.

Dawnlyn knew now why he had summoned them, and, grudgingly, she had to admit a respect for his ability to manipulate people.

"My temper can be great," he continued, "yet I am also a man of honor." He paused for effect, then reached out a black-clad arm toward where Dawnlyn stood and she gasped, so much did his arm resemble a raven's wing. Involuntarily she pressed herself back into the security of the crowd.

"Would the Lady Dawnlyn join me?" he said smoothly, his thin lips smiling very slightly, his spectral arm reaching toward her unerringly in the crush of humanity.

The crowd around her seemed to melt away, leaving a clear path in front of her. What could he want? What game was this?

Slowly, her heart pounding, she walked the few steps to where Gaard stood. His eyes were cool, belying the up-turned lips; they told her nothing.

At the sight of Dawnlyn standing next to Gaard, whispers of speculation emanated from the people.

Gaard raised a quieting hand and a pregnant silence fell over them. "Soon I shall be off to my homeland for a time and my man, Sweyn, will tend the lands here. I hope to be gone but a short time and when I return . . ." His gaze moved from the crowd and rested on Dawnlyn's uptilted face. ". . . when I return, there will be a marriage between your Lady Dawnlyn and myself."

Great cheers of delight sounded in the courtyard, and then he was asking her something and she couldn't hear so

79

loud was the roar of voices and so swift was the beat of blood pounding in her ears.

"What?" she asked inanely, trying desperately for control. "What did you say?" And all the while she couldn't believe the evidence of her ears. All that she'd wished and planned for had come to pass. Why, then, did she feel so defeated?

"I said, does my betrothed wish to say anything to her people?" And then he bent closer to her ear. "Collect yourself, woman, you look about to swoon."

As the cheers died down, and Dawnlyn stood mutely facing Gaard, a high-pitched voice sliced through the air, drawing Gaard's attention.

He raised a silencing hand. "Who wishes to speak?" he called out.

"I," came the voice, disengaging itself from the rest.

"Step forward."

Agnes, the midwife of St. Abb's, moved her small, aging body forward. "I wish to know why the Lady Dawnlyn Renfrew," her old voice crooned, "the child whom I, myself, pulled into this world, is to be married? She was brought forth to join our church! She was to be a nun. You call marriage to a heathen," she cackled, "an honor? Posh, I say! You force the child!"

The throng shrank away from the old woman as if she were tainted with the plague, while Dawnlyn's breath caught in her throat.

And then Gaard took a furious step forward. Quickly Dawnlyn grabbed at his arm. "Please," she whispered, "Agnes is old, she's half senile, Gaard. Please . . . let me speak to them . . ."

With great restraint, Gaard turned toward Dawnlyn. "Make your speech good, woman, or this Agnes will have to pay the price of trying to humiliate me. I cannot let this pass."

Dawnlyn took a deep breath, faced her people. "I, myself," she began, "have sought this union. There is no force involved." Dubious grumbling sounded from the people. She tried again. "It is true!" And a thought came to her then. "Your new laird even offered to allow me to return to Coldingham," she lied abruptly, feeling his gaze burn into her flesh. "Aye," she went on swiftly, "he did offer, but I have had a change of heart and wish to marry."

The crowd stood silently assimilating the news, and eventually even Agnes's hard glare softened. Their eyes seemed to say, Dawnlyn Renfrew, the sweet young novice of Coldingham, would not deceive us.

"Why would you say such a thing?" asked Gaard in a low voice.

"To convince my people, Gaard. It seemed too hard for them to believe I would so easily give up my life in the church. I will pray for forgiveness to my God . . ."

"You are a woman of many sides," he replied thoughtfully.

The feast went well; food swelled on the many long tables and ale poured from kegs. Dawnlyn, though, had little appetite as Gaard on her left and Sweyn on her right ate venison in frumenty, haggis, roast goose and quinces in comfit.

She was thinking of her strange fate, marriage, and she was thinking of her kinsmen, below, probably half-starving.

"Are you not hungry?" observed Sweyn, drinking heartily from his flagon.

"Nay." She looked at Gaard. "I have little appetite when so many rot below us. Why can they not join us, Gaard? What harm would it do? The people would honor you." Her tawny eyes reached into his.

"They are fighting men, Dawnlyn, not so easily set down as these you see at the tables."

"They are weak and wounded and starving!" she retorted heatedly. "They can do you no harm!"

"Soon, Dawnlyn," he said levelly. "I'll release them soon, but not this day. I have my reasons."

"How easily you gainsay me, Gaard," she hissed. "You care naught for my desires . . . you do everything to further your own position!"

"I told you I have good reason for keeping them below! It

is *my* affair!" Suddenly Gaard pounded a heavy fist on the table, causing drops of ale to fly from his flagon. A respectful hush fell over the great hall.

Anger boiled in Dawnlyn's veins—how dare he dismiss her request as if she were a thrall and then humiliate her in front of the people? He would abuse her no more!

Quickly Dawnlyn gathered her courage and knew what she must do. In spiteful defiance she rose to her feet, forced a smile to her pink lips. "People of St. Abb's. Gaard Wolftooth." She gestured regally to the Viking sitting next to her, a murderous look in his eyes. "Our new master has this day done a just thing. He has decided to allow my father and brother and the wounded to join this feast." For an instant, she thought he would rise and strangle the life from her. But, strangely, he didn't. Instead, with a control she never dreamed possible, he came slowly to his feet, took her hand in his.

Not a soul in the hall spoke; they waited, their eyes fixed on the legendary Viking who stood a foot taller than the woman by his side, his gray eyes cool, unreadable, the scar across his tanned jawline a thin, white line now.

When he spoke, Dawnlyn thought that the bones in her hand would surely break in his grip. "I have decided to free all remaining inhabitants of this tower. It is a gift to my betrothed, who deserves this"—his glance came coldly around to her—"and far more."

Only Dawnlyn caught his true meaning—her nerve fled and she quaked inwardly. The Vikings and Scotsmen, sitting side by side in the hall, rose to their feet and cheered loudly.

Gaard looked over Dawnlyn's head to Sweyn. "Have them brought from the dungeon." His hard, lethal gaze returned to her. "Do you think these people are fooled? They know whose plot this is and that it is against my wishes," he ground out. "You have defied me, woman, when I sought only to honor you. For this you will pay."

But Dawnlyn's fear was replaced by elation when Sweyn and several Norsemen returned from below with her bedraggled kinsmen behind them. Her father blinked his red-rimmed eyes in the unaccustomed light; Ian lagged farther behind, his face carefully blank, his eyes cast downward meekly.

Sweyn led Robert Renfrew to a spot before Gaard.

"Father!" Dawnlyn cried, trying to pull away from Gaard's unrelenting grip.

"Hold!" Gaard's eyes burned into her own. He turned his attention onto Robert. "I will have your word, old man, that from this moment forth, I am to be obeyed as the jarl of these lands."

It was a long moment before the vanquished earl could speak. "I give my word, Viking. You may trust me, as my people trusted me. But know that my word is given in defeat and I ask a portion of land on which to live out my days."

"Granted, Robert Renfrew," said Gaard for all to hear. "You shall have decent land that shall be freely yours until death. At that time it will revert to me."

Again, a cheer rose to echo from the stone walls.

Dawnlyn's heart swelled with joy. And then Robert said, "And I must ask one more thing, Gaard Wolftooth . . ."

"Ask," replied Gaard, his brow arched inquiringly.

"I ask that my daughter be treated fairly also. There must be no beatings."

A dark mask fell over Gaard's face. "I do not beat women, Robert Renfrew. You need only ask this whelp of yours and gaze on her unmarred skin."

"Aye," replied Robert, "I shall trust your word and she does look untouched. Nay, she looks better than ever to these old eyes."

And then Gaard let her go to her father and embrace him lovingly. As he stood watching the warm scene, there came a sharp cry of warning from Sweyn.

"Heed your back!"

Gaard spun around abruptly just in time to duck the slashing blade of the sword that Ian had snatched from an unsuspecting Viking.

Quickly Gaard leaped to the side, unsheathing his own weapon.

"I'll have your head this time!" shouted Ian, moving in for another blow. But Gaard was too quick for him and again sidestepped the thrust.

And then Gaard had borne enough. "Pray to your God, pup," he growled dangerously, "for you shall now taste my sword." He brought the blade up with both hands, crouched into a fighting stance and deftly moved in toward Ian.

Then—it all happened in an instant—one moment Gaard's sword was poised motionless in the air, the next, he had swung it and the young man's sword went clanging to the floor.

Ian was arched backward against the table in a puddle of ale, his arms hanging limply at his sides while Gaard's sword lay against his throat. "Be done with it, heathen!" Ian spat.

Dawnlyn watched the terrible scene, rooted to the spot, clinging on her father's arm. "No!" she screamed suddenly. And abruptly she ran forward, kneeling at Ian's side. "No!" she cried again. "You cannot slay him! No!"

"Step aside," came Gaard's voice, crackling with rage.

But she couldn't. She clung to Ian's limp arm, her stare fixed on the shining edge of Gaard's sword as a drop of Ian's blood darkened it, then ran with agonizing viscous slowness down the groove. "No, Gaard . . . I beg of you! No! He's my brother . . . please!"

Gaard's lips were curved into a thin, cruel snarl. "Get her away, Sweyn," he commanded.

But Sweyn could not budge her, so fiercely was she clinging to her brother.

Finally, exasperated, yet a touch amused, Sweyn said, "I cannot without harming her, my leader!"

"By Odin!" raged Gaard, pressing the edge to Ian's throat with more force. "Be gone, Dawnlyn! I command you!"

"I can't," she wept. "He's my only brother. Spare him, please . . ."

A tangible silence filled the great hall; even the hounds

were quiet, cowering beneath the table. Time stretched out endlessly as the tower's inhabitants stood mutely, expectant.

And then suddenly Gaard emitted a deep roar and just as quickly pulled his deadly weapon away, tossing it aside so that it landed with a furious clang on the cold, hard, stone floor.

Dawnlyn looked from Ian's face to Gaard's and an icy shiver ran up her spine.

"Throw the whelp in the dungeon where he may rot!" Gaard ordered in fury; and for several long moments he stood there, his steel-gray eyes following Ian's form as he was dragged away.

Finally, still unable to quell his rage, Gaard turned to the throng. "I have shown mercy to this Renfrew boy for one reason, and one reason only," he thundered. "The whelp is young and hotheaded but came at me bravely. Still, he is but a pest and not worth piercing with my blade. May he rot in his own hell!"

Then Gaard spun around to face Dawnlyn. "Come here," he said in a deceptively quiet voice. "Sit with me and face these people with what you have done this day, for it is because of your folly that Ian Renfrew must suffer more."

And amazingly, as if forgetting Dawnlyn entirely, Gaard turned his back on her and began feasting and drinking anew as if nothing at all had happened to mar a pleasant day. She was left, quivering with tension and near tears, to face the noisy crowded hall without even a passing word or a second's notice from Gaard for the rest of the endless afternoon. She had to sit at the head of the long table, suffering in silence, the object of everyone's curious attention. She was only too aware of the whispers and glances that fell her way, of the scowls and gossip from her father's old friends. She knew exactly what they were saying of her: "A Viking's whore, an easy conquest, a weak, vacillating, godless woman." Even her father, Robert, who sat at the very foot of the table, was finding it hard to meet her eyes. It was her fault, all her fault, and Ian had to suffer for it!

She could have collapsed on the table in tears, but fierce pride would not let her. She sat, stiff-faced, all through the afternoon and into the dusk.

Gaard, she realized bitterly, could have come up with no better way to punish her if he'd had a hundred years to reflect on it.

Finally, as the shadows lengthened and men fell snoring by the hearth or drunkenly cursed a hound too eager for a tasty morsel, Gaard turned to Dawnlyn, seemingly as fresh and clear-eyed as he had been that morning.

He looked at her carefully, lingeringly, then spoke so that she alone could hear. "Walk with me from this hall quietly," he said in a dangerous whisper, "and do not give me reason to further shame you before these people."

With what dignity she could muster in the face of her trepidation, Dawnlyn obeyed silently and went with him aloft to their chamber. It was like reliving a terrible nightmare, but this time she went quietly, even though she sensed he would show her no mercy.

He banged the door closed ominously, turned slowly, deliberately to face her. "You nearly got your own brother killed!" he said so quietly she had to strain to hear, but his voice chilled her innards. "Did you think the boy was ready to submit? Did you not know why I kept them locked below? Your stupidity has cost us all much, Dawnlyn."

"I . . . I did not think he would—"

"Even *I* knew of this boy's temper! Have you always been so blind?"

"Aye," she wept, "he's my brother! I could not know he would attack you!"

Gaard stood over her furiously. "You will learn to obey me, woman . . . you will learn!"

"I'll try." She brushed away a tear that had slid down her cheek. "I honestly did not know . . ."

Gaard breathed deeply, studying her for a moment, then strode to the tower window. Below, on the ragged cliffs, waves tossed themselves, sacrificed on the jutting rocks, their death glorious in the setting sun, giant plumes of white foam spraying the air, falling back to earth to be forever renewed. His eyes took in the scene while his thoughts dwelled on Dawnlyn, on her sudden, impulsive act.

She was an enigma. Were all women thus? He thought not. In her he sensed a combination of quiet serenity and, contrarily, a strong, rebellious nature. As greatly angered as he was at her thoughtless behavior below, still, he found himself intrigued by this slip of a woman.

His rage ebbing, he took his gaze from the scene below and sought Dawnlyn.

She stood in the middle of the floor, facing him squarely. "I'll understand if you no longer wish to marry me . . ."

"Have I said that?" he replied roughly.

"Nay."

"Then the betrothal stands as before. Furthermore," he said sternly, "an innocent such as yourself, and a defiant one at that, will no doubt be ever finding trouble or brewing it yourself. You need my protection, Dawnlyn. We will be wed, for I do not go back on my word."

They watched each other closely for an endless time and Gaard drank in her beauty. Finally, he said, "It will be some time, however, before we wed. Lie with me now . . . come to my bed again willingly."

Her heart lurched. "I . . . I should not," she breathed, but was unable to move away from him when he came to her and swept her into his willful embrace. She was powerless. She could not move away nor could she relax in his arms.

"Lie with me, Dawnlyn," he whispered.

"I must not again. What happened the other day was a mistake, Gaard. If we were only wed. Why must it be so long before our marriage? Why?"

"There are things I must do . . . places I must go first before I settle myself. But to lie with me now is not wrong. We *are* betrothed. It is binding." His mouth descended and sought hers in a long, passionate kiss. She could feel the swell of her breasts pressed against the hard wall of his chest and slowly, inevitably, her mouth parted beneath his and received him. Her arms, which moments before had hung limply at her sides, came up to feel the breadth of his back. With his hands he carefully began to slip her clothes away while mouth clung to mouth in a ritual as old as time.

All the while she knew she should protest, flee him, but in her heart she truly did not want to. And when he took his lips from hers and her last article of clothing fell to the floor in a sighing heap, she shivered but could not cover herself from his eyes.

"You are to be my wife," he said softly, then reached beneath her knees and swept her into his arms. "I'll not cause you pain this time, Dawnlyn, I'll honor you greatly." His mouth tasted hers lightly. "You cannot know this yet, sweet woman, but you also desire this joining."

"I . . . don't," she whispered, but knew it was not true. Her eyes met his. "I don't know what I want . . ."

For the first time she could remember, a smile reached his eyes. "But *I* do," he said.

When at last he placed her on the big bed, she watched her future husband take his clothes off and still could not fit her mind around the fact that she was to be wed, finally and unalterably, to this man. It frightened her normally practical mind—the shape of her future was a blank, she could envision nothing. She closed her eyes and whispered up a fervent prayer to her God.

The bed sagged on one side; he was coming to her. But this time there would be no confused thought—he was her betrothed. It was not so wrong . . .

Then she felt his fingers on her cheek, stroking her soft skin. He was so close that his breath fanned her warmly. Her stomach clenched; her heart leaped like a wild thing, then settled back and pounded heavily.

"Do not be afraid, Dawnlyn. You will learn tonight of what the minstrels sing. It is time you truly become a woman," he murmured in her ear.

"I am a woman now." Her voice was as soft as thistledown.

"No. I only relieved myself upon you. Tonight *you* will feel the pleasure."

"I do want to know," she whispered, opening her eyes. "I truly do, may the Lord forgive me . . ."

His gray eyes were soft, the pupils so large they appeared almost black. He smiled, showing strong white teeth. "Have no fear, He will forgive you."

His face came closer, blotting out all else until the world consisted only of the two of them. He touched his lips to her forehead, her cheek—soft, lingering kisses—then to her neck and to the place where her pulse beat wildly in the hollow of her throat. His hands stroked her skin all the while, slowly, languorously, as if he had forever to arouse her.

Dawnlyn grew weak, whether from her own confusion or from his caresses she didn't know. She kept very still, fearing that if she moved, the spell would be broken.

Slowly, slowly, his hands caressed her shoulders, her arms, feeling how her skin jumped under his fingers, feeling how her tension began to ebb.

Then, when she was ready, he dared to touch one soft breast, stroking it slowly at its outer edge. She was breathing steadily now, relaxed. He had to be careful, patient beyond imagining with this woman who was to be his wife, but the end would be worth it a hundred times over.

When he touched the peak of her breast, it was already hard. He heard her gasp, then he circled the pink tip with a finger. Her body quivered like a taut bowstring.

Lower, to her belly, her thighs, his sure hands trailed, stroked, patiently, patiently. He felt his own strong need tempt him, but subdued it. There would be time for that later . . .

Then he moved his mouth to her breasts, kissing, sucking, then down to her navel. He was aware of her quickened breathing, the way her body shook involuntarily.

She let out a tiny sigh and he sensed that, at last, she was giving in to sensation, even if it was against her will.

Then his hand caressed the silken, coppery mound below her belly. His heartbeat quickened. She would be ready soon. It seemed like he'd been waiting for her forever, waiting like the skilled hunter ready with bow and spear, waiting for the quarry to come close enough. And now she was approaching, lured by him, put off guard, until the glory fulfilled them both.

Carefully, he touched her within her woman's flesh, feeling at last her core, her inner beauty. Her legs relaxed, fell apart, her white breasts rose and fell, her pink lips were slightly parted. Soon, soon, she would want him as much as he wanted her.

"Gaard," she whispered, her voice wondering, "what is happening to me?"

His eyes smiled into hers. "You are learning how to be a woman, how to love a man."

"It is frightening," she breathed.

"No! It is beautiful. Kiss me. You want to, don't you?"

"Yes. I do." Her eyes were wide, clear as copper flames.

Her arms went around his neck. It was as natural as breathing. She felt the masculine hardness of his arms and shoulder, felt the rigid scar on his back, different from her own body. Yet it felt *right*. He pulled her close, taking her lips with his own. She could not get enough of the sensation. She strained against him, their tongues meeting, blending.

His hand caressed her again, between her legs, and her body began to burn, a hot pain building within her belly, spreading out to her hips, making them press against him as if she wished to be even closer to him than she was, closer than her skin would allow.

His lips left hers, he kissed her closed eyelids, her nose, her neck. "Are you ready now, my sweet Dawnlyn?" he asked.

"Aye . . ." she murmured.

He poised himself over her, his manhood pressing at her. She opened herself to him, wanting something of which she was not quite sure, but knowing she wanted it desperately, more desperately than she'd ever wanted anything.

Then he filled her body and she gave a great sigh of pleasure. But then the need rose again and she knew there was more to the act, even more.

He moved on her, in her; the sensation was both lovely

and unfinished, full of a stabbing pleasure that was entirely new. It began to build, to carry her to the edge of sensation, further and further, until she had no mind at all, but was only sensation itself, moving in a whirlwind with him.

The whirlwind swept her, finally, gasping and shuddering, over the edge into fulfillment. She heard her own cry of release with surprise, as if it emanated from someone else. Then she was aware of Gaard plunging over her until he, too, was finished. And from somewhere in her consciousness appeared the words, formed silently but indelibly in her mind's eye: "This man, this Viking, will be your husband."

As she lay, panting, covered with a fine sheen of sweat, entwined in Gaard's long limbs, she wondered whether the words were a warning of trouble or a promise of exquisite, endless pleasure.

Chapter Seven

ST. ABB'S HALL PULSED WITH PREPARATIONS FOR THE JOUR-
ney across the North Sea. For the past weeks, since the feast
and announcement of the betrothal, Gaard had kept every
able-bodied man busy, drilling them in the arts of warfare.
Most of the men, along with Gaard, had made their camp in
the fields near Coldingham, where his dragon ships lay at
anchor. Only occasionally did Gaard come to the Hall, and
then it was merely to check on one of the tradesmen such as
the smith, to be certain he followed the instructions as to the
forging of weapons or the repair of the chain mail.

He left Dawnlyn totally in charge of the entire Hall: the
accounts, the farms, the sheep herds and the fishing village.
She had been well trained in the skills of management at the
cloister but still, she had a lot to learn in a very short period
of time, as her father had always taken care of these matters,
and she dashed around with the iron key ring constantly
jingling at her narrow waist.

She was busy from sunup to sunset. There were everyday
chores to be directed: the washing, the meal planning, the
rushes to be changed on the stone floors, quarrels among
the servants to be settled. But then there were the behind-
the-scene tasks to be done: ledger accounting, tariffs to be

collected, inventories to be taken both in the tower itself and in the many workshops—the smithy, the bakery, the tannery. And then, too, there was always the worry over the late spring planting: would it rain too much, or too little? Would blight be a factor this season? Were the sheep and cattle healthy?

She barely had time to fret over her future marriage or Gaard's upcoming voyage or even her new responsibilities as the lady of St. Abb's. It was only at night, alone in the big bed that she had shared with the strange, passionate Viking, that she wondered and questioned and tried to imagine what her life would be like as his wife.

She could not picture herself as a married woman—a wife and mother. There was absolutely no connection between *that* woman and the girl, Dawnlyn Renfrew, who had always been destined for a notable position in the nunnery.

She supposed, when she had time to reflect, that it would always be like this—she busily running the keep while Gaard was away a-viking. The knowledge was at the same time welcome and unsettling, but at least now she knew, whatever happened, she would be able to endure—not by calculation, not by knowledge of good and evil, not by high principle, but merely by a curious and shifting sense of equilibrium that defied each of these.

One of her least favorite of chores had been put off long enough. After the village bell had rung midday she tied on an old apron of Gerta's, having to pull it almost twice around her, and descended into the dark cellar of the tower where the dusty, cobweb-draped casks and kegs were stored. Someone had to take inventory of the cider, the ale and the mead, for Gaard had ordered that a goodly number of kegs were to go on the ships with him, and she'd best be certain of the exact tally.

She hated the damp, musty cellar—it was a foul hole and so dark. It seemed as if some terrible, crawly thing was always waiting, just out of the wavering circle of light cast by her oil lamp. She'd hated the cellar always and even as a small child had refused to play hide-and-seek there, although Ian had taunted her unmercifully.

However, mature, dutiful ladies could not indulge themselves in such frivolous fears, so Dawnlyn tried to ignore them and began marking down the numbers of each type of keg, straining to scratch the figures into her ledger in the uncertain light.

A thump and scratch sounded behind her, and she jumped as if burned, stifling a scream of fright.

"My lady?" she heard a voice say, then more shuffles. Quickly, she grabbed at the oil lamp to hold it up and see who it was, but her hand slipped and she dropped the lamp. Suddenly all was oppressively, endlessly black, a blackness so impenetrable that it was as solid as a stone wall.

"By the sweet blood of Christ!" she quavered, cowering back until she hit the piled-up casks. "Who's there? Who is it?"

"Dawnlyn!" The voice came nearer.

"Who is it?" she half-screamed.

More scuffles, a muted curse. "What in hell have you done with your lamp?" came the voice, quite reasonably irritated, not at all unworldly.

"Sweyn!" she breathed.

"Yes, it is Sweyn, and I'm half-suffocated in this dark. Where are you?"

"Here!" Then she almost laughed. Where was *here* to Sweyn, who could see nothing.

"Keep talking, I'll find you."

"I'm so silly. I knocked over the lamp." Her voice quavered. "Have you a flint?"

"Yes, my lady. But it does neither of us any good if I never reach you in this accursed dark!" Then there was a thump and another curse.

"Sweyn, are you hurt?" she called.

"Only a minor wound. Nothing to speak of." Then, "Ah, I've found you!"

And Dawnlyn felt the warmth of another body and then

the feel of a hand on her breast—quickly snatched away—a disembodied hand out of the stygian darkness.

She started, then relaxed. "Oh," was all she said, feeling her cheeks flush in the inky blackness.

"Now, where is that dastardly lamp?" asked Sweyn, and she could hear him scrabbling around on the damp ground for it. She heard the sound of flint striking, and soon there was a dim glow that quickly brightened. Sweyn's blue eyes and drooping blond mustache loomed before her.

"Oh!" she said again. "Thank the sweet Lord!"

"Thank Him that there is a bit of oil left," added Sweyn. "And what are you doing down here like a mole?"

"I had to count the kegs."

"Oh, I see, hard at work, as usual."

"Well, there is much to be done . . ." Suddenly she felt distinctly uncomfortable with the tall, handsome, young Viking standing so close to her in the circle of light. There was something terribly intimate about being alone in the darkness with him, something disquieting that she knew he sensed, too, for he abruptly stepped back from her and an expression of exaggerated unconcern cloaked his features.

"And now that I have found you," he said quickly, "I will give you my message that you may continue your work."

"Aye?"

"Gaard wishes a feast for this eve, as he leaves on the morning tide."

It was as if her heart stopped. And yet she had known that he was leaving soon. She had known all along. Why should she feel this stab of sudden desolation?

"So soon?"

"'Tis not so soon, my lady. It has been several weeks . . ."

"Aye, so it has." Her voice was small and lost in the echoing darkness.

"Now, you must excuse me, Lady Dawnlyn"—his voice was very proper—"for I must needs return to my labors also . . ."

95

"Of course, Sweyn. But I think I shall return to the hall with you. I've had quite enough of this place for today." She gave a nervous laugh and picked up her ledger.

Sweyn took the lamp and, holding it high, led her from the cellar, attentive to every step she took, yet meticulously not touching her to help her up the stairs.

When they emerged into the light of day once more, Dawnlyn breathed a great sigh of relief, then turned to Sweyn to thank him.

He was observing her with a drawn brow, his crystal blue eyes containing an expression of rare seriousness. "Will you miss Gaard?" he asked abruptly.

Dawnlyn cocked her head to one side, studying Sweyn. What an odd thought for the young Viking, whose interests in life seemed only to be wenching, making merry with his fellow warriors, or training with his broadsword. "No," she stated softly, "I think I shall not miss him at all. Have I seen him lately? What difference would it make if he is at Coldingham or across the sea?"

"By Odin, you're right!" Sweyn's lips at last broke into his normal carefree grin. "He is never lazing about the tower, is he? A good leader, Gaard is."

"Aye," Dawnlyn murmured darkly, "he is an excellent leader of men . . ."

She checked the kitchen while Sweyn went to his chamber to bathe, then took some food to Ian, who was still locked below. She and her brother argued as they had for the past two weeks; he was going half mad and kept insisting that Dawnlyn could somehow set him free.

"I cannot, Ian," she whispered so that the sentry could not overhear. "I tried once and you attacked Gaard. It was your doing . . . not mine."

"Get me out of here!" he choked. "I am going insane!" He clutched at her arm. "Please, sister, get me out of this hellhole. Tell the *heathen* I'll do anything . . . anything!"

Dawnlyn left feeling depressed beyond measure and sought the comfort of her own chamber, where she changed into a more suitable gown—a dusty rose linen with long, flowing sleeves trimmed in gold. As she combed out her russet, springing hair, she thought on Ian's plight. But really, there was nothing she could do but ease his days below by sneaking him food and ale. She had even taken him a chess set to wile away his hours, but, in a temper, he had tossed the fine wooden pieces to the floor and crushed them with a boot. Perhaps, she thought, when Gaard leaves, I'll persuade Sweyn to free Ian.

The handsome young Sweyn was already in the great hall when Dawnlyn returned, seeming to have recovered some of his bravado. He walked to the foot of the steps and offered her a brawny arm. "Is this not the proper way for a Scots gentleman to greet a lovely lady?" His clear blue eyes sparkled, teasing her.

"Yes," Dawnlyn said, smiling easily, "you *are* learning, Sweyn."

"And so are *you*, my lady. You have finally learned the art of gaiety."

They strolled toward the long table. "I should take a wife," he said quietly, "but there are none so beautiful as you, Lady Dawnlyn."

He pulled out her chair while Dawnlyn blushed an even deeper hue than that of her rose gown, wondering suddenly what would have transpired if Sweyn, not Gaard, had taken her first . . .

"You know," Sweyn said, a little more seriously now, "a Norse woman has great freedom compared to what I have seen here. She can inherit from her father, she decides her own fate in many areas. By Thor's hammer, she can even divorce her husband for sufficient reason!"

Dawnlyn was aware of Sweyn's eyes on her, gauging her response to his information. "That is a disgusting custom. It could only produce anarchy and destroy the family. It is against God's law."

"Well, my lady, it has not done that, but it *has* released women from unendurable marriages. It is our way."

She was just sweeping aside her flared skirt, disdaining Sweyn's explanations, when they both heard a muffled cough at the double doors and turned toward the entrance.

How long Gaard had been standing there, watching them, neither ventured to guess, although why he remained silent, Dawnlyn could not fathom.

Gaard's eyes traveled eloquently from Sweyn to Dawnlyn's rosy cheeks. "Have bath water sent aloft," he said tightly, then strode across the hall past them and disappeared up the curving stairs without another word.

"You'd best go to him," said Sweyn under his breath. "His mood appears foul."

"No," Dawnlyn replied. "I have duties in the kitchen to see to. Let him soak in a warm bath and ease his mood."

"Perhaps you are right. It may just be that he had a difficult day training your Scots," Sweyn said hopefully.

Gaard descended to the great hall shortly after sunset. Most of his men were already there but had not partaken of the food until their leader arrived. Dawnlyn was in the kitchen, watching over Gerta as the last tray was filled with baked halibut, apple mousse, griddle bread and early carrots from the walled-in kitchen garden.

It was there that Gaard found her. "Leave the work to the servants," he said gruffly, taking her arm with a possessive hand.

As they walked together to the table, Dawnlyn was struck by his change of appearance. Clean shaven once more, his sun-darkened skin glowed. His eyes were a clear gray and his gilded hair shone in the torchlight. He wore a velvet surcoat of burgundy over a clean, white shirt, which was open at the front, revealing the patch of crisp, light hairs over the golden skin of his chest. His features were stern and he appeared to be still preoccupied as a muscle worked in his lean jaw.

Dawnlyn seated herself next to him. "You leave tomorrow?" she asked, attempting to alleviate his mood.

"Yes. On the morning tide." He took a long draught of his ale, began to pile food on his trencher.

"The training went well?" She tried a new tack, wondering at his coldness.

"Umm," he responded, chewing meat from a leg of a spring lamb.

Exasperated, she turned to Sweyn. "Will you be saddened to remain at St. Abb's?" she queried.

"Very much so," replied Sweyn. "I shall miss what promises to be a great battle, but then—who knows?—perhaps I'll find a wife. There will be time now." He watched her carefully at his disclosure.

"You really think you may marry?" asked Dawnlyn, picking at her vegetables.

"Unless I'm lured off by a woodwoman, yes."

"A woodwoman?"

"Why, surely you have them in Scotland," replied Sweyn, a blond brow raised quizzically.

"No. I do not think so," said Dawnlyn thoughtfully. "Who are they?"

Sweyn laughed. "You mean . . . *what* are they!"

"Perhaps Dawnlyn is not interested," said Gaard curtly, turning toward them.

"Oh! But I am," she said quickly. "Please, tell me, Sweyn."

"They are beautiful, Lady Dawnlyn," he began. "So lovely that a man cannot resist their lure, and once he is trapped, it is hopeless, for they hold him in their spell."

Plainly, Dawnlyn was confused. "But . . . women who cast spells are witches . . . they are not usually pretty . . ."

"No, no. You misunderstand," Sweyn smiled. "They are not witches, they are woodwomen." He thought for a moment. "I shall tell you what happened to my father so that you may better understand."

At Sweyn's words, Gaard grimaced and rolled his eyes in exasperation, then turned to his flagon of ale.

Sweyn continued, undaunted. "One day, while my father hunted red deer deep in the tall forest, a great cold fog swept the air and he became hopelessly lost. But my father was a wise man," said Sweyn proudly, "and instead of walking in

99

circles through the banks of fog, he merely waited for it to pass on and sat down under a tall spruce on the mossy floor. And that was when he first saw her . . ."

"The woodwoman?" asked Dawnlyn, caught in the strange tale.

"Yes. She came like a wraith through the mist, and her hair was raven black and her eyes were the brightest blue he had ever seen. She wore virgin white and through the damp material, he could see . . . Well, she was a *most* beautiful woman." Sweyn glanced across to Gaard for approval, then went on.

"My father said her lips were as red as an autumn rose and her teeth as perfect as white, gleaming shells. He rose from his moss seat and approached her. The woman held forth her arms for him and my father gasped at her exquisite beauty."

"She must have been very beautiful," mused Dawnlyn, wondering from where the woman had appeared.

"That she was. And desirable, too," he added, "in a way no man can resist. And he went to her, wrapped his strong arms around her slender body. And that was when he knew . . ."

"Knew what?" Dawnlyn's tawny eyes were as wide as a kitten's.

"That she was not of earth but a woodwoman!"

"Oh!" breathed Dawnlyn, bringing a hand to her breast.

"Yes. You see, Lady Dawnlyn, woodwomen are hollow at the back." He paused to watch Dawnlyn's sudden, skeptical expression. "It is true! And for years my father was under her spell and could see no other woman save her . . . the one with the beautiful face but the insubstantial, hollow back."

Dawnlyn raised a slim brow. "And how, may I ask, did he break this spell?"

"Why, he met my mother, of course. Can't you tell?"

"Tell what?" asked Dawnlyn cautiously.

"Tell how beautiful my mother is. Why . . . all you need do is look on me!"

Then, after a split second of bewilderment, Dawnlyn laughed so hard and so long that she had to hold her sides, gasping for breath. Sweyn, too, roared in delight for some minutes while the noise in the hall mingled with their mirthful chuckling.

Only Gaard did not join the merriment. When at last Dawnlyn calmed herself, her eyes glistening golden with mirth, she took note of Gaard's frown.

"It was a wonderful tale, don't you think?" she asked him, still smiling.

"Yes," Gaard replied, "but I've heard it over a thousand fires. Tonight, I have matters of greater import on my mind."

"Such as?" asked Dawnlyn, vaguely irritated that he would not allow himself to enjoy this last evening with her. And then it struck her—he was preoccupied, true, but his behavior, since arriving back at the tower that afternoon and seeing her with Sweyn, was nothing short of childish!

"There are many things to be done still," Gaard said tightly. "Tomorrow we set sail and all must be in readiness. I must forget nothing. Once we are away, I can relax, but not this eve." And then he turned to face her, a tiny smile at the corner of his well-modeled lips, a casual elbow resting on the table. "I do have a gift for you, however. One that I know will please you greatly."

"A gift?" Dawnlyn suddenly felt a new tenderness toward him—he hadn't forgotten her entirely after all.

"Sweyn!" Gaard looked over her head and nodded. His lieutenant rose and left the great hall.

"Oh, Gaard, what is it?" Dawnlyn cried. "I can't wait! Where has Sweyn gone?"

"Patience," he said, smiling inscrutably.

Sweyn returned a few minutes later and behind him, Dawnlyn saw, was Ian!

She leaped to her feet, blinked her eyes to be certain. Gaard took her hand, began to pull her gently back down into her chair.

"Not yet, my lady. First I must speak to the boy and judge his mettle."

"But—"

"Allow *me* to handle this," Gaard said with a hint of steely amusement. "Remember the last time?" He turned to Ian, who stood on the other side of the table from them. "What have you to say, boy?" asked Gaard sternly.

Ian looked from the fierce Norseman to his sister, then back. His expression was sullenly rebellious, but at least he made an effort to quell his thoughts. "I do not like your being here, but I see the folly of trying to slay you, Viking. It has cost me dearly in sanity."

"So you have decided that to come at my back is folly? I see. And how can I know that you will not change your mind?" Gaard's lips tilted at the corners ominously.

"I wish to live," replied Ian. "Your power is great and I have none."

"And what do you figure I owe you, Ian Renfrew, for these lands that would have been yours one day?"

"To allow me my life will be sufficient," Ian said thoughtfully. "That is all I seek. My life. My freedom."

"Your sister," Gaard said, glancing slowly at Dawnlyn, "has no doubt told you of my forthcoming voyage to Norway. Would you care to join my ranks and perhaps earn a place under me? I require your total loyalty and your brave sword arm."

Ian's mouth fell open in surprise; it was obvious he had expected nothing. "I . . . I would be honored to serve. I am a fighting man. Just allow me my freedom and my sword and, by God, you will have my loyalty!"

"Well spoken, Ian Renfrew. Now go with Sweyn and you will be outfitted. We sail on the morning tide."

"Thank you, Gaard Wolftooth," said Ian earnestly, "thank you."

Dawnlyn was so overjoyed she could have thrown her arms around Gaard and kissed him right in front of everyone. Instead, taking a deep breath, she said quietly, "And I thank you, too. There could be no better gift . . ."

"It's as much my gain as yours."

Directly after the meal, they retired to their chamber, but

Gaard was restless, unable to keep from pacing the rush-covered stone flooring. Dawnlyn had thought there would be a different fate in store for her—and it was not watching this man pace to and fro like a caged lion.

Strangely, she felt a small loss. It was as if he were dismissing her once again, refusing to let her into his life, past the impenetrable male walls he set up about him.

While he paced, she slipped into a night shift of oyster-white linen with lace trim. "You are preoccupied, my lord," she said, standing near the bed, unsure as to what she should do next. It had, after all, been weeks since they had been alone together.

"I am," he admitted, stopping now to face her. "And you are too lovely to ignore, Dawnlyn. Like Sweyn's woodwoman, you have the power to captivate." But he made no move toward her.

"Would you like me to rub your shoulders?" she asked, remembering the times she had done so for her father.

Gaard raised a brow. "Rub my shoulders?"

"Yes . . . to ease your tension."

"Am I tense?" he asked.

"I should think so."

"And I am also being rude on our last night together." He swept a tired hand through the rumpled thickness of his hair. "If it pleases you, Dawnlyn, you may rub my shoulders." He walked to the chair and sat, his long legs stretched in front of him.

She helped him off with his surcoat and began to work at the tense sinews beneath his shirt. And while she kneaded the heavy muscles she thought to herself that he must be terribly ignorant of women. Men—he knew their ways well enough; but women were another matter altogether.

"Oh," he sighed, "that does feel quite good. Such a luxury."

"Have you really never had your muscles massaged before?"

"No," he admitted, relaxing beneath her soft stroking. "And never have I shared a chamber with a woman the

103

night before setting sail. It is the custom of some men to indulge themselves, but I find it distracting."

Dawnlyn felt a curious indignation at his admission, yet she was relieved in a way, too. She wondered if she would ever have the opportunity to see him again on the eve of battle. Would he *really* return from Norway? And how would she feel if he did not?

"I could almost sleep," he said in a husky voice, his head sagging comfortably on his chest. "Yes . . . I might just sleep a few hours, then see to the loading of the ships . . ."

He was drifting off; she let her fingers press into the thick muscles gently, soothing, relaxing him against his will.

"Feels wonderful," he sighed deeply. Then, "Come, Dawnlyn, before my eyes close . . . come onto my lap."

Her heart beating rapidly, she took his proffered hand and moved around the chair, coming quietly to rest in his lap.

The mere contact of her rounded bottom against the hard thighs was enough to send a tingle of unbidden desire coursing down her limbs. He put both arms around her waist and enfolded her slender torso in his embrace. His head rested against the curved swell of her bosom. "I wish to bed you, little one," he said into her breast, his breath warm through the linen. "You put an ache in my loins, so lovely were you when Sweyn held you with his tale . . ."

"Do you mind my talking to Sweyn?" she asked carefully.

"Certainly not," Gaard replied quickly. "You will spend much time with him while I am gone . . ."

"And does that bother you?" she pressed on, sure that he was not being entirely honest with her.

Gaard murmured something under his breath in Norse, then said, "I am not overly pleased to think on it. Sweyn is a handsome young man." He paused, then said, "But I trust him completely. It is *you* I worry about."

"Me?" she gasped. How could he even think she would . . .

"Yes, my little one. Whether or not you know it, you have a passionate nature beneath the cool facade," he said, smiling. "There is a hot-blooded girl whose very nearness to me is quite disturbing!"

His words, the feel of his breath against her, the soft curl of his golden hair brushing her lips, sent Dawnlyn's senses whirling. And she could not deny it—if he said one word about bedding her she would comply. She could not stop herself nor could she deny her longing to feel his skin, all of him, in her hands, against her soft flesh, deep within her womb . . .

"But alas, my Dawnlyn, this night must be for thought. I cannot sap my strength . . . I am the leader. I must be clear of mind when we set sail."

She said nothing but, in truth, she did not understand. It was as if he were an ascetic, deliberately denying his flesh to gain purity for the task ahead. She knew she should be relieved . . . and yet somehow she wasn't.

He stroked the swell of her breast with a single finger; so light was his caress she wondered if she weren't imagining it. His head raised then and his lips brushed hers so carefully, so softly, she suffered an infinitesimal death.

And then he rose, easily, carrying her to the bed and carefully laying her on the eiderdown. Her lips were parted, expectant; her breasts outlined beneath the fine linen rose and fell gently, a place deep within her throbbed slowly, heavily, longingly . . .

Gaard straightened up, gazed on her copper hair spread like a sea nymph's on the quilts, glistening, flowing.

"To leave you like this, Dawnlyn, is more painful to me than you know." He smiled tightly. "But the hours grow short now and I've things still to do."

And without truly thinking, Dawnlyn said, "Cannot Sweyn or Knute see to these things?"

Gaard smiled. "Nay. I must." And then, "You will be . . . all right when I am away?"

"Yes," she whispered softly. "I shall be quite fine. Sweyn will be here, in any case."

"He will," Gaard answered, "and he will protect you

105

while I'm abroad. Do not hesitate to seek him out if you have need."

"I won't forget. He is a loyal man."

"Yes. I trust him and I know he will see to it that you come to no harm."

Dawnlyn's marigold eyes searched Gaard's face. "Will you . . . come to bed later?" she asked hesitantly.

"I plan to . . . even if it is only to kiss you farewell." He left, closing the chamber door carefully, not looking back at her.

Gaard wandered through the dim tower, checking on his men, reassuring himself that all was prepared for the voyage and raid to follow. Some of his men slept heavily from the ale consumed at the meal; others lay about the great hall resting but too tense or excited to sleep.

Gaard then climbed to the turret and checked with the sentry posted there.

The night was cool and a heavy mist rolled in from the sea, wetting the earth softly. As he had no wish to rest, Gaard allowed the sentry to go below for a time and refresh himself. His act was not one of kindness; no, Gaard wished to be alone with the hissing black sea, the cool night sky, his own curiously turbulent thoughts.

He rested elbows on the cool, damp stones of the wall and gazed out over the misty water. The fog met the sky in a line, like a bank of clouds, and above the moon shone through a haze, surrounded by gray clouds.

There was no sight like it, Gaard mused, no sight as wild, as free, as provocative—it beckoned him. The sound of the sea crashing on the rocks far below lulled him with its eternal pounding. His eyelids grew heavy, too heavy to gaze on the silver moonlight as the full orb rode the night sky.

Time froze. With a start, Gaard blinked his eyes, felt the damp stones beneath his elbows, the wild pounding of his heart. He shook his head to rid it of the restless bat wings of the chilling nightmare in which his lifelong adversary, Fenris, had taken Dawnlyn from him. Then he unfolded himself, stood straight as his broadsword, spun around, taking the width of the turret in two long strides, and raced down the tower steps.

He banged open Dawnlyn's door, his breath held in his lungs still.

She was there! Fenris had not taken her, then! It was only a dream vision. And yet . . . it was a powerful sign. Without Gaard at her side there was danger for Dawnlyn. He dared not leave her. And then he wondered fleetingly if he had ever meant to leave her here alone . . .

He strode to the bedside, placed a strong hand on her shoulder. "Wake up, Dawnlyn," he said, "wake up."

She stirred, opened her eyes. "Is it morning?" A frown creased her white brow—the night had fled so quickly.

"No. But you must rise," he said urgently. "And fetch Meg to make ready your things. You are going with me to Norway."

Dawnlyn's eyes opened wide in shock. "I'm . . . what?" she breathed, her voice sleep-clouded.

"Going to Norway with me. Now rise and hurry and Meg will go, too."

"But I can't!" she cried. "I can't leave my home!" But Gaard was already leaving, disappearing through the door. His words bounced emptily back at her from the cool stone walls.

Chapter Eight

DAWNLYN COULD NOT ACTUALLY COMPREHEND THE FACT THAT she was on board *Wind Eater,* even though she was sitting on her sea chest under the awning and watching the Vikings' strong backs bend to the sixty oars that would take them out of the landing at Coldingham.

It had all happened too swiftly. Nothing made sense. All she knew was that one moment she was asleep in her own bed and the next she was being warned to wear her heaviest wool cloak and hustled aboard the skiff that took them out to Gaard's ship.

She could not even talk to Gaard because he was too busy with last-minute details, thus she had no idea why he had decided to take her, nor was she sure whether she was pleased or horrified. She could only sit huddled in a corner of the deck under the awning, out of the men's way, and wait until Gaard had time for her.

The activity she viewed with bewildered curiosity. She had never been on board a ship in her life. It was a fine late-spring day, and the sail bellied out, caught the stiff breeze and began to carry the ship to the northeast, toward Norway.

The sea gulls shrieked and swooped around them, the

stays hummed, and Dawnlyn began to notice the myriad sounds of the sea, endless and varied and new to her ear. She saw the Vikings lean to the oars willingly with cheerful jests and wide smiles; she saw Gaard grinning from ear to ear, taller and more powerful than any, and jubilant, full of the joy of setting out across the leaping, heaving, gray water.

She still sat on her chest, which Gaard had not had time to stow in his cabin, as quiet and timid as a mouse. Her eyes were large and bright hazel, catching the luminous light reflected from the water; her copper hair, bound loosely at the back, sprang about her shoulders wildly from the damp air. With a slim hand she felt her cheeks, sticky now with sea spray. It was all so new to her, so alien—even the ship seemed like a giant, monstrous beast, threatening, with its carved wolf head looming tall above the waves on the bow. And on the ship's sides were hung the shields of the men, gleaming proudly in the sun like the carapaces of giant, colorful beetles. What strange, frightening men these were whose great ships represented might, a promise of danger and death, yet also freedom and adventure.

Meg was with her, wide-eyed and terrified and utterly silent. Dawnlyn was even afraid to stand up, lest she fall, so unaccustomed was she to the rise and fall of *Wind Eater's* narrow deck. She turned her head and watched the gray, fog-hazed line that was the coast of Scotland fade out of sight behind her, and then all there was to view was the unimaginably huge expanse of sea and the four other Viking ships, tiny and vulnerable-looking as they tossed on the waves.

She stared in wonder at her tall Viking and tried to imagine the courage that drove these men to cross uncharted oceans. Gaard's stories came back to haunt her—tales of sailing and marauding from the eastern end of the sun-warmed Mediterranean to the far-off western shore of Vinland, from geyser-sprouting Iceland to snow-shrouded Greenland, to the shores of Cathay and Araby and the giant rivers of the Russ.

What kind of men were these? Surely they were something slightly more than mortal to tempt fate with their confident grins, their rough jokes, their strange ships.

The fact of her body, her shell, sitting on board a Viking ship had no more reality for her than did the fact of her forthcoming marriage to an unchristian Norseman. Her body was there, yes, but her mind could not cope with the actuality of it. She felt dazed, exposed to a gamut of emotional buffetings, uncertain of anything solid and secure in her life anymore.

She and Meg must have sat there for hours before Gaard had time to stop and talk to her. He was windblown and smiling and wore only a thin white linen shirt, which molded itself to his muscled torso. His hair blew about his face in careless waves as he stopped by the two women.

"Do you fare well?" he asked, his flinty eyes light and joy-filled in the sun. "Do you have the seasickness?"

"No, but Gaard, how am I to walk on this moving thing? I'm cold and hungry and afraid to put one foot in front of the other! And Meg, too!"

He laughed, his even white teeth sparkling. "You'll soon get used to it. This is only a short trip—only several days if the wind's right."

"But how do you know which direction to go in? It all looks the same."

"By Odin's beard, such ignorance!" He chuckled. "Do you not see the sun, the cloud banks, the different-colored currents? It's an open book for us. Have no fear. I could put us into the bay near Thorkellhall with my eyes closed!"

"My dear Lord, I hope so," breathed Dawnlyn. "I will pray for us all."

"You do that, my lady"—he grinned—"and meanwhile *I* will sail the ship and see you safely there!"

Then he summoned one of the men and had her trunk carried down below the deck to the tiny cabin she was to share with him. Meg would sleep in a corner of a storeroom, and the rest of the men slept on deck under the awnings, for the entire hold of the ship was filled with weapons, food and other necessities.

"This is no fat-bellied *knorr* or merchantman," explained Gaard. "This is a fighting ship, built in the Stavanger shipyard. She's as stout and as fast as any and has carried me safely from Egypt to the North Isles and back." He took Dawnlyn's chin in his hand and lifted her face to his. He seemed so tall, so proud to her suddenly, with the sun catching in his hair and his eyes deep gray pools. He stood, legs straddled casually, an arrogant pillar of strength. A small smile gathered at the corners of his mouth.

He helped her down the ladder to the cabin, explaining, *"Wind Eater* has been my only wife until now. She may be jealous and not wish to share me with you, so watch that you treat me well, woman." And with that he left her, swinging himself up the ladder to the deck with careless agility.

Dawnlyn sat on the hard bunk and stared after him, wondering whether he'd been joking or serious but couldn't for the life of her decide.

The day and the night went slowly yet steadily. Meg grew quite ill and retired to her pallet with a bucket, moaning and retching. But Dawnlyn felt fine, even venturing on deck again, growing somewhat accustomed to the heaving under her feet.

She stared around her at the endless horizon, the unchanging vistas of white-tressed waves, and tried to understand Gaard's ways. She knew, somehow, that she couldn't understand him without comprehending the sea and his ships. They were, she realized, so much a part of him.

The second day dawned overcast and chilly, a fog bank resting on the sea to the north. Still, the five ships scudded northeast, never slackening their graceful flight before the wind, but Dawnlyn noticed the men's faces were a bit more grim, their eyes watchful.

Gaard did finally spend some time with her that morning, eating his breakfast on the deck at her side. "So you're not one of those puking women who sickens unto death when on the water. Good," he said, and she decided to take it as a compliment.

When they'd eaten, Gaard was called back to duty. Before he left her, he told her to go below to the cabin. "It looks like a gale is coming up," he said. "There is no danger, for I do not wish you to panic, but a woman unused to the life on a ship could endanger herself and thus my own men. Do not mind how the waves toss us. It is nothing to *Wind Eater*." And he was off again, striding with ease into the sea spray.

So Dawnlyn dozed through the afternoon, worked on some embroidery and sat by Meg, who was still not feeling well. She deliberately avoided telling Meg of the gale.

It must have been early evening when she woke from a nap, but the cabin was entirely dark. She rose from the bunk to light the lantern and the next thing she knew she was thrown, as if by a giant hand, across the tiny room and brought up short against the opposite wall. As she tried to rise, she was thrown back to the bunk to lie there stunned while *Wind Eater* rose on end as if she would fly out of the water. With a sickening, sliding drop that made Dawnlyn's stomach rise in her throat, she fell bow-first into the water.

Clambering onto the deck in a moment of unreasoning panic, Dawnlyn was flung to the ship's rail, which now lay under her, flat on the water, so steeply was *Wind Eater* heeled over. She grabbed desperately for the rail, felt her fingers close on something, and then she was lying against the rail, drenched by sea spray, looking directly at the water itself, not many yards from her face. She screamed from pure terror, for it seemed that the ship would be covered in a moment by the monstrous seas, broken apart and swirled below to its doom.

Her hands burned from the pain of holding on. She knew in a moment her strength would fail when suddenly she was being wrenched away and sent sprawling against a hard object as the ship heeled over the other way.

She felt herself half-carried, half-dragged to shelter. Her hood had blown off; her hair was wild and plastered wetly to her face; she felt blinded by the spray and suffocated by the firm hold the man had on her. She whimpered with fear and pain as he pushed her down the ladder into the tiny cabin.

The door closed; the relative quiet collided heavily with her ears. She turned toward the oilskin-clad man.

"Dawnlyn," came Gaard's stern voice, "don't ever do that again!"

"What?" she screamed, past all control. "Don't do that again? You mean don't ever come on board this accursed ship, this *wife* of yours! Is *that* what you mean?"

"No, Dawnlyn." His expression turned grim. "That's not it at all. I simply don't want to have to worry about you all the time!"

"Worry about me?" she cried. "You leave me down here to die . . . ignore me completely . . ."

"I knew you were safe below," he threw at her roughly, "and for Odin's sake, I do not ignore you! You are ever crowding my thoughts, woman. You do not belong here."

"Then why, why did you drag me along! Why don't you throw me overboard and be done with me! Wouldn't that solve all your problems? Then I wouldn't be in your way . . ."

The harsh lines in Gaard's face relaxed. He ran a hand through the thickness of his soaked hair. "All I have been trying to explain, Dawnlyn, is that it is not safe for you to be wandering around the deck in a storm." His voice was surprisingly gentle.

"What on earth difference does it make? We'll all be dead soon anyway!"

"No, little one. This is merely a gale, as I said. It only speeds us on our way. We'll be at Thorkellhall soon. Now, I have work to do." He turned to leave.

"No, please, Gaard! Don't leave me!" The words were torn from her throat; she felt desperate, hysterical. She'd never been so out of control in her life. She felt near death and had no thought for anything but her own black terror.

Gaard stopped at the door of the cabin. Her terror was so plain: the pallid face and wet, tangled hair, the wide eyes, the white lips. He reminded himself again that this was a woman of the land, that she had never been on a ship before, much less in a storm.

"Dawnlyn," he said, "believe me, there is no danger. It is normal . . ."

"Oh, please, I'm so frightened," she moaned, her eyes white-rimmed, her hands clutching at the wet fold of her cloak.

He stepped close to her, pushed a wet lock of dark red hair back from her face. Then, somehow, she was enfolded in his arms, small and trembling like a bird, helpless.

He bent and kissed her forehead, stroked her wet hair. "Have no fear, little one, I will get us all safely to port."

Gaard had always felt protective of women—wasn't that a man's duty? But suddenly he was overwhelmed by a protectiveness at the knowledge of her terror so fierce— a sense of caring so strongly about her welfare—that it shocked him to the core.

It was an alien sensation, alien and thoroughly disquieting and one that he was not at all sure he liked.

It was dusk when *Wind Eater* scudded silently toward the shore of Norway. Gaard met with a few of his trusted men, to finalize plans. He'd left Dawnlyn asleep in the cabin, glad that she was able to finally rest. The storm had abated, but it had blown them so close to their destination that Gaard had to make his plans quickly, before his small fleet was sighted by his brother's ships that were ever scouting the area.

He knew Karl. His older brother left nothing to chance and surely knew that Gaard would make an attempt to clear his good name. Not only would Karl have his own ships on the lookout but every merchantman in the North Sea as well.

So, wisely, Gaard decided to slip into a familiar cove near Thorkellhall and see to his business in utmost secrecy— trying to vanquish Karl face to face would be a deadly mistake. The man was too careful, too slippery, too diabolically clever to defeat head-on. He had to be taken by stealth and cautious planning.

The first order of business was to clear his own name; prove somehow that the charge of manslaughter Karl had brought against him was false. And he had an idea how to go about it, having had weeks now to dwell on the problem.

As the dark coastline came into sight, silhouetted by the glow of the sunset in the growing dimness, Gaard felt his heart pound, then harden into implacable resolve.

His eyes narrowed into slits as he strained for a sight of the familiar shore while he called out to the helmsman, directing him into a secluded bay north of his brother's hall where they could anchor unseen.

His plan went well so far; the dragon ships slipped silently, like sleek nighthawks, into the protected bay, carried on the waves easily like driftwood.

When all five ships were safely at anchor and well hidden in a cove, Gaard finally descended to the cabin.

Dawnlyn was still asleep, and he stood for a moment over her, unable to resist scrutinizing the girl without interruption. It was odd how she'd awakened such disturbing emotions in him. Never before had he even bothered to think, or care, of what went on in a woman's mind. Women were for warming his bed, that was all.

But Dawnlyn was different. She had somehow touched a chord in him; yet truly, he had little time or patience to worry about one particular female. He had other, more important things with which to concern himself . . .

But she lay on the bed, so defenseless, so vulnerable, her hair spread around her white face, her dark lashes lying on her cheek like miniature curved fans. She was so beautiful, so young.

And, he realized suddenly, she had no business at all on a Viking warship. His vision and subsequent idea to bring her along now seemed foolish, almost criminal. What if Karl won? Then where would she be? A prisoner at Karl's beck and call. Gaard felt his hackles rise with fury at the thought of his brother's battle-hardened hands on Dawnlyn's alabaster skin.

He shook off the thought, steeled himself against the night to come. He'd need all his wits about him.

Laying a gentle hand on Dawnlyn's shoulder, he shook her awake.

"What?" she mumbled, opening her eyes. "Is there another storm?"

"Nay, little one. The storm is past. You must have been dreaming. Now sit up and listen to me. I must explain something to you."

She looked at him with suspicion. It was as if she knew, instinctively, what was coming.

"We are anchored south of Stavanger, near Thorkellhall. You will stay here for the night, on the ship. I must go to the Hall . . ."

"At night?" she asked, bewildered.

"Most definitely at night. Would you care to see your future husband without a head?" His lips split in a wide grin at the thought, but Dawnlyn paled to a ghostly shade.

"What are you going to do?" she managed to get out. "Is it dangerous? Oh, Gaard, you've dragged me from my home and I'm all alone here and now you're going off to do something terrible, I know it . . ."

"I am going to disguise myself and find a certain person who can help me prove I never killed that thrall," he said grimly, a far-off look in his eyes. "And then I will take care of Karl once and for all so that his evil nature will never be able to harm anyone again."

"But who will help you? Who is this person you speak of?"

"It is a friend and a most honorable man, a Christian priest, no less. The man who was my tutor when I was a child."

"A *priest?* You call a priest your friend and trust him to help you?" Her eyes were wide with surprise.

"Yes, a priest. I judge the man, not the calling. He is Father Tancred, an English priest, a most learned and intelligent

116

man, a friend of my mother's and, as I said, a friend of mine, too. Although he always despaired of my refusal to turn into a disciple of the gentle Kris."

"And will he be able to help you?"

"We shall see. Very little misses the old priest's eyes, and he will know that the witness against me was paid by my brother to give false evidence."

"Gaard, I am afraid. I will be all alone . . ." Her tawny eyes begged him.

"I will return by daylight. I want you to remember one thing, however. If anything should befall me"—he saw her eyes widen, her mouth tremble—"not that anything will, but if it should, I want you to remember my mother's name. You are to go to her. She will protect you. Her name is Elspeth. Do not forget, Dawnlyn . . ."

"Elspeth. I will remember." But her voice was choked and very, very quiet.

"Come, give me a kiss. A Viking woman smiles and cheers her man off to battle. She gives her body to him so that he is sated and not distracted from his job."

"I am not a Viking woman, Gaard," she whispered, her eyes welling with tears, "but I will endeavor to send you off well. I will pray for you . . ."

"Father Tancred will be much reassured," he said dryly.

He drew her into his arms, kissed her soft lips slowly, thoroughly, but it was not a kiss of passion. Rather, it was one of closeness and comfort—one that was special, given to her alone.

He left the cabin, bidding farewell to Dawnlyn, who smiled at him bravely. Gaard thought that the tremulous smile from the Scotswoman was more poignant than a thousand wild, heedless grins from as many Viking wenches.

But the notion lasted only a split second, then fled as the soft night breeze. The familiar odors and sounds of his homeland enshrouded him and his face twisted grimly once again with purpose.

Chapter Nine

DAWNLYN HARDLY SLEPT THAT WHOLE LONG NIGHT, WORRY-
ing incessantly about Gaard, where he was, what secretive
thing he plotted. She kept telling herself that he was quite
capable, was on home ground and knew what he was doing,
but the nagging fears kept eating at her.

"Elspeth," she repeated under her breath, illogically
terrified that she'd forget the name of Gaard's mother,
equally terrified at the thought of facing a strange woman in
a strange country so very far from her home.

The cracks in the cabin door showed streaks of light when
Dawnlyn heard a commotion, then heavy footfalls on the
deck above. Was it Gaard, returning successfully? Or was it
his cruel brother, Karl, whom Dawnlyn already feared and
disliked just from hearing Gaard's opinion of him?

Having fallen into exhausted sleep still dressed from the
day before, she quickly smoothed her water-stained gown
and combed her salt-stiff hair as best she could, pushing it
under a headcloth. She knew she would feel much better if
she could have a long, hot bath, but that would have to wait.
For now, she'd have to face whatever fate had in store for
her just as she was.

The deck was teeming with men even at this early hour,
and she soon spied the source of their activity. Gaard's

golden head stood above the rest and she caught sight of him easily; but once relieved of her nightlong anxiety she felt uncomfortable in the totally male atmosphere and hung back by the cabin ladder, attempting to be inconspicuous.

Gaard was speaking to his men, grinning and ebullient. Most of the Norse words escaped her, but soon she caught sight of another man with him, a man with hands tied behind his back and a rope around his neck, a man whose head hung down in fear and dejection.

Who was he? Was this unprepossessing-looking prisoner Karl?

Meg joined her on the deck, sleepy-eyed and bewildered. "What is going on, my lady? Such a commotion!"

"I don't know, Meg. Gaard has brought back a prisoner of some sort . . ."

And then Gaard noticed the two women by the ladder and, leaving the prisoner with his men, crossed the narrow deck with long strides. "My lady Dawnlyn," he greeted her, with a satisfied gleam in his steely eyes.

"My lord." She, too, inclined her head, then met his gaze questioningly. He was near to bursting with gratification, she could see.

"I've got Bjorn Thorson," he announced.

"Who?"

"The false witness, the one in Karl's pay."

"Oh, I see. And what will you do with him now?" And her mind filled with images of another prisoner, of Gaard's deadly broadsword slashing through the man's neck.

"I've arranged it all. Father Tancred will bring Karl here to meet with me—"

"Karl—here?"

"Yes, of course. I am denied the privilege of setting foot on the shores of Norway."

"But last night?"

"Ah, that was different. No one saw me. It might never have happened."

"But will Karl come? And if he does, will he not bring an army and try to defeat you?"

119

"He will come," said Gaard with great confidence. "He will wish to see how I fare after his meddling. As for his army, Father Tancred will see to it that only a few men accompany him, and that one of them is the Lawspeaker. It will all be cleared up today and I shall be reinstated at Thorkellhall."

Dawnlyn had an inkling of premonition—something—difficulties that might crop up to mar Gaard's confident plans. Why, she had no idea, but somehow his self-assured words did not convince her.

The morning dawned cool and foggy. The small bay in which they were anchored lay covered by drifting curtains of mist that allowed only a dim hint of sunlight to seep through. Sounds were muffled, echoing, ominous.

The men, at least the Norsemen, ate heartily and appeared to be cheerful. Some of them must have been looking forward to seeing families denied them by their choice of banishment with their chief. Dawnlyn took the time to wash as best she could in a basin of cold water and to dress in one of her more becoming gowns to face the fabled Karl Thorkellson, Jarl of Thorkellhall and one of King Olaf the Gentle's most illustrious lords.

She chose a dark green linen under-tunic and a pale yellow *bliaut,* laced at the sides, to go over it. She had Meg brush out the dried salt in her hair and let it hang free down her back in rippling waves as an unmarried girl was entitled to do. She pinched her cheeks to color them and bit her lips, for the tiny mirror she had brought along told her she was pale and heavy-eyed.

The fog was still lying in eerie patches, resisting the sun's efforts to burn it off, when Dawnlyn and Meg returned to the deck.

She was gazing around for sight of Gaard when she heard a shout from the longship anchored next to *Wind Eater* and went to the rail—there was Ian, waving and grinning from the other ship. On tiptoe she waved back, relieved and glad that Ian had made the crossing all right. She was dying to speak to him, but it was impossible until they reached shore. Still, just the very sight of him was enough to comfort her.

As she stood at the rail gazing into the fog, her attention was drawn by the muted thump of oars and the echoing splash of a boat cutting through the water, but the mist hid the sight of it until Dawnlyn thought the small boat would surely collide with them. And what if the fog hid not one small skiff but a whole flotilla of armed men?

She strained, as did everyone on board, to see through the thick, clinging veil of fog.

And then a muffled shout and the call of the *lur* reached her ears, the hail of one Viking to another, and Gaard was leaning over the rail, calling back.

Out of the cloying fog the prow of a small boat emerged, ghostlike. In it were eight men: an old, white-haired priest, six Norsemen and another, sitting with crossed arms over a broad chest, the undeniable look of leadership about him.

Karl.

Dawnlyn took a deep breath, looked for Gaard, only to see him at the ship's rail, his eyes fixed intently on the approaching skiff, his body as tense and quivering as an animal about to pounce, his virile features an implacable mask.

He was utterly silent until the eight men clambered aboard and stood on the deck; then he greeted them politely, with great dignity, not treating Karl with any particular deference.

But Dawnlyn noticed an unnatural stiffness about Gaard, like a dog greeting another dog; she could almost see his hackles rise.

They were all offered benches to seat themselves on and tankards of ale, which all politely refused. It was as if they played a game, each man knowing the rules and outcome, each going through the motions like a puppet.

The old priest wore a rusty black robe, his bald pate surrounded by a ring of white hair that stood up wildly. He began speaking, in slow, accented Norse so that Dawnlyn, who was growing familiar with the tongue, was able to follow the gist of his speech.

"Gaard Wolftooth, formerly of Thorkellhall, wishes to bring a certain piece of evidence before the Lawspeaker regarding his banishment on a charge of manslaughter. Will you hear it?" His question was directed to one of the other men, a stolid-looking, fair-haired man of middle age, who was dressed richly and wore the golden seal of his office around his neck.

"I myself presided over Gaard Wolftooth's trial some months back and am familiar with the case," replied the Lawspeaker in steady tones. "Present your evidence and I will judge if it be worthy of regard." He turned to the six other men. "You will be my witnesses, all but the jarl, who has a vested interest in the case. Speak."

"Wait," said Karl, holding up a hand.

Dawnlyn's eyes flew to his face, to examine the man who had banished her betrothed. He was nearly as tall as Gaard and of the same fair, ruddy coloring, but he was older and broader in girth. His face resembled Gaard's, and was clean-shaven, but in it all the familiar features lacked the artful carving that made Gaard handsome, Karl's being merely heavy and masculine. And then, too, she noticed, his skin was savagely pockmarked, giving it a dull, faded texture.

"I wish it to be noted that my younger brother left these shores threatening to return and defeat me. His inability to accept judgment has led him to bring about this useless meeting. You can all see he is desperate and will try any ruse to prove his so-called innocence. But, certainly, let us hear his frivolous evidence." And Karl's mouth turned down derisively as he faced Gaard, his heavy arms still crossed confidently on his chest.

Dawnlyn could see Gaard stiffen and his eyes shoot sparks of fury. Thank God, she prayed, that fury was not directed at her . . .

And then the old priest, Father Tancred, laid a gentle hand on Gaard's arm, as if to warn and restrain him. Gaard subsided and made a hand motion to his men.

The unfortunate Bjorn Thorson was dragged from below to stand before the group, his knees quaking in terror, his mouth oozing a trace of spittle from its corner. Dawnlyn could feel a cold, tangible silence settle over the deck, and she shivered as her eyes traveled from Gaard's smug face to Karl's, which was closed and rigid now.

Then Bjorn Thorson spoke, splitting the silence. "My lord Karl, I did not mean to . . . I . . ."

"Shut your teeth," hissed Karl. "Have some courage, man!"

Finally Gaard spoke, his voice thrilling Dawnlyn with its ringing tone, its righteous power. "Speak, Bjorn Thorson, of the things you told me last night."

The man mumbled and shook, trying to turn away.

"Speak, you lying mongrel!"

"There will be no intimidating the witness, Gaard Wolftooth," intoned the Lawspeaker levelly.

And Dawnlyn saw the priest's age-mottled hand touch Gaard's arm lightly again. The stiff lines in Karl's face relaxed and he gave a superior, triumphant snort, as if the whole affair was no more than he'd thought it would be.

"Speak, Bjorn Thorson," said the Lawspeaker, and his voice held the authority of his position and of all the esteemed men who'd held the position before him.

Thorson began to talk, his words coming hesitantly, then faster and faster, tumbling out of his mouth like foul vomit. He was describing how he'd lied at the trial, how he'd been paid, how the man who'd paid him was—

Karl, quicker than lightning, gave a numbing roar, drew his huge sword in one sweeping motion, and slashed. Thorson's head was split from his neck and fell to the pine decking to lie looking up at the assembled men, its mouth still open in a fruitless attempt to continue its confession.

Silence hung on the dank atmosphere for an endless moment; then the raised babble of voices blotted out that moment, negating it.

"Quiet!" The Lawspeaker's ponderous tone cleared the air, and Dawnlyn saw Gaard, half-crouched, his lips drawn back in a feral rage, facing his brother, whose bloody sword was still in his hand.

"Quiet!" the Lawspeaker repeated. The man seemed to

review the happenings for a moment, then shrouded with unassailable authority, faced the assemblage.

"In a case such as this, where the witness is killed before giving evidence, there is an ancient precedent. It was decided, at the *Althing* in Oslo, many years ago, that in this event, the killer is presumed to be suppressing the truth and therefore the charged man is presumed innocent. Gaard Wolftooth, I declare you innocent of manslaughter and your banishment is rescinded."

Then the Lawspeaker turned to Karl, his face giving no hint of his feelings. "Karl Thorkellson, charges may be brought against you by relatives of the dead man and you will be tried by a jury of your peers in that case. Hold yourself available."

Karl sneered, sheathing his sword roughly, totally ignoring the Lawspeaker's words. "You may no longer suffer banishment, Gaard, but may Odin protect you if you even show your face near *my* Hall! I'll slice your body to pieces and eat them for my supper! Stay away from me, I warn you!"

Then Karl's pale eyes regally swept the group, came to rest on Dawnlyn with cold knowledge. "And that goes for your whore, too."

A dark shadow crossed Gaard's eyes like a swift raven's wing. "Say what you will, brother, it means nothing to me." Gaard smiled, an enigmatic, cool turn of his lips. "I am restored to my rightful position now, Karl, against even *your* efforts to have me gone. I spit on your blustering threat. I shall do whatever pleases me. Now, get off my ship. Your presence sickens me! And know this, brother—we are not yet done with each other."

Karl turned and climbed down to the skiff with his five men-at-arms and the Lawspeaker. Father Tancred remained, a frail hand on Gaard's arm as they quietly watched the skiff pull away into the wafting fog.

A huge, collective sigh of relief seemed to emanate from Gaard's men as the boat disappeared toward shore, leaving only the rippled line of its wake written on the water. Then that, too, melted into the ruffled surface of the bay.

Before Dawnlyn could quiet her pounding heart, Gaard turned from the rail and led the old priest to where she stood.

"This is Dawnlyn Renfrew, my betrothed," he said simply. "And this is my teacher and my mother's confessor, Father Tancred. You two should get on well together, dreaming up ways to belabor my pagan brain."

Dawnlyn smiled uncertainly at the old man, uncomfortable at Gaard's sarcastic remark, but Father Tancred seemed used to such blasphemies from his former pupil and merely smiled gently, making the sign of the cross over her bowed head.

"My child," he said, "I must chide Gaard once more for his impetuous ways. This is no place for a gently bred lady."

"Father, I only brought her when I had a vision that warned me not to leave her behind. You know it is not my way to drag women into the thick of a war."

"A war?" asked Dawnlyn quickly.

"Well, not a war, yet," said Gaard. "But you witnessed my brother's attitude. I cannot leave here without a reckoning. By Odin, he would try to prevent me from even visiting my own mother!"

"The lady Elspeth will meet you here," interceded the priest.

"No! I have every right to visit my home and see my mother! He shall not stop me!"

"Gaard, take care. Karl is strong and will brook no disobedience. His hand comes down heavily on any who stand against him. His land is held in an iron grasp and no one dares raise a voice against the man."

"I do!" Gaard's brows were knitted together in a black scowl, the thin white scar on his jaw taut with anger. "I dare. In fact, I challenge him to a duel to decide this thing. Then there will only be a small share of blood shed—his!"

"Watch your temper, Gaard. Karl is no weakling. He would kill you gladly if given the chance," warned the old man, obviously full of concern for Gaard.

"Go and present him with my challenge. Yes . . . a duel to

the death. Go, Father, and arrange it and bring me word of the time and place. It is the only way." His voice was firm and confident, his eyes bright as gleaming metal with the knowledge of certain victory.

"Gaard—" began Dawnlyn.

"No soft words, woman," snapped Gaard. "It is the only way. Ever since my ordeal with Fenris when the Luck came to me, he has hated me. It can go on no longer. That man is a weight on my back that I no longer wish to carry. It is enough!"

"My son, take care in making this decision. It could cost you your life . . ."

"My life is my own to throw away if I wish. In this case, it will be victory, at last."

The priest shook his white head sadly, crossed himself, gave a deep sigh. "I will pray for you, my son. God grant you strength and courage. I think I have always known that this meeting was inevitable. It was ordained."

"A pox on your God's help! I have my Luck and my two strong arms. They are all I need!"

"I warn you, Gaard Wolftooth!" snapped Father Tancred, blue fire suddenly sparking from his faded eyes. "Do not blaspheme my God or He shall punish you! Do not brush off His help, you young pup. You may need it!"

"I beg your forgiveness, Father. I should know better after all these years. Please excuse me to your God." Gaard seemed properly chastened, but a hint of laughter lit his eyes and pulled up one corner of his mouth. "Now, I will send you back to arrange this thing."

Then he gave orders for the priest to be taken back to Thorkellhall and turned to Dawnlyn, who still stood, silent, with pain in her wide, tawny eyes.

"You shall be wed to a rich lord now, little one," he said with a ferocious grin, a silver glow in his eyes. "I will have St. Abb's and this land, too, when I best Karl."

"And if you lose?" she shot at him, angered by his overbearing, mindless, Viking pride. "Then what? I shall be at that man's mercy. Your men and mine, too, will be his slaves! Is *that* your victory?"

"I shall *not* lose. I am Gaard Wolftooth and I have the Luck."

"I curse your fabled luck!" she cried angrily.

"Ah, little one, I see now why you shout at me," he said, his tone suddenly gentle. "You fear for me. Well, it is only natural, I suppose. But still your worry. I always win."

"Oh!" Dawnlyn ground out. "You are prideful and insufferable and I can't bear you!" She turned and began to stride toward the cabin, motioning Meg to her side. But his heavy hand fell on her shoulder.

"Then you should wish for me to lose," laughed Gaard in her ear, "and be spared my company!"

"It might almost be worth it!" she slashed back.

In truth, Dawnlyn was very unnerved over this fight to take place between the two brothers, even more so when she found out she would have to attend the event. It seemed cruel and barbaric and ungodly. And if Gaard were to lose, to be killed, cut down in front of her eyes, covered with his own life's blood . . . She had to keep blotting the images from her mind, steeling herself against the nagging fear.

That afternoon, Father Tancred sent back word that the duel was to be on the practice ground in front of Thorkellhall on the morrow, at dawn.

Gaard still had an air of heedless gaiety about him when he came to their cabin that night. He smelled of strong ale and maleness; even in the near-dark his eyes shone brilliantly, like silver coins.

"Dawnlyn, wake up!" he whispered loudly, sitting on the side of the narrow pallet and shaking her.

"I was not asleep, my lord," she replied dryly. "Your entry was enough to wake the dead."

"Come, now, this may be my last night on earth! Be kind to me." He laughed under his breath and bent to nuzzle her neck. "Come, little one. I am your man and I fight tomorrow. Comfort me."

"You do not sound in need of comfort, my lord."

"Oh, but I am, my little copper-haired vixen." Gaard nibbled on her soft neck, his warm breath raising the tiny hairs and sending an arrow of pleasure darting down her side to her hip.

"Gaard . . ." She tried to sound annoyed, but his name emerged more as a plea.

"Yes, my little one?" His face was buried in her hair, his arms reached around her warm body, crushing her to his rock-hard chest.

And Dawnlyn sensed she would be unable to deny him, especially on this night. It was true—it could be his last night . . .

He kissed her, stroked her with his hands, awaking her passion as easily as making a cat purr. She sighed, giving in to the sensations, and put her arms around his broad back, melting against his strong body, giving to him all that she could.

They sank together onto the narrow pallet, their hands and mouths straining to touch and feel each other's bodies. A hot flame began to burn in Dawnlyn's belly and she moaned with pleasure as Gaard stroked the sensitive spots he was growing to know so well. The flame grew and grew, consuming her with its heat until she seemed to explode in glorious pleasure. And then Gaard, too, stiffened and a low growl of relief reverberated in his throat and his hot seed pulsed into her womb.

Later, when Gaard slept like a babe in its fire-warmed cradle, Dawnlyn lay awake, her thoughts whirling in anxiety, worrying over the question of Gaard's fate, and, finally, praying, her lips moving silently, fervently, as if her faith alone could keep him safe.

The cavalcade of Scots and Vikings wended its way the few miles to the tall wooden gates of Thorkellhall even before the sun's rays gilded the hard dirt practice field. Gaard was at its head, tall and stalwart, dressed in his helmet and mail shirt, his solid black tunic stark against the summer-green meadows they crossed, his wolf-tooth necklace gleaming as if it had an inner light of its own.

His lieutenant, Knute, carried the permitted three shields, and *Lightning Bolt,* Gaard's sword, was firmly sheathed in his belt.

Ian Renfrew had an honored place near the head of the procession. He looked more like a Norseman now than many of the others, fitted out with a helmet, mail shirt, trousers instead of the more civilized hose, a shining-hilted broadsword and a wide, cheerful grin.

The trees cast long gray shadows in the early dimness as they stopped on one side of the hard earthen field where an animal skin had been spread, held down on each side by a laurel pole.

Shortly the gate opened and Father Tancred emerged with a tall blond woman wrapped in a fine, fur-lined cape against the morning chill.

She crossed the ground with queenly grace and went directly to Gaard. Silently she embraced him, her head nearly on a level with his chin, her pale blond hair catching the first rays of the morning sun.

"My boy," she murmured, "this is a terrible occasion to greet you after so long, for I cannot rejoice."

"Mother." Gaard's tone was gentle, full of respect.

"Do what you must. I pray for you both, that this terrible event may somehow be resolved."

He bowed his head at her calm words but had no answer. "Mother, I wish you to know the Lady Dawnlyn Renfrew of St. Abb's Hall in Scotland. She is my betrothed."

Gaard's mother turned to Dawnlyn, and the girl had an impression of cool blond beauty, Gaard's own gray eyes and an immense dignity.

"Lady Dawnlyn, I greet you. I would wish for happier circumstances, by the grace of God."

"And I, too," murmured Dawnlyn. "Gaard has spoken of you, Lady Elspeth."

But then their attention was drawn toward the now-open gates, where Karl's entire retinue was gathering on the far side of the field. An aged, bent woman detached herself from the crowd, walked to the center of the field and held up a gnarled hand.

All commotion ceased and every person's attention was directed at the old crone, the woman called the angel of death by the Vikings, who was in charge of all such momentous events: weddings, funerals, duels, rituals of all types. She began to chant the rules of the fight in an age-old litany. The barely risen sun touched her with a halo formed by the light gilding a million particles of dust given off by her ancient rags.

Dawnlyn's breath stopped. The woman's voice conjured up such primeval practices, such archaic, terrible truths, that Dawnlyn could not bear to listen; she wanted to put her hands to her ears, to cut off the woman's cracked voice that repeated words only the gods should speak.

Then the angel of death was finished. Gaard and Karl stepped forward, each with helmet and mail, sword and shield; they moved to stand on the skin stretched out on the ground, walking on the balls of their feet, lightly, ready for their fate. Each wore a broad, fierce grin on his face under his frightening helmet. They were two big men, poised on the edge of truth, facing each other, both quivering with anticipation, alive with confident hope.

Dawnlyn did not want to look; she tried to close her eyes, but they were held open by a force beyond her control. She had to watch, horror-stricken, terrified, without any choice at all.

The word was given.

The brothers stepped warily, feeling each other out, circling, keeping at least one foot on the skin at all times. The sun rose higher, struck sparks of cold glitter off their swords and shields. Then Karl, as the one challenged, struck first, his sword flashed, clanging on the other shield. There was another curving arc of death from Gaard. Their muscles swelled, wielding the heavy broadswords, swinging, slashing, but striking no mortal wounds.

The shuffle of their feet, the gasps and grunts, the horrid, everlasting clang of sword on shield was like a dirge, a frightful, unending rhythm of destruction and death. On it went, on and on, until hours seemed to have passed.

Sweat rolled from under the vicious noseplates of their helmets, their arms grew heavy and numbed, and still the whistling deadly swing of sword against sword continued.

The two brothers were an even match: both were big men in their prime. Gaard's reach may have been a touch longer, but Karl's heavy shoulders had more power.

Karl swung, struck a powerful blow on Gaard's shield, splitting it in half. Instantly Gaard switched hands, wielding his sword equally well with his left hand, until Knute could hand him a new shield. They went on, battering at each other mindlessly, more machines of destruction than men.

The crowd shifted, the men calling encouragement to their favorite. Dawnlyn stood as still as marble, afraid to move or breathe or speak. She tried to pray but was too distracted.

Then there was a break in the rhythm of the duel. Gaard began to beat back Karl's defense, raining crashing, powerful blows on his brother's shield until it was bent, battered and useless. The ferocious grin on Gaard's lips widened as he leaped to the attack, now heedless of all fatigue. Karl backed away from him, suffering no serious injury, but tiring. Gaard hacked at him, giving no quarter, easily evading his brother's weakening sword.

Dawnlyn began to breathe again, shallow, tenuous breaths of hope. Maybe Gaard *would* win, as he'd promised.

Then she glanced at Lady Elspeth: how could *she* feel? Either man who lost was her son, flesh of her flesh. There was no victory for *her*.

The morning warmed, the dust glittering, rising from the ground where the men fought. The crowd was offered dippers of water by thralls, but for the fighting men, there was no relief.

Still Karl backed away, hampered by having to keep one foot always on the skin.

Then it happened. Karl tripped on one of the laurel poles,

131

lost his balance for a split second. Gaard pressed him fiercely. Karl fell heavily to the ground. Instantly Gaard was on him, standing over his fallen brother, his sword at Karl's throat, ready to plunge it downward, to let out his enemy's lifeblood.

The crowd held its breath; the rustle of air in lungs halted completely. Stillness reigned over the earthen field.

Then Gaard gave a mighty curse and flung his sword aside, unable to kill his own brother. He turned away, disgusted with himself, sucking great breaths of air into his tortured lungs.

Then the scene seemed to slow; motion was arrested, every movement precise and agonizingly slow as in a nightmare, and yet it all happened in the time it takes to blink.

Gaard was in midstride, turning from Karl, reaching up a hand to pull off his helm. A tall young man in the ranks of Karl's warriors stepped forward and shouted a warning to Gaard, who began to turn slowly, slowly, catching Karl's movement out of the corner of his eye. But he was too late. His brother snatched his fallen sword, rose to his knees in one fluid motion and, with both hands, lunged toward Gaard, burying the point deep in his abdomen.

There was a horrified gasp from the assemblage, a slow letting out of a hundred breaths as Gaard stood, watching his lifeblood pour out onto the hard-packed earth. His expression was one of surprise and pained comprehension.

Then pandemonium broke loose. Gaard's men gave a thunderous roar of rage at Karl's treachery; Karl's men drew their swords and crouched, facing the raging crowd across the field.

Frantically, Dawnlyn tried to push her way to Gaard, but the broad backs massed in front of her would not budge. She heard herself screaming at them, but to no avail.

Karl was grabbed by a score of Gaard's men before he could move. Gaard still stood in the field, holding his reddened hands over the wound, trying to make his men listen. But his voice was too weak to pierce the thunderous roar, and his men reached him, gentle hands pulled him down; he disappeared into a sea of men as they tried to care for his wound, all at once.

Finally, a voice made itself heard above the noise—a strange voice—and the slim youth who'd warned Gaard stepped forward into the center of the field and held up an imperious hand.

Somehow the noise abated and the wary men, by their silence, consented to listen to this stripling, this young nobody in their midst who acted as if he'd been granted the authority. He addressed Karl's army, who stood undecided, relieved of their chief. "Men of Thorkellhall, you have just seen here a treacherous act by your jarl. By such an act, he has forfeited your loyalty. He is a cruel leader and has caused much grief amongst his subjects. This is your opportunity—"

His voice was drowned in a roar of agreement from Gaard's men. The youth had to wait for them to quiet to continue.

"—your opportunity to see him gone!" His strong, ringing voice seemed to fill a vacuum, to control the crowd, swaying it to his opinion. "Men of Thorkellhall, you have naught to lose. Gaard Wolftooth will be your leader now. He is the chosen one who bested mighty Fenris . . . He has the Luck!"

"But he is dying!" shouted a voice from the crowd. "His Luck has run out!"

"That is yet to be decided!" answered the youth. "His Luck may carry him through and he shall be your leader!"

A mighty thunder of assent went up from Gaard's men, shaking the very heavens. Knute, of the great red beard and burly shoulders, shook a fist high in the air, shouted, "Stand with us, men of Thorkellhall!" and brandished his sword at Karl, who stood, stolid and regal, held by many strong hands.

One of Karl's men threw down his sword, then another,

and soon there was a resounding cheer and the dull thud of a hundred swords to the ground.

Finally, as Gaard's men surged forward to take the Hall itself, Dawnlyn was able to push and claw her way through the men to where Gaard lay, wallowing in his own blood.

"See, little one," he rasped out, "I won, didn't I?" And then he gave her a triumphant, boyish grin.

Chapter Ten

DAWNLYN COULD HEAR THE UPROAR OF EBULLIENCE THROUGH-
out the entire day, even though the room where Gaard lay
was far from the great hall. It sickened her that the men—her
own brother and the rest of the Scots—celebrated as loud
and as long as the Norsemen. And to what were they
drinking? One man's subjugation of another by brute
strength!

And that one man . . . Her eyes traveled to Gaard's
unmoving form, covered with white linen that outlined his
long, lean torso, covered him as if he were already shrouded
for burial.

Only the faint rise and fall of his chest told her he was still
alive.

Her hand clenched inadvertently in her lap, twisting in the
fabric of her skirt as swift despair gripped her again. She
leaned forward to wipe the beads of oily sweat from his
forehead for the hundredth time. Sickness rose in her gorge,
almost choking her, and fear, too, and she wondered what
she would do if he died.

Gaard stirred, moaning in his deathlike sleep, and
Dawnlyn leaned forward again, as if he were going to say
something profound; but he subsided, and she could only
wipe at the never-ending perspiration that dotted his skin.

"Why don't you try to get some rest?" asked Elspeth finally, her own face ravaged from the ceaseless vigil.

"No, I couldn't," whispered Dawnlyn.

"I suppose not," sighed the older woman. "I never could, either." She tried to smile, but her mouth only twisted in a sad parody of mirth.

It was evening before Elspeth was finally able to force some onion and leek broth past his lips. Dawnlyn held his damp head in her lap, coaxing him to sip the steaming liquid while he tried to tease the women.

"Mother," he coughed weakly, "do you think an onion broth holds the power of life and death? I'll wager not!"

What he referred to, Dawnlyn had learned, was the customary test of the onion soup. Elspeth had informed her: "If several hours pass and his body is clean of the onion odor, then the wound is not deep and threatening. But," she had added, shaken, "if the smell passes through his stomach and emanates from the wound, then he is done for."

And so the women waited, their white hands clasped nervously in their laps, their lips moving in silent prayer. Father Tancred visited several times while they waited, leading them in prayer, his wispy white head bowed solemnly. It was obvious that the old priest was terribly concerned and truly cared for his errant pupil. His pale, rheumy eyes watered constantly, and Dawnlyn wondered whether he was weeping.

Gaard half-awakened; his red-rimmed eyes took in the scene through a haze. "By Odin!" he groaned, "have you no mercy for a sleeping man? Your prayers will surely finish me off!" and he slumped back against the pillow, his face gray.

Dawnlyn gasped. Where the linen bandage covered his wound, a red spot had appeared and was growing larger by the second.

"The fool has opened the stitches," Elspeth muttered, angry and worried in the same instant.

"What if it . . . what if the onions . . ." wept Dawnlyn,

hovering over him now, afraid the telltale odor would rise to meet her nostrils.

Elspeth carefully unwound the cloth from his slender hips. "We shall see now, while he bleeds."

The torn stitches, stuck with dark pieces of linen, oozed blood slowly. Dawnlyn's wide, terrified eyes followed a growing trail of blood as it ran darkly down to his groin, where it wet the linen sheet.

He looked so pallid, so vulnerable that hot tears formed behind her eyelids, burning them. But as Elspeth dabbed at the wound, Dawnlyn steeled herself and bent nearer until her small face was all but touching his flesh.

There was the distant odor of male sweat, of fresh blood . . . but not of onion.

She raised her head quickly, sought Elspeth's glance. "I cannot smell the broth. Does it mean . . . ?"

"It is the best sign we can hope for, Dawnlyn," smiled Elspeth tentatively, patting her hand while Father Tancred left the room quietly.

All the horror, the worry, the long weary hours spent in vigil at the bedside flooded her senses like a tide and Dawnlyn wept. "Will he live?" came her weak voice.

"We shall pray that he does," soothed Elspeth. "We can do no more."

Finally, doing her best to hold back her tears, Dawnlyn helped Gaard's mother replace the several torn stitches, then sat back in her chair. If only she had her own mother's herb chest! But here, in this alien land, how could she know what to use—what healed and what was poisonous? She asked Elspeth about the local herbs—didn't these people use poultices to heal?

"Sometimes," Elspeth answered quietly. "But not as frequently as the Britons do. You see, Dawnlyn," she sighed, "men here virtually laugh at their wounds. To die of a wound and go to Valhalla is an honor greater than life. My own husband died of a wound last year and left me with a smile on his lips."

Sudden anger welled within Dawnlyn and she could abide no more; she rose, pacing the floor. "Nonsense!" she cried. "They thrive on their heathen tales and what good comes of it? How could you bear it . . . all these years . . . ?"

Elspeth, too, came to her feet. She went to the young girl, placed a warm, solacing hand on Dawnlyn's arm. "I know this seems a strange land to you," she said somberly, "but I have come to accept their ways be they Christians or believers of many gods and strange myths."

Dawnlyn worried her full lower lip. "But how *can* you accept such pagan beliefs? And you . . . a Christian. How can you?"

"It was not easy at first, my child. I felt much the same as you, but my husband was a good man; although he was not a Christian, his ways brought him a happy life and he behaved in a Christian manner to all. At my request he brought Father Tancred here to be with me and teach the boys," she finished with tranquil pride.

"But why did your sons not become Christians? I don't understand."

Elspeth smiled slowly, but a hint of pain touched her soft, gray eyes. "Karl *is* a Christian." She paused, studying Dawnlyn's shocked expression. "I should say," she went on slowly, "that he is both Christian *and* a believer in the old Viking ways. I think, perhaps, his choice of Christianity was one of political expediency, as our good King Olaf is a follower of Christ. Karl is a combination of two very different worlds. Perhaps it tears at him . . ."

"And Gaard?" asked Dawnlyn, confused. How could a man be both? How could one even think to combine two such different worlds?

"Gaard?" replied Elspeth. "Now, there is quite another story. I thought for a time that he would embrace my faith. He was such an apt pupil. But then, when he was but a small child, merely seven, he met with the wolves in the forest—"

"You mean that absurd tale about Fenris the Giant Wolf?" interrupted Dawnlyn, amazed that Lady Elspeth sounded so sincere.

"Call it what you like," Elspeth responded mildly. "But there remains the fact of the wolf's teeth that he returned with that very day. My son is not given to lies . . ."

"He found them," said Dawnlyn harshly, turning away from the older woman and looking at Gaard's still form and the tooth necklace strung like white thorns around his neck. "He found them in the woods and made up a silly, childish tale."

"You do not know my son," countered Elspeth sternly. After a moment of pondering on the young Scotswoman's words, she said more calmly, "I did not fully believe the tale myself . . . at first." She let her last words linger on the air. "But then the boy, my own son, changed almost overnight. He grew so strong—he seemed to be charmed and much wiser than most . . . wiser than his older brother, wiser, even, than his parents."

"And he turned from God then, didn't he?" surmised Dawnlyn dismally.

"Yes. He became a true Viking, like his ancestors. By the time he was thirteen, he had slain his first foe, and from that day forth, he chose a life separate from my English ways, from the gentle heritage I gave him. His father, too, was quite amazed at his son's path, for Thorkell, although pleased to go a-Viking in his youth, had taken to a simpler, more peaceful existence by then. Times were changing, Vikings were no longer mere raiders and marauders but had become merchantmen and politicians of great worth and renown."

"Then Gaard's father must have been greatly disappointed in his son."

"No." Elspeth smiled suddenly. "Not at all! His son is the epitome of the ancient, mighty Viking hero in the sagas. A man to be respected and feared, yet a fair man, too. Gaard is a true Norseman, and when you finally come to view him as thus, perhaps you will come to accept him."

"Never!" Dawnlyn ground out bitterly. "Never will I accept his pagan ways! If he lives . . . and *if* we marry . . . I'll never, *never*, accept him! I was to be a nun, Lady

139

Elspeth." She choked on the words. "He has ruined my life, and I must suffer and bear my fate as strongly as I can. But I'll never accept him. My life is doomed."

Letting out a long, sighing breath, Lady Elspeth walked to the door. "It is late, Dawnlyn, and Gaard rests quietly now. I am going to retire. If you need me, you know where my room is." Glancing knowingly one more time on the distraught young girl, Elspeth left the chamber.

For a long moment Dawnlyn stared after her, trying desperately to assimilate the older woman's words. Yet the more she thought on them, the more utterly confused she became. How could a good Christian woman accept, much less believe in, the pagan Viking ways?

Dawnlyn's marigold eyes roamed hopelessly around her as she stood twisting her hands in the folds of her skirt. Where were the familiar, cool, stone walls of her chamber at St. Abb's Hall, the tall, spacious ceilings? This room was so small in comparison and so strange with its dark, smoked-wood walls decorated with gold and silver and carved with odd shapes on the dark walls. The windows, too, were quite different—small, letting little light through the oiled membrane. And in spite of the warm, early summer evening, a shiver crept up her spine.

Gaard stirred, groaned. Quickly Dawnlyn spun around to view him. The bandage was still clean, but his color was terrible, feverish looking in the dimly lit room. All thought of her surroundings fled rapidly as she moved to the bedside.

She thought to call for Meg to bring fresh, cool water, but Lord knew where Meg was—Lady Elspeth had told her that Meg was safely hidden with her own serving girl in a house nearby until the celebration was over. Still, Gaard's body needed swabbing, for when she touched his skin, it was hot beneath her fingers.

Afraid to venture out alone for fresh water, she picked up the wet linen cloth from the basin, wrung it out slightly, then began to mop his brow, the damp curling hair that clung to his neck, his sweat-sheened chest. The bedsheet had fallen away and, keeping her thoughts solely on cooling his flesh, she swabbed his hips around the bandage, his firm, rock-hard thighs and calves, even his feet. And then she moved upward again, rinsing the cloth, stroking the strong forearm, lifting his arm to rest on her lap as she cleansed and cooled the warmest spot in his armpit and up to his broad shoulder. She repeated the process on his opposite side until he stirred.

His eyes opened, red and weary, but recognition lit in them when he saw her bent over him.

"Gaard?" she ventured, afraid that he would not even know her.

"Yes, little one." His voice was weak and unlike his normal ringing tones, but she was so thankful to hear it that she closed her eyes and offered up a brief prayer.

"Are you in great pain?" she asked, then quickly thought: what a stupid question!

"I've felt worse and I've felt better," he said. "I'll live." Then he tried to smile, but his face turned pale and sweat popped out on his forehead. A muffled groan escaped his lips.

"Gaard," she cried softly, nearly beside herself with anxiety. "Shall I call your mother?"

"No. Let her rest. She has enough to bear."

Dawnlyn wiped his forehead, relieved to see his expression relax once again.

"Damn that brother of mine," he mumbled. "I should have killed him. I should have . . ." His face twisted again in torment.

She ignored his ungodly thought, feeling his pain as if it were her own. Glancing desperately at the vial of liquid Elspeth had left, she was tempted to give him some, for it was most effective in stilling pain, but Elspeth had told her not to give him any more for several hours or it could prove deadly. What could she do? She felt so helpless in the face of his pain.

"You look as if you would die yourself, Dawnlyn," he half-whispered. "Do not fret so over me. I have been wounded before. No doubt I shall be again."

"May the sweet Lord save you from this ever again," she prayed.

Gaard grimaced, as much at her prayer as at his pain. "Water," he said. "I have a great thirst."

She supported his head and held the cup to his lips while he drank, wiping the spilled drops away carefully.

Then he seemed more at peace and closed his eyes, his long, lithe frame relaxing under the linen sheet. She thought he was asleep; his words surprised her. "Come close," he said, and her heart leaped in fear—was he dying?—but he went on and she drew in a calmer breath. "Sit close and hold my hand. It helps when the pain gets bad."

"Yes, Gaard, of course." So she sat by the bed while he held her small hand in his large, rough-skinned one, for hours, it seemed, and several times he clenched hers so hard she thought the bones would break, but not a cry did she utter, nor did she try to draw her hand away.

It was the least she could do.

Finally Elspeth returned and made Dawnlyn go to the great hall for food and rest, but she was back within the hour and insisted on staying with him through the night.

The single candle licked Gaard's pallid face with spectral shadows as Dawnlyn watched the pain cross his face on fleet paws, then move on. He turned hot and restless and she had to hold him down, yet he was so weak, it took little effort to do so.

Finally, she could give him a measure of the potent liquid in the vial and he subsided into drugged sleep, leaving her spent and sagging in the chair by his bed.

When she could no longer keep her eyes open, she crawled carefully into the bed next to him so as not to disturb him, feeling, senselessly, that even were she to sleep, her nearness would somehow succor him.

Yet she could not sleep; her fears made her heart gallop and gave her no rest. Every time he moved, she started up and watched him carefully to see if he were failing.

The night crawled on, doggedly.

Once she wondered, trying to be objective, if it would not

be better were he to die. She thought how much simpler, more clearly defined her future would be if he died. The Church would still have her—she could always find a welcome haven there. But her feeling rebelled against the hardness of thought and ached with sorrow and fear at his dangerous condition.

She tried to envision herself wed to him; she looked across at his lean, muscled body, to the swell of his manhood beneath the sheet and to his strong profile outlined in the dim, flickering light. The plane of his cheek was nearly hollow; a deep line grooved it from the nose to his thin-lipped mouth. His facial lines were so strong, so thoroughly masculine—his nose was generous, slightly hooked, fierce looking in profile, while the chin was square and lean.

She studied him leisurely, thankful to have something to do while the minutes ticked by like hours, the seconds like minutes, endless. And it came to her, in the small hours before daybreak, that to have him here, next to her, was better than to be alone. At least, she was forced to admit, his mere presence lent her a kind of security in this barbarous land.

It would be a dreadful thing if he did die. What would become of her, how would she ever get home again? She could not envision life with him as her husband, but neither could she envision a life without him now. The thought left her cold and empty inside.

She must have slept, for when her eyes opened a stray beam of watery light fell across his chest and touched her arm. She propped herself up on an elbow, gazed at his color; the flesh on his torso seemed a healthier hue this morning, even his cheeks held a slight ruddy look again. She reached over and touched his brow carefully. It was cooler.

A tap at the door disturbed her. Not wishing to be caught in bed with Gaard, she quickly rolled to the side, then rose, smoothing her wrinkled gown with hasty fingers.

"*Kom inn,*" she said.

143

A tall, flamelike form flowed into the room, filling it instantly with a strange presence, shocking Dawnlyn, for a moment, into utter immobility.

"Where's Gaard?" demanded the apparition. "Oh, there he is," and the figure swayed past Dawnlyn, leaving behind the sweet scent of perfume and expensive oils to assail Dawnlyn's nostrils.

It was a woman, Dawnlyn was finally able to reason—a tall Viking woman with white-blond hair to her waist and a finely cut red silk gown. The strange female was bending over Gaard, fussing with the covers, turning them back shamelessly to examine the wound in his groin.

"Excuse me," said Dawnlyn with great difficulty, "but who are you and what are you doing here?" She hated the way her voice quavered in the face of this strange woman's audacity.

The Norsewoman's head barely turned, as if Dawnlyn were of no more account than a thrall. "I am Astrid," she said simply, as if that were more than enough explanation. Then, "I am Gaard Wolftooth's woman. When I heard he was wounded . . . Well, you must understand how concerned I was. I came as fast as I could."

Her cold, haughty voice continued, washing over Dawnlyn like ice water. But all she understood were Astrid's words "I am Gaard Wolftooth's woman." They shot through her head like flaming arrows, burning a destructive path, shocking her brain into fumbling paralysis.

"But—but—" she heard herself mumbling inanely, "we are betrothed, Gaard and I."

Astrid did turn from the bed then, her ice-cold blue eyes sweeping Dawnlyn's rumpled figure with calm assurance. "How nice for you," she pronounced sweetly, but her curved lips were as unsmiling as her eyes.

Then the door opened and Elspeth appeared, carrying a tray of food. "I could find no one in the kitchen." She sighed irritably, placing the tray on a table. "I'm afraid those women are still—" Her words were cut off abruptly as she saw Astrid, bent over Gaard's inert form.

"What are *you* doing here, Astrid?" she asked sharply.

"Lady Elspeth." Astrid straightened, curtseyed politely. "I am here to care for Gaard, of course."

"My son is well-supplied with nurses. You'd best return home."

"Surely he will ask for me when he awakens. The disappointment may damage him if I am not here." She spoke in honeyed tones, the glinting, icy eyes hidden by golden lashes.

"No doubt he will manage to live in spite of your absence, Astrid. Now, please do not complicate matters further. Go home."

"Yes, Lady Elspeth," murmured Astrid, "but tell Gaard I was here. Tell him my heart is still his."

"Lord in Heaven, Astrid! There is no time for that. It does not signify! Go home."

And Astrid swept from the room, tossing her silken, pale hair over her shoulders in a shimmering veil.

When she was gone, Elspeth went to Dawnlyn, who sat crumpled in a chair, her face pale and her eyes red with held-back tears. "My dear child," she said, "would that you had been spared Astrid Thorhilddottir. That woman is a menace! Just think! One day, and here she is again, pushing her way into Gaard's very room without so much as a by-your-leave!"

"She said she was . . . she was his . . . woman," half-sobbed Dawnlyn.

"Pay her no heed. In *her* mind she is his woman. Gaard is obviously of another opinion."

"Is he?"

"He is betrothed to *you*, Dawnlyn. Think no more on it. How is he?" asked Elspeth, nearing the bedside, sweeping aside a stray, rumpled lock from his brow.

"He has no fever this morn," replied Dawnlyn. "But he still sleeps so soundly, I don't know . . ."

Then Elspeth turned to face Dawnlyn. A frown creased her white brow. "I am afraid he will be awakened soon in any case. I heard that boy, Leif, talking. The men have summoned the Lawspeaker and . . ." Her voice trailed away and tears showed in her beautiful gray eyes. Quickly, Elspeth turned her head so that Dawnlyn could not view her anguish.

"What is it? What's wrong?" asked Dawnlyn, putting aside her disquieting thoughts of Astrid. Elspeth had seemed thoroughly in control yesterday.

"They want Karl to pay the ultimate price, with the wolves in the pit," she said in a strained voice. "They have called the Lawspeaker to pass judgment and he has agreed on the punishment. They want Gaard there."

Dawnlyn was too shocked to speak, too horrified to offer comfort. All her concern over Astrid fled her mind. Karl was Gaard's brother! Elspeth's son! Surely they would not kill him!

But Dawnlyn could hear voices in the corridor then. They were nearly at the chamber. There was a loud banging on the door.

Her hand came up to her mouth in an automatic gesture of shock. They wouldn't dare disturb Gaard in his condition, would they?

The door opened, squealing on its leather hinges. Leif, the tall young Viking whom Dawnlyn had seen yesterday at the duel, stood there, Knute and Ian at his side. Several others stood behind them hidden in the early morning shadows, their voices loud, half-slurred with drink still.

"Go away!" Dawnlyn cried. "Go away from here!" But she was stopped from saying more when Elspeth's hand gripped her arm.

Tears glistened in the older woman's eyes. "You must not interfere," she said, her voice choked with sadness. "You are to be a Viking's wife. You must behave accordingly."

Leif strode authoritatively to the bedside. "Gaard Wolftooth," he said loudly, "rise and see justice done!"

Gaard stirred.

"Rise! The Lawspeaker has come and if you agree, Karl will face the wolves for his treachery."

Gaard's eyes opened. He looked around the room slowly

146

as if to judge his whereabouts. Automatically, his hand sought the hilt of his sword, which lay next to the bed.

"See, Knute is here," said Leif more cautiously now that the mighty Gaard Wolftooth appeared to be fully awake. "We follow you. Give us the word and Karl will see his evil end this morn."

Gaard touched his parched lips with his tongue, looked slowly from Knute to Ian. "The Lawspeaker has declared this?"

"Yes," replied Leif, watching in fascination as the large muscles of Gaard's upper arm flexed while he pushed himself to a sitting position.

Dawnlyn tensed, would have rushed to him as she saw a flicker of pain cross his eyes, but Elspeth's hand tightened on her arm.

"So my esteemed brother will see his end." A pensive shadow crossed his brow.

"Yes!" cried the youth. "With the wolves, as all treacherous men deserve! A death without honor!"

A tight smile came to Gaard's lips. "A just end . . . yes. Now, help me to my feet."

Dawnlyn's heart clutched. "Gaard, no!" And as soon as the words were out she regretted them, so threatening was the look he shot her.

Leif and Knute and the others who stood on the threshold glared at Dawnlyn accusingly. Their eyes said: how dare you speak to our leader that way! You are only a woman, you would try to belittle him! Even Gaard's quick gaze warned her to silence.

His eyes returned to the trusty Knute. "Assist me." He endeavored to slide his legs over the edge of the bed. His men quickly came to his aid, helped him to dress, heedless of the pain Dawnlyn knew he must be suffering.

Then Gaard stood between Knute and Ian, his arms around their shoulders for support. Dawnlyn could see beads of perspiration pop out on his skin, the hair around his brow dampen.

Slowly, he moved toward the two women. "Mother," he

said levelly, his eyes displaying no pain, no emotion, "will you walk with me to the sacred grove? Will you stand with your sons as justice is meted out?"

Only the slightest tensing of Elspeth's fingers on Dawnlyn's arm gave credence to the woman's inner turmoil. She looked her son squarely in the eyes. "I shall walk with you," she replied steadily.

And Dawnlyn knew that she, too, would have to face the terrible rite to come. God, give her strength!

Gaard's gaze fell on Dawnlyn, cold, closed, frightening. *Honor me and my position,* his glance seemed to say.

Woodenly, Dawnlyn nodded and placed her hand over Elspeth's, following the men across the threshold and down the long corridor.

An exuberant uproar emanated from the throng when Gaard appeared before them and agreed with the Lawspeaker's decision as to Karl's fate.

If it hadn't been for Elspeth's support, Dawnlyn would have shrunk from the scene, weeping hysterically. There were men everywhere in the large hall, women, too, their dresses hanging provocatively off white shoulders, their bright blue eyes glistening in the aftermath of love as they lay across laps or stretched out in burly arms near the fire in the center of the great room.

Ale poured freely from huge wooden casks and the smoke-filled air was laden with the mingled odors of male and female.

Coming close to him, Dawnlyn murmured, "Please, Gaard, your wound . . . let the men help . . ."

He laughed abruptly. "If I'm to make it to the grove, I must do it alone," he said for all to hear.

Cheers filled the air around them again. A voice called out, "Gaard Wolftooth! Our Jarl! He should have been in Valhalla by now! Instead his Luck holds—look at him!"

His *Luck!* The word swung in her mind dizzily. It was all too foreign, too disquieting to ever digest. Again her eyes traveled the room—the shining ornaments on the dark wood walls, gold and silver of great worth, the intricately carved motifs on the door frames, the beams. Yes, it was too strange and primitive to assimilate, and Dawnlyn felt suddenly alone, devastatingly alone among these barbarians.

"Come." She heard Elspeth's voice, felt her hand on her arm once more. "Be brave, Dawnlyn, you must. If Gaard senses your reluctance and . . . yes . . . your fear, he will never forgive you."

Together they walked out into the cool of early morning; patches of mist hung heavily, opaquely, in the glens and nestled themselves against the sides of the many huts surrounding Thorkellhall beyond the tall wooden barricade.

The sacred grove stood to the south of the Hall, in a stand of spruce that rose to the sky, piercing the mist like mighty pillars. Below the secret grove the terrain sloped gently away to meet the pebbly beach.

They had to cross a grassy meadow to reach the spot, and as the entourage neared the lofty spruces, Dawnlyn felt a chill in the air—an eerie, unearthly chill such as she had never known before.

A bank of fog spread before them, reaching its cool tentacles into the stand of trees and laying its fingers upon the mossy floor, where they seemed to embrace every rock, every tree trunk, every crevice.

And it was dark in the grove. So dark that Dawnlyn, when they walked into its grim embrace, thought dusk had fallen and the world was at its end.

If there were a hell, this must be the place. Carcasses of dead animals—goats, sheep, deer—hung suspended from trees, sacrificed to the pagan gods. Some were recent, flesh still draped from bones; others were endlessly old, as old as time itself.

Thin, hungry snarls rose from a pit before them as they walked on through the patches of fog. Finally they came upon the chosen spot for Karl Thorkellson's ignoble end.

Their approach stirred the wolves greatly until the stronger leaped up the sides of the pit, snarling, slavering, their claws clinging to the broken roots in the musty, earthen walls.

Dawnlyn cringed at the sight. Sickness rose to her throat, choking her. She looked tentatively to Gaard, who stood, unattended now, at the edge of the pit.

"Bring Karl," he commanded.

A deathly silence fell over the men and women while they waited. The tall trees seemed to elongate as the fog made its way up the dark trunks, slithering, winding, coiling like insubstantial serpents. A ghostly breeze touched a fresh carcass of a red deer and the body swung ominously before Dawnlyn's mesmerized stare.

And all the while the wolves howled and leaped for their meal.

"My God . . . my dear God," Dawnlyn whispered fervently, feeling her knees weaken.

Elspeth squeezed her hand reassuringly for a moment. "He is here, even now," she said very quietly. "He is here with me to give me courage."

Dawnlyn closed her eyes in silent prayer.

She never knew how long she stood there, chilled to the bone, her heart pounding so loudly that surely all could hear it over the wolves' snarls, but it seemed an eternity passed before Karl stood across from them, at the edge of the pit—the threshold of his doom.

And then all eyes turned to Gaard.

"Do you wish to leap or would you meet your reward with a shove?" His words split the air like a knife; oily sweat dripped from his brow.

The dark assemblage held its breath as one, waiting, their eyes fixed on Karl now.

"I shall leap, you swine!" hissed Karl, and his eyes locked onto Gaard's were bright with hatred. "And as these beasts tear at my flesh, know that my dishonor is your doing and know, too, that my loathing will grow and will live in the bellies of these beasts and in the bellies of their ill-begotten pups!"

Gaard tossed back his leonine head and laughed hoarsely. "So you have no farewell save hatred! No Christian words begging for forgiveness?"

"I die as a Viking. I have no fear."

"Only of me, brother," said Gaard in a low, scathing tone.

"Perhaps . . . for you have at last taken all from me, even an honorable death," spat Karl, dropping his hands to his sides, ready to leap.

Gaard's stare met his brother's levelly. Between them, for a fleeting moment, there seemed to be an odd understanding.

Dawnlyn watched the tangible moment come and go in mute horror. Cain and Abel. Only this time evil would surely die . . .

Across the grove a mist curled and eddied around Karl's legs, making him appear to be disembodied. His eyes still held Gaard's, mute, flashing, eloquent.

Gaard was motionless, his face as ashen as death itself. A terrible battle waged behind his quiescent visage. Then quickly he spun around, took Ian's sword from its sheath and held it above his head.

"Die well then, Viking!" he commanded, suddenly swirling the blade, letting it loose in the air so that the hilt met Karl's hand across the ravenous pit.

To Dawnlyn's eyes the flash of the blade as it spun across the chasm, Karl's hand reaching, reaching, his cry of victory, seemed to take place so slowly that minutes might have passed. Each fraction of movement was set strangely, sickeningly apart from the last, yet they all flowed together as one.

Then Karl's body was in the air, the sword held out before him, and he was falling, slowly, slowly falling into the deadly pit, and his war cries mixed with the hungry howls below.

She was so horrified that Elspeth's own anguish was lost on her that moment and the only thing she could see was Gaard, his frowning face held in stiff lines.

He turned from the pit, his steel-gray eyes meeting hers for an instant, then looking ahead to the path they must follow back to the Hall, away from the demonic rites of the sacred grove.

As Gaard passed by her, she saw blood welling darkly

down his thigh, saw the enormous effort he made to keep from collapsing, saw what she tried to believe was torment in his eyes.

Then an unearthly scream rose from the snarling pit and silence fell over the people in hushed awe. Dawnlyn saw Gaard's back stiffen infinitesimally. But she was so weak, so nauseated that she couldn't be certain of anything. And a dark blanket fell over her eyes suddenly and bright spots exploded in the blackness and she never saw Leif rush up from behind nor did she remember his strong young arms catching her.

All she would remember of that sunless morning was Gaard's relentless expression at the precise moment his brother met his fate.

Chapter Eleven

IAN SET DOWN HIS FLAGON OF ALE, WIPED HIS NEWLY GROWN mustache dry with a sleeve. "I swear, Dawnlyn," he said, "life here is good. Why, the summer days are longer and warmer in Norway than they are in Scotland! It's a miracle."

Ian, Dawnlyn could see, was becoming more a Viking with each passing day. Why, even a week ago, he would not have been drinking ale before the midday meal like this. It must be the influence of all the upheaval recently: first the battle at St. Abb's Hall, his imprisonment and then all the violent rituals here in Norway. It was altering her brother, and Dawnlyn did not care in the least for his new attitude or his new ways.

"You look worried, sister," he said from across the table in the great hall. "Is it Gaard? Is your betrothed not healing properly?"

Dawnlyn shot him a brittle glance. "Gaard is recovering quite well. It is not him, Ian, it is you."

"Me?" he laughed. "But I am fine. Never better!"

"You are becoming like an animal," she said. "Like one of these beasts I see sitting all day in the hall drinking, pinching the serving girls. For *serious* sport you think it fun to play in the meadow with the others, wielding your sword like a child!"

Ian banged his fist on the table abruptly. "Would you have me don a gown and slink around Thorkellhall as you do?" His great temper aroused, he went on cruelly. "Why, this is the first time in a week you have shown your face in the great hall without the Lady Elspeth at your side. What is it, sister," he snarled, "do you think the men will attack you? Ha! No one would dare touch Wolftooth's chattel!"

Sudden tears sprang unbidden to Dawnlyn's eyes. "I am his betrothed, Ian! I am no kept woman!"

"Then why hadn't he married you? Father Tancred would perform the ceremony . . ."

Dawnlyn compressed her lips in painful silence. Why, indeed, hadn't he married her? Ian, intoxicated as he was, was quite right. And then the thought returned, as it had so many times these past days—what was Gaard's relationship, really, with that overbearing female Astrid? What had the woman meant saying that *she* was his woman?

"Well, sister?" asked Ian thickly. "Why don't you two have Father Tancred marry you?"

Her insides quaking, unsure of her position, unsure of anything anymore, for that matter, she was ready to rise and flee Ian's close regard when she felt a hand on her shoulder. Quickly she looked up and saw Leif Haraldsson standing over her. How odd that he always seemed to appear at the propitious moment. "It is pleasant to see you in the hall," said Leif, leveling a hard, warning glance at Ian. "And how is our illustrious leader?" He seated himself next to her, addressing to her a too-bright, beguiling smile.

Dawnlyn tried desperately to collect herself and ignore Ian. "Gaard is much better. He walks with some ease and the wound has begun to heal."

"That is good news." His deep-set blue eyes gazed into hers, holding them. "And you, Lady Dawnlyn, are you well? I feared greatly for your health the other day in the grove. You were so pale."

Dawnlyn smiled timidly, feeling vaguely embarrassed at Leif's unnecessary concern. "I am fine. And I must thank you for carrying me all the way back to the Hall

. . . although"—color rose hotly on her cheeks—"I do not think it was entirely necessary."

With a loud scraping of his bench, Ian stood. "Such pleasant chitchat! I think I'll find a sparring partner and be off to the meadow."

She watched him stride across the hall, then sighed to herself. "I must apologize for Ian's rudeness. I truly do not know what has come over him."

"It is the life here," replied Leif, his eyes leveled on her. "It can do that to some."

"Aye." Dawnlyn moved her glance awkwardly to her half-finished plate of food. "But you are different somehow." She found herself voicing her thoughts aloud.

"Me?" he laughed curtly. "I suppose I am. For one thing, I find their behavior offensive, and for another, I prefer using my wits as opposed to my strength."

Dawnlyn pondered his words, sipping from her mug of cider, stealing a glance at him from under thick lashes. He was—or, at least, he seemed—quite wise for someone who, she had learned, was near to her own age. His blue eyes showed a prudent cynicism beyond his years, and his whole demeanor seemed somehow mature. His profile lent to his air of authority, his nose being generous, slightly curved downward like the beak of a bird of prey.

And he was terribly attractive, she had to concede, tall and lean with healthy, fair coloring, hair the hue of smoked wood and a clean-shaven face.

She decided that he was *one* Viking she could grow to like.

"Have you seen the lands of Thorkellhall?" asked Leif abruptly.

"Why, no"—she looked up—"not really. Gaard has been wounded since I arrived . . ."

"Then . . . might I show you?" He saw her reluctance, comparing her in his mind to a bright flower whose petals close at the sun's heat. "I promise I shall be a perfect gentleman," he added softly, meeting her eyes with a glance of acknowledgment.

Dawnlyn's cheeks burned scarlet. "I never thought you would be otherwise," she said gently.

"Then let us be on our way." Leif rose. "Unless, of course, Gaard might disapprove . . ."

"I did not say—" But Leif was already standing beside her, his hand outstretched. Dawnlyn finally smiled. "Why not? Surely Gaard could not object."

They strolled across the meadows, past the scattered huts of the workers and thralls, and on into a tall stand of aspens whose leaves rustled like so many pieces of rich green silk. Below the trees was the pebbly beach and beyond that, the North Sea glittered in the sun.

Leif, although a touch sarcastic at moments, was an easy companion. When Dawnlyn stopped, merely taking in the strange beauty of the land, he was quiet. When they walked side by side, he regaled her with the story of his parentage.

His mother, he explained, was the daughter of a neighboring jarl and his stepfather was a merchant.

"Your stepfather?" she asked while Leif handed her down to the beach from a grass hillock. "Is your father dead, then?"

A breeze teased at Dawnlyn's midnight-blue skirt, billowing the linen around her slim ankles. Leif's eyes rested on the pretty picture. "He may as well be. You see," he added, deliberately insouciant, "I am a bastard."

"Oh!" Dawnlyn gasped, fidgeting with the skirt that was puffing around her knees.

"It is an interesting story," he went on, leading her to a smooth rock where she might sit. "You see my nose?" He afforded her a view of his profile. "Well, it is said the hook comes from my father, who was a powerful hawk . . ."

"Leif!" She shook her head in dismay. "Not you, too! I refuse to believe in fairy tales."

He laughed, showing strong, white teeth. "I'm not much of a believer myself. Still, it is said the hawk swooped down upon my unsuspecting mother when she was alone in a meadow and—"

"Please!" she rasped out, crimson to the roots of her hair. "Don't tell me!"

"I am sorry . . . I forgot to whom I was speaking," he said, appearing contrite. "At any rate," he went on, "my stepfather is a far better man than I am certain my real father is." He paused for a fleeting moment, a frown creasing his brow. For the first time, Dawnlyn saw the cynical mask fall, the young man's true nature show through it. "My mother said he was a great man—my real father, that is—but how could he be great when he never claimed me or even attempted to see my mother again? Bah! A woman says any man is great who beds her!"

"That is not true!" snapped Dawnlyn, angered at his view of women. "Sometimes we are forced!"

Leif's blue eyes pinioned hers, frank and far too knowing for comfort. "Perhaps," he said quietly. "In any case, I was fortunate with my stepfather, who has been eminently just with me. He showed me things, took me places where few have been." Leif's eyes, as blue now as the North Sea, stared out at the level horizon. "I have been to Constantinople . . . to the shores of Egypt where I saw the wondrous pyramids . . ."

"You jest!" breathed Dawnlyn, her russet-hued hair springing in the soft sea breeze.

"Not at all." He turned to face her, folded his lean frame onto the sand next to her rock. "And I have seen Athens, Rome—"

"But how? How can you have been to all these faraway places? It is simply not possible!"

Leif was suddenly struck by her innocence, struck by the bronze eyes that nearly matched the color of her hair. And her skin was so fair, as fair as the gleaming marble of a Greek statue. Leif had been many places, viewed peoples of every race . . . but this young woman sitting by him now matched easily any of the wondrous sights he had seen.

It was with difficulty that he continued his tale. "I was ten when my father took me and my mother on the journey. His ship carried amber and fur to the Mediterranean lands in trade for jewelry and bolts of bright Cathay silk . . ."

"Silk!" she breathed in delight. "How beautiful . . . how wonderful!"

"He did most of his trading in the capital of the Roman Empire, Constantinople, where we were the honored guests of the Sultan himself!" Pride gleamed in Leif's eyes. "I have never seen a sight as glorious as Constantinople. Dolphins leaped before our prow as our ship made port, and the city rose before us on the lush hills with glorious domed mosques and white, sprawling buildings that reached down to the dock. There were hundreds of ships there, Lady Dawnlyn, hundreds . . ."

"Go on," she begged, "tell me!"

Leif smiled. "How can I tell you all I have seen?" But he endeavored to, holding her spellbound. He described to the best of his ability the Blue Mosque and Hagia Sophia, whose immense ochre domes rose to the sky and beckoned men of all religions. He told her of the great bazaar with the hundreds of shops displaying gold, copper, silver and colorful, intricately woven rugs from far-off lands such as Hindustan and Cathay. He described to Dawnlyn the splashing fountains and huge gardens of the fabulous city and the enormous underground cisterns that supplied water to the people. And all the while he praised his stepfather highly for taking him on the immense journey.

Overwhelmed, Dawnlyn breathed, "I have never dreamed of such things. How did they come to be?"

"All peoples are different," he replied as if to himself. "Just as I am a Christian and a Viking, so are others of mixed beliefs and cultures. And if they come together and jell, then new races are born, new cultures formed, and wonderful cities are built. In the Mediterranean lands, the cultures are so mixed that it takes a man some time before he can assimilate it." Leif studied Dawnlyn for a long moment. "A son born to you and Gaard will be of two very different worlds. Is this not so?"

"Aye," she whispered, overcome by the knowledge. "How can a child know which is best? Which life to choose?"

"He doesn't, Lady Dawnlyn. Ponder on it," said Leif. "The child would embrace both cultures and be that much the wiser for it."

Dawnlyn tried to digest this revelation. "Is Gaard, then," she mused, "the product of such an intermarriage? He seems thoroughly Viking to me—a Norseman to his very soul."

"But he is not," said Leif quickly. "He is staunch and fearless and would have all believe him to be strictly a Viking of the old ways." He paused, collecting his thoughts. "But it is said that he was influenced by his mother's priest, instructed in the Christian ways. And Gaard has seen the places I have. He left his homeland several times and traveled far and wide. It stands to reason that he is versed in many things. It is quite impossible for him to be entirely a Norseman of the old standing. Yet who can know what goes on behind those cold eyes?"

"Who, indeed?" she whispered, losing herself to thoughts of Gaard, thoughts of the many-faceted man whom she was to marry . . . someday. Of course, there was that shameless woman Astrid . . .

While Leif gazed quietly on her, on the way her winglike brows knitted together, Dawnlyn lost herself in the unsettling notions and felt suddenly, miserably insecure. She could almost hate Gaard for that, for robbing her of the peaceful, delineated existence she had known before him. And yet, was it possible to hate a man such as Gaard?

"What are you thinking?" asked Leif, breaking into her disquieting thoughts.

She took a deep breath. "I was thinking about my forthcoming marriage . . . about Gaard." She sighed, then gave a weak smile. "He is a strange man . . . an awesome man. I do not quite know what to think about him. Do you?"

Her eyes turned to Leif.

He was silent for several long minutes. When he spoke again, his voice was deceptively light. "No, I do not truly know him, either. I do, however, know that he is a fearful man, as anyone in Norway can tell you. You may believe as you so choose, but he does have the *Luck*. Yet there are things about the man I fail to comprehend . . . and that I do not like."

"Such as?" asked Dawnlyn, puzzled by Leif's change of tone.

"His disregard for others. There he lacks."

"To whom has he shown disregard?"

Leif's glance fell away. He was quiet for a time; then, strangely, he laughed, but with no amusement in his eyes. "Who can truly know another man or what goes on in his heart?"

Dawnlyn grew pensive. "No one, I suppose, can fathom a man such as Gaard," she replied in a hushed tone. "Doubtless, no one ever shall." She thought then, as she had so many times before, that her future would be a strange, empty place, a place where she would be so awfully alone.

"You will come to Karl's funeral?" asked Leif as if reading her thoughts and attempting to steer the conversation in a new direction. "A Viking funeral is a wondrous thing to behold."

"Aye," she replied, "Gaard has told me I must be there."

"He seems to have you near at hand at all rituals, doesn't he?"

"Aye. Whether or not I wish to be," she reflected darkly. "I truly fail to understand him."

"Perhaps he wants to expose you to our ways." Leif gazed pensively out over the sparkling water. "Yes," he said, "Gaard Wolftooth is a man who requires much understanding. I, for one, would be greatly interested in knowing him better."

They conversed for a time—avoiding further mention of Gaard—and Dawnlyn once again relaxed in Leif's company. She could have stayed on the shore forever that afternoon so lovely was the sea and sky and sun warming her through the deep blue gown. Yet the hour grew late and finally she was forced to rise.

"Gaard will wonder where I have been," she said, shaking loose the folds of her skirt. "He grows bored so easily of late."

Leif, too, came to his feet. "And are you bored also?" He placed a warm hand on her sleeve, urging her to face him.

"Why, no," she replied softly, very aware of his hand touching her. "In truth," she lowered her eyes, "I have had a most wonderful afternoon." She felt his other hand beneath her chin, tilting her head up to meet his.

"Have you?" said Leif so quietly that she had to strain to hear. And her eyes watched his lips, the thin, sensual line of his mouth, which was parted slightly, awaiting her reply, awaiting something else, too, she sensed abruptly.

"I—" she stammered, her heartbeat quickening, "I have enjoyed myself, yes. But now I must—" And she saw that his head was bent nearer to hers, closer than before, and she felt rooted to the spot, unable to move.

"You are so lovely, Dawnlyn," Leif whispered, his breath fanning her lips. "So very, very precious . . ." And his mouth touched hers, his lips parted, featherlike, compelling.

For an incredible moment, Dawnlyn just stood there, Leif's hand under her chin, his lips brushing hers. A thousand thoughts invaded her mind as she realized that in an instant he would kiss her, truly lock his mouth to hers.

Did she want him to? Was her heart beating rapidly from excitement or fear?

She felt his lips, firm over hers. Fear of the unknown, fear that this stranger's mere touch could awaken her senses, caused her to pull away abruptly, a hot, crimson flush staining her cheeks.

"My God," she whispered, her mind reeling. Was it possible for another man other than Gaard to awaken in her feelings of passion? Was she some sort of a wanton? Or did *all* women feel this way when confronted by an attractive man?

"Are you all right?" came Leif's voice.

"I . . . I do not know," she breathed. "I must get back to Gaard . . ."

"Yes," he said, suddenly cool. "You'd best be getting back to your betrothed."

Gaard sat by Astrid's side in the great hall, appearing to be quite interested in her carefree conversation, which lilted above the dull noise of the gathered throng.

Astrid had come to pay him a visit some hours earlier, and at the time he had been glad to see her, to rest an arm on her shoulder as she helped him to walk from his bedchamber to the hall. They had shared an ale together, spoken of old times while her blond head had bent close to his. Yet as the hours passed and food was brought from the kitchen, Gaard had begun to wonder where Dawnlyn had gone—her afternoon strolls did not usually take *this* long!

Astrid was pouring him another ale, her full breast brushing his shoulder, when his attention riveted itself to the open doorway. There was his betrothed, the brightness of the setting sunlight behind her, burnishing her hair to copper fire. Next to her, gilded as well with youth and wholesomeness, was Leif, his head bent close to her shell-pink ear while she seemed to listen to him solemnly.

Astrid's scent, which moments before had held his attention, receded from his senses as did the noise and awareness of the throng surrounding him.

Gaard saw only Dawnlyn and Leif. He saw what a well-suited, handsome couple they made.

Suddenly his wound ached and he felt old and scarred. His eyes followed Dawnlyn's trim form as she moved across the crowded hall with Leif by her side. And then, as she approached the corridor leading to the bedchamber, she smiled warmly at Leif, rested a slim white hand on his sleeve for a moment and then disappeared.

Had she looked in Gaard's direction she would have seen that his mouth was grim and his eyes as narrow and dark as the shadow of a scudding storm cloud—but it is more likely that Dawnlyn would have first noticed Astrid leaning close to him, her eyes resting on Dawnlyn, a smug grin splitting her full, sensuous lips.

"But why must I go to this heathen ritual? You've dragged me to enough. My stomach turns every time and lately I've even vomited afterwards. You pagans slit an animal's throat if anyone so much as sneezes! It's a wonder you've any livestock left at all!" Dawnlyn faced Gaard across the bed, her hands on her hips. "I want to stay here! I can't bear it anymore!"

"You will attend my brother's funeral, Dawnlyn. It is required of you. A man's kin must be there." His face was still pale and thin, his high-bridged nose jutting out more hawklike than ever; his eyes were angry.

"I am *not* your brother's family!" Dawnlyn reminded him tartly.

"You will be," he answered coolly.

"I doubt that!" she snapped. "Not at this rate. You'd rather keep me as your handmaiden!"

"Are you so anxious to be my wedded wife?"

"Aye!" Then she thought of what she had just said, stamped her foot and whirled away from him. "No! Well, you know what I mean!"

"No, I don't. You women are forever changing your minds."

"Just because men aren't subtle enough to understand a woman's motives they fall back on that ridiculous notion!"

"Nevertheless, Dawnlyn," he said soberly, "you *will* be at my side this day at Karl's funeral."

"Yes, my lord," she bit out sarcastically, "I am your willing slave. Whatever you ask I must do. I have no choice at all, do I?" She faced him with hot, angry eyes that sparked with amber flames.

"In some things, little one, there is no choice," Gaard explained softly, implacably.

So Dawnlyn accompanied her Viking, feeling nausea rise in her gorge already, walking by his side slowly because he still hobbled painfully from his wound, it being only ten days since he'd received it. If truth be told, she would have made him stay abed, but there was no telling this man what he would or would not do.

They arrived at the small bay, and the entire procession arranged itself along the shore. Lady Elspeth was there, tall and pale and grieving, fingering her rosary incessantly. How did she stand it? thought Dawnlyn. Her *son,* and not even a Christian burial to set his soul at rest! Leif was there, too, having insinuated himself into Gaard's cohorts without anyone questioning it or really knowing how it had happened. He seemed to hover perpetually at Gaard's shoulder, an eager, expectant expression on his face. Ian, too, stood at Gaard's shoulder, his new pale red beard shadowing his face, and the red-bearded, lantern-jawed Knute was close behind. Father Tancred stood there near Elspeth, his eyes closed, his blue-veined hands clasped in prayer.

And in attendance, too, was Astrid.

The very sight of the flaxen-haired beauty was enough to make Dawnlyn move even closer to Gaard, although, for the life of her, Dawnlyn could not have explained why. Nor could she have said why the woman's mere presence was so shattering, so threatening. It simply made no sense—Gaard was betrothed to Dawnlyn. He had asked *her* to wed him, not that falsely smiling woman whose eyes met Dawnlyn's for a moment, then came to rest possessively on Gaard as if she knew every inch of him intimately.

Feeling a knot in her stomach, Dawnlyn forced her gaze away from Astrid and onto Karl, whose body, black and sunken, was arranged on the silken couch under a tent that had been set up on the ship's deck. Dawnlyn tore her eyes away instantly, but not before she'd seen that he had been dressed in his most elegant clothes with a tunic of silver cloth and a cap trimmed in fur. Drink, fruit and sweet-smelling herbs had been placed around him, along with all his weapons.

They brought one of Karl's gray Elkhounds and the old crone that was the angel of death cut it in half with a surprisingly strong stroke, throwing it into the ship. Then

Gaard stepped forward, as the jarl, and drew his sword across the throat of Karl's fine black bull while the angel of death chanted unimaginable things. It, too, was put on the ship.

Gaard returned to Dawnlyn's side, spattered with bull's blood, grim and solemn-faced. She held her breath and gritted her teeth, afraid the contents of her stomach would rise momentarily.

The old woman's chanting and other preparations had taken so long that it was nearly dusk, yet the entire assemblage stood at attention, watching with ferocious intensity the long, unspeakably archaic events. Dawnlyn's knees were on the verge of buckling from the long, wearisome, ritual-filled day. Yet she knew how vital it was for her to stand tall beside Gaard, to appear a fitting mate for a Viking lord. That was a lesson she had learned quickly, if not painlessly, since she'd set foot on the Norwegian shore.

But now it was coming to an end. It was time for the man who was the deceased person's closest kin to do the final honors—to send the dead spirit to Valhalla speedily, painlessly, gloriously. As the long shadows slid across the pebbled strand, Gaard limped forward to take from the angel of death a lit torch. Slowly, his halting gait more obvious than ever, Gaard made his way across the beach, stepping into the shallow water to stand before Karl's dragon ship.

There was an uncanny silence, as if each person there held his breath, stopped the very beating of his heart. Not a sound could be heard but the gentle lapping of the waves on the shore and the angry hiss and crackle of the torch in Gaard's hand. Calmly, majestically, he touched the hungry fire to the black, pitch-impregnated hull of the vessel. It sputtered, caught, flared into hot, angry life, forcing the crowd to take a collective step backward, the glare of the firelight gilding each face.

Gaard made his way deliberately, unhurriedly, from bow to stern, igniting the dragon ship until it was itself a pyre, the hot orange flames reaching joyously to the darkening sky, sending sparks spraying up in long, graceful streamers of brightness.

Then the men came down to the shoreline and pushed Karl and his ship into deeper water with long poles to drift with the evening tide, a burning altar of death, a gloriously pagan way of ushering Karl into paradise.

Before an hour had passed ship and man had turned to ashes, to drift on the wind and water forever. Then and only then did the crowd disperse, returning to Thorkellhall to celebrate riotously for one last night.

As usual, Dawnlyn thought, as she seated herself in the great hall, Gaard was too busy now to pay her any mind. In truth, her stomach was ready to heave at any moment as she sat there, trying to ignore the mountains of food before her. It was Leif who providentially took note of her distress.

He seated himself beside her. "You do not look well," he observed keenly.

"Nor do I feel quite myself," she replied. "I would that I could retire."

"Then I shall see you safely to your chamber, my lady, and make your excuses to the company. Come." Leif rose, nodded his head toward the dim corridor.

"But Gaard . . ."

". . . is too busy to notice. Come . . ."

And Dawnlyn thought to herself, yes, he's busy—he'll no doubt busy himself with that Astrid! But truly, her stomach was turning so sickeningly, and Leif was right, she should go to her chamber.

She allowed him to walk her down the dimly lit corridor, to open the door for her, and for a fleeting moment their eyes met and locked. Her breath stopped for a heartbeat of time as she recognized the expression in his eyes—it was one of desire, but the desire was curiously tinged with fear and regret and a mockery of all those things, too. Yet he was silent and she felt her blood turn cold in her veins. What kind of man was he? What did he want from her? Surely there were others in the Hall with whom he'd fare better than with the jarl's woman. It was as if he sought her out deliberately. Why?

She tore her eyes away from his. "Good night," she breathed, turning from him.

"Sleep well, sweet Dawnlyn," she heard him whisper.

Quickly she closed the door, and all thought was barred from her mind as she retched weakly into the chamber pot.

Gaard was truly busy as he held court in the great hall, celebrating his new status as jarl, as well as his brother's befittingly splendid funeral.

Yet, he was not joyous at all; his wound ached badly and his mother's distress did not escape him, although her face and bearing had remained stoically unchanged. As for his own feelings, they were mixed: triumph battled caution, pride fled before the guilt of Karl's manner of death. He told himself it had been fated to end this way; he almost succeeded in convincing himself.

Astrid Thorhilddottir sat a short way down the table, next to her father; she stared continuously at Gaard, but on this night he was too drained of emotion, too concerned with his mother's pain to pay the girl much heed. That she was still beautiful he could not deny and that she still desired him was obvious and flattering. He would have to speak to her some time, explain about his betrothal. And Astrid would understand, for did not all great lords marry to further their ambitions?

Gaard sat in Karl's former chair at the head of the long oak table that was scarred and blackened from a thousand feasts. The armed chair was of stone, as was customary, and was very ancient, carved with designs of plants and flowers. His predominant thought was of the last time he'd seen his brother sitting in this selfsame chair—the day Karl had declared Gaard banished from Norway for life. But this time, his own men drank and sported lustily, congratulated him, toasted him with strong, honey-colored mead and sweet cloudberry wine.

He should have been completely joyous.

Young Leif Haraldsson approached him, a touch bright-eyed from drink, tall and slim and well-dressed in an elegant blue surcoat that matched his eyes. A very handsome youth, Gaard registered, attracted despite himself to the boy.

"My lord," said Leif, bowing his honey-brown head respectfully, "I wish to ask a favor of the new jarl."

"Ask then, boy. I am fair to those who help me." Carefully, Gaard studied this young man. Who was he? Why was he here? How had he come, so suddenly and effort-lessly, to be in the center of things?

"I wish to become a member of your household and study to become your Lawspeaker. I am not a warrior, but I can still be of great worth to you."

Gaard considered. Leif sounded most sincere, perhaps *too* sincere, yet his reasoning was solid. "I have a perfectly capable Lawspeaker," Gaard said, locking glances with those opaque blue eyes. He realized, with faint surprise, that Leif was quite as sober as he, Gaard was. Well, then, they were the only two in the Hall that were.

"Yes, but one day . . . It would take me some years to study and learn the laws, in any case. I am willing to wait." The boy was open-faced as a babe, smiling, pleasant, smooth. Smooth as the slippery black rock that lurked under stream water to break a horse's leg. And yet, he was so appealing, with his fresh-faced candor, his friendly ways, his apparent desire to be liked . . .

"I will think on it. Meanwhile you will be a member of my household and will perform any chores that are necessary."

"Any way I can be of help, my lord," replied Leif, hiding his expression in another respectful bow. "But, I must advise you, my talents lie more in the area of mental labor than physical."

"I can see that, boy. My brain is not yet clouded by old age."

"Why, I certainly did not mean to imply that! You are a man in your prime." The frank, open young face, the guileless blue eyes.

"Humph," growled Gaard, dismissing the youth. There was something there, something concealed, veiled by ingenuous blue eyes and an open countenance. Maybe it was only a sharper than average intelligence, an awareness that matched Gaard's own. Or maybe his vague distrust derived entirely from the way Dawnlyn had looked that day, returning from her walk with Leif.

And yet Gaard had the strangest urge to gain the boy's respect and liking, and he couldn't, for the life of him, imagine why. Nor, he reflected, was he sure he *had* respect and liking from young Leif Haraldsson. And he couldn't imagine why he felt *that,* either.

It was a couple of hours later that Gaard quietly closed the door of his room behind him and lit the oil lamp. Dawnlyn slept on her side, still in her clothes, and she was curled up like a child, tear stains dried whitely on her cheeks. He felt a wave of tenderness toward this child with the rare, beautiful coloring and prideful ways. And yet she stood up staunchly, did the things she had to do with precision if not willingness. It had all been hard on her. Now, perhaps, he'd have more time to spend with her, find out what she was *really* like. Now he was secure and the jarl of two goodly lands on either side of the North Sea, *now* his life would resolve itself. He had but a hazy vision of the future but refused to worry over it. What the fates dealt out, he would grasp and turn to his advantage. Didn't he have the Luck?

"Dawnlyn," he whispered, lowering himself painfully to the bed. "Wake up, little one."

She opened tear-swollen eyes, unfocused at first; then remembrance of the funeral flooded them and she turned her head away. "Leave me be," she mumbled.

"I only wish to join you in bed. I am as stiff and sore as an old man. Move over."

She shifted her slim form on the bed and turned her back to him. "That is the last time I attend one of your disgusting Viking rites," he heard her say in a muffled voice. "I am a Christian and I will not sully myself with those events."

"I thought it quite spectacular myself. Never have I seen a better send-off. Just think of Karl in Valhalla this very night, drinking and making love endlessly."

Dawnlyn turned on her elbow to study Gaard's face in the dimness. She was sure there had been a hint of humor in his voice. Could that be possible? Then it dawned on her: Gaard no more believed that fantasy than she did!

"By the love of Christ," she breathed, "I wonder how much of this rubbish you really do believe!" Her voice was wondering.

"As much as I wish, Dawnlyn," he answered harshly. "Now, move over, for I have great need of sleep."

Chapter Twelve

DAWNLYN GAZED INTO THE MIDDLE DISTANCE FORLORNLY, NOT seeing Elspeth's room, not seeing the older woman herself sitting quietly on a pelt-covered chair.

"Oh, what will I do?" Dawnlyn half-sobbed. "What *will* I do?"

Elspeth smiled with patient wisdom. "You will have the babe, of course, the same way women have since the beginning of time."

"Perhaps I'm not really with child . . ."

"We've been over and over the evidence, Dawnlyn. Believe in my judgment—you are. It was bound to happen."

"But Gaard . . ." And she put her head in her hands and wept miserably.

"I shall speak to my son immediately, and tomorrow you will be wed by Father Tancred." Elspeth rose. "Now go to your chamber and await Gaard . . . and for the sake of heaven, dry your tears."

"What if he won't marry me? What if he has changed his mind?" Dawnlyn sniffed, thinking of the lovely Astrid and wiping at her nose with a linen kerchief. "Who will want a fat-bellied woman as wife? Oh," she moaned, "I don't even know if I want to be married. All I ever wanted was to be a nun! I am not prepared for husband and child!"

"You will be married," said Elspeth sternly. "And trust me, you will live through the ordeal, as did I." She paused in the doorway, "Gaard is a good man. He will treat you fairly and make an excellent father."

But how could Elspeth know these things? Everything was happening so suddenly—it was too disturbing, too unfair.

Dawnlyn awaited Gaard in their chamber that evening as Elspeth had told her to do. She was in an agony of trepidation each time footfalls could be heard echoing in the corridor.

Would he be furious, did he even want a child? And what if the betrothal back at St. Abb's had only been to pacify her people—what if he planned no such thing? What if Astrid had reminded him of his ties to *her?* And worst of all, Dawnlyn realized, she was not yet ready for marriage; she herself had not fit her mind around the fact. Her whole existence was in a hideous upheaval.

She moved about the room unable to rest, like a hummingbird, constantly flitting from place to place, knowing that Gaard was being told the news by Elspeth probably at this very moment.

Dawnlyn found herself at the window, taking deep breaths to calm herself while staring out over the darkening vista. The sky was streaked with fingers of color: reds, purples, blues, the full spectrum of light. She had seen these strange lights from the north before, in St. Abb's, but never with such intensity as here in Norway. It was brilliant, twisting about the sky above from an apex on the northern horizon. She could almost believe Gaard's gods were spinning the bright colors as some sort of a sign to him—but that was absurd, a thought as pagan as the land itself! Still, did he see the lights? How would he interpret them? Did they mean danger or promise of a bright future?

When the door did open and Gaard finally stood on the threshold, her heart pounded drumbeats in her ears and she could not turn from the window to face him. What was he thinking? How he must resent her!

"So you are with child," came his deep voice.

She nodded slowly, keeping her back to him, her eyes fixed on the display.

"I am pleased, Dawnlyn."

Her heart lurched. "Are you?" she breathed. And she felt his large hand on her shoulder then, lifting a heavy coil of copper hair.

"I said I was pleased. What more should I say?"

"And . . . and marriage?" she dared to ask. "Are you pleased about that, too?"

The silence in the room was palpable for what seemed an eternity; Dawnlyn thought her lungs would burst from holding her breath in suspense. "I had hoped to wait until we returned to Scotland. But under the circumstances . . ."

A tear, unbidden, fell to her white hand, wetting it hotly. "If you like," she breathed, "we can wait. It is just that I do not wish to give birth to a . . . a bastard."

Gaard turned her around carefully to face him, put a finger under her chin, tilting her head. "Nor do I wish to father a bastard. It is the furthest thing from my mind. We shall be married on the morrow by the priest and you will be my wife." Gently, slowly, his lips descended to her mouth and moved over it with infinite care. Then, just as slowly, he lifted his head from hers. "I do not always have a way with words where women are concerned. If I offended you . . ."

"No," she whispered. "I, too, had thought marriage was still a long way off." And then, "I . . . I am sorry about forcing you . . . the child . . ."

Gaard gripped her shoulders more firmly. "*I* am responsible for this child, not you, Dawnlyn. Your body may carry him, but it was my desire that created him. Do not blame yourself."

Somehow his admission did not comfort her. Instead, Dawnlyn realized that he had agreed to marry her immediately only because of his sense of duty, his responsibility. The thought was far from soothing to her ruffled feelings.

A strange notion occurred to her abruptly, and she could not help but ask, "Will you still find me . . . think of me as . . . attractive when I am horribly swollen?"

He laughed lightly. "Of course I shall. I will place my hand on your belly and know that my seed grows there. It will be a wondrous thing."

She was silent for a time, biting her lower lip, working up the courage to confront him. Finally, she turned her eyes up to meet his level gaze. "Gaard?"

"Yes, little one." His expression was bemused, patient, almost fatherly. Something about it irritated her.

"What will Astrid think of a marriage between us?" she spat out quickly.

"Astrid?" His bemused expression was replaced by one of astonishment.

"Aye, Astrid Thorhilddottir. You know, the tall, fair one whose eyes seem always to seek yours. You *do* know her, don't you?"

"Astrid? What has she to do with our marriage, Dawnlyn?" His tone was one of injured dignity. She could almost believe his innocent posture.

"You'd best answer *that* question, Gaard, for no one knows better than you."

"Why are you bringing this matter up, Dawnlyn? I cannot see that it signifies . . ."

"I bring it up because that . . . that female barged in here when you were wounded and told me that she was your woman!" Dawnlyn's eyes shot copper sparks at him.

But Gaard's reaction put an abrupt end to her anger, converting it to chagrined confusion. He threw back his head and laughed—a seemingly mirth-filled laughter. "Astrid!" He finally chuckled. "That girl! Such stories she tells! So she says she was my woman!" And he reached out to grasp one of Dawnlyn's cold hands.

"Do you deny it?" Dawnlyn asked, trying to hold onto her dignity.

"I deny it. Astrid is no more my *woman* than a dozen others! No, wait, little one!" he said to Dawnlyn's rigid back as she snatched her hand from his. "What I mean is, Astrid Thorhilddottir is no more to me than a past affair like any other. I will marry *you* and only you."

174

"And shall you be faithful to your vows of wedlock or shall you act like the other rutting Vikings?" she demanded.

"Dawnlyn." She shrank a little from his now stern tone. "You must learn to accept our ways without passing judgment on them so self-righteously. It is a naive way you Christians have and does not endear you to the great majority of the world. Now, hear me well. I am an honorable man. In marrying you I make a binding contract with you—that is, I give you my word. I will endeavor to keep my word to the utmost of my ability. Now, that will have to satisfy you."

She had to be consoled with those words and held them close to her for the rest of the evening like a person clinging to a single piece of buoyant wood in a storm-tossed sea. Everything had happened so quickly that she barely had time to collect her thoughts. Gaard busied himself that long summer's eve seeing to the arrangements, sending messengers to neighboring halls, and Dawnlyn barely saw him at all. Yet he seemed at ease with the situation, as if on the morrow their whole lives would not be altered. How could one face marriage so calmly?

Later that night, Dawnlyn spoke with Father Tancred, asked him if the Christian marriage would be binding to Gaard.

"In the eyes of God, yes, it will be binding," he replied, but it was of little comfort to Dawnlyn, who knew Gaard didn't care a whit about her God.

Elspeth, with Meg's assistance, spent long hours helping alter her own marriage gown to fit Dawnlyn; the oyster-white silk gown was too long and too full in the hips for Dawnlyn's slender frame. But when the stitching was done the following morning and Dawnlyn bathed and dressed, the gown with the golden bodice and flowing sleeves trimmed also in gold did look elegant on her. She wore a matching headcloth on her coppery hair and a golden circlet of miniature dragons and serpents to hold it in place—the Greek treasure was a gift from Gaard, who had traded sables for it on one of

175

his voyages and he, himself, had placed it on her head.

The gold of her crown and flowing dress was only a few shades lighter than that of her eyes and hair, and the effect was stunning as Dawnlyn walked solemnly through the great hall and out to the tiny chapel near the main building.

Gaard, holding her arm, commented, "This is as quiet as I have ever heard these grounds. The women are jealous and the men are awe-struck by your beauty. I am proud," he finished, leading her into the wooden chapel with its few benches and raised altar.

Still, Dawnlyn realized, Gaard drew as many nods of appreciation as she. He looked splendid, as handsome as any man she had ever known, in his white linen shirt and burgundy velvet surcoat trimmed richly in silver. His freshly washed hair caught the sun and held it as they stood beneath the altar, a column of light pouring in from an open casement above, gilding them both softly.

Dawnlyn glanced around nervously to catch Elspeth's eye. She felt so terribly alone, so frightened. The older woman smiled warmly, her hands clasped in her lap. Dawnlyn returned the smile, but she was so tense that the corners of her mouth twitched slightly. She cast her eyes down demurely, waited for the Mass to begin while taking deep breaths to calm herself.

The familiar Latin words flowed over her as Father Tancred performed the ceremony. Dawnlyn wondered faintly if the ritual meant anything at all to Gaard but knew that she was grasping at straws—the Christian marriage was for his mother and, she hoped, in deference to her own beliefs.

Gaard seemed confident and relaxed throughout Mass while Dawnlyn could feel every nerve-end tingle, her face frozen in a wide-eyed, unseeing stare. How could this be happening to her? Marriage—it was an endless commitment that weighed oppressively on her slim shoulders. And here she was, carrying *his* child, her breasts already sore, bound tightly by the gold-edged bodice.

When they sank to their knees to receive the body and

blood of Christ, Dawnlyn felt suddenly queasy and was certain she would black out at any moment. And yet there was Gaard, next to her, tall, self-assured, virtually at complete ease throughout the ceremony.

They rose. The blessing came and they were wed, tied together by holy vows for a lifetime. There was no escape now, no hope. Truly she was doomed to a fate that seemed only bleak and without definition.

Gaard was turning her then, tilting her face up to his, his lips caressing hers warmly, intimately, for all to see. She knew he placed his brand on her, and her mouth was seared with the possessive pressure.

It must have been Gaard who held her up, led her on a steady path back to the great hall where they were to feast until nightfall. Then . . . then he would brand her again, and she knew her body would yield all, would arch itself up against him and receive him and would ache for release. Even as she seated herself next to him, Dawnlyn knew a desire for the pleasure he brought to her body, and yet her soul was unfulfilled, spinning impotently in a void.

Minstrels played for them and the hall became alive with shouts of "Skoal!" The celebration of the mighty Wolftooth's marriage began.

Many came and spoke to them; several of the neighboring women brought Dawnlyn gifts that warmed her heart: gold and silver trinkets, a raw silk headcloth from Rome, vases, and jars of rosewater. All the beautiful presents were of foreign origin, and Dawnlyn wondered how many of them were stolen in raids—taken from another.

Elspeth exclaimed over the gifts, imparted to Dawnlyn the special significance of each and kept the young bride entertained while Gaard spoke with his men and the neighboring jarls.

Astrid's absence at an event that would normally draw her was conspicuous, as she and her father were close neighbors to Thorkellhall. Dawnlyn had searched the great hall thoroughly after the ceremony and had been very pleased not to see that blond-white head. Perhaps Gaard had been truthful

177

with her, then, and Astrid's possession of Gaard a figment of her overactive imagination.

Dawnlyn ate little and drank less and thought her knees would buckle from tension when Leif and several others claimed her for a turn to the music. She was kissed by dozens; one even dared to place a hand on her bottom for a moment until he caught Gaard's brooding gaze.

Even Ian forced her to step to the music. "You look absolutely beautiful!" he exclaimed over the uproar in the hall. "But wait! Wait until Gaard fills your belly with child! Think of it," he went on, disregarding her mortification, "my sister, married! You seem so naive . . ."

"Please, Ian," she breathed, "I want to sit down."

"What's wrong?" he asked stupidly.

"Nothing." She spun away, rustling the yards of shimmering white silk, and sought her husband's side.

Gaard was speaking to Leif but turned to Dawnlyn when he saw her plight. "Are you unwell?" he asked with concern, sweeping her frame, his eyes narrowed.

"I am fine," she replied dejectedly.

"That fool Ian has upset you, hasn't he?" Gaard glanced darkly at his brother-in-law, who stood drinking heavily.

"No . . . yes," she said softly. "But it doesn't matter. He has always said the most unthinking things. He is young."

"I should cut his tongue out!" Gaard's whole body tensed, his eyes turned deep gray.

"No, you will not. Please, Gaard! Please, can't you just let well enough alone?"

Gaard shot her a surprised look. "Now that we are wed, you have suddenly grown bolder," he said with a hint of amusement.

Dawnlyn's eyes widened. "Not bolder, my lord. It is merely that I shall not tolerate bloodshed on the day of my marriage."

"*You* will not tolerate!" He laughed abruptly.

"Aye. Is that asking so much?" She stood her ground, hands on hips.

"By Odin, woman," Gaard chuckled deeply, "you soundly amaze me at times!"

Even Leif grinned at Dawnlyn's bemused look—normally, she seemed so timid, so shy in Gaard's presence. And now she dared to tell him what he would and would not do and did not even realize her temerity.

"Come," said Leif. "I would like to claim a dance with you before Gaard has you locked away!"

Still bewildered as to their amusement, Dawnlyn allowed Leif to take her hand and lead her to the slow circling steps.

"So you have lost your fear of our jarl?" said Leif more soberly.

"What?" she asked.

"The way you spoke to him just then—you showed no fear."

"I do not really fear him. At least, I have no reason to," she mused aloud.

"Then the Scotswoman has had a change of heart toward her captor?" His words were the slightest touch bitter.

Dawnlyn thought for a moment. "I don't know, Leif. Truly, the answer eludes me."

He gazed on her for a long moment, his blue eyes caressing her, making her feel quite naked under his glance. "Might I be permitted to say something?" he asked quietly.

"Please . . . don't . . ." she said.

"Oh, Dawnlyn," he said, his arm tightening around her. "Would that you had not exchanged the vows."

"But we have, Leif," she said hastily. "It is done."

"You love him, don't you? Admit it—he is so strong and powerful. Surely any woman would love him." His voice was shaded with regret and anger and no reply came to her mind.

No. She did not love Gaard. That he greatly pleasured her flesh did not constitute love. "Leif," she said, meeting his eyes straightforwardly, "you must not speak that way. What is done is done. I cannot speak of these things with you."

"But you, I suspect, cannot lie to me, either." He led her over to a quieter corner of the hall, still turning her slim body to the tingling music. "You do care about me, don't you?" he said then, unwilling to release her when she began to turn away.

"I don't!" she breathed, her eyes snapping up to his. "You have greatly mistaken friendship for more!"

"Yet you almost kissed me. You cannot deny that to me." He held her arm tightly now. "I felt you trembling that day . . . I know I did!"

"No," she said firmly, gazing at his hand on her arm. "You mistook my fright for . . . for passion." And then, "Now let me be. I am wed now. I should like to remain your friend, Leif, but that is all."

"You are lying . . ."

"No, I am not. Had I allowed the kiss, then you would have just cause for such talk; but I did not." Leif dropped her arm. "It does not matter that we *nearly* embraced, Leif. Don't you see? Nothing happened. It never could have . . ."

Leif did not speak another word to her as they finished the dance, both of them stiff and uncomfortable. Why did he pursue her so? It was as if he could not help himself, as if he were forced to by something beyond him. He did not really *want* her. No, it was something more—a game he played, a ploy to gain Gaard's attention? But that was self-destructive.

Gaard was drinking with Knute and several others when Dawnlyn returned. He paid her no mind this time, apparently satisfied to leave her to her own devices for the time being, and continued pouring ale down his throat.

Without his noticing, Dawnlyn sought Elspeth's company. "I fear my husband is celebrating with great determination," she commented in irritation, wishing the ordeal to end.

Elspeth patted her hand. "Then he honors you, for it shows he is pleased with the day's event."

"Is he?" Dawnlyn glanced over to where Gaard stood, a casual shoulder leaning against a beam. Then abruptly her being was overcome with cold, sweeping alarm. She studied his form more closely.

He was an utter and complete stranger to her suddenly—

a man whose face and figure did not even look familiar, whose mind was as hidden from her as that of the wild boar who rutted in the forest.

And yet he was her husband!

Apprehension squeezed her gut with near panic. My dear Lord, what had she done?

Her face must have shown some of her inner turmoil, for at that moment Elspeth gave a soft laugh. "After one is wed," she observed shrewdly, "the partner looks strange and unfamiliar, is that not so?"

"But why is that?" Dawnlyn stared openly at him now. The way his hair fell in rumpled waves around his face and neck—she'd never really noticed how fair and curled it was. And his shoulders, they seemed broader somehow. Had he grown taller? Had his nose always been quite so jutting, curved down in that arc? "It is most peculiar," she reflected, sensing that everything had changed now that she was married—everything.

"Well," said Elspeth, "is he more handsome or less so?" Her smooth face still held an amused, knowledgeable look.

"He is . . . he is just different," reflected Dawnlyn. "Everything is."

"And you are wondering how you will ever survive these changes in your life."

"Aye. I was thinking just that." Dawnlyn gazed at her mother-in-law with amazement. Was the woman a sorceress to read her mind?

"Everyone feels that way, Dawnlyn. Even Gaard must sense a change."

"I wonder. He seems not really . . . human."

Elspeth laughed. "But he is. And when you realize how very human my son is, then your life will take shape and form, whereas now it must seem amorphous indeed."

"Oh, Lady Elspeth," Dawnlyn whispered, "you are such a comfort. I wish we were not leaving . . ."

A small cloud settled over Elspeth's features. "But you will not be leaving . . . not immediately. You cannot travel across the sea until your child is born."

"But . . ." gasped Dawnlyn, "I . . . Does Gaard know? I'd have thought—"

"Does he know? Of course he knows, my dear. It is *his* plan, not mine."

Dawnlyn lazed in the warm tub of water, wondering how she would spend all these lonely months ahead in Norway. And what if Leif would not leave her alone? What if the handsome youth kept pursuing her until Gaard took notice? God! How she longed to be home. It seemed that she was dealt one blow after another, and everyone expected her to keep turning the other cheek.

In a short while Gaard would come to her, as her husband this night of their marriage. Envisioning him standing tall in the portal caused her heartbeat to quicken. How very innocent of men she had been before Gaard. And now she ached for the pleasure he would bring her—at least, she thought, there was *that* between them if nothing more. It was a strangely secure feeling being held in his arms, and she longed to feel as safe all her waking hours, not just the few rare moments when he held her.

Dawnlyn's hand touched the flat of her stomach beneath the water. Soon she would swell with his child. The notion was both thrilling and, at the same time, threatening. What would it be like to be a mother? Everything was happening so quickly, and precisely where she fit into the scenario eluded her. Where did her worth lie now that she would not become a nun but was instead bound forever to this Viking?

She closed her eyes, letting her thoughts wash over her, waiting for Gaard, wondering how long he would be. And their chamber seemed suddenly very empty without him.

Gaard poured himself another ale. He knew Dawnlyn had retired and was awaiting him, but somehow he wasn't quite ready to go to her.

His men teased him wickedly about his marriage. "No more roving the seas for you!" laughed Knute, his teeth showing through the thick red beard. "Perhaps you better watch your ale consumption! Lady Dawnlyn is a Scot, she'll not appreciate your drunkenness!"

It was all in good humor, and Gaard took another flagon of ale with each jest until his head was buzzing and his vision blurred. But still they would not let him go to Dawnlyn and complained that he was too sober to warm her bed on this auspicious night.

So Gaard drank more, and more, enjoying himself fully, jesting with the others late into the night, while they clanged swords together, wrestled, whirled the serving girls to the cheerful, tinkling music. The women guests had left already; Elspeth, too, had retired as the hour grew late—only the menfolk and sporting wenches remained to usher in the new day.

That Dawnlyn had gone to their chamber half a day ago mattered nothing whatsoever to Gaard when he rested his head on his arm and fell into a deep, drunken slumber.

He awoke with the precocious northern dawn and a headache that felt as if his temples were being pressed together in a vise. Groggy, he rose from the table, stumbled into a chair and half-fell over a sleeping form.

"By Odin's teeth!" he swore, his head pounding so miserably he was certain he would die. Vaguely he remembered he had a wife, but so great was his pain that nothing mattered at that moment.

He made his way, swaying, out into the courtyard. Even the weak morning light caused him to squint and press a hand to his forehead. He took a deep breath, wandered out through the barricade and crossed the grassy meadow. Shortly he found himself on the beach, the fresh salt air mildly reviving him.

Perhaps he would live after all.

He stripped off his fine wedding clothes, letting them fall in a sad heap on the sand, and stood naked in the first tremulous rays of sun.

With long strides his powerful legs took him to the tide line, and then he was walking in, turning his torso against the waves, slicing through the cold water.

Doing an easy breaststroke, his arms carried him surely through the swells. He dunked his head, came up shaking it to clear the cobwebs. He swam until the sun fully caressed the beach and warmed his head. Finally awake, feeling invigorated by the cold water, he walked from the sea, his lean, tanned body dripping, catching the dawnfire gloriously. He might have been a god emerging from the water so beautiful a spectacle did he make—powerful, bronzed, virile, the water running in gilded shining channels down breast and belly and long, muscled thighs.

While he dressed he thought of Dawnlyn, of the fact that the young girl—his wife, now—was still waiting for him in their chamber, waiting, and no doubt irate. And then he asked himself why he had done such a thing to her. He wanted her, as much as any man could ever want a woman. So why? What was there in that room that had kept him away?

Perhaps it was the new responsibility, an unaccustomed burden for him. He was used to watching over his men, his worldly possessions, his ships. But a wife? And one who carried his child? It seemed a weighty encumbrance indeed. For thirty-five years he had made his way alone, and now a terrible measure of responsibility waited in that room.

Dawnlyn was asleep when he closed the door carefully, slid back out of his damp clothes. For a long while he stood at the bedside gazing down on her in the morning light. She *was* young, her flesh as smooth and silken as an exotic Mediterranean bloom, her curves soft and womanly, the breasts beneath the coverlet rising and falling, beckoning to be touched, kissed.

"Dawnlyn," he said in a husky voice. "Wake up."

She stirred, opened her eyes tentatively. "Gaard?"

He smiled, a crooked, lopsided grin. "I have no excuse for keeping you waiting. I drank far too much, then fell asleep."

She studied him for a moment. "Your hair is wet," she observed.

"I swam to clear my head. Are you angry?"

184

"Aye," she replied softly. "I wanted to run away and hide and cause you great worry. But then I fell asleep."

"I am glad. Don't ever run from me, Dawnlyn." He lay down beside her, his head propped on a hand. With the other, he slowly pulled the coverlet away and gazed at her beauty.

She blushed beneath his close regard, then remembered. "Your mother told me that you plan to stay here until the child is born."

"Yes. I would not endanger my wife and child heedless-ly—"

"But Gaard," she interrupted, "I want to return to Scotland. I don't want to spend the winter here!"

"You do not like it here?" His hand moved over the ripe swell of a breast.

Dawnlyn gasped with sensation, felt her nipple harden beneath his hand. "I wish to go home," she breathed. "Everything here is so strange . . ."

Gaard's head followed the path of his hand, his lips lightly brushed the curve of her bosom. "Ah, little one," he said quietly, "you will have me the whole winter long to comfort you. You will grow to love it here as I do."

But would she? Dawnlyn wondered. Then her thoughts became jumbled, and as her breathing quickened she forgot all else save the tune Gaard played on her flesh with his hands, his lips, his powerful male body.

Gaard kissed the whole length of her, her breasts, her hips, her thighs, which he parted with a hand, running his tongue along the soft white flesh. Dawnlyn sucked in her breath when his lips met her core, and she could not have stopped him now even if she wanted to. She let him possess her thoroughly, let him taste of her at his leisure while the blood beat violently in her veins and her womb ached for release. Her legs fell apart farther and her fingers wrapped themselves in his damp hair as her back arched and the pulse of her core quickened until waves of delight washed over her and she cried aloud.

"You were made for pleasure, my wife," Gaard whispered, rising over her to sink himself deep within her moist center.

Dawnlyn received him fully, rising to meet his thrusts, pressing her hips to his in blinding desire.

And she thought fleetingly that, had she become a nun, there would never have been this. How could a woman live without it? How naive she must have been . . .

As she rose to meet his heavy thrusts her body shuddered and again sought release, feeling pulse after pulse of passion consume her whole being until she lay panting beneath him, covered in a pearly sheen of moisture.

Gaard, too, was sated but did not wish to let her go. They dozed, body locked to body, until again he grew hard within her and Dawnlyn twisted beneath him, ran her hands along the hard muscles of his back, unable to know him well enough.

"You sap my strength," he remarked lightly.

She smiled. "It is you who began this, my lord."

And he slipped his hands beneath her hips and brought her up to him, taking her fully, with a demand he had never shown before. She wondered at this, delighting in it, thinking there must be many ways to perform the act and wanting, suddenly, to know them all.

Later, much later, while Gaard slept peacefully, a casual arm flung over her breasts, Dawnlyn thought that if only they could remain thus forever she would live through the ordeal of marriage. Yet she knew it could not be. Soon he would rise and go about his manly duties and she would be left alone again and the loneliness would be unbearable. How would she spend her days, her nights when he was off on his ship? How would she survive? His existence was so clearly defined. Where was *her* worth, *her* destiny?

Carefully, without disturbing him, she nestled closer to his warm, solid flesh, to his undeniable strength and closed her eyes, willing the moment to last a lifetime.

Chapter Thirteen

GAARD HAD BEEN GONE TWO WEEKS ON A TRADING EXPEDITION to Trondheim and Dawnlyn was near to going out of her mind with brooding. He had explained to her that he could not avoid the trip, since it involved some very complicated business regarding Karl's estate. As it was to be a swift journey in, very likely, bad weather, he could not possibly take her along. "And besides, there is my mother to keep you company and all those 'little things' to make for the baby," he had remarked offhandedly.

So he had sailed off into a golden autumn afternoon and Dawnlyn was left behind to stitch and knit and gossip with Meg or Elspeth. And all the while, she was positive that Gaard was bored with her, disgusted by her growing girth, and had gone off to meet with Astrid, who surely knew how to lure a man from a wife forced upon him by necessity.

It was a soggy, gray September afternoon so that she was stuck inside, not allowed to lift a finger to do anything worthwhile for fear that it might "hurt the baby." Hurt the baby! What about *her*? She would die from boredom and then where would their precious baby be?

She sighed fretfully and dropped the embroidery in her lap. She was tired of stitching, too, and that was all the activity Elspeth seemed to allow her. It was not *their* fault, none of them; they only wanted her to be well. She was cranky sometimes, which they all overlooked, infuriatingly, and blamed on her condition.

If only she had something to *do*.

Everyone, except Dawnlyn, was busy preparing for the winter: tanning and sewing furs and boots, butchering, salting and drying fish and meat, pickling vegetables, storing and counting and collecting! And they wouldn't let her help, but refused with such concern that she could not become angry.

The only person who seemed to treat her as a human being and not some sort of *holy vessel* was Leif Haraldsson, but Gaard seemed to keep *him* especially busy, and he was often gone on trips to Stavanger or Oslo or Trondheim as Gaard's representative on matters of trade or on official business. Still, when the handsome young Viking was at Thorkellhall, his company was pleasant, Dawnlyn had to admit. And, too, he had not pressed her of late concerning their "near kiss" and seemed to truly desire her friendship.

She picked up the fine piece of white linen and began to stitch with silk the pale blue wing of an angel; it was to be a new altar cloth for Father Tancred's chapel.

A laughing voice interrupted her self-indulgent reverie. "Lady Dawnlyn, why do you look so glum?" asked a familiar voice from across the great hall.

Quickly she looked up. It was Leif, just returned from an errand, for his cheeks were ruddy with the chill autumn air and his soft brown hair tousled by the wind.

"Oh, hello, Leif. I am not glum, only bored. I should be used to it by now, shouldn't I?"

He strode across the intervening space, so lithe and full of energy it invigorated her just to see him. His lips were creased in a white smile, dispelling the gloom in the hall. "Come, now, you should not be bored! We'll think of something for you to do!"

"If only . . . but there are so many things I'm not allowed . . ."

"Nonsense! I saw my mother bear six fine children, and she worked along with everyone until she was indecently huge. It did them no harm!"

"But Elspeth—"

"She's only overprotective because it's her first grandchild." He smiled. "Now this is our plan." He winked at her while the other bold blue eye laughed at her hesitation. "I'll take you for a short ride on the gentlest horse we have if you promise to walk the horse the whole way. I've a free afternoon, as Gaard is not back from Trondheim yet, and I happen to know Elspeth is visiting a sick thrall."

Lord, but his offer was tempting! Did she dare? "I . . . I don't know if—"

"Come, now!" he urged. "It can do you no harm. And," he added, smiling, "I shall be the perfect gentleman."

"You promise?"

"I do."

With no further hesitation, Dawnlyn rose. "I'll need my cloak and boots. I'll meet you in the stable." And she was off, her tinkling laughter echoing in the great hall, her jewel-hued skirts rustling.

It was nearing the early autumn dusk when Gaard pushed open the giant doors of the Hall and strode in with Knute and Ian at each shoulder like Odin's ravens.

He had begun to shout for bath water to be heated and was searching the great hall for Dawnlyn when he saw his mother standing square in his path, a pale, solemn expression on her face.

He stopped, eyed her questioningly. "What is it? Has the harvest not been going well? Can't it wait? I'm dirty and tired and want a bath."

"Gaard." Elspeth's normally calm voice was brittle.

"What is it? Must I be bothered the minute I return? I . . ." Then his mouth snapped shut, his intense gaze pinioned her. "It's Dawnlyn, isn't it? The baby . . . ?"

"She's all right . . . I think. She went for a ride today. She had a fall."

"A *what?*" he exploded in rage.

"A ride. For Lordsakes, son, we can't keep her immobile for nine months. She said she was bored."

"Bored! She has every luxury, everything she wants or needs and more!" He headed toward the corridor that led to their room. "Is she hurt? I'll flog the craven fool that gave her a horse!"

Elspeth rushed to his side, followed him down the corridor. "Gaard, do not be angry with her. It's frightened her half out of her wits already, though I fear she's more afraid of you than anything."

"Me? But I only want her to be well. Why should she fear *me?*" He turned storm-gray eyes on his mother, his brows drawn together harshly.

"You've a way about you, son, that can be very intimidating . . ."

He burst into her room, stopped on the threshold, suddenly unsure of how he was to behave. Was he furious or frightened? Should he be tender with her or firm? By Odin's beard, this business with women was complicated!

"Dawnlyn?" His voice emerged softly.

She was bundled under the eiderdown in the great, shadowed bed, her copper-hued eyes scared and rebellious as she lay propped against the pillows, her hair like a blood stain against the white linen.

"Yes, Gaard?" Her voice was wary, noncommittal.

He approached the bed, knelt by her side. "Are you well?"

"Yes, I am fine. Nothing happened—"

"You fell from a horse!"

"It was nothing. I was going at a walk and the mare stepped in a hole and stumbled. Your mother is treating me like an invalid! Gaard, please don't scold me."

"Scold you? I only wish for your health and happiness and that of my son."

"We are both well, although why you insist it will be a *son* . . . It could be a daughter, you know."

"It will be a son and he will be perfect and *that* is why you cannot take any chances with your health."

"But, Gaard, what about *me?* I am allowed no freedom, no duties, nothing. Am I worth nothing but a female body to grow sons for you?" She watched him with defiant tears in her eyes.

"You? You are my *wife.*" His tone was one of surprised indignation.

Dawnlyn's lips compressed tightly. "Yes, that is all, *your* wife."

"Is that not enough?"

"It must be, I have no choice."

Gaard looked at her, recognizing the bitterness in her voice but not understanding its source. "Do you still pine for the cloister?" he asked gruffly.

Dawnlyn closed her eyes tiredly. "No. It is too late for that now."

"Who gave you that horse? Who allowed you to go?" Gaard asked, diverting the conversation to less treacherous waters.

"I decided. I wanted to go. Leif took me."

"Leif!" Gaard's iron-gray eyes narrowed, pinned her gaze down.

"Aye," she said stubbornly. "He treats me like a human being, at least."

"I'll have his heart on a plate," snarled Gaard. "I *knew* it!"

"Knew what? For sweet Jesus' sake, Gaard! He's a friend, he took me for a short ride. I enjoyed it! If you touch one hair of his head . . . It was not his fault!" She sat up in the bed, her eyes wild, her tangled hair tumbling about her shoulders.

Gaard's eyes narrowed, he drew back from her. "And why do you protect this Leif?"

"Because you would punish him for something that is *my* fault!"

He hovered over the bed for long moments, weighing her

words. Was there something going on between her and Leif? Was that why she protected him? But no, she looked so innocent, so genuinely disturbed that he feared to upset her more. "I will not punish the boy," he growled out reluctantly between clenched teeth. "I give my word."

"Thank you, Gaard," she sighed, sinking back on the pillows. "I know you are a fair man."

A fair man! He was ready to throttle Leif Haraldsson! The young upstart! The treacherous pup!

"Will you be all right?" he asked, fighting down his anger.

"Yes, I am fine, truly." Then she hesitated, her tawny eyes lowered, shaded by spiky dark lashes. "Gaard?"

"Yes?"

"I am glad you are back . . ."

He was startled, remembering suddenly that he'd just returned from a two-week voyage. "Oh, yes," he stumbled. "I've not seen you for some time, little one, have I?"

"No." Her eyes met his, full of regret and welcome, exasperation and acceptance. "Was it a good trip?"

"Yes," he replied automatically, his mind whirling with puzzled gladness. Never before had he had a wife to welcome him back.

He strode into the great hall straight toward Leif, who stood respectfully, straightening his back even more than usual.

"I wish a word with you, Leif Haraldsson," he growled, jerking his head toward a quiet corner. He saw the young man pale and felt a slight satisfaction.

"My lord," Leif began quickly, "I know what you wish to discuss. It was my fault, my fault entirely. The lady—"

"The *lady* is my wife, you young pup, and I'll thank you not to forget it, not for a second!" Gaard's brows drew together like daggers and his bulk loomed over Leif like a towering mountain.

"Yes, my lord." Leif's head was bowed to Gaard's authority, but, still, something in his voice did not give the impression of humility, at least not enough to suit Gaard. "I know you think it was foolish," Leif continued, "but the lady Dawnlyn was so sad, I only wanted to cheer her a little. I meant no harm."

"What you *meant* has nothing to do with it! She or the baby may be harmed and I will count it your fault!"

"Yes, my lord, I will accept any punishment you deem worthy of my crime." The words were said contritely but with the barest hint of insolence underlining the word *crime*. It made Gaard's eyes snap around to meet Leif's more intently.

"I promised my wife not to punish you, more's the pity," grated out Gaard menacingly.

"Then I benefit from the fact that you are a man of your word," said Leif very quietly, meeting Gaard's angry gray eyes with his own bright blue ones. There was something significant in his gaze, but Gaard could not grasp it, so quickly did it fade, to be replaced by one of calm acceptance. "I thank you for your mercy and understanding, my lord."

But somehow the smooth words did not seem the least bit remorseful to Gaard.

As it turned out, there was nothing at all amiss with Dawnlyn's pregnancy from the fall, as she told Gaard and Elspeth repeatedly, but they were both loathe to let her out of bed until she took matters in her own hands and appeared in the great hall the next morning to join the household in breakfast.

"I may not be built like a horse, as these Viking women of yours are," said Dawnlyn with a hint of smugness in her voice, "but Renfrews have been populating St. Abb's for four hundred years. And I am much more durable than you seem to think. I refuse to stay in bed."

"Perhaps she's right, my son," said Elspeth, patting Dawnlyn's hand. "We've been overzealous in watching her."

"Mother," began Gaard, then noticed the two women ranged against him, one hopeful, the other totally self-assured. He gave up. "All right," he growled. "She can do what she wants, *within reason,* but no more riding."

"Yes, husband," said Dawnlyn meekly, but golden laughter spilled from her copper eyes. She began to eat a hearty meal of black bread, butter and cheese and autumn apples, planning with Elspeth between bites just what household responsibilities she might assume.

Gaard himself had to admit Dawnlyn was more cheerful when she began a regular routine at Thorkellhall. Elspeth gave her the dairy for her realm, and Dawnlyn was quite happy there, overseeing the milking, skimming, churning butter, making the rich, golden-brown goat cheese and the pale, sweating rounds of milder cheese from cow's milk, then counting and storing the lot.

"You smell like sour milk!" complained Gaard at the evening meal, wrinkling his nose.

"At least I am busy. What's a little dairy smell? Look"— she spread her slim white hands, palms up, with a wide grin—"I have blisters from churning. Isn't that wonderful?"

"Wonderful! You're a foolish girl," said Gaard, frowning.

"I am no *girl,* my lord, nor am I foolish. Our lord God says, 'Idle hands are the devil's plaything.' "

By early October, Thorkellhall was well provisioned, the ships were ready to be dry-docked for the winter and the store rooms were bursting with game enough for many weeks. Gaard found the time growing heavy on his hands and almost envied his busy, blooming wife her duties.

At night she was tired and fell asleep early while he remained in the great hall with his men, playing games with the walrus-tusk dice, drinking, listening to the bard retell the old sagas. It was a mundane existence, one he'd rarely tasted before, never having had a hall of his own nor a family. He wondered if Sweyn was just as bored back in Scotland and wished for some small reason to launch *Wind Eater,* or swing his sword, *Lightning Bolt,* or make a small excursion to punish an offender of the law, even in a minuscule matter. But nothing came up; the Hall ran smoothly and his subjects were happy. Even King Olaf had informed Leif that he accepted Gaard as the new jarl at Thorkellhall. And the autumn remained unseasonably mild.

Late one afternoon there was a sudden rain squall that blustered damply off the North Sea. Gaard had been overseeing the tarring of the ships for winter but left off as the rain began to slant in and run under his collar.

Shaking the drops off his woolen cloak as he stepped into the Hall, he did not at first notice the visitor sitting by the fire, seeking shelter from the sudden storm. It wasn't until he heard his name being called from across the room that he noticed who had arrived at Thorkellhall in his absence.

"Gaard, my friend, it has been so long! Why, I haven't seen you since before your marriage." The soft, insinuating voice reached across the intervening space and curled softly into his ear.

"Astrid," he said, surprised. "And how have you fared this fine autumn?"

She had risen and was walking with her characteristic hip-rolling gait toward him, her long flaxen hair swinging in rhythm, her lips red as ripe cherries and smiling. "I have been very sad and my father says I am impossible to live with." She attempted a pout, but her eyes flashed mischievously at him through the fringe of her lashes.

"Why are you sad?" asked Gaard. "Are you unwell?"

"Yes," she pouted, "for you have not been to visit."

"Me?" He was genuinely surprised. "But I am a married man."

"And are you thus dead and buried to your old friends?" she asked, hands on hips. Then she relented and smiled beguilingly at him, linking her arm into his. "Tell me how you are settling down to married life. Does it suit you?"

They sat on a bench by the fire and Gaard gestured to a thrall for refreshments to be served before he answered. "It suits me right well. I have no complaints."

"But no joyous ravings either, I take it?" laughed Astrid archly, showing all of her even white teeth.

"I did not say that," replied Gaard seriously. "Astrid, there is something I wanted to talk to you about. I did not have the opportunity before."

"Well, here I am, Gaard, at your beck and call. Speak." And she pressed herself against him, somehow managing to brush his arm with the side of a full, ripe breast.

"It is about my marriage. I wanted to explain that I'm sorry if I left you expecting a betrothal. But then there was that fiasco with Karl and my banishment. I had to find lands elsewhere and thus I took the Renfrew's keep. You can see, of course, that I had to take the woman, also—to keep the peace."

"And did you have to *marry* her, too?" asked Astrid, for the first time allowing a gleam of enmity to dart from her ice-blue eyes.

Gaard was silent for the length of a heartbeat. "It seems that I did," was all he said.

"Nevertheless, you are still my *friend,* are you not? You are welcome at my father's Hall still."

"Yes, I am your friend, Astrid, and will try to visit your Hall one of these days." He nodded, wondering why, indeed, he had not been to any of his neighbors' Halls of late.

"Good! That is settled, and now I wish to be entertained while I wait out this accursed storm. Shall we play with the dice, or would you prefer a game of chess?"

"Make it chess, for I am weary unto death with dice. I have lost a dozen silver coins to Knute this week."

So they wiled away the rainy afternoon playing chess by the fire and talking of old times when Astrid and Karl and Gaard had been children romping together in the Norwegian forests.

Astrid took great care not to appear too forward, or to disturb Gaard's cautious friendship. It was obvious he took his marriage vows more seriously than she could have wished, but soon he was relaxed and laughing, having fallen into their old pattern of bantering and bawdy jesting. It was true he won every game they played, partly because Astrid let him, but also because she could not stop herself from hungering for his masculine beauty, or from being distracted by his painful nearness.

Dawnlyn awoke from her nap and saw that it was raining outside, the autumn light fading rapidly. She wondered whether it had interfered with Gaard's work today, then decided to see if he was in the great hall. Perhaps he had some time to spend with her since the weather was so inclement.

She brushed her hair and donned a clean gown—a pale lilac wool—that almost succeeded in disguising the growing swell of her stomach. She turned sideways to the polished silver mirror and stretched up on her toes to examine her profile. Yes, she was definitely becoming quite pear-shaped. Gaard always told her he liked her new shape, but she didn't put much faith in his words. How could *anyone* like such a bloated figure?

She slipped down the darkening corridor toward the great hall and paused on the threshold, searching the big room for Gaard. It was, as usual, half-filled with men and women— warriors, servants, thralls, traveling merchants—gathering for the evening meal.

The fire threw a dancing glow over the people in the hall while she searched for Gaard's tall, golden-haired form.

There he was, sitting by the fire, bent over a chessboard. She began to make her way toward him, then stopped in her tracks like an arrow-pierced doe.

Opposite Gaard, bent over the chessboard, too, was the white-gold head of Astrid. As Dawnlyn watched, the Viking girl's face rose to Gaard's, spoke some words and he smiled fondly at her. Then Astrid put out a slim alabaster hand loaded down with jeweled rings, touched Gaard intimately on the arm and spoke again, her ruby lips moving slowly, sensuously.

Dawnlyn stood there, hurt in her heart, unable to move or think for a moment. Then, when she could, she slipped back into the dark corridor as quietly as a mouse, her heart lurching sickeningly, unshed tears welling in her eyes.

She was completely unaware that Elspeth stood on the threshold of her own room and had viewed the entire scene, shaking her head with chagrin over Dawnlyn's pain. The older woman had seen the restless gleam growing in her son's gray eyes; whatever its source she knew it presaged trouble.

Chapter Fourteen

CHRIST'S MASS AND THE VIKINGS' WINTER SOLSTICE CELEBRATION came and went. December had seen little sun in Norway, and when it was visible through the gray, it was merely a weak, watery orb arcing low on the horizon. It seemed dusk was always upon them, and everyone awaited spring doggedly, especially Dawnlyn, who wanted only to see the child born and return to St. Abb's.

The time came for Gaard and his men to make ready for a long hunting expedition. Dawnlyn watched, wishing he would not be gone the full two weeks. And yet, she knew, he must go and provide for the people of Thorkellhall—he would always be going or returning from somewhere, from places of which she had never even heard. The thought did not comfort her in the least.

"I have decided to leave Knute here to watch over you and Mother," he told her while checking his fur coat and hunting gear one last time.

"Why Knute?" Dawnlyn asked. Knute was such an oaf—kind, but bungling and dull.

"He is trustworthy." Gaard suddenly stopped sharpening a small knife, met her eyes with his. "Would you prefer Leif to remain at the Hall?"

"Of course I would," she replied honestly. "Leif is a most interesting man."

"A pup! He's hardly a man yet and unproven in battle. How could he protect you?" Gaard's eyes were dark now, stormy—she saw in them a strange, barely controlled emotion that made her repent of her words. "Knute stays here. That is final." He turned away from her and sought the others who awaited his orders.

"Fare well," Dawnlyn whispered, wondering why Gaard had not kissed her, or even said good-bye this time. Perhaps, she thought darkly, she was too swollen, too hideous for him to bother with now. If only the child would come, she mused, if only her time were nearer.

Abruptly another thought seized her: perhaps her admission that she would have preferred Leif's company had angered Gaard. Was it possible for her husband to be jealous and keep the emotion to himself? If he were jealous of her friendship with Leif, well, then, he should simply come out and say so. Then she thought that when Gaard returned, it was time to air this thing—this ridiculous jealousy of Leif and perhaps, too, her own hidden feelings toward Astrid.

Aye, Dawnlyn decided, these things that cropped up between them would most definitely be brought to light, and soon . . .

On horseback, Gaard led his fur-clad men away from the Hall toward the northeastern forests where they would hunt and fish. The supplies they needed were packed on shaggy, sure-footed ponies: dried fish, warm fur robes, hickory skis on which they could trek silently through the deep snow or cross a frozen lake to ice-fish.

The going was slow—even the compact, thick-furred Norwegian Elkhounds had trouble moving through the deep snows of December. They crossed rivers, meadows, the lake country, until the heavily wooded forests of the hills lay before them, promising red deer and elk, perhaps ptarmigan —a tender treat.

Gaard made camp at the edge of an aspen grove, a short distance from a wide meadow where hopefully the deer and elk would winter-feed as the deep snow drove them from the glacial forest. Within a few days they had hanging in camp a bull elk and three red deer. He was pleased with the kill, pleased with the performance of his men and dogs in spite of the temperatures, which nipped hands and feet painfully.

On the fourth evening, they sat around the fire, huddled beneath their fur blankets, sipping on mead stored in skin pouches. Gaard was quiet, pleased with his own skills that day while fishing a deep lake. He glanced at his men, smiled at their ribald jokes—they were a good, hardy lot.

Light, powdery snow had begun to fall gently, nestling itself in their fur, dusting caps and shoulders and crossed legs. But the men were accustomed to the long winter, to the frequent snows that would feed and swell the rivers that spring. Only Leif seemed ill at ease, hanging back from the group, chewing sullenly on dried venison.

Gaard observed him carefully. The boy was an enigma, had been since the first. He had almost too easily given his allegiance to Gaard, too easily ensconced himself in the fold. And why? The answer eluded Gaard. It might be for Dawnlyn—Leif had obviously taken to her fragile beauty almost at once. Still, Gaard had a gut feeling that she was peripheral to Leif's true objectives, whatever they were.

The boy was intelligent, wise beyond his years, in truth. And Gaard sensed that he would be an excellent Lawspeaker some day. But there was something there, something behind the observant eyes, something hidden that Gaard did not wholly trust. At times when talking to the lad he itched to know what lay behind the smooth words, the too-easy smile.

Leif, as if sensing eyes on him, looked up, caught Gaard's pensive gaze. And then Gaard rose, walked towards the boy.

"I am pleased with the deer you felled yesterday, Leif," he said, easing his tall frame down beside him.

"Thank you," Leif replied. "It was my first."

"Then you are glad you rode along?"

"Yes. Although I would have preferred to remain at Thorkellhall. I have much studying to do if I am to prove my worth to you, my lord."

Gaard's eyes narrowed slightly. Was that the *only* reason the boy would have stayed behind? "And why must you prove your worth? There are years ahead to do so. Why is it, Leif," he said slowly, levelly, "that you are in such haste to please me?"

Leif opened his mouth to speak but then seemed to change his mind.

"Could it be," Gaard went on, "that it is not me you wish to please but my wife?"

"No!" Leif's eyes snapped around to meet Gaard's. "No. That is not true."

"You don't find her attractive, then?"

"I do . . . but that is not it. I only wish to have a good position someday. I am anxious to secure my future."

Gaard was oppressively silent for a long moment, then said, "You are lying, boy. I do not know why, but I shall tell you one thing and you best hear me well . . ." His tone was dangerous now, low and as deadly as a knife's blade. "Keep away from my wife. I will not have you near her or near my son, for that matter, when he is born. Do I make myself quite clear?"

A murderous look flashed across Leif's eyes in the patterned firelight, then fled quickly. "You have made yourself clear, Gaard Wolftooth. I shall not go near the Lady Dawnlyn lest I *taint* your son." The young boy rose, turned his back on Gaard and walked toward the trees, where he disappeared into the quiet veil of snow.

It was not until hours later, as the Viking men slept peacefully, that the sentry posted to watch for bears awakened Gaard.

"It is Leif," the Norseman said, stooping beside Gaard. "The dogs barked a while ago, and a mount is gone."

Gaard's heart pounded furiously in his chest as he leaped

to his feet. For the first time in his life, he knew fear. "I ride to Thorkellhall," he said quickly, his gray eyes black and lethal.

Dawnlyn was awakened in the quiet hours of early morning by a small sound in her chamber. It was the type of disturbance that did not fit into the usual pattern of nighttime noises and she sat up instantly, alert.

"Lady Elspeth?" she whispered, straining her eyes into the dark, her heartbeat quickening. "Gaard? Who is there?"

Slowly, while she held her breath, she could make out a shadow, a figure, near the door.

"Who is it?" Fear clutched at her sickeningly.

And then a voice, a young, stricken, male voice, reached across the chamber. "It is your fault . . . If it were not for you, Gaard would not be so blinded."

"Leif?" Her small voice quavered. "Is that you?"

"If he were rid of you then he would know—"

"Answer me! It's you, Leif, isn't it?"

Silence.

Slowly, slowly she slipped from the bed, gauged the distance between herself and the door. The shadow moved stealthily toward the bed, opening a path of escape if she were quick.

Not stopping to think, wanting only to escape this man— Leif, her mind kept repeating—she rushed for the door and was amazingly free, racing down the long corridor toward the great hall as fast as her burden would allow.

Where was Knute?

She could hear the man's footfalls behind her and felt the breath in her lungs snatched away. Why? her mind screamed, why would he want to harm her? What did he mean, "If he were rid of you . . ."?

There was no one in the firelit great hall. Desperately, Dawnlyn looked around for help. Where could she run?

Then suddenly there was a hand on her arm, spinning her around, and her eyes met Leif's cold, threatening, ice-blue gaze.

"Knute is gone from the hall on a false errand," he said. "There is no one to come to your aid."

"But why?" she cried. "Why do you want to harm me?"

"Gaard sees only you. He is blinded by your beauty and the precious burden you carry." And Leif placed a hand at the back of her head, wound his fingers into the thick, loose tresses.

"No!" she screamed, a thin, terrifed wail. "No!" But Leif was too strong for her and she could not pull away as his lips descended to hers. She twisted and fought against the assault but to no avail. And then he tore his mouth away and his hand covered her breast, squeezing it painfully while his lips moved to her neck.

Dawnlyn's mind reeled—was he going to rape her, in her condition? No! He couldn't, not Leif, not this young man who was her *friend!* No!

"Stop this, Leif!" she cried, struggling. "Stop!"

"There is no way to reach him," Leif groaned, "save through you . . ."

His hold had slackened slightly. Quickly Dawnlyn seized the moment and spun away, almost succeeding in freeing herself except that Leif had hold of her arm still, pulling her back toward him. They struggled that way, it seemed endlessly—a frozen tableau of conflicting wills.

Then, as she was losing ground, abruptly Dawnlyn was freed, falling back against the wall as Leif's grip on her was released.

It all happened so quickly it was moments before she realized Gaard was there, lifting Leif off his feet, slamming him into the unyielding wooden wall, then slamming him again and again until Leif crumpled at Gaard's feet, blood welling from a cut in his lip and one on his cheek.

Then Gaard drew his sword in a powerful swing and held it dangerously out to the side, ready to take the boy's head off.

"He didn't hurt me!" Dawnlyn cried. "Oh, no! Don't! Don't!"

"Go ahead," Leif choked, his eyes glaring defiantly up

into Gaard's. "Kill me! Kill me, you pig, and watch your own flesh and blood drip from your sword. Go on!"

Instant, horrifying revelation dazzled Dawnlyn's senses and she knew, realized she had always known. "Oh, my sweet Lord! Gaard! You mustn't!" And she lunged at Gaard, his arm ready to strike the death blow. "Stop!" she begged desperately, clinging to his arm with every ounce of strength she possessed. "He's your son!" she wept, breathless. "Look at him, Gaard, look! He *is* your son!"

The tension in Gaard's arm slackened imperceptibly. "What?"

"That's right, *Father*," hissed Leif. "I am your son. Go ahead and kill me and may you suffer a thousand more painful deaths!"

"My son?" Gaard's eyes searched the youth's face—his blue eyes, his hawkish nose, shaped so much like his own, the thin, cruel lips that turned downward now in loathing. "Are you . . . ?"

"Yes! I am your *bastard!*"

Gaard stood mutely frozen in his stance, his gray eyes wide in shock, his mouth hanging open, the sword still clasped in his strong hand. "My son?" he breathed, and his voice rang with utter bewilderment.

Chapter Fifteen

It was Dawnlyn who finally took command of the situation and tried to help Leif to stand. Gaard stood stock-still, his hand still gripping the sword's hilt, his eyes roaming the boy's face in disbelief.

"For God's sake, Gaard!" Dawnlyn cried, still trying to get Leif to his feet. "Fetch me a cloth so that I can clean Leif's cut. Go on, hurry, now." She managed to help Leif over to a chair in the hall and force him into it. "I'll get you an ale," she said quickly, seeing how the young man's hands shook with terrible emotion.

But Gaard could not move at first; all he could do was stand there numbly, stare at the boy—his son—thinking of the difference a split second could make: in that whisper of time he had nearly killed his own son.

Dawnlyn was at the ale keg; she turned to glance at Gaard from across the large room. "Gaard! Please," she called. "Leif is hurt!"

Without conscious thought, Gaard slowly sheathed his gleaming sword, forced himself to react to Dawnlyn's plea. And then he was by her side with a wet cloth, handing it to Dawnlyn. He went then to the keg and drew himself an ale, too.

"I'll do that myself," said Leif harshly, taking the cloth from Dawnlyn, his eyes still glaring hatred at Gaard and his wife.

Gaard took a long, pensive drink, wiped his mouth. "Who is your mother, Leif?" he asked, his tone more even and controlled now.

"As if you do not know!" spat Leif.

"If I knew," Gaard's eyes narrowed carefully, "then I'd not be asking you." Then, after a moment's thought, he added, "Whether or not you believe it, I had no knowledge of impregnating a woman before Dawnlyn. That is the truth."

Leif studied his father cautiously, his eyes filled with distrust. "You do not remember Helga? The Jarl Harald's wife? She was here not so long ago, at your *wedding* feast," Leif hissed, rubbing at the cut on his lip harshly.

"Helga is your mother?" asked Gaard, his mind racing back over the years.

"Tell me you never slept with her! Go ahead, deny it, Gaard Wolftooth!"

"But of course I did," replied Gaard simply. "It was before my three-year journey to the Mediterranean. I recall her well, in fact. A beautiful girl . . ."

Dawnlyn, embarrassed, thinking she should not want to hear these things, shrank away from them a few paces but still within earshot, unable to keep herself from listening.

"How easily you remember!" raged Leif. "And now you will tell me that you left not knowing her condition!"

Patiently now, with infinite care, Gaard replied, "That is correct. All you need do is ask Helga."

The boy was speechless for many moments. A display of conflicting emotions crossed his handsome features, the thoughts tormenting him. "She has always told me this," he whispered painfully, shaking his head. "But I merely assumed she protected your mighty legend, your *good* name. Can it be true? Did you really not know?"

"I did not have any idea she carried a child. When I

returned, I suppose I heard she had married. It's been so long, I truthfully do not recall. I was—what?—sixteen years old."

Then Leif's head snapped up, angry, questioning. "Would you have left had you known? Would you have married my mother? I think not!"

Gaard fell silent, looked for long minutes on Leif's face. "I cannot say. I was young, younger than you. I was filled with the longing to see the world, to be with my men and my ships. In truth, I do not know, for the past is gone now."

It took some while for Leif to assimilate this information. Finally, he sighed wearily, put his head in his hands. "I have hated you since I first found out from my mother that I was a bastard. And she bragged to me that I had the finest, most powerful of fathers in all Norway and that I should be proud! Proud to be your bastard!"

"Why did you not tell me this from the first? Why did you let me think—"

"Because I thought she lied about your not knowing of my existence. She was in such awe of you, I thought she protected you. You cannot imagine how my hate ate at me . . . I do not know what to say or think or do . . ."

Gaard placed a hand on Leif's tousled hair. "And to think what I said to you earlier—that you were not to be near my son. It is no wonder . . ."

Suddenly Leif's shoulders hunched and Dawnlyn saw him fight tears. "I would never have hurt Dawnlyn," Leif groaned. "She is the finest woman I have ever known." His eyes, filled with moisture, looked over at her. "I was so undone by what Gaard said to me . . . I don't know what madness overcame me."

Madness, yes, Dawnlyn thought, and hate and spite. Leif had used her—or had at least tried to use her somehow—to get to his father—to hurt Gaard through her. And then she wondered just how much Gaard had seen of Leif's attack; had he only seen Leif pulling at her arm or had he seen Leif kissing her?

Oh, dear God, she prayed silently, please don't let Gaard ever know what really happened . . .

"Oh, Lady Dawnlyn," Leif was saying, "I know I could never have hurt you . . . never!"

"I know," Dawnlyn whispered fervently. "I know you would not have."

Then Leif looked at Gaard. "Can you ever forgive me?"

"If you will forgive me my neglect for the past eighteen years. You should have been with me, Leif. We have much to make up for, do we not?" A tentative smile split Gaard's lips; his gaze fell steadily on the youth.

Then Dawnlyn watched a scene that filled her with hope and joy; she tried to focus the sweet pain into something she could stand. Gaard took Leif's shoulders, brought him to his feet, embraced him with gentleness and understanding until Leif, torn and hesitant, wrapped his arms around his father and let quiet tears wet Gaard's sturdy chest.

Confused and embarrassed, it was finally Leif who broke the contact. He stood away from Gaard, his eyes uncertain, staring at his father. Dawnlyn saw in him the pain and bitterness born of eighteen years of hatred and wondered if Leif could ever forgive the sin his father had unwittingly committed against him. The moment stretched out—Gaard expectantly awaiting Leif's next move, Leif not knowing what to do, his world of bitterness abruptly crumbling at his feet, leaving him alone and naked, unguarded by his resentment.

Gaard's expression was unreadable but sure and steady. "I want you here at the Hall . . . by my side, Leif. We will get to know one another as we should have years ago."

"I . . . I do not know. It is difficult," replied Leif, fumbling for words. "My whole life I have thought you truly knew about me. I thought you shunned my mother and she only protected you . . ."

"I understand."

"And now . . . it is too difficult . . ."

"Then I will take charge," said Gaard simply. "I will try to make amends and perhaps you will see the way in time."

The following evening Gaard summoned the inhabitants of Thorkellhall along with many neighboring houses to feast with them. Of course, Astrid and her father were there. Dawnlyn tried her best not to notice the way Astrid preened and strutted whenever Gaard's eyes turned in her direction. It was a painful and wearisome chore to be in the same room with the woman, but it was one she must face this night.

After the food was served Gaard stood, raised his gold and silver flagon and made the announcement that Leif Haraldsson would hereafter be called Leif Gaardson and would be left in charge of the Hall when Gaard was absent. "And," he continued, "when my son reaches the age I deem him matured, he will, with the King's permission, be given the Hall and be your next jarl."

Dawnlyn sat demurely by Gaard's side, watching the assembled Vikings but really quite removed from the emotions they displayed so boisterously. The women of the Hall, thralls and freewomen alike, cheered lustily at the announcement, for the smooth-spoken Leif had a way with words that caused the female heart to blossom like a wild posy. The men cheered, too, surprised at the revelation, but accepting it gladly and with good heart, for Gaard was a well-loved jarl and his offspring would be accepted as easily unless he proved otherwise.

Leif sat to the right of Gaard's stone seat, managing to look very self-important, very ill at ease and very young, all at the same time. Dawnlyn hid a smile as she watched Leif's expression change from intense happiness to discomfort to elation to embarrassment and back again. It seemed that the ultimate goal of his life, while greatly desired and sought after for years, was difficult to assimilate when achieved. It left him, for the first time in his life, as unprotected as a babe.

Still, she wondered if Gaard and Leif would ever truly trust one another; so many experiences, so many years stood staunchly between them. Then, too, she tried to explore her own feeling regarding Leif: her son would not be Gaard's firstborn. Did it matter greatly? she asked herself, for her son would still be the heir to St. Abb's Hall and all of its lands.

Leif had risen and was speaking, holding aloft a gem-studded flagon of mead. His voice was so youthful tonight, choked with emotion. "I am pleased to be accepted by my father and found worthy of his trust. I hope to live up to his faith in me. And"—here he stopped to gulp and take a deep, wavering breath—"I will endeavor to make him proud of me, although perhaps not in the fighting man's way. I am of a new generation and we must abide by our own times, which are those of the merchant and politician. Yet we all know of the tales of Gaard Wolftooth and are proud of the Viking heritage that he keeps strong! Let us drink a toast to my father"—the word was stumbled over, unfamiliar on his tongue—"and his lovely wife!"

He sat, his eyes meeting Dawnlyn's for an instant, then sliding away. He drank his mead much too quickly.

Helga and Harald were present that night and Gaard spoke privately with them both. Dawnlyn was not included in the meeting and felt somewhat left out in the cold. Even Elspeth's reassuring words could not soothe her discomfort.

"Gaard is not a young man," said Elspeth, sitting next to Dawnlyn. "There are many things in his past in which you cannot share. You must console yourself that you are his future, you and your son."

"But he has a son now."

"He has a son who is *virtually* a stranger. A boy whose life he did not mold nor share in. It is very different."

"I suppose," murmured Dawnlyn, glancing over to where Gaard sat with Lady Helga and her husband. And what was Gaard thinking when he spoke to the lovely Helga now? Did he recall the bed they had shared—or the way the woman's flesh had felt beneath his strong fingers? How could the three of them even sit together like that and speak? It seemed so terribly awkward. But then they were Vikings, and perhaps their feelings were guided by a different set of rules.

211

The great hall was alive with merriment and Dawnlyn felt that many eyes were upon her, wondering if she, too, would give the great leader a son. It was odd, but after a few awkward glances in her direction—and quite a few drinks—it was finally Leif who came to her side and spoke to her; she was immensely relieved, for Leif might just as easily have set up a permanent barrier between them.

"And I will have a brother," he was saying, "and a stepmother as kind and understanding as any. I wish you did not have to return to Scotland, but when my life is settled and my thinking straight, I'll come for a visit from time to time."

"Oh, Leif," she said, "I honestly hope you do. But it's such a very long way."

"Not for a Viking," he said more firmly. "It is merely one sea to cross and a small one at that!"

"You are a strange lot," Dawnlyn reflected. "Strange indeed."

She sat long hours after Elspeth had retired thinking of Leif and his father, wondering if they could one day be true friends. Ian and Gaard talked and drank while Leif finally relaxed in the attention of many a young girl from neighboring halls. Girls, Dawnlyn observed, with bright blond hair and tall, slim frames, their necks heavy with gold and silver chains, their arms circled by bronze serpent bracelets above the elbow.

Eventually Ian stode over to her, the lovely Astrid, several years his senior, on his arm. He was flushed and jubilant.

Dawnlyn noticed instantly that the girl had partaken of too much drink, for her eyes were glassy and her coloring high. Yet she was beautiful, Dawnlyn had to admit. Tall and slim as a sapling, with white-blond hair hanging straight and thick as a heavy silk curtain to her waist. Her eyes were a pale, shining ice-blue and two spots of rose touched her cheeks. She was dressed in a cherry-red gown with a low neckline that exposed the tops of her white breasts and reflected blushing highlights onto her skin. Around her waist was a girdle of gold trimmed with white ermine tails, and a tiny jeweled dagger hung from it. She looked utterly untamed and sensual and made Dawnlyn feel as unattractive as a mouse, and a bloated one at that.

"You know Astrid?" grinned Ian, his eyes resting possessively on the beautiful Viking woman.

"Aye, we have met," replied Dawnlyn, attempting civility. Her pride would not allow her to be less than courteous. "How fare you this eve, Astrid Thorhilddottir?"

"Exceedingly well, Lady Dawnlyn," she smirked. "Thank you."

Ian looked from one woman to the other aware, even in his befuddled state, of a peculiar tension between them. Women, he thought, bemused.

"I have not yet congratulated you on your marriage, Dawnlyn," gushed Astrid, her light eyes sparking challenge. "My father was . . . indisposed and therefore we could not attend the celebration, so I bring you our good wishes now. and also for the babe that you carry," she finished pointedly.

It was obvious to Dawnlyn that Astrid's remark insinuated that Gaard had been forced into an unwanted marriage. Hot anger flushed her cheeks. "Thank you so much." She smiled, feeling her face would crack with the effort.

Then, thankfully, Ian swept Astrid away to dance to a gay tune.

Quickly, with as much dignity as she could muster in the face of her humiliation and anger, Dawnlyn rose to leave them all to their celebrating.

But Leif suddenly placed a hand on her arm. "You are offended?" he asked, having overheard Astrid's remark.

Tears glistened unbidden in Dawnlyn's eyes while she watched Astrid, like a tall red flame, fly gracefully across the floor to the music. "Aye, I am sorely offended. I cannot stand to think—"

"—that Gaard has bedded others?" he finished for her. And then, "Perhaps you are wrong about Astrid. Perhaps

Gaard pays the woman no mind since his marriage." Leif's gaze fell away. "If you were mine . . . I would not look upon another."

Dawnlyn flushed hotly. "Thank you," was all she could force out, knowing how difficult the compliment must have been for him. And yet, he had broken all the way through the ice now and she was glad—it would have been awful to leave Thorkellhall knowing that her presence would always make Gaard's son uncomfortable. Perhaps now it would not.

"I should retire," she said finally.

"Because of Astrid?"

"Nay." Then she thought a moment. "Well . . . yes. I do not like her kind."

"And what *kind* is that?"

"A woman who hops from bed to bed fornicating like a rabbit!"

Leif's thin lips split into a grin. "It is your Scots' upbringing. Come," Leif said, pressuring her arm, "sit back down and ignore Astrid. You behave with jealousy and Gaard will not understand."

Unsure whether to flee or stay, Dawnlyn held her ground for a moment, glaring hotly at Astrid, who had somehow slithered her way to Gaard's side now, her full lips pink with delight.

"I'll stay," Dawnlyn whispered, holding her back stiff, wishing more than anything that her body was once again slim and desirable.

Gaard was oblivious to Dawnlyn's anguish, however. For what seemed like hours he chatted with Astrid, eventually placing an arm around the woman's smooth, white shoulders. The full swell of her breasts rose above the gown's bodice, round and creamy and enticing. Astrid coyly leaned forward, pressing the succulent mounds together with her arms, affording Gaard a most tempting display of her charms.

Dressed this night in a simple blue and yellow gown that was cut high around her neck, far too matronly, Dawnlyn felt like crying. Then she thought better of it and decided she should scratch the wench's eyes out. And all the while, she could not understand her reaction—Astrid was merely a woman he had bedded, he had not married her. She hoped—as Leif had suggested—that he had not been with her since his return from Scotland.

And yet she knew it had been weeks and weeks since Gaard had relieved himself in her own flesh, and the notion turned Dawnlyn's stomach sour. She suddenly felt horrible —depressed and alone—and the ugly, dark thoughts she was having disgusted her. She hated the whole, sordid mess, and, mostly, she hated herself for reacting so pridefully and immaturely.

Fortunately, Leif kept returning to her side—at least *he* understood Dawnlyn's plight. Even Ian roamed over once more, his eyes red-rimmed with drink.

"Poor sister," he slurred. "We make merry celebrating Leif's good fortune and all you can do is sit and wait for the baby!"

Gaard finally untangled himself from Astrid and strode over to her. "You should be abed, Dawnlyn," he said protectively. "The hour is late."

"I know." She arched a slim brow. "But you have been so *occupied* that I hadn't the chance to bid you a good night."

His lips drew down in a thin line. "I'll see you to our chamber," he said, wondering at Dawnlyn's twisted words.

He stayed in the chamber while Meg helped Dawnlyn out of her gown and into the full nightshift, then told the serving girl to leave them.

Dawnlyn stood in the center of the room, the firelight flickering on her warmly, causing her hair to glow a rich russet shade. Her fully rounded stomach protruded against the linen material, silhouetted by the orange light, and Gaard was heartened at the sight.

He leaned a casual shoulder against the closed door. "It will not be long, little one, before we have a son."

She turned to face him then. "No, I suppose not," she

said automatically, still envisioning the tall, blond Astrid in those strong, sinewy arms.

"Something troubles you," Gaard said.

She was quiet for a moment, her stare fixed in the middle distance between them. "I am only tired tonight and tired of this swollen belly."

"But you look lovely—"

"Ha!" she scoffed curtly. "Lovelier than your Astrid?"

"Astrid . . . Of course you are."

"And can you deny that when you leave this room to rejoin the guests you will not go straight to that buxom wench?"

Gaard's glance grew dark. "Why would I deny such a thing?"

Dawnlyn spun away from him, her arms folded tightly across her chest. "Then you have bedded her?"

"Many times in the past." And then he added unthinkingly, "But she is not the only one."

Tears welled hotly behind her eyelids. "How can you brag of such things? How would you feel if I continually threw up to you men I have bedded?"

"But you haven't, so how can I say?" He grew impatient then. "You have no need to be jealous, Dawnlyn. I have placed you above all others, haven't I? I wed *you*, not Astrid or Helga or any other."

Her chin held high, she retorted, "It comforts me little when you wed me only to gain the loyalty of the people of St. Abb's."

"I could have done that anyway. I need not have married you."

"Then you wed me because of the child," she threw in bitterly.

"Yes. And because I gave you my word that I would." Running a hand through the thickness of his sun-streaked hair, he went on, "I was ready to marry. A strong man must continue his stock . . ."

"You care nothing for *me* . . . nothing!" The tears began

to fall, but her head was turned away so that he could not see her pain and anguish.

"This is ridiculous," he muttered angrily. "I have told you a hundred times that I honor you. I married you, didn't I? Well?"

"Aye," she bit out. "Now go to your pleasures and leave me to rest."

"I shall." He opened the door. "I am a man, Dawnlyn, not a puppet on a string. If I choose to enjoy the company of one I have known since boyhood, I shall." And he closed the door behind him, leaving Dawnlyn alone with her torment, sobbing into the pillow until no more tears would come.

Leif and Gaard were gone from the Hall frequently over the next weeks. At times there was a tenuous companionship between them and they occasionally laughed together, yet Leif still seemed to withhold a vital part of his inner self from Gaard. It was as if he sometimes pulled the resentment back around him, as if it were a shroud too habitual to abandon.

Dawnlyn's burden grew heavier until walking itself tired her, and often she sank into a chair, too weary to even stroll about the hall.

She had not spoken to Gaard again about Astrid or any other but sensed his trips around the countryside included visits to Astrid's hall. Yet Dawnlyn knew if she pressed Gaard on the subject he would toss her words off as inconsequential. So she remained silent, dying a small death each time he returned, his cheeks ruddy from the cold, his lean body ever on the move, ever seeking sport of some kind.

Once she voiced her anxiety to Leif, "I would that my husband were a short, balding oaf whose only sport was staying about the hall, seeing to business within these walls." And Leif had laughed heartily as if she had told a bawdy tale.

The sun had broken through the gray one late January

217

afternoon. It poured goldenly through the high windows and lit the great hall splendidly. For the first time in weeks, Dawnlyn's spirits were lifted, as Gaard was there with her, regaling her with tales and myths, cheering her as if that were his plan.

They sat close together, Gaard's hand resting on her arm, his hair golden-light where the sun struck it, his eyes warm, the color of wood smoke this day. No one disturbed them, sensing that the jarl and his wife were enjoying their pastime. Dawnlyn smiled and laughed and blushed, secure now with Gaard at her side, his attention solely on her.

He had just asked her if she would care to walk a little about the courtyard in the sun when Ian came up to them.

"There's a rider coming," he said. "Should I go see who is there?"

Gaard gave Dawnlyn's arm a slight squeeze. "No. I'll see to it." He rose, smiled at Dawnlyn, then strode to the door.

She was praying that whoever had come would not stay long or perhaps was not here at all to see Gaard, when in walked Astrid, her black sable hooded cape catching the light richly through the portal. Dawnlyn's heart sank miserably as she watched Astrid toss aside the elegant fur, exposing her tall frame, her gold and jewels winking across the room.

"Come and see Dawnlyn." Gaard took her arm above the gilt, serpentine bracelet.

As they approached, looking like they fit together perfectly, Astrid said, "Oh, yes . . . Dawnlyn. Poor dear, she's so swollen, isn't she?" And Astrid batted long, pale lashes up at Gaard, her frame in the snug-fitting green velvet gown molded to his side.

Dawnlyn also wore a deep green, but seeing the emerald of Astrid's gown against the glittering necklaces, her rich, almost white hair flowing down her back, made Dawnlyn cringe inwardly.

Astrid was beautiful, a tall, ice-eyed goddess whose proud carriage fitted Gaard's perfectly. She seated herself on the bench Gaard had occupied, forcing him to sit across the table from the women, and Dawnlyn sensed instinctively that Astrid wanted him to compare the two.

"Oh, my," Astrid breathed, seeing the fullness of Dawnlyn's gown, "you *are* near your time! Oh, my! How uncomfortable to be so heavy!" And a hand fluttered to her white bosom in sympathy.

Dawnlyn felt hot fury envelop her but somehow managed to clasp her hands in her lap demurely. "I am large with Gaard's child. He says it will be a son."

"Isn't it wonderful!" She turned huge eyes onto Gaard. "You must be so proud!"

"I am," he replied, sipping at his cider easily, unaware of the tension crackling between the two women.

"And here I have disturbed you," Astrid went on, "and I am afraid it's business."

"Of course," Dawnlyn murmured, her cheeks flaming.

Astrid laughed then, patted Dawnlyn's knee as if in understanding. "Poor girl, I must ask Gaard to accompany me to my father's Hall. He is ill with sniffling and cannot venture out. He said it was most important . . ."

"I am certain it is," said Dawnlyn, barely in control now. "Business is business."

Finally, Gaard raised a bemused brow. "You will be all right if I go?"

"I shall be perfectly fine, Gaard," she managed to say. "I would not dream of asking you to stay when dear Astrid has traveled all this way to fetch you." She turned narrow copper eyes onto the blond. "Still, I suppose when one has nothing better to do with her time, a ride must help wile away the long hours. We must not let Astrid's journey go for naught." And Dawnlyn prayed that her meaning was not lost on Astrid.

Oblivious to his wife's sarcasm, Gaard rose. Even though she was furious to see him leave, Dawnlyn felt a bold surge of triumph wash through her at Astrid's outraged expression.

Gaard came around to Dawnlyn's side. "I shan't be long, I promise."

"We wouldn't dream of keeping him," said Astrid tightly, swirling away abruptly.

But Astrid did keep him—through the evening meal and until nearly daybreak the following morning. And all Dawnlyn could envision the whole sleepless night was Astrid's pale white body arching itself beneath Gaard's lean hips, her full, white mounds cupped in his hands, her blond head straining backwards at the moment of complete fulfillment.

When Gaard did finally slip into bed beside Dawnlyn, she feigned sleep. Even when he placed a hand on her belly with great care, she froze inside at his touch. And she thought angrily of all her prayers that long night, of the many pleas to God to return Gaard to her side—and she felt betrayed: not only had God refused her prayers but her husband did not care about her.

Still, as she lay there in deep, pained thought, Dawnlyn knew one thing: everyone in the world could turn from her, but she would never, never turn from herself. Inside of her was a deep instinct for survival, and she would fight tooth and nail for that which was hers. If Gaard had taught her nothing else, he had taught her to hold on in the storm.

Chapter Sixteen

THIS HALL NEEDS ATTENTION!" ANNOUNCED DAWNLYN ONE morning as she sat at breakfast with Elspeth.

"It is in good order, is it not?" asked Elspeth, looking around her in surprise.

"I cannot bear it. The rushes are old and dusty, the cooking pots are black, the table needs scouring . . ."

"But it is midwinter! Surely those things can wait till spring."

"And my bedclothes need beating and sunning."

"But that is never done before the first croaking of frogs in the spring!" reminded Elspeth.

"It must be done now. I will do it!" And Dawnlyn pushed herself up from her bench, so heavy and unwieldy now with child that Elspeth was amazed at her movement.

"You will not! Gaard would have my head!" warned Elspeth.

"But Gaard is not here. He will never know . . . nor will he notice the changes when he returns. You must admit that."

"It is true. Men never see the things we do for them. But they live better because of it and *that* they appreciate, even if they don't know the cause," laughed Elspeth. "All right. But you will do nothing, only direct the women, and we'd best be done before Gaard returns from Stavanger."

"Oh, thank you, Lady Elspeth. I feel like I will *burst* if I do not see these things done!"

"Ah, your time grows near, then. All women get that feeling when they are about to deliver. Thorkell found me on a stool scrubbing the walls just before I had Gaard." Her gray eyes grew misty with memory.

"Well, it means nothing, I am sure. *This* baby will never be born!"

Elspeth covered Dawnlyn's faintly puffy hand with her own. "It will, my child."

"Never."

So, to the tune of much grumbling from the thralls, the rushes were swept out into the gray February snow with their accumulation of winter's filth; the pots were emptied and scoured with sand and lye soap; the trestle table and benches were taken out into the dim, watery sun and scrubbed.

In short, the Hall was turned topsy-turvy, an unheard of thing in midwinter. Dawnlyn moved about as fast as her bulk allowed, scolding a thrall here, a serving boy there, ordering more soap, turning rooms inside out, much to the inhabitants' distress. Then she began on her own room, tearing the bed apart, airing the linen and eiderdown, beating them with a hazel twig, which assured the removal of any vermin.

Dawnlyn's face beamed happily when it was done; she stood with hands on rounded stomach, surveying the newly cleansed hall. Elspeth watched her affectionately.

"I feel better now!" declared Dawnlyn. "Now let the mighty Gaard Wolftooth come home, for we're all done."

"He is to arrive late this eve or on the morrow, I believe, depending on how quickly he can arrange everything with the king. I know he will hurry because of your time being so close. He almost didn't go because of it." Elspeth beamed. "He has taken quite well to marriage, better than I could have expected. You are good for my wild son, Dawnlyn."

"I am not so sure of that, Lady Elspeth," said Dawnlyn pensively. "He turns to other women already . . ."

"Astrid?" asked Elspeth knowingly.

"Aye."

"Pay her no mind. She's an old friend."

"Friend! Rather more, if appearances are to be believed!"

"Once, perhaps. Not now. Do not be jealous, my child. Gaard has eyes only for you."

"Me! I am repulsive." She gestured at her swollen shape. "He will not touch me. He hasn't for ages! And if he is pleasant to me it is only because I carry the child."

"He is only *afraid* to touch you. Wait until after your confinement. He will be with you again. It is his first experience with birth, too, you know."

"He is tired of me. I will be alone from now on except when he wants another child."

"No. He wants you above all others. He chose you, did he not?" asked Elspeth, trying to cheer her daughter-in-law. The poor child was in the last state of frenzy and depression before she gave birth. What a time for her insensitive son to renew a friendship with Astrid!

"He chose me because I asked him to marry me. It was my father's idea."

"I would like to meet your father—a man of much wisdom." She smiled. "But surely you know Gaard well enough to see he would never do something because he was *asked.* He *wanted* to, I swear to you."

"Well, he has repented of his decision, then," replied Dawnlyn bitterly.

"It will work out. You will find that Gaard has a great sense of duty and loyalty. He will be a good husband to you." Elspeth patted Dawnlyn's hand.

"I pray you are right," Dawnlyn sighed, "but still, I feel afraid of the future—a babe every year, Gaard gone half the time on dangerous forays or with another woman. There is so little *meaning* to it all. My life was to be so much more ordered in the cloister, even more important. Now I am nothing—a wife amongst a thousand others. There is nothing special in it."

"Dawnlyn, my dear child," said Elspeth, "you are looking at it all backwards. As a wife and mother your life is ordered by the very laws of Creation and of God, for did He not say, 'Be fruitful and multiply'? To me there is more good in one child raised well than a pack of nuns praying for a hundred years." She crossed herself contritely. "Forgive me, but I feel that, truly. A mother and wife provides the strength from whence comes all greatness in this world. It is so, Dawnlyn."

"Your words make sense, but I cannot make my heart accept them. I am not *unhappy,* it's just that something is missing."

"You will be so busy when you have your own Hall to manage back in Scotland that you will have no time to even think of that missing piece to the puzzle. And soon after that you will realize that the piece was there all the time but you couldn't see it. It will happen so," said Elspeth fondly.

"You are very comforting, my lady. I pray you are right, for I cannot bear the thought of an empty existence. There must be some *meaning* to life, you understand?"

"Yes, my child, I know full well. And there will be. Lord above, there already is!"

"But when do you think we will be able to sail to Scotland?" asked Dawnlyn, her mind fluctuating, as always these days, between thoughts of the baby and the trip home.

"In March or April, when the winter gales pass, and when the baby is strong enough to travel."

"So long . . ."

"It will pass quickly, my dear, you will see. And now there is Leif to take over Thorkellhall, so your departure will not be held up for any reason."

"Yes, I am so glad those two could agree on something. I was afraid, for a while, that it would come to a terrible fight, like the one with Karl."

"It was fortunate, I agree. Yet I am not sure Leif will not always feel some bitterness, and Gaard some distrust. It is a difficult situation," said Elspeth, "and yet, now that Gaard has petitioned the king to officially acknowledge Leif as the heir to Thorkellhall, we can pray that they meet with more friendship."

"I know that boy adores his father," said Dawnlyn, idly pouring a cup of cider. "All those years he thought his father had forsaken him deliberately. It left scars . . ."

"We all have our scars. And we learn to live with them quite handily. It is out of your hands, in any case. It is between them." Elspeth rose from where she'd been sitting with Dawnlyn in the great hall. "I want you to rest now, after your cleaning fit. Then it will be time for supper and maybe Gaard will be home."

"I *am* tired, as usual these days." Dawnlyn smiled wryly. "As for supper, I can do without it. I feel quite without appetite."

Elspeth gave her a quick look. "Then I will not wake you. Go, child, sleep. You need your strength." And she watched Dawnlyn walk slowly, heavily toward her room, as ripe as any fruit ready to drop effortlessly from the tree.

A bitter winter storm blew from across the North Sea while Dawnlyn slept, causing the dim winter afternoon to darken even more; then the snow blew in with the wind, slashing, freezing, piling up in corners where the vicious wind whipped it. Elspeth noted the storm, worrying that it would delay Gaard and Leif on their return from Stavanger. She spun wool swiftly, tirelessly, even as the light in the Hall faded, for her fingers knew their way with the fleece better than her eyes, and all the while she listened to the howling storm, knowing that Gaard might have to stay his trip in the face of the weather and wondering just how soon her daughter-in-law would go into labor.

Dawnlyn slept peacefully for over two hours, awaking abruptly to an odd sensation. She'd felt, in her sleep, a strong kick from the baby, and then a strange pop, as if the kick had made something inside her give way. She searched her body mentally; there were no cramps or pains or anything unusual. But then she felt something hot and wet on her thighs and her eyes opened wide in silent wonderment. Her water had broken! By the Virgin Mary's holy breath, so she *was* going to have this baby, after all!

Carefully, she got out of bed, lit an oil lamp in the dark and wadded up a piece of linen to stop the trickling flow of her water.

She came upon Elspeth in the great hall, just finishing dinner. Gaard's mother took one look at Dawnlyn, who was leaning on the doorframe, a scared, joyous expression on her small, piquant face, and knew.

"Heat water!" she ordered a kitchen thrall, then strode quickly to Dawnlyn, taking her arm. "Come, daughter, you and I have work to do."

Gaard and Leif set out from Stavanger a day late under a cold, thin sun, the horses having to plunge through drifts in places, breaking into a sweat despite the freezing temperature. Gaard was impatient, pushing his mount unmercifully; Leif just hung on, gray-faced, and followed. It took until the winter sun had reached its insignificant zenith in the low, grainy sky for them to reach the Hall, with Gaard swearing to every god he could think of the whole way.

Gaard threw his reins to a stable boy and half-ran to the heavy front door, throwing it open with a bang. The servants all looked up, startled, then went on about their duties. Gaard stood on the threshold, looking frantically around the great hall.

Finally he saw the red-bearded Knute in a corner, busily oiling his battle harness. "Knute!" he bellowed across the cavernous hall. "Where is my wife?"

Knute's head raised in surprise. "Oh," he answered mildly, "she's in her room with your mother. She's been there since last night."

But Gaard never gave him time to finish. He dashed down the corridor to his chamber, threw open that door, too, with a bang, stopped short.

Elspeth's head snatched around to see what the commotion was. Quickly she rose from her place by the bed and rushed to her son's side. "Gaard, thank God you're back."

"The storm . . ."

"I know. It has already started."

"Dawnlyn?" His usually strong, ringing voice was quavering now.

"She is fine, but she is working very hard and it's taking a long time. The baby is so big, you see, and she has such slender hips . . ."

"By Thor's flaming beard! And I gave her that big child! What if it kills her?" His gray eyes had gone haggard and dull. "She's such a little thing."

"Gaard. Be brave. This is what women are made for. She's strong and healthy. It only needs time."

"Let me see her," he begged.

"All right. Just for a minute. She's working very hard, remember. She's a good, brave girl."

Slowly, torn between fear and marvel, he approached the bed he'd shared with her these months. She lay on the bedclothes, in only a long white nightshift, her face pinched, her hair pulled back into a neat braid that lay over her shoulder in a thick copper coil. Her swollen stomach seemed to dominate the room so that he hardly noticed the midwife and her assistant or the pallid face of Meg.

Dawnlyn's eyes were closed, her eyelids blue-veined and delicate as white silk. She was breathing deeply as if she'd run a long way.

"Dawnlyn, little one." It was a broken whisper.

Her eyes fluttered open, revealing tawny pupils that gazed into his, yet were not wholly cognizant. "Gaard?"

"Yes, little one, I am here."

A beautific smile lit her face. She reached for his hand, squeezed it weakly. "I knew you would come in time." Then her brows drew together, a look of utter concentration came over her features and she began to breathe hard again, unable to speak.

He held her hand while the contraction lasted, horrified at

227

the pain his son was causing her, helpless as he'd never been before. When she relaxed, his breath whistled out between his teeth and he realized he had been holding it.

He felt Elspeth's hand on his arm.

"Go now, my son. I will let you know how things progress," came her soft voice.

He turned to his mother, his face a mask of fear. "How can she bear it? Can't you do something?"

Elspeth smiled condescendingly. "It is always this way. It was like this when I bore my sons. It is the price for our sins."

"A pox on your cursed sins! Dawnlyn never sinned! She was as innocent as a babe when I had her! *She* should not suffer!"

"Go," sighed Elspeth. "I do not have time to argue theology with you now. She will be fine."

And so he left the room, his broad back bowed down with anxiety, and returned to the great hall to throw off his fur coat and plump himself down on a bench, where he stared moodily into the fire, jumping nervously at every noise.

"How is she?" asked Leif quietly.

Gaard swung his leonine head around toward the lad. "Suffering all the agony of the damned. And it's all my fault."

"God's blood, my lord, she's not the first woman in history to bear a child!"

Gaard eyed his newfound son angrily. "But this is my first wife and *I've* never been through it before. It's *Hel.*"

Leif threw back his tousled brown head and laughed. Gaard was forced to acknowledge his own ridiculous words with a sheepish smile that quickly melted into a worried frown again.

The hours dragged on. Gaard tried desperately to busy himself: sharpening his sword, playing dice with Ian and Knute, even attempting to review the hall's account books. But when he realized he'd read the same figures twenty times without understanding them, he gave up, sat in front of the fire and stared into the leaping flames.

That the other denizens of the great hall smiled understandingly at him he was not in the least aware, nor would he have cared if he had known.

When Elspeth came to him and touched his arm, he jumped as if a red-hot poker had burned him and turned on her with wild eyes. "Yes?"

"She is still in labor. There is some progress. She said to tell you not to worry." Elspeth's face was tired and her eyes lined with blue shadows. "It is taking a long time. Poor little thing."

Gaard slumped on the bench. *His* fault, all his fault! The torment she suffered, had been suffering all these endless hours! And she had thought to comfort *him* in the midst of her untold agony. He put his head in his hands and groaned. When he looked up again, Elspeth was gone.

The hour grew late, the thralls barred the huge doors, snuffed out the candles, returned to their own straw pallets. Gaard remained by the banked fire, tense and weary with the awful waiting. He sat looking at his hands while worry ran sideways across them like crabs.

He had no idea how long he'd been sitting there when his mother appeared in front of him, her mouth curved in a tired smile, her gray eyes beaming proudly. He tried to jump up, but his stiff muscles refused to move fast enough; half-bent, he cried out to Elspeth. "Well? Tell me? Is Dawnlyn still alive?"

"Gaard, she is fine. The baby is born—a boy, a big lusty boy-child!"

He sank back, his cramped muscles screaming their protest, put his face in his large, battle-scarred hands. "Thank Odin and Thor and Freya and even your Kris," came his muffled voice. Then, "A boy? A healthy boy?" His face turned up to his mother's, a smile beginning on his ravaged features.

"Yes, my son. Would you like to see him?"

"My son?" breathed Gaard, and then it struck him that his first thought had been for his wife, his little Dawnlyn, and, for a moment, the unknown baby had been merely secondary.

He entered the chamber as quietly as a wraith this time,

afraid to disturb Dawnlyn. The midwife held a tiny wailing bundle swaddled in white linen, which she crooned to and rocked. But Gaard's eyes were only for Dawnlyn, a tiny heap under the eiderdown. He knelt on the floor, afraid even to sit on the bed and make it sag.

"Dawnlyn, I am here." He held his breath for her reply.

Her eyes opened tiredly, she turned her drawn face to his, gave him a tremulous smile. "Does he please you?" she asked softly, her voice no more than a breath.

"Who? Oh, yes, of course. But *you*, my little one, how are you?" He reached out a big hand and gently brushed a sweat-soaked tendril of hair from her forehead.

"I am tired, Gaard, very tired. But content. What a long time he took to get here, didn't he?"

"Longer than eternity, my wife," Gaard whispered.

Dawnlyn's hand rose from the eiderdown, touched Gaard's cheek. "You look tired, too. Get some rest, my lord."

His heart squeezed with an odd, alien emotion at her words. Still, after all this, she worried about *him!* "Sleep now, Dawnlyn. You have accomplished a hard task this night." Then he bent over and kissed her bloodless lips, barely touching them, but as fervently as if he were a true believer and she a holy relic.

The next morning the whole world looked much more reasonable to Gaard. The weather had turned mild, the snow melting to slush, and everyone in Thorkellhall congratulated the new father, making his breast swell with pride as if he had done something quite unique. The long, terrible wait for his son's birth was banished from his mind and a broad grin split his face as he swaggered about the great hall receiving his accolades.

After breakfast he decided to visit Dawnlyn and the baby. After all, he had not even seen the new baby yet, a fact that he refused to admit to anyone.

A weak light straggled in through the oiled membrane of the window, casting soft shadows on Dawnlyn's face as she sat up in bed holding the baby. Her face lit up with happiness as Gaard entered the chamber. "Good morn to you, my lord. Will you hold your son?"

He stopped, studied her carefully. "You are well recovered," he said softly.

"Yes, I am fine after a good night's sleep. All except my bottom"—she made a move of distaste—"which is very sore from the size of this enormous son of yours."

Gaard approached the bed, curious now, bent over Dawnlyn and warily pulled aside the blanket that covered the baby's face. The tiny, red, puckered visage looked strange to him, and so did the miniscule red fist resting by his son's fat cheek and the nearly bald pate with its fuzz of pale blond hair.

"I wish to call him Eric Robert, after my grandfather and my father," said Dawnlyn.

"Eric Robert . . . Well, I believe I had a grandfather named Eric also, and several other kinsmen of that name. It is as good as any."

"Good, that is settled. I will tell Father Tancred. He will be christened in ten days."

"*And* there will be the Viking name-rite, too," began Gaard. "He will be consecrated to Odin, the god of wisdom."

The newly named baby woke, drowning his parents' words in hungry howls. Dawnlyn bared her breast and put him to it; he quieted instantly.

"Isn't he beautiful?" sighed Dawnlyn. "Elspeth says he looks like you."

"Beautiful? I cannot say, having known very few babies to compare him to."

"Of course he's beautiful! He's a miracle. After all those months, then those long hours, he is precious to me already." Dawnlyn looked at Gaard with wonder and love shining from her eyes.

"And you, little one, are as precious to me as he is," said Gaard tenderly. "I only came to realize it last night. I was so worried . . ."

Dawnlyn's face was hidden, bent over the baby. She stayed that way for an endless heartbeat of time, her head bowed as if in prayer. Then she raised her face to his, her tawny eyes filled with uncertainty and hope. "Gaard? Do you mean those words? They are not just spoken in your new pride?"

"Dawnlyn, you have grown very dear to me these past months."

"I find that hard to believe when you act as you do with that blond wench, Astrid," replied Dawnlyn softly, her copper eyes meeting his levelly.

"What?" he asked, confounded.

"Sleeping with another woman does not display your respect for me very well, Gaard."

"Sleeping with . . . Astrid?" His voice was filled with disbelief.

"Gaard, you have behaved disgracefully with her and it hurt me very badly. There I was, swollen and hideous while you were gone half the time, disporting yourself with that slut!"

Gaard stood stock-still, his face a mask of bafflement; then a grin began to twitch at the corners of his thin lips. "You are jealous, my wife," he announced self-importantly.

"I am not!" cried Dawnlyn.

"Yes, you are, so it will do you no good to deny it. I'll tell you a secret. I recognize the feeling so well because I have felt it also. I confess. I was jealous of Leif. For a short time only," he hastened to add. He reached for her hand, pulled it to his lips. "Do not be jealous, little one. You are my wife. I respect you above all others."

Dawnlyn searched his face long and deeply. "You did nothing with her, then?"

"She is like a sister to me. We laugh and joke and ride together. She drinks far too much in the Hall with the men and tells bawdy tales. She should have been married years ago, but her father is weak and can do nothing with her. And besides, Ian has caught her eye now."

Dawnlyn weighed his words carefully; he had said much

but so little—he had not actually denied bedding the girl. In fact, he had pointedly avoided mention of it.

Should she press him further? Did she *really* want to know? And in truth, his admission that he respected her above all others was of great comfort. It should be enough.

"Now, let me see this new being we have made together to make sure he has all his . . . parts," said Gaard, steering their conversation to a safe ground.

They unwrapped the baby together, laying him on his back on the eiderdown until he squalled at the ignominy of it all. Gaard marveled at the way he kicked and howled, his little face turning bright red, and Dawnlyn forgot all thought of Astrid while she watched him. He felt his son's tiny biceps, assuring her that he would be a mighty swordsman some-day, then pinched a fat thigh and swore he would sit a horse like a Mongol prince. As for his tiny pink rosebud, Gaard swore he would equal the mighty black men of Timbuktu, for everyone knows they are the best endowed of any in the world.

They swaddled the baby in his clothes and he fell asleep in Dawnlyn's arms while Gaard watched them. What an idyllic picture they made—his beautiful young wife, her russet head bent over the fat babe at her breast.

Then Elspeth came in, insisted that Dawnlyn rest and tried to bustle Gaard out of the room.

"I will go," he laughed, "but first my wife deserves fitting thanks for giving me such a fine son." Then he bent, tilted Dawnlyn's face up to his and kissed her lingeringly on the lips.

Elspeth coughed judiciously nearby and Dawnlyn drew away, red-cheeked. "Gaard! What will the Lady Elspeth think?"

"She will think that I like my wife very much indeed, which is quite true!" he grinned. "Now I will go celebrate this event in a manner befitting its significance." And he left, leaving Dawnlyn and Elspeth to chuckle together over the proud new father he had become.

Chapter Seventeen

THE DAY HAD ARRIVED AT LAST WHEN THEY WERE TO LEAVE FOR the Northumbrian coast of Scotland. It was mid-April; March had been stormy and gray and Gaard had decided to await the calmer seas of April before crossing. For a time, Dawnlyn was certain he delayed because he had changed his mind and decided to remain in Norway—but that was not so. Gaard's itch to be away, to take to the seas once more, was intact.

He came to their chamber the morning before departure. His face was boyish, exuberant, eager to be gone. "Has Meg finished with the packing?" he asked, glancing around the room.

"Yes. It is all done." Dawnlyn looked up from the baby, who was nursing at her breast. "You are cheerful this day," she observed.

"I am!" he laughed. "To feel the sea beneath my feet once more always pleasures me. And I have just mastered Father Tancred in a theological argument, which always cheers me."

"I'll wager he feels just as sure he's mastered you!" she quipped, a grin touching her rosy lips.

"You may be right," Gaard smiled, "for I let him have the last word."

"Oh?"

"It was my way of saying farewell to the old man." His expression sobered. "I fear I shall not see him again. At his age . . ."

"You will miss him?"

"Yes, believe it or not, I will. He is a good man, a fine teacher and a loyal friend. I asked him to come with us, but he refused. He said it was his fate to live and die among the heathens. A strong soul, that one."

"Yes, a strong soul . . ." And Dawnlyn thought of the frail old priest who had sustained Lady Elspeth's faith through so many years, who had educated Elspeth's two sons so well, who had prayed with Dawnlyn over Gaard's mortally wounded body and married her and Gaard. She, too, would miss the old man.

Gaard stalked the bed chamber restlessly as if the walls could not hold him, as if the confining space within them were a prison. He was so bursting with energy that Dawnlyn thought if she touched him he would crackle with current.

"You are always so anxious to be gone?" she ventured.

"Yes, little one. It's in the blood. I cannot help it, even if I wanted to." He grinned boyishly, happily, as if his words were ultimately reassuring.

A frown appeared on Dawnlyn's brow. "And how long will it be before you are off again from St. Abb's?"

"Now, little one, we have been over this subject many times before. When I choose to leave, I shall."

"And Eric? What will he do for a father?"

"You can see," Gaard smiled, looked on the growing baby at her breast, "that he needs a mother now. When he is older, he'll go with me, of course."

"Of course." She bent her head to study Eric and thought about how much she would miss the child when Gaard took over his life. But by then, she hoped, there would be other children to comfort her.

Suddenly her heart clutched. Would there be? What if Gaard decided never to bed her again? And she recalled the last time, several weeks after Eric had arrived and Gaard had held her at last, stroked the full curve of her breast, touched her carefully, intimately. And then he had entered her and she had felt a stabbing pain and cried out and he had quickly withdrawn, an arm thrown over his forehead. She had not known what to do to ease his discomfort and had only been able to soothe him with words, telling him it would be a little while longer, fearing desperately that he would seek his pleasures with Astrid.

And he had declined to touch her since and she dared not bring up the subject, so great was her embarrassment to have to ask. Yet she longed to feel him inside her again, to have him hold her so close that their bodies would be as one.

Gaard came to her, bent, kissed the top of her head. "I have a surprise for you," he said. "My mother has decided to return to England . . . that is, Scotland."

"She has *what?*" Dawnlyn gasped.

"She sails with us on the evening tide." He stooped down next to her. "Are you pleased?"

"Why . . . yes, I can hardly believe it!"

"Lady Elspeth says there is naught to hold her here after so many years. I am her only son now, and there is you whom she has grown to love, and, of course"—he stroked the baby's soft-down head—"Eric."

"But her whole life has been here."

"Most of it, yes. And now she longs to step on the soil of her birthplace once more. She still has family in York and will visit them. I feel it is a most sound decision. If she is unhappy there, then I'll simply bring her home."

"Oh, Gaard," Dawnlyn smiled excitedly, "think! I'll truly have a mother now!"

"And Ian has informed me that Astrid wishes to accompany him to Scotland also," added Gaard matter-of-factly.

"Astrid? With Ian? What are you talking about? She's so much older!" asked Dawnlyn, stunned.

"I told you before, he has been keeping her company of late. I see no harm in it. They'll tire of each other soon enough."

"She'll not live at St. Abb's!" slashed Dawnlyn.

"Don't be silly, little one. Where is she to live, then? Have no fear, she'll keep out of your way. After all, *you* will be the lady of the Hall."

"And this does not bother you," asked Dawnlyn, her eyes narrowed, "her coming as Ian's guest?"

"No, why should it? They are both grown and responsible for their own actions. And Astrid can keep you company when my mother visits her family in York," he added ingenuously.

"You cannot imagine what the thought of her company means to me!" grated out Dawnlyn between clenched teeth. Was she never to be rid of the beautiful Astrid? And why, suddenly, was the woman playing up to Ian? Was this all to cover up the fact that Astrid and Gaard intended to continue their relationship? A cloud settled on Dawnlyn's horizon, even as her heart danced with gladness to be going home.

At least, she thought, Astrid would be on board Ian's ship—not Gaard's.

They sailed on the evening tide and the sky was ablaze with the setting sun. Mighty fingers of red and fuchsia spread over the western sky and fell warmly on the ships, lighting their sails to a richer shade of crimson. Dawnlyn was reminded of another radiant sunset, another Viking dragon ship that had slipped over the horizon many months before. Only that ship had leaped with flames and carried Karl's body to its final resting place.

Their arms grew tired of waving to the crowd assembled on the shore. Father Tancred's bent figure and Leif's taller one remained in the center of the throng, and Dawnlyn was sure she saw the old priest's frail hand raised in benediction long after it could have been possible. And Leif's face remained in her mind's eye, too. They had embraced warmly upon parting, and in Leif's eyes she had seen his thankfulness for her wisdom, his gratitude that she had never mentioned to Gaard the things that had truly gone on between herself and Leif. And she was heartened. She knew, too, that his promise to sail for St. Abb's within a year was sincere. Gaard and Leif might never be close, yet there was hope. There was always hope . . .

She glanced over at Elspeth, who stood also at the rail, watching the golden shore grow smaller, diminishing until it seemed only a low bank of pink clouds on the horizon, and then even that was gone.

Sensing Elspeth's need, Dawnlyn locked an arm with hers. "There is a lifetime of memories on that shore, is there not?"

"Yes," the older woman sighed. "And it seems just yesterday that Thorkell brought me here, a young captive, terrified and so alone."

"I know," whispered Dawnlyn. "I do know."

The crossing took only a few days, as a strong wind blew at their stern and the five sturdy ships scudded easily over the choppy sea. Gaard pointed out to them a cloud that gathered at their stern, its billowing white puffs resembling a massive beard; he told the women it was the god Thor and that his breath was with them. When Dawnlyn giggled at the tale—although the cloud was most impressive—Gaard winked at her. Even Meg did not complain this trip, and the women were able to stay on deck in the sun for most of the journey. Eric, too, was comfortable, and several times Gaard came for him and walked him about the ship, pointing out its features as if the baby could understand.

The men were polite, going about their duties efficiently, their wild beards sprayed with sea salt, their fur caps set jauntily on their heads. They certainly were a happy lot, Dawnlyn decided, then could not help but recall her earlier fear of these huge Norsemen with their fierce blue eyes and carefree, sporting ways.

It was odd, but when they slipped into the Coldingham harbor, when Dawnlyn felt for certain it would be the Northumbrian coast that thrilled her, it was instead another sight, one more powerful, more spellbinding that held her captivated. Gaard stood at the helm, tall, his thick golden hair swept back by the wind, his lean cheeks tanned, his resolute jaw scored by the old scar, crinkle lines around his gray eyes while he leaned over the rail, pointing, calling out orders to his men.

He presented such a strikingly virile picture that her breath was snatched away, and then she could not help but envision him a year ago; he must have stood on the same spot, called out to his men the same orders, his lithe body bent into the wind in the same way. And then, that very day, she had first seen him standing so powerfully, so terrifyingly tall in the portal of the chapel . . . Lord how she had feared him! But he had not harmed her, not really. And now she was here with him, his child in her arms, and they were a real family.

What would this next year bring? What kind of existence awaited her in the future with this Norseman as husband? Would she be lonely when he was gone or would his child and mother comfort her? Surely she would be busy with the baby and the running of St. Abb's Hall. But at night, when he was gone, what would their chamber be like, how lonely and empty would it be?

At first sight of the swift dragon ships, Sweyn had called the men to arms. Minutes later, while he stood on top of St. Abb's battlements, he had recognized the sleek ships to be Gaard's. With a gleaming, curved horn—a *lur*—he had signaled to the ships as they rounded the inlet, heading to Coldingham. The sound was by now familiar to Dawnlyn—a Viking call, a rich, golden string of notes that spread over the waves and rang brassy and confident in the air, greeting them.

They waited at the harbor and unloaded the ships until Sweyn arrived with horses and wagon. Sweyn leaped from his horse, ran to Gaard and they both slapped each other's backs with such hearty blows of friendship that Dawnlyn feared they'd knock each other down. Such a spate of Norse jabber and jubilant laughter! They were like boys again, so glad were they to see each other after almost a year. A Viking homecoming was always an event for rejoicing, as often enough the dragon ships were lost at sea despite the uncanny skill of their pilots.

Dawnlyn knew this, but nevertheless hated the delay. She was anxious to be home, to step inside the familiar Hall once more.

She was standing with Elspeth, pointing out features of the land, when Gaard approached them.

"Has Dawnlyn shown you the nunnery?" He nodded his head toward the sprawling stone structure on the hill above.

"Yes," Elspeth replied, "she has." Then she smiled knowingly at Dawnlyn.

Gaard placed a hand on the small of Dawnlyn's back. "Are you still thinking of running away and hiding yourself in the cloister?"

"I am not," she said defensively, eyeing Astrid, who had just been brought ashore from Ian's ship. "Have I ever run from anything? I was raised by my father to stand and meet life face on, Gaard."

"And you do it grandly." Taking both Elspeth's and Dawnlyn's hands, he led the women across the rocks and over to the horses and Sweyn.

"Greetings, Sweyn!" Dawnlyn called, smiling, suddenly glad to see his friendly face once more. "Is the Hall still standing?"

"It is!" He laughed and embraced her warmly. "I see Gaard has a son," he said, nodding towards Meg, who held the baby. "Congratulations!"

"Thank you."

"And I, too," he beamed widely, "am soon to have a child."

"Oh, Sweyn!" she breathed. "You are married, then?"

"That I am. To a beauty from Coldingham—Colleen, whose father had her studying at the cloister."

"I know her well," Dawnlyn laughed, thinking that Sweyn did indeed choose the most comely girl of all.

"She is most fortunate," he teased, "don't you agree?"

Giggling at Sweyn's tremendous ego, she mounted her horse and waited impatiently for the others. To be home again! Her heart swelled with joy at the mere thought.

Gaard and Sweyn rode ahead of them a few paces while Ian, with Astrid close behind, rode with Dawnlyn. "Ask Sweyn," said Ian quietly, "how father fares."

Dawnlyn gave her mount a kick and came abreast of Sweyn. "Is my father well?" she asked, keeping her eyes on Sweyn—she had no idea how Gaard would react to the question and feared to upset him during their homecoming.

"He is well and living at the Hall." He gazed at Gaard. "I had wanted to wait to tell you, but there has been trouble of late . . ."

"Trouble?" The thin line on Gaard's jaw grew tense and white.

"Yes. It began with several unaccountable fires in the village and then missing cattle. I was forced to call on Robert Renfrew for advice."

"Sweyn!" Gaard thundered. "You were left in charge!"

Sweyn met his rage straight-backed. "And I did my best, Gaard. I managed to take captive one of the men who had set another fire close to the hall, and from him I learned the name MacDougal."

"The MacDougals!" Dawnlyn whispered in remembrance.

"Exactly," said Sweyn, keeping his eyes on Gaard. "Then I was told by the Scots here that there has been an ongoing feud with that clan for many years. I wished to learn all I could about their methods, so I summoned Robert from his house up north and bade him remain at the Hall. That was two months ago."

Gaard was silent for a moment, then said, "For the safety of the Hall, you did the right thing. I only wish I had been here." He thought a moment longer. "Has there been trouble since?"

"Some missing ewes and stolen horses from the crofters. Robert says it is their devious way." Sweyn sat up taller in his saddle. "I longed to raid the MacDougal's Hall, Gaard, but Robert wisely stopped me for, as he was quick to remind me, the majority of fighting men were in Norway with you

241

and the decision to battle should lie on your shoulders." Sweyn sighed. "I decided to await your arrival, figuring you would sail in the spring."

"Good," said Gaard. And then Dawnlyn saw his facial muscles relax and a slow smile gathered at the corners of his mouth. "So these MacDougals want a fight," he finally grinned. "Well, Sweyn, perhaps we'll just have to oblige them!" And the two men laughed heartily together.

St. Abb's tower looked the same yet different somehow to Dawnlyn. She couldn't be certain, but it seemed smaller. Robert Renfrew came hesitantly forward from the heavy double doors, his eyes searching Gaard's face for approval or some sign that his presence was not threatening to the Viking.

"Greetings, Robert Renfrew," said Gaard noncommittally, looking from Dawnlyn's face to her father's as he dismounted. He walked to Meg in her wagon and took Eric from her arms. "Your daughter and I have a gift for you," he said, handing the child to Robert, who drew a breath.

Before embracing her father, Dawnlyn went to Gaard's side. "Thank you," she whispered fervently, amazed at the simple act of kindness from her husband. Ian, too, was bewildered at Gaard's change of attitude toward his father and almost said as much, but he held his quick tongue this once.

After Dawnlyn and her father had embraced warmly, Gaard helped his mother down from her horse and introduced her to Robert Renfrew, who was several years her junior. "There will be no squabbling over the grandchild," Gaard said to them both, gazing proudly on Eric.

The entourage entered the great hall and sought refreshment. Gerta bustled around the kitchen and all but ignored Dawnlyn when her mistress came in dutifully to order food served.

"Nary a soul will tell me when to cook or when to serve or how many there are to feed!" the plump cook complained, her plump rear end waddling about the large kitchen efficiently.

"Are you not glad to see me?" Dawnlyn held back the urge to giggle.

"I'll have time to be glad when this meal is served, my lady," and Gerta went about her business.

While the servants carried trunks and possessions to the various chambers, Dawnlyn seated herself in the great hall with the others. Food was brought finally, and when they were finished eating, Gaard rose and sought the group's attention.

"I have thought long on my position at this Hall," he began, "and have concluded that since my marriage things must change. That Robert Renfrew is here already may prove of benefit to me. Under this roof," he glanced around at the expectant faces, "are two families. This is our home, and we now have a child who binds these families together through blood. I wish to live here as a single unit." Dawnlyn was so surprised and pleased that she could do nothing but stare wide-eyed and openly at Gaard. "I am your master here and expect to be obeyed at all times. I may seek counsel from one or another member of my family but hold the right of final decision. We will live as one now. What say you?"

There were murmurs from Robert and Sweyn and several of the Scotsmen present. The Vikings were the first to cheer and call for more ale, but it was Ian who rose to meet Gaard's words with a raised flagon. "I say, my laird, that your announcement is nothing short of a miracle!"

Dawnlyn gasped. "Ian!"

But Gaard merely grinned. "Do not fear, my wife. I have come to know Ian well, and although his choice of words is often poor, his meaning is clear to me. You must understand that Vikings now live throughout the civilized world and are peaceful denizens of their chosen homes. I, too, wish for peaceful cohabitation here." Then suddenly Gaard laughed, his head tossed back in mirth. "Of course," he grinned, "if any of our neighbors or the Normans to the south wish to break our peace . . . well, then, we must accommodate them!" And a great, thundering roar of delight echoed from the stone walls as Vikings and Scots alike leaped to their feet in agreement.

When the merriment finally abated, Dawnlyn said, "How can you speak of peace and war in the same breath as if they are one?"

Gaard leaned down. "At heart," he said, "I am a Viking and always will be. And as a Viking, I have learned that the two go hand in hand. Without war there is no meaning to peace and vice-versa." Then he chuckled at her expression. "Think on this, Dawnlyn . . . open your mind to the reality of our world."

Evening came upon them softly, gilding the Hall in warm spring light that promised summer to come. Dawnlyn sat by the hearth, contentedly nursing Eric while Gaard spoke to Robert and Sweyn concerning the recent trouble with the MacDougal clan.

Astrid did, of course, choose a time to approach Gaard when Dawnlyn was unable to defend her rightful place by his side. Dawnlyn had to look on, a most unwilling audience, while Astrid sidled up to Gaard, took advantage of a lull in the men's conversation and linked her arm through his.

"My lord," Dawnlyn heard her say, "such a large and comfortable Hall this is! You must show me the rest of it if I'm to live here. Why, it's so immense I could easily get lost!"

Dawnlyn sat feeding Eric and fuming at Astrid's gall. Oh, yes, Astrid's timing was exquisite! And then, to her dismay, Gaard grinned, seemed to swell with pride at the Viking woman's praise and, like a lamb to slaughter, was led docilely by Astrid from the great hall to show her around.

It was their first night home! Had he missed Astrid so much on the short sea journey that he must rush off with her so quickly? And to do so in front of everyone! Dawnlyn felt hurt to the core, humiliated, forgotten. She bent her head over Eric, glad to be able to hide her face from the pitying, prying eyes. She fought back hot tears of frustration and pain.

It seemed forever before the couple returned, and by then

Ian was there to lead Astrid away, seemingly unconcerned by her short dalliance with Gaard.

Were all men so heartless? Dawnlyn wondered. She could not reconcile Gaard's tenderness with his betrayal of her no matter how hard she tried. Her mind whirled and she wondered if her brain was, indeed, completely muddled.

Eric was finished. Dawnlyn decided she had to make an effort, had to defend her own claims on her husband. A Renfrew did not yield easily, especially to such a shallow, selfish, *useless* female as Astrid Thorhilddottir!

She took a deep breath, broke into the men's conversation. "I think I should like to stroll about the meadows for a time before retiring," she said, eyeing Gaard meaningfully. "With your permission, my lord?"

Gaard rose from his seat, stretched. "Yes. Enough of this talk for now. I'll accompany you." He took her arm beneath the elbow and led them to the door. "You *were* asking if I would join you?" He arched a brow.

Dawnlyn drew her soft cape around her. "You are learning, husband," she replied, her tawny eyes lit with purpose.

They strolled together through the courtyard as dusk stole over the land, then ventured out to the wide stony lea overlooking the white tresses of the sea far below.

"I cannot tell you how pleased I am to be home," breathed Dawnlyn, beginning to relax, easing her slender frame down onto a rock, her eyes staring warmly over the familiar scene.

"You need not try to tell me, little one." Gaard gazed on her pensively. "I know."

They sat together until the earth cooled around them and the first star shone in the eastern sky. Dawnlyn was all too aware of his nearness, of the casual, strong arm encircling her shoulder. She was aching to confront him with his perfidy, recognizing the need within herself to hear him reassure her, even if his words were lies, but she fought the temptation. It would only anger him—she'd tried that tack before and it did not work. Gaard cherished his freedom above all else, and she could not curtail it, else she'd lose him completely. She tried very hard to put the image of Astrid from her.

"Gaard?" she whispered, breaking the long silence.

"Umm . . ."

"You know I am no fragile thing," she began, feeling heat rise to her cheeks. "If you . . . if you wanted to . . . we could—" She bit her lip, mortified.

"If I wanted to what?" Gaard turned his head, studied her through the darkness, a smile splitting his lips.

"Pay it no mind . . ."

Slowly, gently, he turned her face toward his with a hand and his lips touched her eyelids, her nose, sought the warmth of her mouth. He played with her carefully for long moments, his tongue teasing her lips, and then her mouth parted and he drove his tongue into her, his lips crushing hers with growing urgency.

Dawnlyn's arms came around his neck and she ran fingers through the tousled thickness of his hair, felt the corded muscles of his neck.

Suddenly he broke away. "I have waited a long while for you to be ready, and I can wait no longer," he said in a husky voice.

They stood together, silently, then walked back to the Hall. Dawnlyn checked the baby, who was sleeping in his cradle next to the hearth, Meg by his side.

"Come," said Gaard, taking her hand, "Eric is fine. It is I who need you." And they walked side by side up the curving stone steps to their chamber.

Dawnlyn looked around her, amazed at how very different everything appeared after so long an absence. While she gazed around the firelit room, Gaard undressed, tossing his clothes to the floor heedlessly.

Naked, powerful and lean in the golden glow, he came and stood before her. With a hand he unfastened her hair from the braid and ran fingers through the red coils until they sprang around her shoulders and down her back. Then slowly he drew her gray velvet *bliaut* away, and the linen dress beneath followed the same path to the floor.

Dawnlyn stood quietly before him, her eyes glistening like copper, her breath catching in her throat. And then he removed her last article of clothing, her undershift, and tossed it carelessly aside. She stood before him as naked as he and for endless, agonizing minutes, he merely reveled in her beauty.

Finally he ran a hand across the full, swollen breasts, stopping to tease at the nipples, then moved his touch lower, across her flat stomach and onto a curved hip. With his other hand he cupped a buttock and drew her length against him, bowing his head to taste the hollow at the nape of her neck. And then she was in his arms being carried to the soft bed, where he eased their bodies onto the eiderdown and propped himself up on an elbow to view her.

"The birth of our child has only served to make you more lovely," he said tenderly. "I like this new fullness to your body." He began to fondle her with his hands, and his mouth followed their sensual path. First he aroused her nipples, drawing them into his mouth, releasing them in rhythm to her desire. Then his head moved lower, his tongue encircling the belly button, sending shivers of delight coursing through her.

With his hands he gently spread her legs apart, stroking the white flesh of her inner thigh, moving his touch upward until his fingers caressed her intimately.

"Your sweetness drives me insane to have you," he breathed, then lowered his head between her thighs, taking her with his lips, his tongue, until her senses reeled and pulses of pleasure seized her womb and she cried aloud at the peak of climax.

Before she could think, before she could catch her breath, Gaard raised himself above her and drew her legs up around his lean hips. "I'll try to be gentle," he whispered, then sought her entrance.

Dawnlyn tensed to receive him and felt his swollen member slide within her slowly, so slowly she moaned in delight. And she was filled with him, her back arching to give him all she could.

Alternately he filled and emptied her until again her desire grew uncontrolled and she moaned for release from her aching senses.

But Gaard held back, teasing, delighting in her response, holding himself in check until she scratched at his back and cursed him half-furiously, half-pleasurably. Finally he thrust himself deep into her womb again and again until she twisted mindlessly beneath his powerful body. Then Dawnlyn cried as wave after wave of delight washed over her, drowning her with its intensity, and it was a triumphant cry.

She lay beneath him spent, perspiration glistening on her naked body. Slowly they drifted on a soft cloud of sleep together until Dawnlyn awoke, knowing that Meg must be frantic below with the baby—surely Eric was hungry by now.

She rose quietly and pulled on a robe. But when she returned with Eric and sat with him nursing on a chair, Gaard was awake.

"How long will he be?" Gaard asked, rising to stoke the dying embers in the fireplace.

"A while longer."

"Well, tell the hungry lad to hurry, for I have a need also." And Gaard's smile warmed her as much as the nursing infant.

Eric slept through the night in his cradle, but Dawnlyn and Gaard did not. It was as if they had to rediscover each other's body—to touch and stroke flesh until it was once again committed to memory.

Gaard took her in many ways that long, splendid night, and Dawnlyn thought she would surely perish from exhaustion. Still, she could not stop herself from rousing to his demands, and each time he entered her, she gasped in pure pleasure. He was an expert at arousal, she thought sometime before dawn, well-versed in the art of making love. And yet, she, too, was learning and had found ways to pique his interest, which caused him to sit up once, saying, "A fine nun you would have made!" And she reddened hotly, recognizing the truth of his statement.

The following afternoon, when Gaard had finished meeting with his men over the MacDougal situation, he again came to their chamber and sought Dawnlyn.

"I am surely bewitched," he taunted. "Take Eric to Mother and return at once, for my need is great again."

Dawnlyn laughed. "And if I don't?"

Scowling, he said, "Do you recall our first meeting? I may have spared you that time, but now that I have tasted of you . . ."

She smiled. "Yes, my lord. But do not ever try to force me again, for I'll scratch your eyes out!"

"Then don't deny me, wench. And hurry, for Odin's breath arouses me."

Dawnlyn did as she was bade, wondering at Gaard's sudden, renewed interest. But she was too content to question his motives. Whatever they were, she was ecstatically happy, and she found her heartbeat quickening as she remounted the steps to their chamber.

When she entered, Gaard stood at the window, his back to her, shirtless now, the strong, ropelike muscles with their twisted scar beckoning to be stroked, caressed. And then he turned to face her and his features were unreadable—he seemed suddenly to be a stranger once more, and she wondered if she would ever truly understand this man.

As she unfastened her clothes, her eyes never leaving his, she did know one thing: this tall, fierce Viking had breached her heart, and the fissure was growing ever larger now, leaving her heart more open, more vulnerable than she could have ever dreamed possible.

The thought welled within her strongly and she could not say if she were pleased or terrified. She had somehow opened herself to this man, and beyond that portal there was the promise of great happiness; yet, too, there was the promise of overwhelming pain should he desire to wound her.

Dawnlyn's clothes fell to the floor, and as Gaard moved

slowly, inevitably towards her, she prayed silently that he would take great care with her exposed heart, as great a measure of care as he did with her flesh.

Her lips parted softly, her arms received the strong breadth of him and her mind repelled all rational thought as his body played its tune on her senses once more.

Chapter Eighteen

THE SMITH HAMMERED AT THE BLADE WITH MIGHTY STROKES, sending showers of sparks scattering, then plunged it into the trough of water, where it bubbled and hissed angrily.

"There, my laird," said Duncan, the smith, "all straightened out."

Gaard took the sword by its still-warm hilt and sighted along its length. "Good," he said. "Now there are others to do and a dozen or so axes to repair as well." His mouth pulled up into a slanting grin. "We'd best be ready for anything the MacDougals might do. And my men have grown fat and lazy with inactivity. It's time for some action to sweeten their tempers!"

"Oh, there you are!" came Dawnlyn's soft voice from behind him. "I've been looking all over for you. Gaard, I must talk to you." Her voice seemed strained and a touch frantic.

"Now, what can it be that's so important? I'm busy with Duncan."

"Gaard." Her tone was hard with warning, her eyes lit with copper sparks. He'd grown to know that when Dawnlyn sounded like that, he'd do best to listen.

He rolled his eyes up with exasperation: the smith,

Duncan, grinned sympathetically. "All right. Walk with me to the stables and I'll hear you out."

Dawnlyn had on an old brown dress with an apron over it; her hair was pushed back under a headcloth with only a few recalcitrant strands escaping. Still, to Gaard she looked as fetching as a young girl, with familiarity only generating appreciation. He stopped her as they rounded the corner from the smithy and pulled her into his arms.

"Give me a kiss, my pretty," he laughed. "You've been so busy I can hardly catch you alone lately."

She pushed against his iron-sinewed arms with impatience. "Gaard, I've no time for that! The baby's waiting to be fed and I still haven't finished the sewing or spinning, and now the head shepherd's come to me with another task! Gaard, please stop!" She shivered at his nuzzling of her neck. "I don't have time to do it all!"

He stepped back, a frown creasing his strong features. "But you have servants for that! Surely I'm not to be cheated of my own wife's attentions. Come now, Dawnlyn."

"The servants have their own tasks. Remember, Gaard, you've just doubled the size of the household with your men and I can't seem to manage it all myself."

"Ask your father to help," growled Gaard.

"He *does* help! But he's off to Berwick now for the sheep fair and must then go to Edinburgh with the yearly tithes for the king. And remember, you asked him to present your land charters and patent of earldom to King Malcolm and Queen Margaret, legitimizing your position here. The Lord only knows how long *that* will take!" Her eyes brimmed with tears. "Gaard, I've tried so hard not to bother you with these details. I know you don't wish to be a landlord, but I can't seem to manage by myself! There's so much to do, and with the baby . . ." A single crystalline tear slid down her cheek, and she brushed it away roughly. "I've failed you. I'm useless! You should send me to the cloister, for all I seem to be good at is praying!"

Gaard studied her, his hands on her shoulders, astounded

at her speech. He hadn't had a hint of this turmoil in his wife; he'd thought things were going very smoothly indeed and had been enjoying a relaxed spring hunting and skirmishing with his men.

"Perhaps if your mother were here," choked out Dawnlyn. "She's so efficient. But she's gone to York to visit her family."

"And she's had forty years of practice at running a household, too," said Gaard softly. "You should have told me sooner, little one."

"But if I'm to be *worth* something . . . I feel so useless."

"Now, come with me. We'll go to the Hall and sit down and you will tell me everything. If I am the jarl, I must be aware."

"But you always said you hated it and had no interest!" wailed Dawnlyn.

"Sometimes a man must do things that are . . . unsavory to him. I'll survive," he said dryly. "Come now, cease your tears."

So they sat in the great hall and Dawnlyn fed the baby while Gaard listened to her enumerate the things that had to be done. The list staggered him; he'd had no idea. Elspeth had easily handled Thorkellhall, and St. Abb's had seemed to run itself last year, but perhaps he hadn't been aware of Dawnlyn's labors then. And, he recalled, there had been no baby.

"I see," he mused when she had finally finished. "It is somewhat more complicated than I thought. How did your father manage?"

"He worked from dawn till dusk," she said simply, "and the household was much smaller."

Gaard stared off into space. He dare not ask Sweyn to lend a hand, for he'd promised his lieutenant freedom from landlord's chores forever in return for his services the past year. And Ian—well, Ian was practically useless except in war and the hunt and, after all, St. Abb's was not *his*. So, that left no one but he himself.

"By Odin's breath!" he muttered. "So I'm to be a fat-gutted landlord after all!"

"I'm sorry," came Dawnlyn's strained whisper.

"No, little one, don't blame yourself. You've performed miracles here. It is all my fault. A man must watch his holdings. You should not be expected to do everything." He stroked her small straight nose with one big finger. "Eric is the most important thing now. You must save yourself for him."

"I'd heard of a wife in the village who just lost a baby and thought of asking her up here to wet-nurse Eric," ventured Dawnlyn, "but I don't want to, even though it would give me more time."

"No! Eric will drink his own mother's milk! That is final!"

"I'm glad. I didn't wish to give him up so soon. Oh, Gaard, are you angry with me? I'm a failure."

"No, I'm only angry with myself. Now, today you rest and I shall whip that lazy Meg if she can't see to things for a few hours. Then I'll go out and see the shepherd about his lambs. Thor's hammer! The Viking way is far simpler!" And he stalked off, muttering, to find Meg.

He instilled the fear of Hel into his wife's skinny serving wench and left her shaking in her red leather slippers. Then he went to the kitchen and began on fat Gerta. But the rotund cook merely turned on him with a fierce glare and raised skillet and shouted that "the kitchen was run right well and you'd do best to leave me to my work!" At least that satisfied him and he left Gerta's realm feeling quite virtuous.

He walked to the dairy and shouted sufficiently at the head dairymaid, then to the stables where, at least, he knew the man in charge. The stableboys were galvanized into action at the sight of his fierce scowl and surprisingly sharp words and breathed a collective sigh of relief when he rode out of the keep on the big, dappled destrier.

The warhorse was half wild at the best of times but was worse than ever now, having been hardly ridden all winter while Gaard was gone. It gave him a merry battle all the way to the protected valley where St. Abb's prize black-faced sheep were grazed. They were met at the valley's entrance by four bristling sheep dogs, whom the gray immediately tried to brain with his heavy front hooves until Gaard pulled him up sharply.

"Good morn to you, laird," called the shepherd, whistling to his dogs. "Come to count the spring lambs, have ye? The old laird always did." He spoke as if the Jarl of St. Abb's had a duty to *him,* for Odin's sake, thought Gaard, tying the vicious stallion to a sturdy tree.

"Come on, let's get it done, man," growled Gaard.

"I asked for the lady Dawnlyn herself," replied the one-eyed shepherd ponderously, "seeing as she knows the sheep better than a seaman like yerself, beggin' yer pardon, my laird." He sighed lugubriously. "But I reckon you'll do."

So the morning was spent making the tally of spring lambs, ewes and rams until Gaard's nose was clogged with the thick smell of mutton and he learned about the quality of wool, the birthing habits of ewes, the diseases and eccentricities of sheep, and had occasion to witness the incredible skill of the four Shetland sheepdogs.

Gaard left the valley a great deal wiser and full of respect for the one-eyed shepherd and his huge task. He also realized how very much he had to learn and was filled with shame for tossing all the responsibility off on his young wife, whose willingness to save him trouble ate at his heart. He even felt the initial stirrings of interest in just how St. Abb's worked—from farmyard to great hall. It was a challenge worthy of a *man,* if not a *Viking.*

At dinner that night Gaard found a greatly refreshed and gaily dressed Dawnlyn anxious to hear about his foray into the world of landlord and farmer.

Her marigold eyes and smiling lips rewarded his hard work that day, and he even thought the tower servants treated him with greater respect.

"Gaard, was it awful? Did you find old Alfred?" she had asked nervously.

"Oh, yes, I'm not helpless, my lady," he laughed. "We counted lambs until I near ran out of numbers!"

"And was it a good year?" she asked anxiously.

"All I know is that Alfred seemed content and we had a cup of ale together after we'd done."

"Oh, well, then, it *was* a good year. Alfred was celebrating. Did you give him his tithe?"

"His *what?*"

"Oh, sweet Lord, forgive me, I forgot to tell you. Alfred gets a penny a head if the spring crop's good. I'll have to ride out tomorrow and take him—"

"No, you will not! Am I not the jarl here? *I* will take it to him. Can't I be trusted with anything, woman?"

"Yes, of course, Gaard. Forgive me. I'm just accustomed to worrying over such details."

"Details! Is a man's life to be governed by *details?*" he grumbled.

Sweyn laughed and slapped Gaard's back. "I had my taste of it, now it's *your* turn. It has a way of tying down a man's life, I'll tell you." He threw back a pint or two of mead. "But still, it has its rewards, and my Colleen's one of them." He leaned across to kiss his pregnant wife on the lips, whereupon her fair skin colored prettily.

The next morning Gaard mounted his gray destrier again and fought the wily beast all the way to Alfred's meadow with a leather sack of pennies, one for each new lamb that had lived, and a leather skin full of the Hall's best ale to replenish Alfred's supply.

He wasn't to think it odd until later that the four Shelties did not challenge his way at the valley's entrance, or that Alfred's shrill whistle did not break the silence. But by then he had spied the column of smoke lifting from the shepherd's rude hut and the four sad, bloodied heaps of bone and fur.

The valley, of course, was completely empty but for the tracks of the stampeded sheep and the faint smell of blood and charred turf.

"Alfred!" bellowed Gaard, automatically drawing *Lightning Bolt* and kicking the stallion into a heavy gallop down the middle of the lush valley. "Alfred!"

A faint cry drew his attention to a stand of leafy maples. He reined the gray toward the trees, hoping against hope, and threw himself from the saddle.

"Here, my laird," quavered a weak voice. "Oh, they got me for sure this time."

Gaard found Alfred in the shadow of the trees, his face half-charred, his hair and eyebrows gone, a deep gash on his forehead. He cradled the old man's head in his lap, held the skin of ale to Alfred's lips.

"Who did this, man?" he rasped, no longer the mild landlord-farmer, transformed instantly into the Viking out for bloody vengeance.

"MacDougal," whispered Alfred. "MacDougal and his God-cursed kin. They killed me precious Shelties, killed them like they was nothing!" A tear squeezed out of Alfred's rheumy eye. "They near burned me in my cottage, but I heard the dogs growl and barely got out before the thatch fell in. Oh, me poor babies that are dead and in heaven now!"

"MacDougal!" Gaard's voice was low and hard as forged metal. "He'll be sorry he ever did this, or my name's not Gaard Wolftooth and I never charmed Fenris out of his teeth!" His gray eyes gazed out over the low green hills that rimmed the valley and they were filled with resolve and utter confidence.

The next morn Gaard became a stranger, a hard-eyed, predatory warrior in helmet and chain mail and battle harness. The men with whom she spoke and ate every day were unrecognizable, anonymous, fighting machines— beastlike in their cruel helmets. Her husband gave a savage Norse war cry, making his gray destrier rear and paw the air, and the men raised their swords, brandishing them in the pale dawn, causing the ground to shake with the thunder of their roar of fury. Then they were off, hooves pounding sparks on the cobblestoned yard, laughing and joking with bloody, exultant glee.

The aftermath was a day of waiting, a day of dull, nerve-wracking horror that caused Dawnlyn to work herself into frenzied exhaustion just to keep busy, busy, always busy, so that perhaps for a moment or two she might forget.

Afternoon came and went; the long spring twilight began, softening further the dull, misted light. Dawnlyn kept the huge gates manned and ready to be opened at a moment's notice, kept a full score of torches lit on the top of the walls in front of the Hall, kept savory stews bubbling in the pots and cooled ale kegs ready. She was just putting Eric to bed in her chamber when a commotion downstairs made her hasten to tuck in his cover and fly down the curving steps to see what it was.

"They're back!" cried Colleen, her white face suddenly joyous, "and I saw Sweyn!"

"And the others?" began Dawnlyn, but Colleen was already gone with a flurry of skirts.

Quickly Dawnlyn followed her to the front doors of the Hall, which had been thrown open, her heart pounding against her ribs, her stomach tied in a sick knot. How many had returned? How many saddles were empty? How many widows and orphans had been made tonight—and how many cripples?

She stood on the top step, staring at the mad charade in the courtyard as the men poured in through the open gates. It was near dark; the torches reflected off the mist and confused the eye with glare, gilding a white-toothed smile here, a horse's mud-streaked flank or a blood-crusted sword there. The noise of horses' hooves, men's shouts, women's cries all combined to make a hellish cacophony of sound.

Dawnlyn held back, pressed against the door frame, paralyzed by apprehension. What would she do if . . . ? But then she could not bear it another second and ran into the mass of humanity, her eyes frantically searching for Gaard or anyone she knew. They all looked the same to her in the flickering, taunting light of the torches. They were all mud-spattered, bloody, grinning victoriously beneath their fierce helms.

Where was Gaard?

She realized she was screaming his name, pushing her way past horses and coarse chain-mail-clad bodies, past women clinging to bloody lovers, heedless, her hair loosened from its headcloth and springing around her shoulders and face like gleaming copper wire.

He was not there. Her small fist pounded on the arm of a giant warrior. "Where is Gaard?" she begged him. "Where is the jarl?" Her voice rose strident with panic. "Where is he?"

The grinning Norseman backed away from her onslaught. "My lady, take care, that's my wounded arm," he said, grimacing.

"Where is he?" she cried shrilly.

The man looked around. "Can't say, my lady. I don't see him. Do you?"

She backed away from the grinning warrior, a fist of icy dread squeezing her heart. Her hand went to her mouth, jammed against her teeth in terror; her eyes were white-rimmed with fear.

Finally she saw his head across the mob, his dark blond hair plastered to his skull from wearing a helmet all day. She pushed her way toward him, near collapse with the agonized relief of seeing him safe, her way slowed nightmarishly by the throng.

"Gaard!" she cried, sobbing out his name. "Gaard!"

Then, at last, half mad, she reached him—but he was not alone. He stood there, tall and familiar and safe—but his head was bent in earnest, oblivious conversation with Astrid, whose face was turned up to his, open and smiling and joyous like a flower in the sun.

Dawnlyn wanted to shrink away, to be unseen, to disappear in the pouf of a necromancer's spell. Her heart stopped dead, the pain so intense she thought it might never start again. She felt herself sag with fear and weakness and hurt.

Then suddenly he was at her side, saying her name, and she didn't even care that a moment ago he had been with Astrid. Now, *now* he was safe and he was with her and she melted with weak relief against him.

"Dawnlyn," he said, his mouth against her hair, "where were you? I went to the Hall . . ."

"Where was *I*?" She laughed weakly, sagging against him. "Where were *you*?"

"Why, I merely went to take Alfred the MacDougal's finger. I promised him his head, but the man was as slippery as a greased pig and all I got was his finger."

"His *finger*? Oh, Gaard." She pressed herself against him, laughing and crying at the same time. "His *finger*?"

Dawnlyn was following Gaard through the great hall when she caught sight of Astrid, in a secluded corner, smiling brightly at one of the Viking men.

Dawnlyn knew suddenly what she had to do.

"Gaard?" He stopped at Dawnlyn's soft voice. "Would you mind if I join you upstairs in a few minutes? I've something I must see to first." And while Gaard went to the chamber for his bath, Dawnlyn walked slowly, purposefully toward Astrid.

She tapped the blond woman on the arm. "Astrid," Dawnlyn began, "I wish to speak to you." And then, glancing at the tall Viking with her, "*Alone.*"

Dawnlyn took a deep breath. It was now or never, she thought to herself, steeling her nerve.

She plunged in, amazed at her uncharacteristic temerity. "This is the last night you will spend at St. Abb's, Astrid. You will pack your belongings and be gone from here on the morrow."

"What?" gasped Astrid, her entire body growing rigid.

"You heard me. I have borne enough from you. And for that matter"—Dawnlyn gazed over to where Ian stood with the men—"so has my brother."

"Ian? How dare—"

260

"You care naught for one another. Not only is he too young for you, but you have deceived him evilly, as you have eyes only for my husband!" The words, once spoken, purged Dawnlyn's soul of a heavy burden. She would not relent now, and it was not as difficult as she would have guessed. Sometimes, thought Dawnlyn, impulsive behavior did provide a solution.

"Ian will not let me go!" choked Astrid. "Nor will Gaard! This is *your* idea, isn't it?"

"Aye," Dawnlyn admitted calmly. "It is high time I fight for what is mine."

"This is outrageous," Astrid spat. "We shall see what your husband has to say—"

"*I* am telling you," Dawnlyn said harshly. "What Gaard says will not matter in this case. *I* say you will go."

"Ha!" Blue sparks flew from Astrid's eyes. "You are insane!"

"Perhaps." Dawnlyn turned to leave. "But it matters not to you. Just be ready in the morning and a ship will be prepared to take you back."

Astrid suddenly grabbed Dawnlyn's arm. "You little . . . why, how dare you! They will not allow this! You can't do this!"

Dawnlyn looked down dangerously at the beringed hand on her arm. "You have no place here, Astrid. Go back to Norway. You will never have Gaard, never."

"You think you have won, don't you?" the Viking woman rushed to say. "But I'll wager Gaard will not let me go." Her eyes flashed brilliantly. "Yes . . . go ask your *husband!* You'll see!"

Snatching her arm away from Astrid's grasp, Dawnlyn narrowed her eyes. "I am lady of this Hall, woman, and Gaard Wolftooth's rightful wife. I am on my way this very moment to tell him that you are leaving. And leave you will, Astrid Thorhilddottir, on your own two feet, or by the blood of our sweet Lord, flat on your back!"

And, regally, Dawnlyn swept her skirt aside and walked

toward the curving steps. But even as she held her chin high and mounted the steps, Dawnlyn could not help but think on Astrid's words: "Gaard will not let me go." Dear Lord, she thought, how in heaven's name was she going to tell her husband what she had just done?

While Gaard sat in the metal tub, soaking himself, Dawnlyn paced, working up the nerve to tell him about Astrid. Over and over she told herself that she was Gaard's wife and lady of St. Abb's. *She* did not need to put up with her husband's mistress under her roof any longer. And she *would* not! Gaard might shout, might even strike her when he found out, but, by the sweet blood of Jesus, she'd be rid of Astrid for good this time!

"My lord," she began.

"Yes?" asked Gaard, his face a mask of weary triumph.

"I wish to speak to you of Astrid . . ."

"Odin's miserable teeth, not again!"

"Yes, again," she said finally.

"I warn you, Dawnlyn . . ."

"And I warn *you*, Gaard," she snapped. "I will not have that woman under my roof another day! If you wish to make love to her I cannot stop you, but you have not been discreet and you have shamed me! She *will* go!"

"Shamed you!" he roared, rising from the tub, rivulets of water streaming from him and splashing her gown. "I have not touched the brazen wench!"

"I don't believe you!" shouted back Dawnlyn, her hands on her hips.

"Take care that you do not become a fishwife and get a beating from me!" he warned, stepping from the tub.

"She is going! And your reluctance to get rid of her only proves my suspicions!" raged Dawnlyn. "She will leave tomorrow and I have already told her. I know I have done wrong in your eyes, so go on, beat me! Hit me and I will show everyone in the tower my bruises and tell them why and you will be ashamed!" And then she began to undo her

262

clothing, hysterically, pulling at the laces of her *bliant*, ripping at the buttons of her tunic, panting in her fury and her haste. "I will undress that you may beat me with more effect!" she cried, pulling at the stubborn fastenings with trembling fingers.

Gaard stopped his angry advance. By Freya's soft skin, his wife was truly demented. She really *did* believe he'd been in Astrid's bed!

He struggled to comprehend just what had set her off, why she was so undone just now.

"Dawnlyn," he said, going to her and putting his hands on her shoulders, stopping her frantic struggles. "Calm yourself and listen to me."

She stopped her attempts, but her face was red-splotched and almost ugly with anger and fear. She still panted with exertion.

"I do not have any feelings for Astrid, except perhaps memories of a childhood playmate"—he held up a hand at her snorted protest—"and I insist that you believe me. In fact," he said, eyeing her carefully, "I had been about to do what you have already seen to—to send her home to Norway with the very next ship that sailed. It is true."

"You just decided that to placate me!" cried Dawnlyn. "And you will go to her there and I will be left alone!"

"No, Dawnlyn, this is not true. I have never lied to you, have I?"

Dawnlyn looked at him, wanting desperately to believe, yet terrified of being hurt again. "You will let her go?" she whispered.

"Let her go? Willingly! She means naught to me!"

"I am afraid to believe you. You lied to me about her so many times before . . ." Her molten copper eyes begged him, bottomless with pain and fear.

"I never lied, Dawnlyn, never. The lies were all in your mind."

"But all those times you went off with her, or spoke with her . . ."

263

"They were precisely that—a conversation, a walk—on *my* part anyway. I admit, she can be a temptress and loves to display her charms."

"Gaard," she sighed, relaxing in his arms, "I do not know what to believe . . ."

He pulled her to his still-damp body, wetting the front of her gown, but she uttered not a word in protest and pressed against him. "Believe me, little one. You are my wife, the mother of my child. You please me greatly. Why should I wish to dishonor you?"

"I am a fool, Gaard." He felt her soft lips moving against his nude chest.

"Yes, you are, little one, but never mind. You shall grow in wisdom from now on." And he chuckled fondly.

"And Astrid will be sent home?"

"Tomorrow, as you wish it," he replied gravely.

"Tomorrow, then," Dawnlyn answered, turning her face up to his, a radiant look of joy on it.

Gaard bent down and covered her lips with his, thinking how peculiar and difficult wives were, yet how sweet and soft they were, too . . . at times.

Later, in the great hall, after the men had cleaned themselves and bound their wounds, Dawnlyn sat on the arm of Gaard's chair, her hand possessively on his shoulder as if to protect him from further harm of any kind. She picked the best, most tender morsels of meat and fed them to him from her own fingers, one at a time. Her cheeks were rosy from wine and her hair was loose, flowing down her back in tangled waves.

The men relived the entire battle, recounting over and over how they had surprised the MacDougal clan in their poorly defended tower. "With their pants down," laughed Sweyn.

"As if they never thought we'd attack them!" growled Gaard. "And there, penned up in front of their walls, were my sheep!"

"They had the gall to leave them out in the open,"

marveled Ian. "As if we'd let them take the sheep without raising a hand."

"Stupid," agreed Knute, taking a loaf of bread from a serving wench and ripping off a hunk. "But it was a good fight."

"A good fight!" chorused the rest of the men, raising their flagons.

"The MacDougals rallied bravely, I'll give them that," said Gaard. "We killed many and burned what we could, but they're not finished. They'll fight back, if I'm any judge of men."

"More fighting?" asked Dawnlyn.

"But they'll not catch *us* with our pants down," grinned Gaard wolfishly. "And they'll not take one thing that belongs to me ever again—not a cow or sheep or dog or grain of rye."

Dawnlyn was to remember those words later, when their significance would be brought home to her in the most hideous way she could imagine. Tonight she laughed with the rest of them, her white teeth flashing in a triumphant smile that would have reminded her shockingly of a Viking woman's grin if she'd been able to see it.

Chapter Nineteen

DAWNLYN HAD HER ACCOUNTS, HER TALLY SHEETS AND ABACUS spread out before her on the trestle table in the great hall, her goose-quills ready and her ink mixed, but her eye kept straying to the great double doors that were open to the balmy summer's day. It was as if she were a child again, wishing to escape the Abbess' lessons and run among the grass and heather and buzzing bees. She tapped her full lower lip with the tip of the quill, her tawny eyes staring into the middle distance, thinking back on those innocent child-hood days of lessons and prayers and praise for her cleverness. Then she shook her head ruefully and bent to the task of figuring the month's accounts.

She had nearly finished when she was distracted by a commotion outside in the courtyard. Was it Gaard returning from Coldingham? Surely not; it was far too soon. Indolently she rose and stretched her cramped muscles, then moved slowly toward the door to see what the interruption was.

But she hadn't far to go, as the open portal was suddenly filled with glaring white, swishing skirts, like the billowing sails of a ship, and the stout, portly figure of a nun in full regalia.

Dawnlyn gasped, stopping short, then gave a glad cry and ran to the familiar, bustling figure. "Aunt Gabriella!" she cried, throwing herself into the woman's plump arms.

"Child! How many times have I told you not to call me Aunt Gabriella! So undignified!" The nun's face was square and cheerful, but her expression right now was stern. Then her mouth split into a good-natured smile and she hugged Dawnlyn to her round chest. "But I forgive you . . . again! Only because I haven't seen you in a year or more!" She pushed Dawnlyn out to the farthest extent of her short arms. "Let me look at you, child! Why, you look well, quite well. You've put on some weight. Good." She pulled back the long, wide sleeve of Dawnlyn's pale blue undertunic and examined her arm carefully. "He doesn't beat you? I see no bruises."

"Beat me? Who?"

"Why, your husband, of course!"

"Gaard!" Dawnlyn laughed. "No, he doesn't beat me, Aunt."

"Well, then, he's a minority of one and so much the better for you." Gabriella cocked her wimpled head and studied Dawnlyn, her brown eyes keen and knowing. "Oh, my dear girl, I've missed you and prayed for you. Why didn't you visit me? I've been half crazy with worry, and finally I decided I had to come, I just had to."

Dawnlyn averted her eyes. "I was away in Norway for many months . . ."

"Aye, child, I know all that. Robert's been to visit me and told me the whole sad tale. It's your soul I'm more concerned with and how you are *inside*." Gabriella turned her eyes up to heaven and struck her round breast with a small clenched fist, then gathered her stark white robe in her little hand and swept over to the bench, where she plumped her round derriere down and patted the empty space next to her. "Now, come here and sit with me and we'll talk. But first"—she held up a pudgy finger—"you'll order drink and food from your kitchen so that I may refresh myself. It's hot as the flames of hell today."

Dawnlyn went out to the kitchen and asked Gerta to send something up quickly as the Mother Abbess Gabriella was visiting; then she ran her hands over her braided hair to smooth the escaping tendrils and pulled her skirt straight. Her aunt's sharp brown eyes never missed a detail!

Reentering the great hall, Dawnlyn took a deep breath. Her aunt was a formidable woman despite her sweet, plump appearance, and she kept the nunnery running like clockwork, with every novice in mortal terror of her sharp tongue. Dawnlyn loved her aunt and had always desired to emulate her, but Gabriella could be an intimidating person if she chose. Dawnlyn had known for months she should visit the cloister but had been strangely discomfitted at the thought and had put it off. And now the venerable Mother Abbess of Coldingham Nunnery was here.

"Auntie, I'm so glad you've come," she began, seating herself gracefully next to Gabriella. "I did wish to visit, but it would have been difficult—"

"Say no more. I understand perfectly. You betrayed your vows. Oh!" she held up a plump white hand, "I know you were forced. Robert told me, but nevertheless . . . it must have been awful for you, my poor child."

"It was, at first, but now I'm quite content. I have a son, you know." She refused to give in to her aunt's condescending attitude.

"Of course I know! I must keep myself informed, mustn't I? Where is he, this child?"

"He's asleep upstairs, but when he wakes, I will have him brought down for you to bless. He is a wonderful child— beautiful and so strong already!"

Gabriella eyed her niece suspiciously for a long moment. "You sound awfully like a new mother," she said wryly.

Dawnlyn colored and looked down at her clasped hands. "That is what I am, Mother Abbess. One cannot always help one's reactions when forced into a situation." She hated to sound apologetic. Why did she feel as if Gabriella put her on the defensive?

"I'm sorry, Dawnlyn, child." Gabriella put a hand on her

niece's arm. "I'm only a servant of God and have no right to judge you. It's my unholy pride and my disappointment that you did not join our ranks. Now, enough of that. Tell me of this man, this Viking you married."

"I hardly know where to start! Let me see . . . Well, at first, of course, he terrified me, so tall and fierce-looking and that wicked laugh! But then I found he was a man, a human being like others. But no, Gaard is not quite like other men. He is so strong and brave and so . . . confident. Nothing daunts him."

"Nothing?" queried Gabriella, an eyebrow raised.

"Nothing," repeated Dawnlyn proudly.

"Hmmm. He must be quite a man." There was an ironic edge to her voice.

"Aye, he is." Dawnlyn's voice was faintly smug. "He won a victory over the MacDougals last month when they stole our sheep . . . and didn't lose a man!"

"But, Dawnlyn, he is not a Christian!"

"I know." Her head came up, her small pointed chin held high. She would *not* act the penitent under her aunt's superior gaze. "But he is a good man."

"A raper and killer of Scots—a good man? Come, now, child. There's no need to defend him to *me* just because he's the father of your child!"

"Aunt Gabriella," said Dawnlyn coldly, "I would prefer you not to speak of my wedded husband in those terms."

"Ah," the warm brown eyes narrowed knowingly, "you feel something for him. Do you *love* this pagan Norseman?"

"Love?" Dawnlyn was nonplussed. "I respect him, I *like* him. But *love?*"

"It's nothing you need to consider in marriage, my child. What you feel is obviously enough. It is your duty now." This was stated matter-of-factly. "Love is merely for the troubadors, in any case, and the poets."

Just then Gerta's kitchen maids delivered a small feast and began to lay it out on a bench: fresh buttermilk, saffron cakes still hot from the oven, a cold strawberry tart.

Gabriella cocked her head, watching the entire process

269

carefully. "A nice repast, Dawnlyn. The Hall is running smoothly?" She picked up a bun, nibbled on it.

"Excellently, auntie. I learned my lessons at Coldingham."

"And do you remember *all* your lessons, child?"

"Aye, of course."

"Do you still keep your faith in God? Or does your pagan husband forbid you to worship Him?"

"My husband is a very learned and broad-minded man," Dawnlyn replied stiffly. "He knows of all religions and respects them all but has chosen his own way. He allows me to worship as I please."

"Good." Gabriella studied Dawnlyn closely once again. "Do you miss the cloister? Do you regret . . . ?"

Dawnlyn examined her own mind, framed her answer carefully. "I do not regret my marriage and my child. I miss—sometimes—the order and wholeness of the cloister, perhaps, but I could no longer live there, for I have too much stake in this secular world now."

Meg came up to Dawnlyn then, curtseying and crossing herself in honor of the Mother Abbess, and whispered into her mistress' ear that Eric had awakened and was hungry.

"Excuse me, Aunt Gabriella, I must feed the child. Then I will bring him down to you."

The necessity of holding Eric and feeding him calmed Dawnlyn's agitation. Why did her aunt have the power to unsettle her so? Every statement she'd made in favor of her new life, her husband, her child, had been twisted by Gabriella to sound superficial and undistinguished. Did all nuns look down upon the laity like that? It dawned on her that *she* herself had, at one time. Did she still? A qualm of misgiving shot through her breast. Was she then, in her aunt's eyes, a commonplace drudge, a person of no significance in this world? God forbid, did her aunt *pity* her?

Dawnlyn stroked the baby's soft cheek and smiled down on him. No, her Aunt Gabriella was wrong—*he* was worth everything. Only women who had borne a child would understand that, and to them, the majority of women on the face of the earth, their rewards were so obvious that they did not even bear discussing. No, the nuns were deprived of this particular fulfillment; *they* were the ones bereft.

The baby had finished his nursing. Dawnlyn changed his linen, dressed him in his long white lace christening gown and carried him down the stairs to meet his commanding relative.

"Aye, he is a strong, fat baby," agreed Gabriella. "A worthy heir of the Renfrews."

Dawnlyn beamed her pride. "Do you want to hold him, Aunt?"

"God forbid it! He might soil my robe. It's a new one and cost many pieces of silver. I shall appreciate him from afar, my child."

And *that*, thought Dawnlyn, was how her aunt—and all nuns—appreciated life itself—from afar.

The baby cooed and kicked his pudgy legs, then whimpered and insisted on being held upright so that his little fat feet danced a jig on his mother's lap, as if he practiced for the day he would begin to walk.

Soon it was obvious that his cries and gurgles were distracting to Gabriella, who wanted to know the details of the Hall management and whether the cloister could trade for some of St. Abb's valuable fleece in the fall.

"He certainly is a noisy little boy, isn't he?" she asked, half smiling, half critical.

Dawnlyn tried to put him in his cradle, but he refused; his loud wails let them all know he wanted complete attention—his rightful due.

"Meg," called Dawnlyn, looking around the great hall for her maid. "Where *is* that girl?" She was only too aware of Gabriella's disapproving glances and pursed lips. "Excuse me, Auntie. I'll find Meg and have her take Eric."

Quickly she located Meg in a corner of the stairway, giggling and smooching with her latest beau—a young blond Norseman who should have been on guard out at the gate. Dawnlyn chastised them both soundly, then handed Eric to Meg. "For goodness sakes! Behave yourself, at least while

271

the Mother Abbess is here! Now take Eric out for a walk and give me some peace!"

She returned, outwardly smiling and serene, to her aunt and continued the conversation, but in her heart of hearts there was a small seed of resentment growing—resentment of Gabriella's superior ways, resentment of her own responsibilities that kept her so busy and distracted, resentment of Gaard, who had put her in this position against her will. And—last but not least—resentment against her own inner weakness that allowed her to take her aunt's unknowing barbs so much to heart.

It was with a sense of relief that Dawnlyn promised to visit and saw the Mother Abbess off in her gaily colored cart driven by the ancient servant who always drove the Mother Abbess on her rounds.

After Gabriella was gone Dawnlyn tried to concentrate and finish her accounts, but the scrawled figures danced in front of her eyes and made no sense to her. She pushed it all aside and leaned on an elbow, her forehead creased into a frown.

Her aunt's words came back to her: "Do you regret . . . ?" *Did* she regret her loss of the pure, holy life No, she decided, it was not really that. Her life now had more than adequate compensations and maybe . . . just maybe, she had come to realize, it wasn't the holy life she'd desired so adamantly, but the power and dignity and respect the position of nun would afford her. And didn't she have a position of influence now? She was lady of the Hall, in charge of hundreds of lives besides her own family. Did she not carry the heavy ring of keys at her waist to display her authority? And did not everyone look to her for answers and decisions? Yes, her worth was proved.

Why, then, this nagging presentiment that something was wrong with her life, some piece of the puzzle still missing? Why was she not wholly satisfied? What *more* was there to have?

Then she remembered another thing her aunt, the Mother

Abbess, had asked: "Do you *love* this pagan Norseman?"
But her mind began to whirl in agitation and she backed
quickly away from the thought.

The sun beat down hotly on Gaard's head, sweat ran in
rivulets down his neck, wetting his tunic until it clung to his
back. And to his further discomfort and irritation, his mount,
which had been tied on the beach while he worked on his
ship for long hours, was frisky and ready to gallop the whole
way. Actually, if the blooded gray weren't trying to best him,
Gaard would have let him have his head; but he was
thoroughly sick of everyone and everything fighting him this
day, so he kept the horse well reined in.

Back in the courtyard he dismounted and threw the reins
to the stable boy, who hurried off when he saw the dark
scowl on his jarl's face.

Grumbling under his breath, wiping futilely at the salty
sweat in his eyes, he entered the great hall, banging the door
behind him viciously. "Bring me ale and fetch bathwater!"
he commanded the first girl he saw. "And for Thor's sake,
hurry!" The servants all froze in their stances, cowering.
"Damn it!" Gaard roared. "I said hurry!"

Suddenly skirts were lifted and small feet began to scurry
about in fear. And then he saw Dawnlyn among the women,
her hands on her hips, a frown creasing her brow. Something was on her mind . . .

He strode purposefully toward her. "Your temper looks as
vexed as mine," he growled. "And something else, my wife.
Whatever is bothering you must keep, for I am in no
mood—"

"It will *not* keep, my lord!" Dawnlyn said defiantly. "My
needs are as great as yours, and I won't hide in the corner
simply because your day has been hard." Her eyes traveled
quickly over his appearance, then dismissed him. "I must
speak with you and immediately."

"Oh, no!" He took the flagon of ale from a trembling
servant. "I will first have my bath. Do not try me this day."

And he turned his back on her, striding toward the steps. "That water better be ready before I finish this ale or someone's hide will suffer!" he yelled over his shoulder.

Dawnlyn stood for several minutes debating; his mood was as vile as she had ever seen, and yet hers was not much better. She needed to speak to him; there were things on her mind, questions that plagued her and could not wait for an answer.

She made her decision, whirled around and went to the kitchen, where she checked on the kettles of water for his bath. Satisfied that it would not be long, she went back through the great hall and purposefully mounted the steps.

Gaard was peeling off his stained clothing, tossing the tar-smelling articles helter-skelter. He did look exhausted, she noted, picking up his clothes piece by piece, stacking them in a neat pile.

"Where is my water?" he muttered.

"In a minute, Gaard . . . in a minute." She went to the chamber door, tapped her foot impatiently until several girls appeared carrying the steaming buckets.

Gaard finally sank into the warm water, dunked his sweaty head and came up shaking it until Dawnlyn's clothes were splattered.

"You needn't take your anger out on me," she said, picking up a rag to scrub his back. "I have my own concerns, Gaard."

"And well you might," he said irritably. "These Scots of yours are useless."

"Aye, my lord," she replied, having heard his complaint before and knowing now that the repair to his ship must have gone poorly. "But I do not wish to discuss my people, Gaard. I must talk to you about us. About—"

"I am in no mood, Dawnlyn," he interrupted. "We will talk later."

"We will talk *now*." She went on throwing caution to the wind. "My aunt came today . . ."

"The almighty Mother Abbess?" he scoffed. "And I suppose she has said things to upset you?"

"No. She was most gracious," Dawnlyn said defensively, growing angry at Gaard's attitude.

"It is said that she is never gracious save when it suits her to be so. I do not trust her from all I have heard. No doubt she came to see if I have embraced your God . . ."

Dawnlyn laughed bitterly. "Hardly that! We have all given up on *that* subject . . ."

"Then what did the great lady seek?" Sarcasm dripped from his voice.

Her temper flared hotly. She threw the linen cloth in the water and stalked to the window. "My Aunt Gabriella only came to see how I fared." Sighing then, she turned to face him. "Perhaps you are right; we should talk when you are less vexed."

But Gaard was ready for an argument now that Dawnlyn had started this. "No. We will speak now," he said. "Pray, what has put this burr under your saddle, my wife? What gracious words spake Aunt Gabriella?"

"You are quite impossible," Dawnlyn replied. "I told you, my aunt said nothing. She only began me thinking on my marriage."

"You mean, I am certain, that she wanted to know if you are as happy married as you would have been a nun."

"Something like that," Dawnlyn admitted. "And I have been tormented by doubts—"

"But I have given you everything!" Gaard sat up in the iron tub, gazed on her wonderingly. "Our marriage is good! We profit well together! And there is Eric . . ."

"Yes. Everything you say is true. But I feel somehow unsettled within myself. It is as if something is missing in my life and I know not what."

"Nothing is missing," Gaard said darkly. "I have given you all. Why should you complain?"

"I am not wholly content," she said pensively. "I feel something lacks."

"Then I will do more chores. Perhaps you are merely tired."

"I am not tired. My life is quite in order, Gaard. It is more . . . more that something *inside* me is not whole."

"That is ridiculous." He then muttered under his breath and reached for his ale.

Dawnlyn studied him with a frown. Even though his temper was terrible at times, even though he would never be a Christian, none of these things truly bothered her anymore; she had grown used to his ways. No, there was something else, some part of him that seemed held back from her and, she thought suddenly, some part of herself that she had not yet given him.

"I do not think it is ridiculous to want one's life completely ordered," she said to him then. "If I feel that something is lacking then I must know what it is."

"Women," he muttered.

"Men, to me," she said quickly, "are just as perplexing. Men never speak of things from the heart."

"The heart?" He arched a brow.

"Yes. Should we not discuss the way we feel?"

"But I feel fine!"

"Oh, Gaard!" she whispered in exasperation. "I mean, how do you feel about me? About our marriage? Do you merely tolerate me, or do you *care* about me?"

"You speak like a poet or some such thing. Of course I care about you. It is an inane question."

"But," she murmured quietly, "do you . . . do you *love* me?" And she knew then, the moment the word fell from her lips, that all along love was what stood between them, that love, or the lack of it, was the unsolved enigma in her mind. How simple! she thought abruptly. She should have seen it months ago! If Gaard truly *loved* her, then somehow she knew she would be whole, that her worth would be total.

"Well?" she asked again, seeing the bemused look on his face. "Do you?"

"Do I love you?" he replied in great wonder. And then, "What does it matter? I have never thought about such

276

things. I am a fighting man, Dawnlyn, not some court fop who has time for such nonsense."

There was nothing he might have said that could have pained her more. He did not love her—there was no room in his heart for such a *small* thing.

Not even knowing why, she fought back tears of pain and anger. She threw him a look of pure loathing, then spun around and fled toward the door. And then she shot over her shoulder, "I do not love you, either!" and rushed from the room.

Still weary from the long day and now angry, too, that Dawnlyn was carrying on so ridiculously, he rose dripping from the tub and snatched the linen towel around his waist. "Come back here!" he bellowed after her, but Dawnlyn was already below, stalking the hall in fury.

He strode to the door, down the corridor to the curving steps. "Come back up here!" he thundered, then began descending the stairs. Finally he stood in the great hall, a puddle of bathwater growing at his feet. Dawnlyn had seen him, as did the servants, and was fleeing to the kitchen, hot tears of anger wetting her cheeks.

"Don't you *dare* walk away from me!" he called. "We are not done with this talk you insisted on. Now get over here!"

"Oh!" she cried, turning around to face him, hands on her hips. "Don't you order *me* around! I am no thrall!"

"You treat me worse than a slave!" he retorted, scowling at the servants, who tried to melt away from his notice. "I come back to my home from the worst day of labor I have had to endure in months . . . I am hot and weary . . . but you do not care in the least!"

"That is not true . . ."

"Then you insist that we talk when I have begged you to put it off, and you have the gall to ask me such a ridiculous question!"

"It is *not* ridiculous!" she wailed, wiping at her tears with trembling fingers, "It is most important to me!"

"We are married. The question is moot and foolish and female and I—"

But whatever he was going to say remained unspoken as suddenly a commotion at the doorway snatched his attention. Meg was there, he saw, surrounded by servants and a sentry who helped to support her. On her head was a nasty gash and she seemed about to swoon.

Dawnlyn was the first to move toward her, and Gaard saw a look of fear on his wife's face that caused his heart to thud heavily. Then he, too, walked quickly to Meg's side.

"Meg?" Dawnlyn was whispering so quietly, so fearfully that Gaard had to strain to hear. "Meg? Where is . . . where is Eric?" The words were torn from her breast.

Suddenly cold fear coiled inside Gaard's stomach. "Where is my son?" he asked dangerously.

Meg's terrified eyes rolled up in her head. "I was playing with him," she choked, "on the grass . . . then everything went black . . ."

"Where is he?" Gaard thundered, catching Dawnlyn to his side.

"He's . . . gone." Meg wept and Dawnlyn felt all the blood leave her face as she clutched at Gaard in terror, her tawny eyes wide and stricken.

And Gaard knew then, for the first time in his life, a real fear—one so deep and painful that sickness rose from his stomach. Only through sheer will was he able to keep it down.

"Eric . . ." he whispered. "My son . . ."

Chapter Twenty

LONG BEFORE JAMES MACDOUGAL'S MAN RODE UP TO ST. Abb's hall with a white cloth wrapped around the hilt of his sword, Gaard knew who had taken his son. And the ransom note was no surprise, either.

"Five hundred pieces of gold!" gasped Sweyn. "Why, MacDougal is insane!"

Robert and Ian, along with Dawnlyn, who held herself together through sheer faith, stood close to Gaard as if to glean his strength in this terrible time of despair.

"MacDougal must think his losses were great indeed," said Robert darkly, shaking his gray head.

"They were," Gaard replied, "but hardly worth so much gold or the life of my son. I'd give all to be able to storm their tower."

"But you must!" Dawnlyn sobbed, her head in her hands. "You must ride there at once and bring Eric back!"

"Yes!" Ian shouted. "To arms! That blackguard must meet his end!" And with Ian's exuberant cry, roars of agreement sounded from the men of St. Abb's as they stood en masse in the great hall. Only Gaard remained silent, a look as cold as death masking his features.

Finally Gaard raised his hands above his shoulders. "No!" he called above the heavy din. "Silence!" And slowly the uproar ebbed and swords were resheathed in belts until the men faced their leader in hushed respect. Satisfied, Gaard went on. "If we lay siege to the MacDougal he will surely kill Eric. No. We will ride there, in force, and I, myself, will call the coward out! It is the only way." Then Gaard raised his hands again, stretching his arms high in the air. "Are you with me, men?" The hall came alive with the beat of their willingness and like a living heart, the men pulsed with excitement, with anticipation of the moment when their worthy leader would meet the MacDougal face to face.

While they made ready to ride—sharpening blades, testing leather—Gaard drew Dawnlyn to a far corner of the hall where they could speak privately.

"Are you certain you should not raid them? Perhaps we should pay them the ransom!" Her stricken eyes searched his with desperation.

"You must trust me, Dawnlyn." He took her face in his hands. "I know what is best."

"I do trust you," she sobbed. "I just can't think properly right now . . . I am frantic with worry . . ."

"Nor should you have to think on it. It is in my hands now . . . mine alone."

"If only there were something I could do! Some way I could help!" Then Dawnlyn shook her head from side to side and wept as she had for the past several hours. When she looked up again, her cheeks streaked with tears, she said, "Eric hasn't even eaten! Look at me!" Gaard's eyes gazed at the dark spots on Dawnlyn's dress where her milk seeped through.

"I'll murder that son of Hel! I'll have his head or by Odin's breath I'll die trying!" And he knew his words were borne of rage and that his great temper was of little comfort to his wife. Why must she suffer?

"Oh, Gaard . . . when will you be back? How long must I wait here alone and in this torment?"

"We may not be back here until early tomorrow morning. It is a long ride."

"But will he let Eric go?"

"I cannot say. I should imagine he will make us strain at the bit for a time, then surely he must accept my challenge."

A sob tore from Dawnlyn's throat. "Why? Why little Eric?"

"He is the most dear to us." Then Gaard said pensively, "More dear than I had realized. I do not feel a whole man without him. It is as if a leg has been severed from me."

"I, too, feel a part of me gone. We were so happy . . . the three of us . . ."

"Yes," he muttered darkly, "we did not truly appreciate it, did we?"

Much to her amazement and comfort, it was Gaard who suggested she go to the chapel and pray. "Remain there and I will come back to you."

"With Eric . . ."

"With our son." He then hugged her gently. "Do not fear, little one," he said. "Between your prayers to Kris and mine to my gods, Eric will soon be with us again."

"Yes," she replied, her lips against his shirt, "we will both pray. You to your gods and I to mine. It cannot hurt to have all the heavens on our side."

Gaard smiled tightly, putting her at arms' length. "Don't tell me you have come to accept my gods?"

"Nay," her eyes met his steadily. "But my God will hear your prayers, too. And even though you pray to the wrong one, He will see your grief and anguish and know that you are a good man, Gaard."

"Well enough. Now go to the chapel."

Dawnlyn remained in the ancient, candlelit chapel for most of the night and gave her prayers to God. But the silent pleas did little to comfort her; time after time a traitorous thought seized her mind: all the prayers in the world had not half the strength of her husband. If little Eric were to be saved, it would be Gaard's doing, and once she even found herself praying that his Luck would hold true. The thought was unsettling. If God knew what was in her heart, where her faith lay in this ordeal, surely He would be angry. And yet, did not God join a man and woman and give them children to protect? Certainly *He* would want her to place trust in Gaard's hands.

"The Lord helps him who helps himself," she whispered, and abruptly a great truth was known to her: she had not misplaced her faith by putting it in Gaard—the Lord had placed them on this earth, had ordained this marriage so that there would be continuance.

And so she prayed through the long night that Gaard's Luck would endure and that God would give him strength and protect him.

While her understanding of her marriage grew, Gaard led his men across the glens, the bogs and primeval shell-mounds of Northumbria north to where the MacDougal's tower stood. It was no wonder at all, Gaard thought, that James MacDougal coveted the St. Abb's land; MacDougal's tower sat inward from the coast on marshy terrain that would never produce in a rainy year, nor would cattle and sheep survive well on these empty moors.

It was nightfall by the time Gaard's troops reached the boundary of MacDougal's land. Heavy fog lay silently in the splits of the earth, swept across the moor coldly like a veil cloaking the horses' hooves so that they appeared to glide on a cloud, footless. The men grew restless, not caring for the strange atmosphere that brought to mind tales of mist monsters and *wendols* and men who rode heedlessly into the moor, never to be seen again.

A weak moon rode the cloudy sky like a skiff on high seas, but they were afforded enough light to continue. Gaard was certain by now that their approach was known by Mac-Dougal, who must be readying his forces for battle. But Gaard was not going to storm the tower; he merely rode to challenge the laird alone and to display his forces.

It was nearly daybreak before they reached the tower, which loomed above them on the crest of the hills like a giant, dark-stoned monster. When they had been there the month before it had been daylight and the monster had seemed less threatening, less sinister.

Gaard raised a quiet hand indicating for them to halt. He

would await daybreak now before riding up the hill to trade words with MacDougal. And as he dismounted to rest, he thought of Dawnlyn, alone at the hall, alone and worried sick, and now it would be midafternoon before he would be back at St. Abb's—home and with Eric safely returned to his mother's breast.

First light was slow to come. It began as a faint pearl glow to the east, illuminating the banks of thick fog to a dim gray hue. A few trees were visible finally, their gnarled, burned branches twisting eerily, silhouetted by the insipid light. The tower against the sky seemed to almost breathe as the clouds of mist rose to touch its massive stone walls. Soon it would be time to ride across the barren moor and call out the MacDougal.

Gaard checked his gear: the edge of *Lightning Bolt,* the thick handle of his war axe, the nose plate on his helmet, which was slippery wet with mist.

"It's Godforsaken land," whispered Robert Renfrew, who kneeled by Gaard's side. "There is ever a chill here that seeps into a man's bones."

"Yes," Gaard agreed. "There is good reason for Mac-Dougal to seek our land to the south. I fear the only way to stop him will be to see the man dead."

"Aye," Robert grumbled pensively. "It is something I should have done in my youth."

"The deed will be done this day." Gaard rose, summoned to his side Sweyn, Ian and Knute. "I shall ride alone before you to the tower wall. Keep the forces well behind me in a line so that there will be no mistake of our intent this day. I do not want that devil to think we are attacking or Eric might be . . . Eric may suffer."

And so they mounted their steeds and formed a long line across the rough, striated land. The horses were restless and strained at their bits, nervous from the lifting banks of fog; the men sat rigid in their saddles, their helms and shields dull in the weak light.

As Gaard rode ahead of the line he drew comfort in the familiar sounds and odors of men ready to do battle: the sound of leather squeaking, of horses chomping at the bit, of metal slapping against a firm thigh. The air was pungent with dampness, with anxious male sweat, with horseflesh—and from these things he drew a great strength.

Atop the turret a sentinel call could be heard echoing across the valley, and then Gaard saw other shapes gather around the sentry, straining their eyes through the mist.

When he was directly below the tower walls, his gray stallion prancing nervously beneath him, Gaard raised a sinewy arm to his foes. "I am Gaard Wolftooth!" he called. "I shall spare this tower if the laird shows himself!"

"Hold!" the Scots sentry shouted from above. "The MacDougal comes!"

Impatient, trying to keep thoughts of his son's danger from seeping into his mind and sapping his will, Gaard waited. His destrier continued to prance beneath him, occasionally trying to rise and paw the air as Gaard's own tension relayed itself to the beast. Then finally James MacDougal was on top of the wall, leaning cautiously over the side, a white bandage still visible on his hand even after so many weeks. Suddenly Gaard was glad the damage he had done to MacDougal still caused him trouble.

"If any act of aggression is committed against my tower," he called to Gaard below, "then your son's life shall be taken!"

Gaard's heart squeezed painfully. "I have ridden to your walls, MacDougal, seeking to do battle with you alone. My men are at a safe distance from you." He swept an arm across the line of warriors behind him. "The fight is between us now! Let my son go!"

MacDougal studied him for a long moment, turned and spoke to several of his mail-clad soldiers, then leaned over the wall again and laughed, the sound of which reminded Gaard of a death knell. "Did you not receive my ransom note?" he said. "I want gold! Why should I do battle with you when you *must* pay me?"

It ran swiftly through Gaard's mind that MacDougal was taunting him—the man could not possibly ignore a personal

challenge. Why, his clansmen would know he was a coward!
"You must come out and battle me, MacDougal! Surely you
cannot hide behind my son's life."

"Ha!" MacDougal spat. "I am no fool! Bring the gold!"

"No!" Gaard cried, raising a fist to his foe. "Would you
have your men see your cowardice? Have you no honor?"

Then there was a movement behind James MacDougal
and suddenly Gaard saw a bundle handed to him. The
blood raced through Gaard's veins, pounded in his temples
sickeningly. "No!" he roared, the sound of his rage echoing
ominously across the moor.

"Bring the gold, Viking!" MacDougal then held the
bundle over his head and the coverlet fell away, exposing
the child to Gaard's horrified stare. "Do you see your son?
What is he worth now? Bring the gold!" And Eric began to
cry, an infant's wail that tore at Gaard's guts as nothing
before had ever done.

Slowly he became aware of movement behind him—his
men were advancing, their muted roar of outrage reaching
him, their swords unsheathed, gleaming dully above their
heads in the wan light.

Gaard quickly gathered his wits and spurred his horse
toward them, yelling, "Stop!" until he thought his lungs
would burst.

Seeing his frantic signals to them, the men finally reined in
their mounts and held fast until he was upon them.

"We cannot attack!" he cried. "MacDougal will kill Eric
immediately. Now turn, quickly, we ride to St. Abb's!"

There were several calls of discontent, which Gaard
handled severely. "You *will* obey my command or I, myself,
will cut you down!" And to prove his words, he drew
Lightning Bolt and held it above his head. "Turn your
horses! Now!"

As the dissenters slowly obeyed, Sweyn rode abreast of
Gaard. "That vomit-filled pig!" he growled between
clenched teeth. "That filthy coward!"

"Hold your wrath," Gaard ordered, "or the men will turn
on the tower again. Now lead them away and give me a

chance to think!" But on the long ride back, no plan came to Gaard's mind. He rode some distance ahead of his troops, unable to think properly. All that came to mind was the image of Eric's helpless body held above the coward's head.

Hate writhed within Gaard like a coiled serpent, hate and disgust and self-doubt. And Dawnlyn—how would she receive this news? She was the babe's mother, yet what protection could he give her against the reality of danger to Eric's life?

As they approached the walls of his own tower, Gaard began to feel less than a man. He was returning home defeated, useless. He would have to pay the ransom, give in to MacDougal's demands like a worthless coward himself.

Dawnlyn raced out from the great double doors, her eyes filled with hope and joy. When she saw Gaard, the tormented look on his face, his empty arms, she froze in her path, swift despair gripping her.

"Eric!" she whispered, and then as Gaard dismounted and strode toward her, his shoulders sagging, she swayed and gave an unearthly cry. "Oh, my God! Eric!"

Gaard swept her into his arms, pressed her head to his chest with a hand. "He is alive and from what I could see, he is faring well." He went on to tell her precisely what had taken place and why he could not allow his men to storm the tower.

Trembling, Dawnlyn walked beside him into the hall. "But Gaard . . . we must pay the ransom at once," she sobbed, half falling into a chair. "We must! There is more than enough."

"No."

Her head snapped up and her eyes met his; he could hardly bear the anguish that brimmed in them.

"We cannot give in to this treachery."

"But we *must!*" she wailed.

"I said no. Would you have the father of your children put his tail between his legs and run like a lowly dog? Is that the sort of man you wish to bed you? Is that the kind of man I must become?" he shouted, his gray eyes as black as night.

Dawnlyn was struck speechless, and it was her father who came to her side and tried to comfort her. "Your husband is a man of great strength and honor, lass. You cannot ask him to crawl on his knees before the MacDougal, for it would surely kill Gaard to do so."

"But . . . but Eric . . ." Hot tears fell to her hands, clasped whitely in her lap.

"Eric is not lost to you. Gaard will think of a way. Have faith in the man whom you have married."

Gaard remained as silent as an ancient Greek statue, but his brain seethed with worry. How could Dawnlyn have faith in him when he, himself, was slowly losing control of his own will . . . his Luck?

After calming herself as best she could, Dawnlyn looked up at Gaard. "Have you a plan? There must be some way."

"There is," he said solemnly, "but as yet, I do not know exactly what is to be done."

"But Gaard," her voice quivered, "surely you have some idea of what we must do. I . . . I know you to be the strongest . . . the most wise of all. Surely you can find a way."

A look of pain seized his features, twisting them. "I am glad you have faith in me," he rasped out bitterly, "for I have all but lost trust in myself."

Slowly she came to her feet and reached out to touch him. "Gaard . . ." And then she was in those strong arms, half crushed to the hard wall of his chest. "You will think of something . . . I know you will," she breathed, listening to the heavy thud of his heart as it pounded with self-contempt.

Later, as Gaard sought solitude wandering the grounds aimlessly, he found himself standing on the cliff overlooking the writhing, eternal sea.

Perhaps it was the lulling effect of endless waves pounding the headland, the expanse of sea meeting horizon that calmed him, but after several hours alone on a rock overlooking the North Sea, Gaard was once again becoming himself. A Viking, he mused pensively, draws his strength from the seas and the open heavens above and this he was doing. "Spirit of Odin. Come to me . . . tell me what is to be done . . . give me strength of sinew and give me Luck . . ." And eventually one-eyed Odin seemed, indeed, to visit his mind's eye on that lonely rock; the god's spirit, clever beyond man's ken, invincible, powerful, seemed to enter Gaard's brain until his ears rang and Gaard grew dizzy.

So profound were the thoughts buffeting his mind that he had to hold onto the boulder for support: "Embrace my adversary Kris," came the thought in a thunderous rush, "and go to the MacDougal as a lowly, begging, mendicant monk. Gain entrance and take thy son to your breast, and when the boy is safe, take down the walls of the tower so that I may laugh!" The spirit of the god of wisdom seemed to draw in a deep breath, and it was as if all the air had been swept from the earth. "Go, now! I will be with you in case you have need of me. But hurry, bester of Fenris, I have others who call on me!" And Odin's image exploded before Gaard's closed eyes in a sudden burst of light and he was gone. Only grassy meadow and sea below met Gaard's steady gaze as he reopened his eyes.

The air returned. Gaard drew in a deep breath and rose, walking with renewed purpose and strength back to the hall.

When he strode in, Dawnlyn ceased her frantic pacing and came to him. "Have you a plan?" she asked, but the question, she could see, was unnecessary. On Gaard's face was a look of utter competence and self-assurance. *This* was the man who had taken her long months ago from the chapel, who had driven himself into her body and given her a child—this was her husband, her proud Viking.

"Summon the seamstress and bid her fashion on me a monk's robe with hood. It must look lowly and well-worn. Now hurry!"

While Gaard gathered his men for a war council, Dawnlyn oversaw the stitching of his garment—a loose, brown, homespun robe with a large, pointed hood. She herself wove the rope belt and rubbed into it grease and soil to make it appear well-used. When the robe was sewn, she followed the same procedure to age it as she had done with the belt, then for good measure rubbed some manure into it to make it seem like the wearer had taken shelter many nights in a stable.

While her hands worked feverishly, she tried to comprehend Gaard's plan: someone must be going to dress as a monk and gain entrance to the MacDougal tower. But who—who would Gaard trust save himself?

Her task completed, she returned to the great hall and handed him the garment. "It is for you?" she asked quietly.

"Yes." His eyes met hers for a moment. "I must go there. Now wait for me aloft in our chamber while I finish reviewing my plan with the men."

Dawnlyn awaited him impatiently in their room while Gaard went over the last details of his plan with Ian, Sweyn, Knute and Robert. She walked the cool stone floor anxiously, wondering how she had ever survived without her husband. And then it struck her that she might have been taken by a cruel, horrible man who beat her and smelled of onions and ale all the time. And what of Eric? Would she ever have borne such a wonderful child by another man? Surely not. And even in her desperate, tormented state, Dawnlyn could not help but count her blessings and vow to give up each and every one if it would help to regain her son.

Gaard came to her at dusk still clad in his chain-mail shirt, trousers and high leather boots. Silently, for no words were necessary between them, she helped Gaard into the loose robe, then knotted the belt around his lean hips.

"You have guessed my plan," he stated levelly.

"Yes. And you will need a heavy cross about your neck. Gerta has one . . ."

Her eyes met his for a moment, then quickly she looked away. She was afraid for him . . . afraid for Eric; but it would not do to display her emotions. She stood back and surveyed him. "You are too tall, but if you stoop. And Gaard," she said abruptly, "can you cross yourself?"

With the hood over his fair head, stooped as much as his great height would allow, he made the holy sign of the cross.

Dawnlyn gasped. "No! It is the opposite way across your chest!"

Again he made the sign, only this time properly. "Am I humble enough? Do I look the role of a wandering monk?"

Dawnlyn smiled tightly, her hands on her hips. "No. Not to me. But then, I know you too well."

Gaard walked toward her, tossing the heavy wool hood from his head. "Send your prayers with me, little one." He tipped her chin up with a gentle hand.

"I will pray," she said, "but my prayers will be for you and not for God's help." Her luminous amber eyes caught the fading evening light. "You see, my husband, I have learned through this ordeal that the Lord cannot do all for us; some things we must do on our own so that we become stronger."

His head bent and his lips brushed hers carefully. "Then you have learned much and I respect your God for granting you this wisdom." He kissed her thoroughly but without passion; in his demanding touch there was need—his mouth seemed to say, "I want you . . . I cannot go it alone . . ."

Dawnlyn responded to his hard, searching lips with her own need, and never had she felt so close to him; she was so at one with his soul that her breath was snatched away.

When Gaard stood back from her finally, his eyes were a soft, gentle gray, the clear color of the sky after a spring storm. "I do not want you to worry while I am gone," he whispered. "My Luck is with me now and all will go well."

"Was it Odin who gave you this plan?" she asked pensively.

"Yes. It came to me in the meadow and my Luck is as great as ever." Then Gaard smiled. "You do believe in Luck, don't you?"

Dawnlyn met his look steadily. "I think so. If there is such a thing, then you possess it and I will not be afraid."

His smile broadened, making him appear boyish, as handsome again as any man she had ever seen. "Someday, little one," he said, "you may just make a good Viking wife!" Then he sobered. "Now I must be off."

"God speed," she whispered fervently. They embraced

warmly once again; then Gaard hid a long, two-edged dagger in his boot, gave her one last reassuring smile and left the chamber. Save for several of his trusted men led by a middle-aged veteran named Godfred, Dawnlyn and the servants were quite alone in the large Hall. Shortly after Gaard's departure, Sweyn, Ian and her father had also ridden out with the forces, and Dawnlyn wished Elspeth were there with her, to comfort her. Yet she knew the thought was purely selfish, as Eric was most dear to his grandmother and she would be worried sick. No, she realized, it was best Elspeth was still in York. When she returned they would all sit around with Eric and the past would be a mere ugly memory.

And so Dawnlyn kept company with Meg during the long night, and surprisingly the frail serving girl was a great comfort to her mistress, having felt Eric's loss deeply, too. Still, time sidled along unevenly—minutes crept by like hours, each hour like the rising to the setting of the sun. But Dawnlyn did not lose hope—if anyone could bring back little Eric, it would be his father.

Gaard rubbed his eyes, realizing he had not slept in so long he could not remember.

The MacDougal tower lay before him once again, and Gaard's men were to the south, hidden in the banks of fog, quietly awaiting his signal.

He reached down and checked to see if the dagger was in place, then felt beneath the robe for the tiny cured leather pouch of sleeping drops given to him by Robert.

He was prepared.

Pulling the hood over his head, stooping his shoulders humbly, he walked steadily along the rocky path leading to the rear gate of the tower. He knew he would be stopped by the sentinel posted there, but that could not be helped. All he could hope for was that the MacDougal had left no instructions to the guard as to what should be done with beggars. James MacDougal was looking for a full-fledged raid, not a lone monk seeking a handout from the kitchen.

Then he heard the inevitable "Halt!" from atop the battlements and came to a slow stop like an aging nag. "What is your business, monk?" called the sentry.

Gaard's head came up wearily. "I shall give a Mass and blessings for a simple meal, my son."

"We have no time for Mass this day, friar."

"Surely a blessing, then? I am weak from my wandering. I have great need of a meal." Gaard's shoulders hunched lower.

"Well . . . all right. Go to the postern gate and you'll be given entrance by the sentry."

Inwardly, Gaard sighed in relief; he was all but there now. He began his slow progress again toward the rear gate. As it was barely dawn, he hoped most of the inhabitants would still be sleeping and he would have to deal only with the women in the kitchen who prepared breakfast.

He gained entrance after knocking on the thickly planked door, and the weary sentry barely gave him a second glance, merely nodding to the right, across the courtyard, to the kitchen. Once inside the kitchen Gaard saw three women bustling about—they, too, hadn't the time to cease their labors and truly pay him mind.

He seated himself on a bench at the wooden table, brushed away a flour smudge and rested his arms on the surface. Then he remembered that his hood was still on and he slowly slid it to his back.

"You're a fair one," the eldest cook observed, kneading dough with her age-splotched hands.

Gaard forced a smile but felt thoroughly exposed now. "Aye, daughter of God," he said, "my father used to say I had the light both within and without."

"Tall, too," she went on, eyeing him keenly now. "Never seen one quite like ye . . ."

Gaard smiled more broadly, with as much ease as he could manage. It was not that he couldn't handle these women if necessary, it was simply that he preferred as little commotion as possible.

"My height shortens with lack of food, woman. I would appreciate what little scraps you can spare."

One of the others brought him a cider. She was young, darkly pretty with a small child clinging to her skirts. When she plunked the mug before him, her eyes widened at his appearance and a rosy blush touched her cheeks. "Would you bless my girl?" she asked timidly, glancing at the child at her feet.

"Fetch me food and I'll speak with the girl," Gaard said while praying silently that the woman would leave the child at his side while she went for food. It would not do to let her hear his blessing, for he hadn't the slightest idea what was said. Why hadn't he asked Dawnlyn?

Mercifully, all went well with his mumblings and gestures and the child only cried once when left alone with Gaard. He glanced out the open kitchen door. It was daybreak—in a few minutes the sentinels would spot his men, the call to arms would be heralded and pandemonium would spread throughout the tower. Then he would make his move.

Gaard had just taken his first bites of cold oat gruel when the call echoed in the courtyard. The kitchen women froze in their tracks, their eyes huge with fear. And then they were scurrying about like mice with no direction.

"Go to the chapel and pray!" Gaard rose from his seat. "Go! I will join you there."

The two younger women and the child disappeared; only the older one remained. "The men must be fed," she grumbled, unconcerned. "Prayers will not fill their bellies."

Gaard's features drew down in rigid lines. "Then cook, woman. I go to the chapel." He walked past her and into the great hall, wondering if she would still be there when he returned.

In the great hall there were men rushing everywhere, half-dressed, their swords dragging behind them on belts. No one paid Gaard any mind, but he was certain someone would notice when he began to mount the tower steps instead of heading toward the chapel.

Then suddenly, as he slowly crossed the hall, he felt a hand on his arm. His heart began a heavy pounding as he carefully turned around.

"Bless me," said a young boy about the age of his own son Leif. "We do battle this day—bless me, Father."

Gaard let out a long breath as the lad bowed his head. He made the sign of the cross over the boy's head and folded his hands in prayer, his lips moving as if mumbling words to God. Then the youth rose, smiling tentatively. "May your . . . May God be with you this day," Gaard said sincerely, gazing at the smooth, nearly beardless skin of the boy.

"Thank you!" The lad hurried off then, following the others out into the courtyard.

And Gaard was alone in the hall. He went quietly to the curving steps and began to mount them two at a time. He stopped and looked around on the first landing—which room? Was Eric even on this level? He tried several doors, only to be met by empty chambers. He rushed up the steps again to the next landing. How long could his Luck hold out?

As if in answer to his question a door opened and he could hear a man's voice and then a woman's reply. Quickly he ducked into an empty chamber room until he heard footfalls pass the door and ascend the tower steps leading to the turret. When it was safe again, he stepped back out into the corridor and began checking rooms once more.

No Eric.

He climbed to the third level—surely the boy was here, for on the fourth and last level were the chambers of James MacDougal and his kin. Eric would not be kept there.

Gaard carefully opened the first door in the dimly lit corridor and his heart lurched in relief when he saw Eric, wrapped in a snug coverlet, nursing at a young wet-nurse's breast.

The woman looked up in fright, then gasped.

"Do not fear," Gaard said quickly. "I have been sent by MacDougal to take you and the babe to the chapel."

"Thank God!" she breathed, her eyes still wide in fear. Then she rose and came towards him.

Gaard thought quickly. "Give me the child and go on ahead, girl. See yourself to safety . . . I'll be close behind."

She hesitated for a moment, then handed Eric to Gaard. It was all he could do to keep from hugging the child to him. "Go on now, lass," Gaard said sternly, "be off to the chapel. Hurry, the Viking is nearly upon us!" And with that she fled rapidly from the room.

When she was gone, Gaard reached under his robe and took the pouch of sleeping drops from his belt. "I am sorry, Eric," he whispered as he rubbed the liquid on the infant's lips. Then he kissed his forehead gently and loosened the burlap sack from under his belt, easing Eric into its depths. The sack was loosely woven and he had no fear that Eric would not be able to breathe. Soon the child would sleep, and when he awoke, he would be in Dawnlyn's arms.

Gaard hung the sack gently over his shoulder, then stooped down, checking the dagger in his boot. He left the chamber and began making his way back down the steps. Once he heard footfalls rising from around a curve in the stairs. Breathing hard, he turned quickly and retraced his way to the second landing, where he hid around the corner until the man passed, heading to the turret.

His plan was going more smoothly than he had dared to dream. He crossed the hall undetected and headed toward the kitchen. Suddenly he remembered the old cook. Was she still there? He entered the kitchen and began to cross it as if it were the most natural thing on earth to do. The cook was indeed there, busy at the ovens. Gaard had almost reached the door when her voice stopped him.

"What thievery is this?" She gazed hard at the sack over his shoulder, took several steps toward him.

"It is not thievery, woman," he said quickly. "Come and see."

Hesitantly, she approached while he carefully placed the bundle on the wooden table.

She reached Gaard's side. "What is in there?" she accused, leaning over to view the contents.

Then Gaard moved. He clamped a hand over her mouth and began dragging her toward the pantry cupboard. The woman struggled frantically, but even her great bulk was no match for Gaard's strength. When he had her safely in the pantry, he turned her rapidly around to face him. Before a wail reached her lips, he cuffed her on the chin with just enough force to knock her out cold.

"I am sorry," he said, carefully propping her inert form against the wall of the closet. She would have a sore jaw, but at least she would live.

He retrieved Eric and slowly opened the kitchen door leading to the courtyard. From his vantage point, he could see a single sentry at the back gate, as the attention of the MacDougal forces was on Sweyn's men, who were gathering at the front of the tower.

With slow, deliberate strides, Gaard crossed the yard and approached the sentry. "Let me out," he said to the hefty man, startling him. "I have blessed your people and must be on my way before this battle begins."

The sentry grumbled darkly under his breath. Then he noticed the sack. "What's in there?" He took a step toward Gaard, his hand on the hilt of his sword.

"Scraps from the kitchen." Gaard eased the bundle from his shoulder while stooping to place it on the ground. At the same moment, he reached slowly under his robe's hem and grasped the handle of the dagger, drawing it from his boot. When he straightened, he made his move swiftly, for there was no time for indecision. With a deadly, painless slash, he laid open the sentry's throat, then quickly dragged the body around the corner from the gate.

Taking up Eric once more he slipped out of the gate carefully, leaving it ajar. He then shed the cumbersome robe and pressed himself to the wall, hoping he could not be seen from above, and made his way slowly around the east side of the tower until Sweyn's form could be seen below mounted on a white steed as prearranged.

With Eric held closely to his chest, Gaard raised an arm

and slowly waved it from side to side in signal. He strained his eyes to see Sweyn's reaction and a slow smile gathered at the corners of his mouth when his lieutenant turned his horse in a clockwise direction. In a few moments, Gaard knew, Eric would be safely away. A breeze touched him suddenly, and Gaard smiled broadly, knowing that Odin was still with him. Was that not the god's breath stirring the air?

Chapter Twenty-one

THE CHOSEN MEN QUICKLY CLUSTERED AROUND GAARD LIKE silent bees on a rare blossom, their swords drawn like lethal stingers. Quickly Sweyn handed him his long broadsword, and Gaard strapped it on, heaving an inward sigh of relief; a Viking is not a whole man without his weapon. Then Gaard gave them the layout of the MacDougal's tower, as close as he could recall. They nodded soundlessly, their helmets making them appear to be savage beasts of prey, their eyes glinting with gleeful ferocity at the thought of the coming battle.

Robert ran up behind them, panting, his normally calm features flushed and fearful. "The babe?" he rasped out.

"He is here, safe." Gaard indicated the bundle he held protectively. "Take him to his mother." He paused, handed his son to Robert, held the man's gaze. "And may your God help you if anything befalls my son, Robert Renfrew, for my gods will seek revenge."

"Naught will happen to the child, man," answered Robert coldly, matching Gaard's dagger-sharp look. "He is my grandson and of my blood, too." He took the baby, unfolded the flap that covered the child's face as if to reassure himself that Eric was truly safe.

"Farewell and make haste, Robert," warned Gaard.

"Soon this place will be safe for neither man nor beast." Then he turned to the ten stalwart men he'd chosen for the most dangerous part of his plan: Sweyn and Knute and eight others—four Vikings and four of St. Abb's bravest Scots. "Now, pray to whatever gods you wish, men, but pray for a strong arm and a full measure of Luck. Let us go!"

They would have preferred a clashing, howling entrance, but Gaard's plan called for stealth and cunning—at first. They made their way past the kitchen, down the corridor that led to the great hall. The hallways were empty; obviously the MacDougals were still massed on their battlements expecting the attack to come from Ian's forces, who were allowing themselves to be seen, even shot at by Mac-Dougal's archers, drawing all the attention.

Crouched, their bodies tuned to a hair-trigger pitch, their backs prickling with the warrior's sixth sense, the eleven men slipped into the great hall, where a few elderly servants gaped at them, stunned. Then they were out the wide front doors, crossing the courtyard under cover of the various shelters built there for work places. They had nearly reached the great, tall wooden gates when a cry rang out from one of the Scots on the wall.

"Now!" hissed Gaard and the men fell, like clockwork, into the well-rehearsed formation they had planned: a four-sided phalanx, shields raised, practically impenetrable to MacDougal arrows. Gaard's ten close-ranked warriors moved slowly but inexorably toward the huge, tree-thick log that barred the gates, while swift arrows rained down on them and a score or more Scots scrambled down from the battlements to attack. They had only a few minutes at best until they would be overwhelmed by MacDougal's forces.

It would be close. They had twenty yards to go, then fifteen; already their shields sprouted arrows like the raised hackles on a mad dog's back and a few of the quicker Scots were bearing down on them, screaming ancient Gaelic war cries, their battle axes raised for the kill. Soon they would be inundated by the superior numbers, engulfed by the Mac-Dougals, borne down and slaughtered by the mass of men.

"The gate!" gasped Gaard as they inched their way onward, now having to fight off the slashing swords and axes of their foes as well. But the MacDougal's ravening hysteria to destroy Gaard and his men perversely aided their cause—the arrows raining down from above interfered with the Scots attacking the phalanx from the ground and even resulted in some of their own men being wounded.

Suddenly the arrows ceased when the MacDougal's archers finally realized they were killing their own. The men on the ground, swelling in numbers each moment, rushed in to the attack, but the cessation of arrows gave the staunch warriors of St. Abb's the split second they needed to advance toward the gates, open their ranks into a semicircle, backs protected, and fight off the screaming Scots, whose own numbers hindered rather than helped them in their attempts to reach Gaard's men.

Gaard and the huge, hulking Knute, protected by the others, worked at slipping the giant log out of its supports. Gasping and cursing, blood mingled with sweat running into their eyes, they struggled to unbar the great bolt while the rest of the men fought like wild animals, silent and dogged, cutting, stabbing, catching blows on their shields, their legs straddled immutably, powerfully, the pile of corpses growing to their knees, then their thighs.

The bolt slipped out! With a thud it fell to the ground and the huge gates creaked inward, pushed by Ian's men waiting just outside. The MacDougals paused in their battle for an eye-blink of time, then gave a resounding howl of fury and terror and comprehension of their doom. They fell back as the gates crushed inward, sweeping all in front of them, and Ian, at the head of the St. Abb's forces, rushed into the fray giving a convincing, bloodcurdling imitation of a Viking war cry.

Gaard's small group faded back thankfully into the fresh troops that rushed into the breach, exhausted by their heroic stand, their sword arms swelled and burning with exertion. They were as close that moment, the eleven heroes of the victory over MacDougal, as if the angel of death herself had

300

slit their veins with her razor-sharp dagger and ritually blended their very blood together and made them brothers.

"Come!" shouted Gaard, straightening up. "We're not finished yet, men! There is still a fair bit of fighting to be had this day." He threw a flashing white, wolfish grin at his men and followed the tail end of the St. Abb's forces as they hacked and slashed their way across the blood-slick cobble-stoned courtyard of the MacDougal's dark tower.

Soon Gaard was at the forefront of the fighting, at red-haired Ian's side, his iron-hewed sword arm cutting down the MacDougal men in his berserker's fury as easily as a pendulum cuts the air. Yet the MacDougals fought fiercely, giving ground only a begrudging inch at a time.

The inferno caught each man up, lending him greater courage and strength than he possessed, but the men from St. Abb's were stronger and fresher and fought with the abandon of jungle beasts with their stormy-eyed jarl at their head. In the blood-hot, screaming confusion, Gaard battled with a cruel grin uptilting one side of his mouth, feeling nothing but the need to purge the sick fear and horror of his son's kidnapping from his mind. Only the feel of *Lightning Bolt* slicing flesh, cracking bone, eliciting screams from the enemy cooled his white-hot Viking fury.

A young boy, not more than sixteen, fell under his sword, only wounded but no longer a danger to the St. Abb's warriors, so Gaard let him lie, moaning and holding the spurting puncture in his shoulder. Then Gaard heard a cry, insane with rage, behind him and whirled around just in time to catch an axe blow aimed by the MacDougal on his shield. The man yanked out the axe with a shriek and came at Gaard again.

"My son!" screamed James MacDougal. "That was my son you just cut down. A boy!"

"I treated him with better grace than you would have my son!" Gaard's voice was as cold and brittle as the frost king's sword.

The MacDougal opened his mouth in a frenzied cry and swung his axe at Gaard for answer. It sucked a blast of hot air in its wake, a scant inch from Gaard's head. The man was powerful and insane with rage. He seemed not to tire but attacked again and again, screaming all the time incomprehensible Gaelic curses.

Gaard sidestepped, luring the man to his right, feinted with his sword. The MacDougal immediately raised his axe and came in to Gaard's unprotected left side, his whole body reaching, stretching out, committed totally to the blow. But the axe never reached its mark, for Gaard twisted sideways, let the axe slash harmlessly by him and brought his broadsword down with a satisfying chop that severed helmet, chain mail, flesh and bone. The MacDougal's head was cleft from helm to shoulder, and he toppled slowly and majestically to the blood-stained ground.

Then and only then did the berserker lust begin to fade from Gaard's blood. When he had the presence of mind to look around him, his forces were in the process of finishing off the last of the badly wounded enemy and surrounding the living to take them prisoners.

Carnage was everywhere. Tangled limbs and blood and fallen weapons littered the ground. Moans and shrieks came from the less seriously hurt. The metallic, rusty breath of spilled blood filled the air, making it heavy and choking to breathe. It was a Hel on earth, the courtyard of the MacDougal's tower.

"Sweyn!" bellowed Gaard amidst the infernal noise and horror.

"My lord," came the answer immediately, and Sweyn came limping up, a broad grin on his handsome face.

"Are you bad hurt?" asked Gaard, eyeing his lieutenant's bloodied leg.

"A mere scratch!" laughed the irrepressible Sweyn.

"Knute?" Gaard searched the milling warriors for the huge burly shoulders and red beard of Knute.

"Oh, I saw him not long ago. He'd lost a finger or two, but was well otherwise. And Ian's there." He pointed to the young man's slim form across the courtyard. "I put him in charge of the prisoners. You were busy at the time." Sweyn laughed.

"How many did we lose?"

"Not more than five or six men, and ten wounded. Only Inge Borson is mortal wounded."

"We were fortunate. Those MacDougals fought well."

"A worthy foe, my lord."

"And a harmless one now. I will leave the rest to you, Sweyn, for I must return to St. Abb's. I will send back a wagon for the wounded when I reach there." He paused, looked about the courtyard. "I want this tower and everything in it burned to the ground and the MacDougal's men scattered to the four corners of the earth. You will see to it, Sweyn?"

"Yes, my lord, willingly."

"And tell Ian Renfrew for me that he proved his worth today and I will give him these lands for his own. Henceforth he will be the lord of his own Hall. Now I must get back and see if my son is safe."

Sweyn stood, hands on hips, watching his jarl stride away toward the warhorses, swing upon his big gray destrier and gallop off across the moor toward St. Abb's. The young lieutenant shook his head ruefully. Not long ago Gaard would have stayed on to drink and diddle the women and trade jokes with the men. But now he rode off even before the battle was properly over to see if his son was safe! If that's what the responsibility of a family and lands did to a good Viking, Sweyn was not at all sure he wanted any part of it. Maybe Colleen would like to sail off to Byzantium—or somewhere—when the baby was born. This settling down business was as frightening as a gale out of the northwest and much, much more permanent . . .

Gaard rode hard the long miles back to St. Abb's, throwing the reins of the sweat-streaked, nearly foundered horse to a stableboy, and stalked into the Hall.

Godfred Bandylegs challenged him at the door, saw who it was and lowered his sword, grinning from ear to ear. "Good fight, my lord?"

"Yes, a good one, Godfred. Did Robert . . . ?"

"Renfrew returned hours ago with the babe as safe as the day he was born." Godfred eyed his jarl, saw the relieved sagging of the great shoulders, the relaxing of the whole battle-stained frame. "Here, my lord, you're a man who needs a good measure of ale if I ever saw one!" He handed his jarl a flagon.

"You're not far wrong, Godfred. It's been a long day."

"But a good one, my lord."

"Yes, a good one. The MacDougal's dead, along with near all his kin. Ian Renfrew will build a tower there and the land will be his now," he said in strong, ringing tones.

"A friend on the north border, that's it, my lord?"

"Yes," said Gaard, then downed a pint or two of the golden liquid, wiped the back of a scarred hand across his lips. Then, "Have a wagon sent for the wounded and a keg of good ale and food. The men won't be home before tomorrow, I wouldn't think."

Still holding the flagon, Gaard made his way toward the curving stone stairs. He felt oddly calm, cleansed of all his berserker's fighting fury, of all fear and anxiety over his son. Now there was time to reflect on things, on the past and the future, on all the aspects of his life. He was a man who had fulfilled every dream. He had two healthy sons, fertile, secure lands on both sides of the North Sea, a fleet of swift dragon ships, the respect of his warriors and a beautiful wife.

As he climbed the familiar curving stairs to his chamber, Gaard's thoughts turned back to the point in time when Meg had brought the news of Eric's capture, the last time he had had thoughts of anything but revenge and fighting and anxiety. He pictured in his mind's eye Dawnlyn's face that afternoon, tearful and angry and hurt. What had she been so upset about?

Then it all came flooding back: the heat and his irritation —which seemed a small thing now—and her ridiculous desire to know if he *loved* her. Love? A word for the poets, a word used by the Christians to speak of their God. Merely a sound made by the lips and tongue.

Meaningless.

Yet it had been important to his wife, or so she had cried to him that day. Was it more than a mere word, then? His mind seemed sluggish and tired; fanciful notions flitted through his brain. Did he *love* Dawnlyn? He liked her, he respected her, he adored her slim white body and calm, strong, feminine ways. Was that love?

He was still asking himself the question when he pushed open the door to his chamber and entered the familiar room. The late afternoon sun lit the chamber with a golden glow, gilding Dawnlyn's bent head as she nursed Eric. Instantly, as he entered, she looked up and her copper eyes met his across the room, her gaze heavy with emotion and desperate relief.

"Gaard." Her words held a wealth of meaning, a significance beyond the mere sound of his name.

He went to her, knelt by her side and touched his son's head. "He is well?"

"Yes. My father brought him hours ago, squealing with hunger." She put a hand out and stroked Gaard's cheek. "And you?"

"I am unhurt. Your brother is well."

"Thank God," she whispered fervently. Rising, Dawnlyn went to the cradle and laid Eric down, then turned to her husband, holding out her arms. "Come here and let me feel if you are really back and in one piece."

He went to her and she melted into his embrace, uncaring of the blood and sweat and battle soil on his clothes. She felt good in his arms, warm and sinuous and right. Why had another woman never filled his arms as she did? And why was the feel of Dawnlyn so unique?

And then it struck him like a blow—it must be *love* that he felt. Or else why did his heart squeeze with poignant response to her nearness? Why did he want her by his side always? Why did he think only of her among all the women in the world?

His brow furrowed with puzzled concentration, and then he became aware of Dawnlyn's frightened gaze on his face.

"Is there something wrong, something you haven't told me?" she asked breathlessly.

He smiled down at her, pressed her closer to him. "No, little one. I was merely thinking."

"Of what, my husband?"

"Of you. Of us. Of the future."

"And what were your thoughts? You looked so serious."

Gaard released her and rubbed a big scarred hand over his face. "It was"—he felt peculiarly sensitive bringing up the subject—"what you were wailing about to me the other day, before Eric was kidnapped." He paused, finding the task harder than planning a battle. He looked to Dawnlyn to aid him, but her face was very still and oddly closed to him—watchful and expectant. "I was thinking about . . ." He strode across the room and stared out of the small, deep-set casement that was open to the summer breeze. The slight breath of air cooled his cheeks. ". . . about what you asked me that day." He stopped, helpless, unable to go on.

Then he was aware of his wife's presence at his back; her arms crept around his chest and her cheek rested against his broad back. "About love?" she whispered.

"Yes." His voice was subdued, unlike his normal strong manner of speaking. "Is it still important for you to know?"

"Always, my husband," came her answer.

"Well, then"—he still could not face her—"I suppose I do love you . . ."

"Suppose?"

"I do love you," he said more firmly, but the words were still uncomfortable on his tongue.

There was utter silence in the room. Only Dawnlyn's heart beating against his back told him she was still there. Finally the tension in him became too much to bear and he forced himself to turn and face her.

"Dawnlyn?"

But he could see how she felt; it poured from her like the holy light he'd seen emanating from the man Kris in Christian paintings. Her lips were parted, her eyes lit as if a copper flame was kindled within them. "Gaard . . . do you mean it? You're not just trying to humor me?" She waited for his response as if it were the most important thing in the world to her.

"I mean it, little one. It came to me just now, but it is very hard for me to . . . express myself. I am not a man of easy words."

"Never mind easy words! I'd trade all the easy words in the world for one of your difficult ones! Oh, Gaard!" She glowed with a kind of rapture. "You make me so happy."

It was worth all the trouble of getting the words out, he realized, seeing her joy. And it was true, every word of it, he knew with a surety he'd rarely felt before except in matters of war. A weight lifted off his chest and a great illumination filled him. "And you, Dawnlyn, how do you feel?"

She came to him, cupped his face between her two slim white hands and imprisoned his gaze with hers. "I love you, Gaard. I have loved you for a long time, but I only knew it . . . well, a few days ago."

He drew her toward him, lifting her feet off the floor, and swung her around so that her skirt flared out behind her. He bent his head and kissed her warm lips, then drew back and looked at her, his eyes warm and shining with a silver glint. "Are you happy now, little one?"

"Yes. I am happy. I am utterly, completely content now!" She laughed. "And how can that be? For you are a pagan Viking warrior and I am a pious Christian girl who once thought to be a nun. How is it that we have come to love one another? Tell me, Gaard."

"It was meant to happen. Our blood was meant to mix in our children. Odin and Thor and Freya willed it."

"And my God did, too, for his ways are mysterious and full of wonder!"

"I'll grant you that, my love," he smiled. "Now, for the sake of all our Gods, fetch me bathwater and grant me some peace in my own Hall!"

Epilogue

DAWNLYN BORE TO GAARD WOLFTOOTH SIX HEALTHY CHIL-
dren, two daughters and four sons. The daughters both
stayed near their birthplace—one married, one became a
Mother Abbess of great renown. The sons, like their legendary father, were rovers.

The two youngest males ventured out together one
summer's eve and traveled as far as Constantinople, where
they established a trading house in that city, their venture
taking them as far as Cathay. Both married and resided in
the Byzantine capital when they were not, themselves, off on
their ships exploring.

The middle son, Olaf, journeyed to Norway, where he
made a good home near the birthplace of his ancestors and
befriended his older, half-brother Leif, who also spawned
several children, all of whom used their sharp wits to
advance themselves.

But it was Eric who was most like his father. Although he
did return to St. Abb's several times in his manhood, Eric left
his home at age seventeen on the ship he and his father
handcrafted themselves. His ventures took him to lands
even Gaard had never heard of and, being the handsome,
virile man that he was, Eric left his seed sprouting in many a
willing female body. Over the centuries there was born to an

DAWNFIRE

occasional woman a child with eyes the color of storm-tossed seas and hair as golden as the age of the Vikings. It is odd, but these tall, prideful descendents of Gaard Wolftooth —the one who bested Fenris, the Giant Wolf—were ever thirsting for new adventures, they themselves leaving their Norse seeds to germinate in the dawnfire of the expanding world.